C000258983

I have been interested in ghosts and the unexplained all my life. I first remember sensing a presence when aged about six or seven, and had many supernatural encounters in my youth. My parents consequently thought that I was a child who was 'afraid of the dark'. I suffered from strong poltergeist activity at the age of sixteen, and my parents then began to believe that the incidents were not my imagination – well, mainly my father – my mother with some reluctance. Previously, it had been an uphill struggle to convince them that I was not 'playing up'.

My late aunt on my mother's side of the family professed to be psychic, but I understand that she may have 'embroidered' her stories. The upshot was that my parents did not have much time 'for all that nonsense'.

I believe that being an only child has made me an independent and self-reliant woman, but it was sometimes a lonely existence as a psychic child, with unsympathetic parents.

I lived in a very haunted apartment in Harrow on the Hill. My husband and I witnessed many different types of phenomena there.

I have experienced a variety of supernatural happenings, at many places, up to the present day, including Avebury Manor, Wiltshire, houses in Penge and Croydon, and time slips at Ascain, France, on a train near Victoria Station and at Waltham Abbey, Essex. I was formerly a member of the Ghost Club.

Having said all that, my life does not revolve around spooks. I had a successful career in finance, which resulted in a move to the Hertfordshire/Essex borders. My adopted hometown is Bishop's Stortford, which I find fascinating, and the surrounding countryside and counties, captivating.

My other interests include medieval French history, the Tudors and the Stuarts, jazz, classical music (I was a singer in a choral society – a lady tenor!) and continental cuisine. I am also a semi-professional artist and I have included some illustrations in this guide as an ambience to the narrative.

Jenni Kemp

GHOST TOURS OF HERTFORDSHIRE AND ESSEX

AUSTIN MACAULEY PUBLISHERS™

LONDON • CAMBRIDGE • NEW YORK • SHARJAH

Copyright © Jenni Kemp (2019)

The right of Jenni Kemp to be identified as author of this work has been asserted by her in accordance with section 77 and 78 of the Copyright, Designs and Patents Act 1988.

All rights reserved. No part of this publication may be reproduced, stored in a retrieval system, or transmitted in any form or by any means, electronic, mechanical, photocopying, recording, or otherwise, without the prior permission of the publishers.

Any person who commits any unauthorised act in relation to this publication may be liable to criminal prosecution and civil claims for damages.

A CIP catalogue record for this title is available from the British Library.

ISBN 9781788484817 (Paperback)
ISBN 9781788484824 (Hardback)
ISBN 9781528954488 (ePub e-book)

www.austinmacauley.com

First Published (2019)
Austin Macauley Publishers Ltd
25 Canada Square
Canary Wharf
London
E14 5LQ

I would like to thank my husband, Jack, for his patience and the solitude he had to endure whilst I spent a mammoth amount of time researching and compiling this book. Also, for his tolerance at my constant requests that we drive to far-flung corners of Hertfordshire and Essex.

My thanks also goes to Lisa Hockley, Steve Hockley, Colette Entwisle, Stephen Wood and Alan Gardner.

Also by Jenni Kemp

Haunted Bishop's Stortford

Table of Contents

Foreword

Ghosts, whether you believe in them or not, have experienced them or not, have intrigued humanity since the dawn of time. Stories of spirits reappearing long after death can be found all over the world and despite 21st century technology and advances, remain an enigma. In recent years, television has played a big part in the 'science' (and entertainment) of hunting ghosts. During my time spent working with Lion Television for the UK Horizons series 'Ghost Detectives', our investigation team spent 24 hour shifts in a myriad of haunted locations using the most up-to-date technology together with the ancient ability of clairvoyance. Ghosts were with us, we felt them, experienced their presence and the tricks they played but what the cameras failed to catch was the most primordial excitement and sense that we were not alone and that some unfathomable energy was with us at certain times.

Ghosts do not behave in predictable ways, maybe this is why capturing one on camera or interviewing one is always just out of our grasp. There are ghosts that replay a significant event over and over on a particular anniversary, ghosts that appear to be aware of their mortal neighbours and actually interact with them by moving objects, rapping answers to questions or physically pushing the curious human. The cause of these phantoms is often unknown but over time the belief has been that these spirits are somehow trapped on the earth plane. This ability to remain un-pigeonholed makes it difficult for science to answer the question 'what is a ghost'. However, there are theories emerging which are linked to explanations of natural energies, electromagnetic fields and even human brainwaves. For now though, ghosts remain unexplained and perhaps this is why we continue to find them such a deep-rooted fascination.

Many books have been written about ghosts but *Ghost Tours of Hertfordshire and Essex* provides the reader with individual tours to haunted sites accompanied by map references and historical information. For anyone who wishes to actively pursue ghost hunting in the Home Counties, or just sit by the fire and enjoy the thrill of a good ghost story, this book is one to add to the personal paranormal library collection.

Ruth Stratton

About the Guide

The guide has sixty-two tours, which incorporate over two-hundred and eighty towns and villages, and more than eight-hundred haunted sites. Some sites have several ghosts.

I have included map references in many cases (to the nearest square) using Ordnance Survey maps. The investigator does not necessarily need a map, but it is a useful tool.

Satnav users will be disappointed that I have not used postcodes. The reason being that post codes will not necessarily take you to the exact spot. For example church ruins at Thundridge or Minsden are best found on a map. The satnav screen will not give you the finer details or tell you anything else, but a map will. Using an Ordnance Survey map makes the whole area come to life. History is spread out on the sheet. As you are making your way to a site, the map will show you where a battle was once fought (by the symbol of two crossed swords with a date), names of country houses, or strange names of farms and woodland, give one the feel of the area and its history.

Some sites are off the beaten track and in certain cases the Ordnance Survey Explorer maps are more useful, in that they may show more detail and footpaths and bridleways are clearer. They also give names of roads and lanes.

Dates are given for cyclical hauntings together with map numbers you will need, at the start of each tour.

All tours can be lengthened or shortened as to the investigator's wishes. Some tours are quite long, and others small, so the tourist may cut down a tour, or add from an adjacent excursion.

Some of the manifestations in this guide are described in précis. There are many books one can read that give a fuller account of the hauntings, and can be found in the Bibliography.

Many people are interested in ghosts, and the purpose of the guide is to enable the serious enthusiast to seek and observe. The counties are awash with fascinating stories, legends, history, and lovely old villages, market towns and pubs. Consequently, I have included 'notes of interest' or 'history notes' to some tours.

I would strongly request that the tourist respect people's property and privacy at all times. The inclusion of a property in this guide does not necessarily mean that it is open to the public. I have visited numerous sites and where possible spoken to people who work or reside in these places, in order to obtain authentic accounts.

There is no guarantee that the investigator will see a ghost. Ghosts are unreliable, and do not turn up when you expect them to. Even the anniversary ghosts.

Apart from the reported sightings in this guide, there are many sightings that go unreported. Ghosts are ubiquitous. You just need to be in the right place, and under the right circumstances, which can be when you least expect to see one.

The ghost hunter can add his own search to the tours in this guide. There are many places where one may encounter a ghost. For example, stately homes open to the public, abbeys, priories, churches, graveyards, battlefields, castles, places of previous accidents, and sites of murder and execution.

Look up local history in the library or on the internet. Nowadays perhaps the village pond looks pretty and tranquil, but it may have been used as a ducking pond for witches, with a baying rabble. The village green where now cricket is being played, may have been the site of executions, with a jeering mob. Crossroads are maybe where a gibbet or gallows once stood.

Shops or use of buildings may change, but were correct when compiling the tours.

What Is a Ghost?

What is a ghost? Dictionaries describe ghosts as spirits of the dead, but some apparitions are not, for example, the phantom car in Ware, or the apparition of the house at Fobbing. Some apparitions are of the living.

People have believed in ghosts since more or less caveman times. Surely, not all sightings are imagination (or hoaxes). Otherwise, it is a disturbing thought that intelligent people have been deluding themselves throughout the centuries.

There are many sceptics, but also those who are afraid to admit their belief because they do not wish to appear gullible or be ridiculed.

Often more than one person has witnessed a ghost at the same time on the same occasion. Likewise, people have witnessed the same ghost independently, on separate occasions. So, the 'it is all in your imagination' theory does not hold up.

It would seem that certain hauntings are somehow recorded in their surroundings. The buildings are a kind of stone videotape. Intense emotion, for example, of a murder, or suicide has penetrated the physical fabric of the environs. These types of haunting often fade over time and then disappear completely, as if the 'tape' has worn out.

Important historical events, like battles are re-enacted. Maybe this is this due to extreme rage, passion or zeal that the force of energy on a large scale is replayed. Interestingly, these manifestations often appear on the anniversary of the event.

There are crisis apparitions where someone who is about to die, or has just died, visit loved ones. People appear in photographs who were not there when the photo was taken.

Most ghosts go about their haunting and seem not to be aware of the living. Only occasionally is it reported that a ghost looked as shocked to see us, as we are to see it. Poltergeists seem to want to attract attention, and the often-frightening phenomena stop just as suddenly as it started.

Then there are time slips where one appears to enter another dimension. The surroundings and atmosphere seem to have retreated into the past. Often buildings and trees appear flat like stage scenery, or the vision is like a large videotape being played out in front of the observer.

Time means nothing to a ghost. A haunting can peter out over time, but something can start it up again. Refurbishment and building works seem to trigger a dormant haunting.

The night before a full moon is believed to be propitious for a sighting.

SO, WHAT IS A GHOST? Surprisingly, in this age of extensive technology, it is something that remains unanswered. But one day, hopefully soon, we will have an explanation. There is a school of thought that ghosts do not exist because we cannot prove their existence. In 1800, photography and television would be fantastical. In 1900, the mobile phone a pipe dream. So, one day…

Tours

Tour One
Hertford

OS Map 166
Cyclical and Notable Dates – 12/13 May – Sheffields Chemist
30th September – Marshalls Store

We start with the county town of Hertford.

Fore Street in Hertford seems to have a haunting in nearly every property.

At Prezzo, phenomena started when the original charity shop was being converted to the previous bistro Café Uno. There is said to be a strong sense of evil. The women who worked at the shop did not like to use the lavatory as they said it had a creepy, forbidding atmosphere. They would rather trudge to the public Ladies' Conveniences in Gascoyne Way car park.

When the premises were refitted, builders experienced some peculiar happenings. Often, I have noticed, a refurbishment disturbs or disrupts the spirits that have lain dormant or unobserved. (See Maslens Store and Alliance & Leicester on the Bishop's Stortford tour No. 21.)

Pieces of timber propped up against a wall suddenly moved across the room of their own volition, witnessed by three workers.

Wires that had been clipped to the ceiling were discovered to be unclipped and hanging precariously. Bricks left in preparation for the next day's work were found to have been moved. No logical explanation was found.

A strange mist arose from the basement, and on another occasion, marching shadows were seen against walls.

Early one morning the cleaner was working alone on the second floor when he heard a tumultuous crash below. He fled downstairs to see what had happened, but all was normal, and no cause for such a sound was apparent. The only difference was that a chain which was always placed across the top of the stairs had been removed.

The Red House at number 119 Fore Street (circa 1600s) was apparently part of Christ's Hospital for orphaned children. The upper stairs are haunted by a former matron carrying a tray.

At Threshers wine shop (at the time of writing closed down and vacant), employees have reported an eerie feeling in the cellar. Often staff arriving for work found a tap turned on flooding the floor even though the premises had been locked overnight. The most spooky occurrence was when a loud crash was heard, which appeared to come from the bottle store. Workers found six bottles placed in the shape of a star, and no explanation for the noise.

Sheffield's Chemist, 64 Fore Street has had some manifestations. In 1997 I worked with one of the pharmacist's sons in Harlow, and he told me of some strange happenings. The hauntings usually happen around 13th May.

The pharmacist heard curious knocking sounds which followed him around no matter where he went in the building. Medicine would move by itself in front of witnesses. A shelf collapsed noisily to the floor. It would seem that the poltergeist or spirit wanted to tell the chemist and his employees something involving the past. A two hundred year-old prescription book was found on a toilet seat, and a bottle of strychnine suddenly appeared from nowhere. In the distant past strychnine was used as a medicine, but nowadays it is classed as a poison. The bottle was immediately taken to the police.

A member of staff used to talk to the entity. It would reply with one knock for 'yes' and two for 'no'. The ghost managed to convey its story by a series of taps which depicted letters of the alphabet. The troubled spirit had been murdered by its brother in order to own the premises.

In 1996 there was a serious fire at Marshalls Furnishings Warehouse, at the back of the shop. Concerned about looters, the police arranged an overnight presence. A woman police officer was situated at the rear of the building. She glanced up and saw a man looking at her from one of the upstairs windows. She described him as having long black curly hair, a moustache, and wearing apparel pertaining to the Cromwellian period. She radioed for help and when fellow officers arrived, they went inside the skeletal, burnt out shell of a building, but found no one. Apparently, the officer remains convinced of what she witnessed.

Not long ago a psychic could sense the spirit of a forty-six year old man but no other information could be gleaned, and a customer sensitive to spooks felt a presence. Look out for the ghost on 30th September, which is the anniversary of the event.

Albany Radio 63/65 Fore Street was once a Georgian private residence. A lady dressed in costume of that time appears upstairs. The house was called Cupboard Hall.

The Corn Exchange in Fore Street was once a theatre. The caretaker would attend the building when it was empty and hear scenery being moved, musicians tuning in instruments and voices – but the place was void of people.

History Note

This building stands on the site of the former municipal jail, opened in 1702. It was filthy, overcrowded, and the inmates suffered from typhus and smallpox. Many died of the gaol fever. A prisoner was brought out from one of the dungeons as dead, and on being washed under the pump, came to life. There was no chapel or infirmary. The town's residents blamed the non-ventilated gaol for frequent epidemics. As well as the gaol Hertford had a cage, whipping post, pillory and ducking stool. Sometimes a gallows was erected outside the gaol.

At Gays Newsagent 28/30 Fore Street, here the ghostly strains of a violin can be heard.

Baroosh Bar 78. Fore Street is haunted by a woman in Victorian dress.

Pearce's Bakers, 23 Railway Street suffers from poltergeist phenomena and smells of tobacco in the eerie cellar.

History Note

Railway Street was previously known as Back Street. It was a slum area and in 1899 was the scene of a bloody and shocking crime. The overcrowded place in a way resembled the Victorian East End of London, in that it had many lodging houses, an itinerant population, and known for its poverty, drunkenness and violence. 'Rotten' Smith murdered his cousin Mercy Nicholls by stabbing her fifty-nine times, and left her in the gutter to die. Various residents saw Mercy being kicked and assaulted and heard her screams and cries for help, but did nothing. Eventually, a member of the public went to the police station in Queen Street at 3.40 a.m. and another a while later, but the police were slow to act – under the pretext of only one officer on duty which turned out to be false – and police did not arrive at the scene until 6.00 a.m. Apparently, the police constables had an arrangement where they would cover each other in order to go home early and not report back to the station before going off duty. Passers-by saw Mercy lying in the gutter, with clothing torn, covered in blood, and whimpering. Due to the police fiasco and the callous behaviour of the witnesses, Mercy died at Hertford Infirmary around 10.00 a.m. due to loss of blood and hypothermia. According to the coroner, the stab wounds although many, were small. If the public had helped her and the police had acted promptly, she would have survived.

Smith was found to be insane, and unfit to plead. The verdict of the court was that he was a danger to the public, and sent to Broadmoor Lunatic Asylum

Now visit Hertford Museum in Bull Plain. Here phantom noises are heard and there is a creepy feeling in the building especially a cold spot and draught around the stairs.

The Hertford Club in Bull Plain was owned by Sir Henry Chauncy in 1700. The sounds of footsteps, squeaking floorboards, laughter and voices can be heard coming from the snooker room when it is empty. On entering the snooker room knowing it to be void of people, a barman saw that the cues were shaking in their racks. Ruth Stratton and Nicholas Connell who wrote *Haunted Hertfordshire – A Ghostly Gazetteer* describe this event "as if a game of snooker had been abandoned".

Chauncy was the recorder at the witch trial of Jane Wenham in 1700, and helped to get her pardoned. (See Walkern – the last reputed witch in England. Tour No.11.)

St Andrew's Street almost competes with Fore Street for ghostly activity.

The shops on the corner of Old Cross and St Andrew's Street boasts at least three ghosts. A lady in Victorian garb, a man with white hair, and something unseen that purveys a sense of evil in the attic. Members of staff and the public have mentioned feelings of unease on the premises, and it is said that dogs growl or whine at the foot of the stairs. Could the Victorian lady be the same shade that haunts The Natural Health Shop? She glides around with a gentleman wearing a high collar.

A pub in St Andrew's Street formerly the Three Tuns, now the Baan Thitya, and previously a workhouse, is haunted by the image of a young female who looks forlorn and in tatters. She walks through a wall, and then appears to ascend stairs which are no longer there.

A former shoe shop in this road is haunted by an old woman wearing an unhappy expression who descends the stairs and passes through a wall where it is believed a door once stood. At night, sounds of someone running up and down the stairs can be heard but no one is seen.

Wallace House, 5/11 St Andrew's Street also has three ghosts. A man loiters in a corner of a room, another peers out of a window and the third manifests in an upstairs hallway.

Pound Stretcher, 16 Maidenhead Street is the site of the old Woolworths shop. Here poltergeist activity takes place in what was the storeroom. Garments were scattered and clothes rails moved by no human agency. This building stands on the site of a demolished pub named the Maiden Head.

A spectral, middle-aged man wearing black frequents the upstairs of the Salisbury Arms Hotel. Spectators say he suddenly vanishes. Room number six is reputed to be haunted, and a man in Cromwellian dress appears. Could this be the same spectre that the policewoman saw at nearby Marshalls?

In close proximity the previous premises of the Hertfordshire Mercury in Fore Street, now the Hertford House Hotel, and weird phenomena occurred. When the premises belonged to the local newspaper, door handles rattled and turned off their own accord, lights flashed on and off. Doors slammed on unoccupied floors, and keys moved in their locks when no one had touched them. Some believe the offices were haunted by the spirit of an employee who died upstairs.

At one time police were summoned as someone working alone witnessed the above phenomena, and thought that there may be a prowler in the building. An extremely frightened police dog 'flew' out of the cellar with its hair standing on end. Needless to say no trespasser was found.

The cellar is supposed to be haunted by the shade of a murdered kitchen maid.

Employees at Monsoon in Market Place have reported hearing footsteps or someone vacuuming on the shop floor when it is closed, and all staff are in the storeroom in the basement.

Before we explore the haunted areas on the periphery of the town, take a look at the Old Vicarage in Church Street. Apparently, two Roman Centurions stand in the front of the gate. This premises was occupied by an Osteopath, and patients have seen a woman in Victorian dress in the entrance hall and waiting room. Her feet are not visible. This is probably due to a different floor level at some time. There is a macabre feature to the premises – which later became tearooms – the garden path is made from gravestones!

It is said that a man in Quaker's clothing haunts Port Hill as well as the old Quaker burial ground, which is situated opposite the gates to Hartham Common. My hairdresser was walking across the meads with a friend. They saw a strange looking man who suddenly vanished. They may have met the ghostly Quaker. However, they were so frightened they fled, and ran all the way back to Ware.

At Gallows Hill off the Ware Road, B1502 here one may hear the sound of rattling chains and shouting, or see a vision of a person in grey. This may be an 'imprint' of a person about to be hanged surrounded by noisy ghoulish spectators. Gallows Hill was once known as Chalk Hill. Hartham Place Housing Development now stands where the gallows once stood, and the bodies were usually buried nearby in unconsecrated ground.

Balls Park Mansion originally belonged to Hertford Priory, then Hertford University, and now has been converted into luxury apartments. A grey lady appears under the balcony in the wood panelled vestibule. According to legend a woman hurled herself off the first floor balcony into the lobby below. The haunting takes place in the autumn particularly in October. She has also been observed in the corridors on the first floor.

In recent years a member of Hertford University staff one evening was walking towards this seventeenth century mansion when he was suddenly forced backwards by an unseen entity.

Bengeo is a district of Hertford. On the corner of Cross Road there is a turreted house which has on occasion's aromas of wood smoke or perfume when there is no apparent reason for an olfactory presence. The spirit of a woman has also been witnessed here.

Hertford Castle – the castle ruins can be found behind St Andrew's Street. The castle dates back to the tenth century. A monk haunts the grounds of the castle holding an apple. No one seems to know who he was, or the importance of the apple. The refurbished castle is now offices for a solicitors' practice and council offices.

History Note

The castle's dungeons were used to house prisoners. The Knight's Templars, David 2nd of Scotland, King John, Prince Philip of France and James 1st of Scotland, were all imprisoned there, but may not have been ensconced in the dungeons.

John of Gaunt 1340-1399 lodged at the castle with each of his three wives, Blanche of Lancaster, Constance of Castile, and Katherine Swynford, who was formerly his mistress.

Elizabeth 1st, Mary Tudor and Edward 4th as children resided in the nursery at the castle.

The castle was considered to be close enough to London, for hunting and country pursuits to be enjoyed, and in addition one could easily make the journey on horseback to and from the capital.

Leahoe House is to be found in the grounds of County Hall, Pegs Lane. Here it is said a nun haunts the top of the staircase. She wears a long black and grey habit.

For further reading, in my view one of the best, and well-researched books on Hertford and its environs is *Haunted Hertfordshire* by Ruth Stratton and Nick Connell.

Map of Hertford

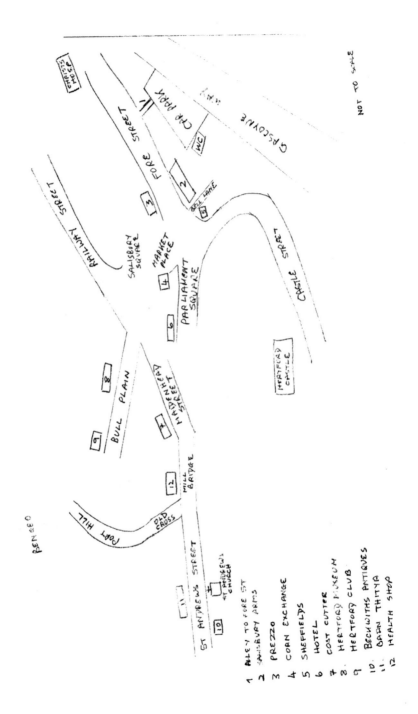

1. ALLEY TO FORE ST
2. SALISBURY ARMS
3. PREZZO
4. CORN EXCHANGE
5. SHEFFIELDS
6. HOTEL
7. COSY CUTTER
8. HERTFORD MUSEUM
9. HERTFORD CLUB
10. BECWITHS ANTIQUES
11. BARN THITYA
12. HEALTH SHOP

Tour Two

From Hertingfordbury to Welwyn Garden City, Lemsford, Hatfield, Welham Green and Essendon

OS Map 166
Cyclical Dates: Essendon January and August
Welwyn Garden City 23rd–27th July.
Hatfield House 31st December.

On leaving Hertford take the A414 towards Welwyn Garden City.

On this road you may witness a hitchhiker who suddenly vanishes. Apparently, Hertford police are aware of this apparition, which occurs at a curve in the road just before the turn off for Hertingfordbury.

At a signposted roundabout, turn left to Hertingfordbury. Here a shining sword was seen to hang in the sky over the Rectory way back in the seventeenth century.

Notes of Interest

Spencer Cowper of Hertingfordbury in 1699 was charged with the murder of Sarah Stout whose body was found floating in the Priory River at Bayford. It has been argued that Sarah committed suicide after Cowper finished their relationship. Cowper was acquitted, some say due to his predominant, political family, but also because the judge hearing the case became ill and could not sum up as his memory was impaired. Cowper was never retried.

Jane Wenham, the last condemned witch resided here – See the Walkern tour eleven.

Go back on to the A414 to Welwyn Garden City.

The staff toilets of the John Lewis Department store are reputed to be haunted.

Also the Queen Elizabeth 11 Hospital (known locally as the QE2) has an unearthly lady who wanders around the wards and passageways.

Guessens Court stands on the site of a fourteenth century farmhouse. A knight installed his mistress in the building where his wife also lived. It is said that the wronged wife set fire to the property, which was razed to the ground, killing the mistress. The furious knight decapitated his wife. It is not certain which lady haunts the area, whether the wife or the mistress. A possible time to encounter the phenomena is 23rd–27th July.

The Barn Theatre in Handside Lane appears to have a malevolent presence, amongst other phantoms. The stage area has been reported to be particularly creepy, and the old wardrobe room, which is now the kitchen, is always cold and clammy. Children's voices are heard, and a small boy has been seen. I have often thought that there is something eerie about an empty theatre, and it would seem that others also feel this. Workers and builders toiling through the night, in the empty theatre have experienced the sound of footsteps in corridors and on stage. Also, stage lights would be turned on and off through no human agency.

In addition, there has been a strange glow on the stage, when the rest of the building is pitch-black. Apparently, an exorcism was carried out after a frightening séance had been held in the bar at the Barn.

On the fringe of Welwyn Garden City is Black Fan Road, which has woodland to one side. There is a wide path through the trees, which is used as a shortcut. A strange man with a stick, possibly a ghost, is seen walking between the trees. He has been seen lying down, as if unwell, but he cannot be found when approached. This happens late at night. Then he is suddenly seen again – just watching the people in the wood.

West of Welwyn Garden City is Lemsford.

Here you will find Brocket Hall. The spooks here are said to be of lovers Lord Byron and Lady Caroline Lamb. It is said that the macabre re-enactment of Byron's funeral cortege passes in front of the elaborate gates. At other times there are supernatural smells of perfume. An employee, the last to come off shift one night – it is now a golf club, restaurant and conference centre – on locking up definitely heard someone near him cough.

Lord Palmerston's ghost has also been sensed here.

In 1994 an exorcist was called in to lay to rest a little girl calling for her mother, and a nineteenth century carpenter who fell to his death.

History Note

The eccentric Lady Caroline Lamb, miffed at a rejection by Lord Byron on one occasion, had a pyre lit in the grounds. Village maidens, dressed in white, were made to dance around it whilst she read an elegy and burned Byron's portrait.

Travel South to Hatfield

The old coach house at Hatfield House is now used as a restaurant. The ghost of a little girl vanishes after being told to go away. There is also the spirit of a tall dark man who looks very unhappy.

On New Year's Eve a coach with four black horses is said to race up the long drive like a bat out of hell, pass through the doors and ascend the main staircase where it disappears.

Queen Elizabeth 1st has been sensed here, and the spectre of a veiled anxious woman, possibly the mistress of Charles 2nd who is desperate to pass a message to him.

The shade of the first Marchioness slides along the Long Gallery. She was burnt to death in a fire at the palace.

In the Old Palace footsteps have been heard in a corridor, followed by the sound of a door opening. Then the footsteps trudge hesitantly as the phantom descends some stairs.

The misty figure of a female has been seen at the Gateway where she floats over Fore Street. The apparition dissolves at the church door.

The Todd building at Hertford University Campus is haunted by a hazy something that plays with the lighting.

Bush Hall House is said to be haunted by its former resident Sir Christopher Chester. The building is now a hotel, and Sir Robert has been seen ascending the stairs and in bedrooms.

A train driver reported that on one occasion when he was behind time on the Great Northern Railway, the train was passing through Hatfield without stopping. A serious looking man in black appeared. He seemed to have stepped off the platform and put his foot on the footplate brake. The man put his hand on the regulator, and the driver put his hand there also. The touch of the man in black was like ice. The steam had been extinguished and the train slowed. The signal showed the line was clear. The stoker had not seen the man in black and was annoyed when the train stopped at Hitchin. They both then saw that there were two trucks on the line. The ghostly man in black had prevented a train crash. The driver, stoker and passengers would have been killed.

Now Take the A1000 to Welham Green

A house which was previously a café on the Great North Road is believed to be haunted by the café owner, who is buried in the garden. The mischievous ghost manifests her presence through varied means of poltergeist activity.

Go Northwest to Essendon

You may hear someone knocking on the door of St Mary's church, to be let in the locked church. This is likely to be witnessed in August. Or you may see the ghost of a young woman on horseback wearing a green habit and tricorn hat. A likely time to meet her is on a January morning.

Camfield Place is situated just outside the village, and is the former home of both writers Beatrix Potter and Dame Barbara Cartland.

It has been reported that Beatrix witnessed, when alone in the drawing room, twelve candles being stifled, one at a time. Ghosts are said to haunt the stairs and hall.

Camfield Place is also haunted by 'Jimmy', a cocker spaniel who once was Dame Barbara's pet. The ghost of the dog was seen by the writer and a maid after it was 'put down'. Also, other pet dogs were troubled by Jimmy – a bad tempered spectre. The dogs would back away from their food bowls and yelp as if being bitten.

Tour Three

From Hertford Heath to Jenningsbury, Hoddesdon, Broxbourne, Wormley, Flamstead End, Cheshunt, Enfield and Brickenden

OS Map 166 and OS Explorer 174.
Cyclical Dates: Enfield 28th June, October generally, 25th, 26th and 31st December.
Hoddesdon Christmas time.
Jenningsbury pre-Christmas

From Hertford Take the A414/B1197 to Hertford Heath

The area around Haileybury College and Hertford Heath is haunted by soldiers who re-enact the murder of one of their men. The sound of baying dogs can also be heard. It is an historic fact that Cromwell's army had passed through here, and an execution had taken place.

At Jenningsbury Farm, Hertford Heath, a man drowned himself. His ghost has been seen here, and in the road, often just before Christmas.

Take the A10 to Hoddesdon

At The George, 8, High Street, the publican's dog refuses to descend the steps to the cellar where poltergeist disturbances have occurred.

Priory Close stands on the site of Yew Arbor House where a lady wearing a green dress haunted the place. I am not aware that she haunts the new dwellings.

The Bull Inn is reputed to be haunted at Christmas time by a white entity.

Local hearsay reports that a spectral nun walks from St Augustine's church.

History Note

Goose Green is just outside Hoddesdon (OS Exp 174 Ref 3509). On Sunday 12th July 1891, Sarah Dye aged fourteen went for a walk with her friend and two young men. They lived at Hertford and made their way towards Hoddesdon. When they reached the Green Man at Goose Green (now The Huntsman) they stopped for some ginger beer.

There was a group of young men seated outside. Their ages ranged from sixteen to thirty-seven. Sarah and her friends left about 8.45 p.m. and decided to go home via Box Wood. As they did so, the four were accosted by the group of men. The four went back to the pub, the men pursuing and stalking.

For some reason Sarah's friends left, leaving her alone to find her way home to Hertford. The group of men stalked her. One grabbed her around the waist, and the others assisted him in dragging her to the ground. Two men assaulted her whilst another dozen men watched. One of the men clamped his hand over her mouth to prevent her cries being heard. They then left her.

Sarah then proceeded to walk home again. A little way along she was accosted again. Her clothes were torn from her and she was dragged into the bushes where she was again raped by one of the older men whilst the others once more looked on. Unsurprisingly, she then fainted.

When she recovered she tried for home once more. This heinous game of cat and mouse continued, when one of the men caught hold of her but she was able to fend him off. She arrived home at 11.00 p.m.

Apparently, she did not tell her parents but on the following Wednesday she reported the matter to the police.

The police were able to round up some of the men, and Sarah was able to identify several. A few of the men said that they had tried to come to her assistance but were unable to do so due to the number of men participating. In fact one had received a black eye for his trouble.

Some of the men had said that Sarah was willing to this escapade but the doctor who examined her confirmed that there were signs a grievous assault had happened.

The outcome was that Wells, the thirty-seven-year-old was sentenced to ten years penal servitude, and the others were sentenced to nine months and five years. The judge commented strongly to Wells, that as a man of thirty-seven he should have come to Sarah's aid, not joined the others in raping her.

Sarah Dye must have been very brave in going to the police. She had to endure the 'shame' of a public trial, and regardless of the outcome her 'reputation' would be sullied for the rest of her life.

No wonder she did not tell her parents at first. It was noted that during her first ordeal she said, "You had better let me get up because if my father was to know I would get a good thrashing." Such was the general attitude of the time. Have we become unprejudiced today? Not in some communities, I fear.

Carry on down the A10 and Turn off to Broxbourne

An apartment in Cozens Lane East (off B176) had violent and disturbing poltergeist phenomena. A child saw the ghost of a man after the local vicar had blessed the rooms. (Poltergeist activity can sometimes become worse rather than better after a blessing.) Apparently a psychic exorcised the spirit. The best description, in my opinion, of this event can be found in *Ghostly Hertfordshire* by Damien O'Dell.

The woodland near Broxbourne is reputed to have been haunted by a woman in white.

Carry on to Wormley

Holy Cross Hill is off Church Lane (OS Exp 174 Ref 3405). Here you may encounter a policeman standing in the middle of the road indicating motorists to stop. He wears an old-fashioned uniform and gradually disappears.

In woodland, Paradise Wildlife Park (OS Exp 174 Ref 3406) is said to be haunted by a man in black, believed to be a departed man of the cloth. He disappears through a solid wall in an area that may have been the site of a plague pit.

Further along White Stubbs Lane to the west is Wormley Wood (OS Exp 174 Ref 3206). Ancient soldiers' spectres stalk the area.

Go Further South to Flamstead End

Cheshunt Great House dated back to 1450. The house no longer exists due to fire, but it is rumoured there were tunnels to Waltham Abbey, secret portals and phantoms. Do the tunnels still exist, and if so are they frequented by ghosts? The house was haunted by a grey lady, and there was an irremovable bloodstain upstairs.

The Rose & Crown at Trowley Bottom has the phantom of a young girl who befriends men in the Gents toilet! She has also been seen sitting on a trunk in one of the bedrooms, and on the edge of a bed where the impression of her body has been observed. Legend says this is the spectre of a young lady that was murdered in a barn at the rear of the pub. Her body disappeared without trace.

At The Three Blackbirds Inn, the restaurant area is believed to be plagued by the apparition of a woman in a white blouse and mobcap.

The residents of Britannia Cottage have reported sounds of heavy phantom footsteps. Also the vision of a woman wearing a shawl who walks through a wall.

On a winter's morning, just before light, you may encounter the shade of a lady in grey shawl and bonnet with a small child in tow, in Delmerend Lane. The same vision has been seen in River Hill. Also, an apparition in white sometimes materialises.

Further South Is Cheshunt

Old Palace House in Theobald's Park has many spirits.

Note of Interest

The entrance to Theobald's Park is a huge monument designed by Sir Christopher Wren, which was first erected in Fleet Street in 1672 at Temple Bar. It was dismantled and re-erected here in 1888.

Further South is Enfield. Enfield is in Middlesex, but it is easy to take this in on this tour. You can also take in Waltham Abbey on this Tour. See tour thirty-one.

A phantom stagecoach known locally as the Enfield Flyer, travels at breakneck speed down Bell Lane. It usually appears after dark, about five feet above road level, then suddenly disappears. (Part of Bell Lane is now Eastfield Road.)

The black coach, with two lady passengers sporting noticeable hats, has also been observed dissolving into the River Lea, or Albany Park. Reports of this sighting have been muted for a number of years.

The coach with a team of black horses makes no sound and is surrounded by a phosphorescent blue light. The driver wears a tall black hat and carries a whip. Children have seen the coach in the early hours of Christmas morning, but it has also been witnessed in mid-summer. One recorded sighting was on the 28th June, and others on or near Christmas.

One of the warehouses beside the canal suffered from poltergeist activity. Employees would hear noises like someone working on the top floor, which was empty. An employee's pet dog (brought in for company one Saturday morning) refused to ascend the stairs, and backed away snarling and whining. Mysterious shadows and a peculiar moaning sound would emanate on this floor. Staffs were pushed around by unseen hands.

Enfield Chase Is to the West

Here you may see the spirit of a red-cloaked knight who frequents the pastures and footpaths.

Retrace your journey up the A10 to Turnford and then take the A1170 back to Hoddesdon. Turn left into Cock Lane to Brickendon – a village west of Hoddesdon (OS Map 166 Ref 3608, Exp 174 Ref 3608).

The lid of the dessert freezer at the Farmer's Boy Pub is sometimes difficult to open. Only when staffs ask the ghost of a playful little girl to get off can they get at the contents.

Lights turn on and off, uncanny banging noises occur, and a phantom walks through a wall because it cannot open a door.

One night a staff member was sitting in her car after closing time, when the pub was in darkness. Suddenly, the bar was flooded in light. She saw a man who was not a pub employee, get a drink from one of the optics. He then came over to the window and stared at her. She realised that he was a ghost, and she drove off in a fluster. She described the spirit as approximately forty years of age with dark unkempt hair.

Charles Barclay died in the library at Fanshaws. The olfactory presence of cigar smoke wafts around when his shade is observed near the Hall.

Tour Four
Saint Albans

OS Map 166 Exp 182
Cyclical and Notable Dates: Abbey-spring and summer generally, 24th December.
Verulamium Park – summer and Christmas time
Wheathampstead / St Alban's Road (B651) November
Bernards Heath – 17th February
Chequers Street – 22nd May
Ivy House – Christmas time
King William Pub – August
White Hart Hotel – August
Strutt & Parker– summer

Just outside St Albans to the west are the remains of the Roman city of Verulamium, and parkland, where you will find the River Ver. Ghosts have been witnessed here in the recent past. A mounted Roman centurion – often seen on summer mornings – suddenly appears from nowhere.

You may encounter a white sparkling mist that materialises into the form of a cavalier. He wears a tunic with silver buttons and tassels, baggy trousers, high boots, has long curly hair, and brandishes a sword. He is seen around Christmas time and floats towards Verulamium Lake.

You may also hear the tramp of marching feet. A battalion of phantom Roman soldiers then appears. Are these men on their way to fight Queen Boudicca of the Iceni who razed to the ground the Roman garrison at the spot in AD61?

Legend

Tradition says the witch Mother Haggy who lived circa 1616 can still be seen flying around the town on her broomstick and crossing the River Ver on a kettledrum, during daytime. She could change into a cat or a hen. She was never tried as a witch, and died of natural causes. However, her ghost some say haunted Battlefield House in Chequers Street.

The grounds of nearby Gorehambury House is host to the souls of Roman soldiers. Hill End Farm near here boasts phantom footsteps of the gravelled pathway.

Just northeast of here is Batchwood Hall. Renovations taking place set free an unseen spirit who likes switching electric lights on and off, unlocking padlocks and moving articles around. This may be the unhappy spectre of a man who died whilst trying to save his wife from the burning building in 1905. It is said that he searches for his wife's missing body. There was another fire in 1995 and people fleeing from the fire witnessed an image of a woman with a shovel spreading burning coals. (See Borley Rectory, Essex, tour forty-three for similar phenomena.)

The Pre Hotel, now the Garden House, is in the vicinity, where the form of a child can just be made out in wedding photos taken in the gardens. It is believed this may be the doppelganger of someone now an adult, who once lived in the house as a young girl. She loved the gardens and is still covetous of them.

A driver travelling along the road from Wheathampstead to St Albans (B651) late one November night saw a legion of Roman soldiers marching with a standard bearer leading. Her passengers could hear the stamping feet and the chinking of harnesses but saw nothing. Apparently, many people have witnessed this phenomena.

Drop into St Albans via Bernards Heath by way of the B651. The author Betty Puttick once 'walked' into a time slip here. I wrote to Betty Puttick about my own supernatural experiences, and she graciously replied. Many authors do not bother. In brief – she was walking her dog there when she noticed the trees in the wooded part of the common looked strange and the locality was uncannily quiet. (See my experience at Clophill, Tour fourteen.) As she entered the wooded area she encountered a battle. Horses were neighing and rearing up. Swords were clashing amongst shouts and cries. She then saw a man seated against a tree trunk. He wore a leather cap, jerkin, boots and leggings. He had a bow and arrows. He appeared wounded and in pain. He gradually melted away. She may have 'wandered' into the second battle of St Albans, 17th February 1461. To understand the full extent of this fascinating and scary story, one should read her own account in her book *Ghosts of Hertfordshire*. I have read many books on retrocognition (the opposite to precognition) and this would seem to be a classic case. I was so enthralled that I visited this spot with my husband on the anniversary of the battle. Unfortunately, we did not experience anything. I did think the place had an eerie feeling to it but this may have been autosuggestion. Apparently, others have heard the sound of hoofbeats on St Peter's Street, which overtook them, travelling towards Bernards Heath. (OS Map 166 Ref 1508 OS Exp 182 Ref 1508.)

The magnificent Abbey houses many a ghost. St Alban himself has appeared with a golden glow around him. Numerous sightings through the ages of ghostly, cowled figures have been seen inside and outside the Abbey.

A procession of Benedictine monks walks through the walls. Four monks seen leaning alternately to one side then to the other as they walk, seem to be carrying a coffin.

Some people living near the Abbey hear beautiful music when the building is locked and empty. An authoritative and high-ranking clergyman heard the music and recognised it as the composition of Dr Fayrfax who died in 1521 and who is buried here. Summer and springtime seems to be the best time to witness the supernatural strains of music.

During World War Two a firewatcher heard the plaintive strains of the Fayrfax Albanus Mass. He saw the keys being played on the organ, but hands were not visible. He could also see the music, a lighted candle and a congregation of monks. This happened on Christmas Eve.

Music has been heard in the early hours of the morning (circa 2 .a.m.) by many people. Shades flutter around and the spectral smell of incense sensed.

A bride (formerly a novice) saw the ghost of her groom, who had been murdered on the way to their wedding. She expired instantly. Her bridal wreath was preserved here until around 1950.

A visible and audible spectral monk speaking Latin haunts Romeland Cottage which overlooks the Abbey churchyard. It is believed that the cottage may have been built on the site of the charnel house, where monks awaited burial during the plague.

Nearby at St Albans School, the sound of hobnail boots belonging, it is said, to a deceased caretaker may be heard stomping along the empty hallways.

The Gateway was once a prison, and sometimes the sounds of screams pervade the area.

On All Souls Day, 1st November, an apparition of a procession of monks both inside and outside the Abbey has been observed – likely to be seen in the early morning.

Near to the Abbey is Chequers Street. This is the site of the Battle of St Albans, one of the fiercest combats of the Wars of the Roses, 22nd May 1455. Battlefield House once stood in this street where modern shops are now. The house was said to have a gloomy, creepy feeling about it, and one had the sense of constantly being watched. Chequers Street is haunted today by the sounds of an ancient war. Horses neighing and whinnying, the sound of sword on metal, voices, and shouts of torment around 22nd May can be heard. The shops in this area are reputed to be haunted by nondescript shadows, ghostly footsteps and a strong smell of flowers.

Ghosts galore haunt St Peter's Street. A house in this road is haunted by a soldier who walks down a staircase which no longer exists.

A butler committed suicide in Mallison House. He appears at a window wearing a white wig and butler's garb. He has also been seen on the stairs – minus his legs.

At Pemberton Almshouses, a bed would produce an indent as if a weighty person had lain on it coupled with the strong smell of tobacco.

The Grange is in the centre of this road. A grey lady loiters around the building. She also stalks the area of the Alban Arena, which was built on the site of gardens belonging to the Grange.

A servant girl is obsessed with polishing the staircase handrail at Ivy House. She is believed to have been walled up in a chimney of a house which previously stood on this site. She also cleans the cellars. This young blonde wearing white, stands at the top of the stairs. Her footsteps can be heard approaching the entrance hall around Christmas time.

Christopher Place is a shopping precinct, and is built on the site of the old Wellington Inn, parts of which are still there. The Blue Boar previously occupied the spot. A little boy who lived at The Blue Boar was killed when he ran under a coach and horses just outside. The changing rooms at Country Casuals have an eerie feeling. I was trying on some garments, and had the strong feeling that something did not want me there, and I had to leave. At the time I knew nothing of the ghostly activity here.

Staff at the opticians have reported feeling damp cobwebs cross their faces. Lights turn on at 4.00 a.m. and cc cameras prove the building is empty. No electrical faults were found.

Employees of a butcher's shop that used to be at 26, Market Place have reported poltergeist activity – sounds of banging, crashing, punctured car tyres, cobwebs skimming faces and lights turning on and off. A small hazy figure has been seen as well as a man standing in the area who vanishes.

In need of refreshment? Visit one or two of the following pubs:-

Ye Olde Fighting Cocks – supposed to be one of the oldest pubs in England. Articles disappear only to reappear somewhere else. Monks dressed in brown habits are visible from the knees upward. They surface from the cellar, creep across the bar and settle by the fire before disappearing.

The Tudor Tavern – George Street – over six-hundred years old. A shade follows bar staff around, and may chase you out of the building. You may meet 'Harry', the resident poltergeist. The usual old poltergeist tricks apply – lights on and off – plates and glasses thrown around. Is this the same spirit of a man seen sitting at a table, jug in hand, with dark curly hair, beard, black tunic and a 'bunch of lace at his throat'? (Quotation: *The Highwayman* by Alfred Noyes.)

The Boot Inn – Market Place – circa seventeenth century. Supernatural happenings with electrical equipment, lights on and off, and the juke box playing of its own accord.

The Hare & Hounds – Folly Lane. Here a barmaid came across an intense black something that wanted to engulf her. She said it was the epitome of evil. At one time an odious and foul goo seeped from the cellar walls. The adjoining bricked-up wall was once part of the city gallows. The dead bodies would be flung into a pit which is now the cellar. In the bar the front door opens and closes by itself. Then a door at the other end does exactly the same, as if someone has walked in from one end and exited at the other.

The Goat Inn – Sopwell Lane – circa 1500. The spook here has a staring, demonic face. Things get moved around. There are cold spots, weird noises and an obnoxious atmosphere in certain parts of the premises.

White Lion – Sopwell Lane – sixteenth century. A young girl watches at a window, waiting for a lover who unbeknown to her was hanged at the gallows. The indistinct impression of a face appears at a window in the bar. A figure has been seen sitting at the fireplace even though the bar is closed. A spectral hand has been witnessed on the stair rail to the cellar.

King William IV – 1937. A tall phantom dressed in khaki uniform frequents the cellar here. He could be a past patron who was a member of the Home Guard. August is a likely time to see him.

The Verulam Arms – 1853. Poltergeist activity.

Six Bells – sixteenth century. Phantom footsteps and a spook in the kitchen.

Fleur De Lys – French Row. A feeling of being watched and ghostly footsteps are heard.

The Three Hammers – Chiswell Green. Poltergeist activity.

White Hart Hotel – Holywell Hill – fifteenth century. People experience the uncomfortable feeling of knowing a presence is around but can see nothing. The cellar door locks itself without a key. Lights turn on and off. Room 8 is particularly scary. Messages by an unseen hand have been daubed on a mirror, and towels are scattered about the room. In Room 7 a fireplace that had been bricked up was consumed in flames. A little girl sits by the fireplace in the bar. The image of a lady in Georgian dress walks here. Paranormal investigation teams held séances here. Many strange things happened and clairvoyants contacted various spirits. The stories revealed were then corroborated at the Hertfordshire Archives. August may be a good time to experience something.

A coach pulled by headless horses climbs up Holywell Hill. An amorphous faced ghost wearing a white ruff and black skullcap resides in White Hart Cottage, Holywell Hill.

Estate Agents Strutt and Parker are visited by a mysterious monk and a pipe-smoking cavalier. A haggard face appears between the filing cabinets. These manifestations often happen in summer. Other buildings in Holywell Hill have ghostly activity.

Shops in the High Street, particularly No. 17, are haunted by a young girl who was incarcerated by her father because she had fallen in love with a storeman. She committed suicide. Her departed spirit is believed to be the miserable looking grey lady that dwells here.

Adjacent shops have had poltergeist activity. Stock is thrown around and yet another monk manifests here.

The Gables in Market Place, is haunted on the upper floor by a man with a malevolent expression and an old lady sitting by the window making lace or embroidering. She is said to transmit the desire in the onlooker to jump out of the window. An adjacent shop has a ghost who befriends children.

W H Smith inhabits the ancient Moot Hall building. This premises has been a courthouse and a gaol. Here you may meet 'Henry' who likes to tamper with the lighting. He is apparently a benign ghost who may have been tried here during the Peasant's Revolt of 1381.

Some of the premises on George Street are very old, which may not be apparent due to the modern facades. The wraith of a little girl stands on the stairs of Long Tall Sally. Another business has a troublesome ghost who moves stock around.

The apartments above the Alban's Antique centre are haunted by a transparent lady wearing a lace dress who vanishes through a wall. Is she the unseen being responsible for turning on taps in the middle of the night?

Fishpool Street was once a slum area where policemen would only patrol in two's. A number of ghosts reside here. You may meet a grey man, a man wearing a top hat, a nurse clad in a grey uniform, a cavalier and two white ponies pulling an open carriage, driven by a man in a panama hat.

A lady in a blue dress prowls between the houses in the street at 3.00 a.m. She constantly wipes her tears with a handkerchief. It is believed she mourns the death of her daughter who she accidentally asphyxiated.

Another property houses a ghost that tries to strangle the residents. Luckily for the inhabitants next door, their ghost is a genial lady.

The list of supernatural visitations in Fishpool Street goes on: a spook lifts latches and closes doors, dogs and cats watch something unseen by humans, a disabled woman still taps on the floor for attention, a soldier from the Boer War manifests – he may wish to shake hands, beware for they are ice cold, furniture is moved around, a cavalier slides around a cellar.

A spectre in Welclose Street appears at a kitchen window. A woman in Victorian dress drifts along a hallway and bedroom. Screams are heard in the middle of the night.

Kingsbury Water Mill boasts the singing soul of a departed miller.

A woman wearing a straw hat holding a trug may be seen in a Verulam Road garden.

You may espy an elderly man in Hill Street who stands by a bonfire as if warming his hands.

Footsteps resounding on a stone floor aisle have been heard at St Stephen's church. The extraordinary thing is, the aisle is carpeted!

A sister has been observed usually during the winter evenings at St Alban's Hospital in Normandy Road. Her feet and ankles are not visible as she walks on the original ground level.

Kingsbury Avenue and Camlet Way are believed to be built on the site of a Roman burial ground. Roman soldiers appear here.

On the periphery of St Alban's is an area known as The Camp. Roman soldiers can be heard tramping on gravel in an area that is soft grass. The Camp' pub is here.

Also on the edge of the town is Frogmore Village. A pilot that crashed killing two people on the ground is said to haunt here.

St Michael's Manor Hotel on the outskirts of St Alban's dates back to 1512. A ghost walks down the main staircase. In St Michael's Street the fetch of a middle-aged lady in white wanders around a restaurant in this road.

Map of St Alban's

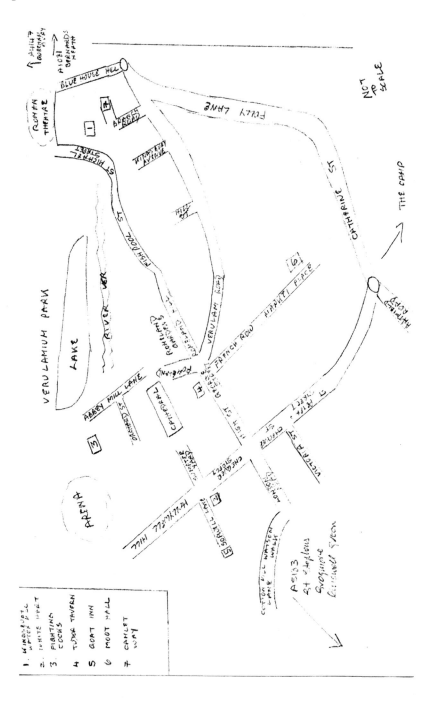

1. KINGSBURY WATER MEAT
2. WHITE HART
3. FIGHTING COCKS
4. TUDOR TAVERN
5. GOAT INN
6. MOOT HALL
7. CANLET WAY

Tour Five
From Tyttenhanger to Salisbury Hall, London Colney, South Mimms, Shenley, South Barnet and East Barnet

OS Map 166 Exp 182
Cyclical and Notable Dates Barnet – 24th December, Easter Day or 14th April

To the south east of St Alban's is Tyttenhanger.

Here a mansion is haunted by a man believed to be Sir Henry Blount, who wears a satin dressing gown which rustles as he perambulates the corridor to his library on the second floor.

Due south is Salisbury Hall (South of London Colney) (Exp Map 182 Ref 1902 and OS Map 166 Ref 1902).

A handsome, young cavalier haunts here. He wears a frilly white shirt, dark knee breeches and large silver buckles on his shoes. His long blond hair is tied back. He was carrying secret papers when he was surrounded by roundheads and took refuge at Salisbury Hall. He could find nowhere to hide, and so realising he would be caught, committed suicide.

Some say he 'fell on his sword', others that he used his firearm. Spectral footsteps may be heard. Do they belong to this troubled cavalier?

Charles 2nd installed his mistress Nell Gwynne here. Nell, dressed in a blue shawl, flits around the great hall and a bedroom. A cheerful ghost, she has also been seen on the lower part of the staircase. The bedroom over the porch is frequented by something horrific that shakes the bed.

Phantom laughter can sometimes be heard in the garden.

On leaving here, take the B1081 to London Colney, and to the west is Napsbury Hospital. A resident of the cottage in the grounds was troubled by the spirit of an old lady, who would turn doorknobs and frighten pets. Faltering footsteps ascending the stairs were heard. A grey phantom would then enter a bedroom and fling off the bedclothes. The resident spoke to the image. The old lady then materialised only to slowly fade away. She is not so troublesome now, but is seen on occasions standing by the fire.

Sounds of phantom trotting horses can be heard at the Colney Fox Pub, and strong poltergeist activity emanates at The Bull Inn.

Take the B556 to South Mimms

The fourteenth century vicarage is haunted by a previous vicar's wife who was murdered by her husband in the seventeenth century. Her screams are heard and a tall lady in a grey dress walks down the stairs. Nurses at a nearby sanatorium witnessed a spectral lady wearing grey.

In the church a priest may be seen kneeling at the altar. He then proceeds to rise and float to the vestry door where he disappears. At night, weird noises emanate from the tombs where blue lights dance about.

At a crossroads in the village, an old man with a long beard raises his cane in acknowledgement of the villagers passing by. Many a traveller has been held up by a highwayman, in this area as this was a principal thoroughfare to the north. The road is reputedly haunted by these robbers and muggers who are said to be buried in the churchyard.

Just a mile north is Mymmshall Wood, where the ruined motte and bailey of South Mimms Castle can still be found. The ghost of Sir Geoffrey De Mandeville clad in battle attire haunts the castle mound.

Take the A1081 to High Barnet

The junction of Barnet Hill and Meadway in High Barnet is haunted by a young woman and child. They stand in the middle of the road and traffic passes through them. It is believed that these are the ghosts of a woman and child who were killed at this spot one Christmas.

In east Barnet, the spectre of Sir Geoffrey De Mandeville, dressed in a red cloak with silver spurs appears here. He is sometimes accompanied by a lady in grey. Christmas Eve is a good time to catch sight of him. He is supposed to appear every six years. Next one 2022.

A re-enactment of the Battle of Barnet on Easter Day, 14th April 1487, can sometimes be caught. Legend has it that at the top of Hadley Church, a wizard conjured up a heavy mist to aid Edward fourth's army. Sometimes a fog manifests on 14th April, during the repeated image.

De Mandeville is also seen at Trent Park, now a university campus. There is an old trench fortification in the grounds named Camlet Moat. The moat can be seen on the south side of Hadley Road.

Dick Turpin haunts this area. He is seen riding furiously across the surrounding common land and roads, his cloak flying behind him. He is also observed wearing a tricorn hat, riding coat and boots, skulking between the trees.

A spirit of an old witch creeps around the moat. The figure wearing black is said to be a crone who lived in nearby Enfield Chase and was well known to be a witch. She was executed in 1622, but now she is seen at the moat stepping falteringly forward using a stick to ease her way. In addition, a ghostly man chases travellers here.

The cellar of a house near The Grange in East Barnet is disturbed by a transparent spirit. (Houses named The Grange are nearly always next to a church.) Rumbling sounds, tapping, and indistinct voices are heard.

A headless black figure haunts Oak Hill Park, East Barnet. It drifts around the pavilion and then turns in the direction of the onlooker.

Another entity frequents here. He wears a large flamboyant hat and Edwardian clothing. He sits on a bench and then vanishes. He has been caught on film.

A ghost train appears on the line near Hadley Wood South tunnel. It leaves a cloud of smoke behind and is audible.

Tour Six

From Watford to Bushey, Elstree, Aldenham, Radlett, Bricket Wood, Abbots Langley and Kings Langley

OS Maps 166 and 176 OS. Exp 182
Cyclical and Notable Dates – Radlett – Wintertime
Aldenham – Wintertime and February
Watford – 9th March
Abbots Langley – 1st November

Scene painters and workmen at The Palace Theatre at Watford have heard footsteps on an empty stage at 3.a.m. The curtains then separate as if something has walked through them. Footsteps are heard elsewhere in unoccupied spaces. Three past employees have died here. Also, the theatre is believed to be built over a graveyard where Napoleonic French prisoners are interred.

A premises in the High Street just above Jackson's the jewellers is haunted by an old Tudor man. He wears a doublet, stockings and a ruff. He appears in a grey, murky mist and walks at a lower level, where the original floor would have been. He has been witnessed by many employees when it was Copperfields Restaurant.

Number 97 High Street stayed empty for many years and was haunted by the previous occupant, a frail old lady, who died there.

St Mary's church and nearby shopping centre is haunted by a spirit of a schoolteacher who died in a fire, rescuing the children.

Watford Library has the shade of a male librarian who dislikes female librarians.

The tunnel near Watford Junction Railway Station was constructed underneath the site of an old churchyard. Bones and broken coffins fell onto the railway builders. After the construction was completed, at a certain area, the steam engine plate men reported that the boilers would spit coal back, causing some workers to be badly burned. On investigation, it transpired that this happened under the old graveyard. Could this be caused by revengeful spirits?

Cassiobury Park lies just to the west of Watford. At one time the grounds were extensive and a magnificent mansion stood there. Now, the public park is much smaller, but has a lake and part of it borders the Grand Union Canal. The ghost of Lord Capel of Little Hadham Hall, appears here on the anniversary of his execution, 9th March 1649. He has also been seen other times, sometimes headless, and occasionally with long hair and a moustache. Why does he not appear at Capel House or Hadham Hall (both premises at Little Hadham)?

Jack o'Cassiobury was a Negro slave employed by a rich lady whose property was near the Grand Union Canal. She disliked the bargees that frequented the watercourse that abutted her land. Jack's daily task was to harass the boatmen, and generally create merry hell. One day he fell in the canal during a fight and was knocked unconscious. He drowned. His tormented ghost now prowls around Iron Bridge Lock

The Grove, now a hotel, is situated just to the north of Cassiobury. The ghost of Lord Doneraile has been observed many times, usually on stormy nights – naturally. He joins a phantom foxhunt, complete with an unearthly Reynard and baying hounds.

An area near Station Road and the railway bridge is troubled by spectral noises. It is believed that someone had been hanged, and unhappy souls amass here.

Mill End Community Centre has the presence of a mischievous poltergeist. Also the spirit of a lady in Edwardian dress loiters in the ladies' lavatory. If you speak to her, she will give you a curt reply, then vanish.

The canteen of the Watford Observer newspaper offices are haunted by a spiteful ghost who pushes and jabs people. One employee was knocked to the ground by an invisible force. Strange banging and whistling have also been heard.

The Bramfield Estate, Garston, in the north of the town is where the unaccountable smell of urine permeates the area on occasions. No cause can be found and some locals think it is of supernatural origin.

Otterspool can be found just on the fringes of Watford to the northeast. You may meet the ghost believed to be of a foreman who died in a factory here. He wears a white overall and smokes a pipe, is of stocky build with grey hair. His features are indistinct.

Take the A411 to Bushey

The Royal Masonic School was bought out by the International University. This building was used by TV companies. The former students' residential section is reputed to be haunted. The usual spectacle of electric lighting switching on and off by non-human agency occur. A little girl's spectre drifts around the stairs. There are underground tunnels underneath the building, in the past used as easements. These are checked periodically and ghostly whispering and unmistakable sounds of sobbing are heard.

Another ghost is said to be Hillary, the daughter of a previous headmaster. Some say she flung herself from one of the towers, others that she fell from a horse. Galloping hooves are heard. However, it has recently transpired that Hillary died of natural causes, but her ghost has been witnessed in the chapel where her hazy image has been captured on film.

Ghosts of boys playing football and generally messing around are seen only to disappear. Also, amongst other ghosts is that of a former school matron.

Now the university has been converted into apartments. It would be interesting to know if the residents have experienced anything spooky.

Continue on the A411 to Elstree

The Holly Bush public house in the High Street is haunted by a bearded man who has plodding footsteps which are audible. Some dogs become agitated in the car park, which, apparently, is the site of a former undertaker.

Carry on along the A411 – Deacons Hill to Borehamwood.

Legend

A story handed down through the ages tells of Tommy Deacon who rode his horse like a madman down what is now Deacon's Hill, that he broke his neck. Some say that he is buried at the foot near the crossroads, others that his grave is at the top, where the earth is always dry come rain or shine. There is a patch of ground which fits this description, but local sceptics say that this is due to porous chalk.

The Gate film Studios at Borehamwood were haunted by a variety of ghosts – a former makeup artist, a previous workman, another man and a bearded man seen by numerous people on many occasions. The studios were demolished in 2006, and housing now occupies the site.

Take the A5183 to Radlett

The Wagon & Horses Pub can be found on this road. There is a small lay-by on the opposite side of the road. Here a spectral coach and horses stand. A man in a three-cornered hat, jacket and knee breeches, assists a lady in grey to alight from the coach. They then cross the road and enter the inn. This apparition is usually seen in wintertime.

Take the A462 from Radlett to Aldenham

Note of Interest

Off this road lies Gills Hill Lane. It continues down Loom Lane to Butlers Green. Loom Lane can also be found off the A5183 (the old Roman road), near the Cat & Fiddle Pub.

A notorious murder was committed in Gills Hill Lane in 1823, and dubbed the 'Hertfordshire Tragedy'. A boxer murdered a solicitor who had cheated him at cards. He was shot point blank, his throat cut, and dumped in a pond in Gill Hill Lane. For a full and detailed account of this fascinating story, see *Crime in Hertfordshire. Vol 2* by Simon Walker.

At Wall Hall Mansion, the ghost of a woman believed to be a former housekeeper, appeared, mainly in February, wearing a long grey skirt and white blouse. There were also reports of a grey lady. Were there two female ghosts here, or were the sightings of one woman? Children's laughter was sometimes heard when no youngsters were around. Swishing sounds like a long skirt trailing on the floor were also heard. Expensive homes are now on this site, and one wonders if the ghosts still haunt.

Retrace your journey to Radlett. Travel north and at Colney Street turn left into Smug Oak Lane, Bricket Wood. (OS Exp. Map 182 Ref 1502.) Here a phantom female stands in the middle of the road and then vanishes. Sometimes a figure in an overcoat is seen.

To the west and just north of Watford is Abbots Langley.

The vicarage is haunted by Mary Ann Treble, a servant girl allegedly ill-treated by a former vicar's wife. She looks out of a bedroom window, and has been witnessed sliding towards St Lawrence's Church where she meanders around the gravestones. She has been seen on three consecutive All Saints Days – 1st November, praying in the church. (These are just the recorded sightings – there may be other unreported glimpses of this spectre.) It is believed that she died a terrible death of pneumonia after she either fell or was pushed down the stairs. Repairs to the fireplace in her room never stay mended. Is the fireplace connected to her death? Further reports indicate that she rises from her grave in St Lawrence's churchyard, and floats to the vicarage.

Leavesden aerodrome now used as a film studio is haunted by an airman in RAF uniform, who was accidentally killed one stormy night.

Kings Langley lies to the North West, where a procession of ghostly monks walks in the remains of the Priory orchard.

Tour Seven
Redbourn and Hemel Hempstead

OS Map 166

From St Alban's take the A5183 to Redbourn.

Beware of a nasty bend in the road near the Pre Hotel. Motorists have accidents here. Cars develop unexplainable faults only to be resolved once past this area. Apparently, in the days before the motor car, horses would shy here near some trees, would not go forward, and would have to be turned back.

Redbourn village has many pubs with a ghostly history.

The Cricketers, circa 1800, overlooks Redbourn Common. Saucepan lids went missing, then reappeared when new landlords moved in. This happened with other objects as well. The ghost responsible for this phenomena is known as mischievous Martha. Dogs will not go near the function room at the top of the stairs.

The Bell and Shears, over four-hundred years old, has ghostly footsteps which can be traced along the upstairs corridor – again animals avoid this area. Drinkers in the bar can sometimes hear the footsteps even though the passageway is carpeted. There are no historical legends to account for the haunting.

The Bull, is a sixteenth century hostelry. The blue room upstairs (no longer blue) is reputedly haunted by someone who was left to die here. A spectral someone resembling a milkmaid loiters around the bar area. The cellar has noises of rolling barrels, but when inspected all is as it should be. The pub is also haunted by a former deceased landlord.

Take the B487 to Hemel Hempstead

The Jarman Park Cinema, now Cineworld suffers from poltergeist activity. At Picotts End a five-hundred-year-old cottage has some unique monastic paintings. Poltergeist activity has been reported and a vision of a monk nearby.

Ye Olde Kings Arms, reputedly haunted by a big fat man who sits on a bed and laughs. A lady in white has also been seen. The inn dates back to Tudor times and guests report of 'restless nights' in a certain bedroom, where strange noises are heard.

In the White Hart (circa 1530 in parts) the ghost of a man who seems scared out of his wits, appears in black and white, similar to a photograph negative. Some believe this is the image of a man who was killed on the stairs while trying to escape a press gang, and his screams can still be heard. Disembodied voices have been heard coming from an empty bar.

A former work colleague of mine also witnessed some spooks at a farm in Gilston, Essex. They were farm workers wandering around some silos, but they too were in black and white, like a photograph negative. What should have been black was white, and vice versa.

The Crown, circa 1523, is where a presence is felt in a cold spot. Also orbs have been photographed here.

Tour Eight

From Rickmansworth to Chenies, Sarratt, Chipperfield and Bovingdon

OS Maps 165 and 166
Cyclical and Notable Dates – Chenies 9th September

Rickmansworth lies to the southwest of Watford.

A supermarket that stands on the site of The Swan Hotel has the ghost of an old man who wandered around the hotel. It would seem that he still haunts this spot. Although he is no longer seen, his presence is sensed and some employees have been touched by phantom fingers.

The headless figure of a woman is seen late at night in a churchyard near Long Lane.

The Feathers pub has a poltergeist.

A ghostly image haunts Moor Lane.

The ghost of Admiral Lord Anson of Moor Park Mansion perambulates the grounds. (Moor Park is sometimes addressed as Northwood, Middlesex.)

Take the A404 to Chenies (strictly in Buckinghamshire, but included here) where the manor house is haunted by at least two ghosts. Heavy, distinct footsteps and creaking floorboards are heard in the middle of the night. They have been traced to an anteroom used by Elizabeth 1st. Also, at about 2.00 a.m., noises of limping footsteps start outside a bedroom and travel to an ancient gallery, once used as a dormitory by two-hundred of Cromwell's men .However, other researchers are of the opinion that the limping ghost may be that of Henry 8th .He had a jousting wound on his leg that was ulcerous and would not heal. The monarch stayed at Chenies from time to time.

A priest's hiding hole was discovered in recent times adjacent to the pink bedroom. There is an almost decipherable date of 9th September 1660 something. The priest hole is now used as a built-in wardrobe, but on the night of the anniversary of 9th September, something unseen opens the doors and windows of the pink room and walk-in wardrobe. Chenies Manor is a private residence but open to the public on occasions.

To the Northeast Lies Sarratt

Here at Rose Hall, the grandparents of the eminent ghost hunter Peter Underwood once lived. The house is said to be haunted by a headless man wearing a bright, blue coat with gilt buttons. He is supposed to have been murdered here – apparently by decapitation!

A little way north you will find Chipperfield. A one-storey property in Megg Lane is haunted by a large Roman soldier, a monk and a praying priest.

To the Northeast Is Bovingdon

In Box Lane a mysterious shining presence has been reported. A house in this road suffered from violent poltergeist activity. In the dim and distant past a murder was committed in St Lawrence's churchyard. It is said that restless spirits dwell here due to the locality having been polluted by the butchery.

Tour Nine

From Ware to Wareside, Stanstead Abbotts, Great Amwell, Ware Park, Thundridge (Cold Christmas) Wadesmill and High Cross

OS Map 166 OS Exp 194
Cyclical and Notable Dates Ware – 8th September
Great Amwell – June Evenings

The Great Bed of Ware, dates back to 1493, and was mentioned in Shakespeare's *Twelfth Night*. The bed was intended for the use of royalty and the gentry. It measures approximately eleven feet square, has posts eight feet high, and an ornately carved bedstead.

It is reported that occupants who try to sleep in the haunted bed, end up with scratches, pinches, bruises and exhaustion, as the ghostly assault goes on throughout the night. The bed was moved around the taverns of Ware. It is thought to be haunted by its creator Jonas Fosbrooke. It now resides in the Victoria & Albert Museum in London.

I stayed at Fanham's Hall on two occasions when it belonged to the Chartered Building Societies Institute. However, I did not encounter any supernatural activity. The only spirits I came across were in the bar! For an excellent comprehensive history of this fascinating house, refer to *Ghostly Hertfordshire* by Damien O'Dell. The ghosts of the Hall are numerous and varied. For example, running footsteps and clattering about on the top unoccupied floor. The old music room fleetingly reflects something in a mirror, and plaintive melodies emanate from the empty room.

Another mirror, this time on the main staircase has shown the reflection of a woman in a long medieval dress and pointed headdress. The sound of crying children seems to come from an area under the stairs. Other phenomena are, icy hands felt around one's neck, a feeling of an unseen presence, indistinct voices, one's name being called, hair pulled by unseen hands, objects flung around or moved by invisible hands before the observer's eyes, a man in a waistcoat who looks out of an upstairs window, a feeling of a crowded room which is empty, a strong smell of tobacco, a lady in a brown and white dress, a grey lady searching for something, the usual poltergeist tricks with electrical goods and lighting, accidentally bumping into someone who is not there, a haunted cellar, the sound of breaking glass, doors opening and closing in deserted areas and ghostly laughter in the drawing room. The list goes on! (OS Map 166 Ref 3715.)

In the mid-1880s several clergymen were spied laying a ghost at midnight in St Mary's cemetery. Could this have been connected with Katherine Fanshawe from Ware Park, who was interred here secretly at night, but not in the Fanshawe family vault? (See Markyate Cell, Tour nineteen, and Nomansland Tour eighteen.)

A house in New Road was haunted by something that turned on taps, opened doors and trudged upstairs.

Another council property in Tower Road has the unhappy spirit of a woman who is likely to follow you upstairs

Old Hope House near Ware Lock was demolished in the 1980s by Glaxo Smith Kline to make way for their new offices. Two cats belonging to the house were so terrified of an entity that they were killed – one vaulted out of an upstairs window and broke its neck, the other scampered away from something so fast it collided with a cellar door and died. Rooms would always be icy cold whatever the weather, and constant footsteps perambulated an upstairs corridor. When the house was demolished, a number of Roman coffins were found, but previous residents believed the ghost was of a man who hanged himself there. It would be interesting to know if the Glaxo Smith Kline employees have experienced ghostly phenomena on this site.

The Waterfront public house stands on a roundabout at the High Street. It is here that a female motorist had to perform an emergency stop one evening. She nearly collided with an old-fashioned car which suddenly appeared, driven by a stern looking man who took no notice of her. She could see him clearly as the street lamps gave sufficient light, but his car had no lights on. The apparition then vanished suddenly.

Presdales School woods are reported to have an entity that wears a black cape and hood. The spectre's skin is covered in scars, and it has bright yellow-green eyes. If it sees you, it will chase you. (OS Map 166 Ref 3613.)

History Notes

On 8th September 1617 Margaret Bownes of Ware met with her husband William who was working in East Field, and discussed pawning a petticoat. William disapproved and struck her head with a cudgel. She died instantly.

Ann Sickling and Anne Packer were indicted for eavesdropping in 1660. They were standing under the eaves of a house in Ware listening to a conversation, their intention being to cause trouble between the occupants of the house and their neighbour.

To the East of Ware You Will Find Wareside

A former employee at the Chequers told me that as she walked by the side of a laid table, all the cutlery rose into the air. This was witnessed by customers.

Just southeast of Ware, is Stanstead Abbotts. The Red Lion pub is said to have a priest hole and is possibly haunted. (OS Map 166 Ref 3811.) Opposite the pub, at a bend in the road (B181) towards Harlow, if driving, the sensation of colliding with a tramp occurs.

Partly retrace your journey and you will find the village of Great Amwell off the A1170

Here the New River turns into a lake known as Amwell Pool at the foot of a steep path. In the middle of the water lies a small islet surrounded by willow trees. On the islet is a grave, allegedly, of a Victorian girl whose ghost flits around here. It is rumoured that on occasions you can hear her weeping. Haileybury Madrigal Society – very much alive – sing here on June summer evenings. This usually tranquil place can become quite crowded with the local audience. No seats – standing only on the side of the river. The island and trees are floodlit, which makes the area and evening enchanting.

You can reach this spot by way of another turning off the A1170, but it is much more picturesque and atmospheric to go via the hamlet's church and pub. (OS Exp 194 Ref 3712 or OS 166 Ref 3712.)

Amwellbury House lies a mile to the south of Ware. A procession of chanting monks is seen and heard here, usually just before snowfall.

Now Take the 'Old' A10 Road to Thundridge

The old church ruins at Cold Christmas can be found about half a mile east of the village of Thundridge mainly down a footpath (OS Map 166 Ref 3617 and OS Exp 194 Ref 3617). Approximately sixty graves are still visible, with many headstones either broken or leaning over. Ghostly music has been heard.

On one occasion, recently, some people decided to visit the site at night, as they had heard it was a strange place. As they were about to leave in their car, a sudden mist came down that enshrouded the vehicle. They then heard someone trying the door handles but they could not see anyone outside the car.

The site between the River Rib and the church ruins is haunted by soldiers wearing helmets and breastplates. There is shouting, a disturbed atmosphere, and the ruins appear to be on fire.

A policewoman told me that she felt the 'new' Victorian church of St Mary's had a very strange atmosphere. She had been called out to an incident, but could not wait to get away.

Wadesmill is part of Thundridge. Still on the 'old' A10 going north—The Feathers pub dates back to 1615, and was once an old coaching in which stabled one-hundred horses. Here the ghost of a fair-haired girl playing a violin lurks. She is believed to have been crushed by a coach and horses.

Carry on up the 'Old' A10 to High Cross

A private house in this vicinity was haunted by a skull and a man dressed in a cape. Items went missing and dogs barked at an unseen something. The reflection of the ghost was shown in a mirror, and caught on camera.

Tour Ten

From Buntingford to Layston, Great Hormead, Anstey, Braughing and Standon

OS Maps 166 and 167. OS Exp 194
Cyclical and Notable Dates Standon – 12th September
Buntingford – 26th December, November and winter
Time generally
Braughing – 2nd October, 10th May, Christmas

The most famous Buntingford ghosts resided at Bell House, now the Bell Gallery, which dates back to 1450. The premises was originally the Bell House Coaching Inn which was let out in three apartments in the 1940s. All these families complained of strange occurrences – door handles turning and no one there, noisy footsteps in empty rooms, a baby crying and a woman sobbing quietly. Residents awoke to feel an invisible weight pressing down on them, or a sensation of being strangled. A séance was held here and the sitters 'got through' to a Hannah Bedwell. She indicated that she was fifteen years old, and had had an illegitimate child. The father, a porter at the inn had been killed. Hannah was concerned that she would be dismissed and evicted, so she killed her baby by lying on it. The spirit informed the circle that she was arrested, imprisoned in Bedford gaol and hanged at Newgate. The members of the séance decided to look into the information received, and it was confirmed in parish records that a Hannah Bedwell had resided at the inn and she was hanged at Newgate for infanticide. There was also a record of the baby's birth.

According to Hannah, there were other troubled spirits here who were patrons of the inn, 'bawds and cut-purses'. For a more comprehensive account of this story and details of the séance, please read *The Mummy of Birchen Bower and other Ghost Stories* by Harry Ludlam.

Other ghosts reported in this building are a man in black who descends the stairs, a grey lady, and the door handles still turn of their own volition.

A house in the High Street has the ghost of a young girl in a nightdress who walks into the dining room. She has also been heard pacing about upstairs. Doors open and shut, and children's toys are moved around. A lady in white appears to any children living in the house.

Number 87 High Street, was once the White Hart, and here footsteps are heard.

An apparition of a monk has been seen in Monk's Walk. Years ago, it is said, that a monk drowned a child in a pond near here, but it is no use looking for the pond as it no longer exists, but you may espy the monk!

On November evenings if you walk beside the river near Chapel End, you may experience the sparks and moving lights under the water in the middle of the river. The ghost lights surface and cross the road into 'Totties Ditch' and then stop behind The Crown.

Also at dusk in wintertime, you may see a white something cross the road at the rear of St Peter's Church.

Aspenden Hall lies to the southwest of Buntingford. Here, it is reported that the ghost of a nursemaid searches for a child she accidentally drowned in a lake, and the child's eerie cries can be heard.

Just outside Buntingford, to the northeast are the ruins of St Bartholomew's Church (although some of the building is still intact). You can walk to this site through Church Street, Buntingford.

The medieval village of Layston was a ruin by 1700, but people still worshipped at this church up until the Second World War. However, the bells are now rung by ghostly campanologists after dark. On one occasion, the bell ringers of Buntingford heard them herald evensong, and went to see who was in the locked church. When they arrived they found the church lit, but as soon as they entered, the lights were extinguished and the ringing ceased. The place was deserted!

Take the B1038 to Great Hormead, and on the way you will pass Alswick Hall on the right. Here, phantom sounds of a coach and horses re-enact an accident. The lady of the manor and her coachman were drowned in the pond when her carriage overturned. Tradition has it that the horses were alarmed by a supernatural spectacle and bolted.

At Great Hormead a house formerly named Rectory Cottage, experiences ghostly footsteps. The spirit is thought to be male due to the heaviness of the tread. The sounds usually descend from the attic, but sometimes come through the front door and climb the stairs.

The driveway leading to the church from the road is haunted by a figure wearing a pale robe. It glides unfalteringly as if snooping about. Some say it is the monk that haunts Brick house, which can be found off the minor roads to the northeast of the village. Legend has it that a murder took place here, and maybe the monk was implicated in some way.

Nearby is Anstey. A secret tunnel runs from Anstey castle mound to Cave Gate in Wyddial to the west. In 1831 a fiddler known as Blind George entered the tunnel with his dog. He played his fiddle so that those above ground could follow his route. Suddenly, there was an awful screech, then all was as quiet as the grave, not a sound. Villagers saw the terrified dog pelt out of the cave, its tail missing and with scorched fur. George was never seen again, and noone has ventured down the tunnel since. Apparently, its trail can be seen in winter because the snow melts first here, and it has been said that crops will not grow on the land above. Apparently, on occasions one can hear the plaintive sounds of music where the tunnel runs underground. Interestingly, there is an area of Anstey called Snow End, but this does not appear to be on the track.

From Great Hormead, Take the B1368 to Braughing (Pronounced Braffing)

Just before entering Braughing, the sewage works are on the left hand side of the road, just before Hay Street. Here an unpleasant feeling – not smell – of an evil presence abounds. Before the sewage farm was in existence, it is rumoured that a man died a horrible death in this vicinity after committing a crime – possibly theft.

The road from Braughing to Horse Cross (Stortford Lane) is haunted every five years on the 10th of May by five monks, and they have also been witnessed at the lower end of Upp Hall Lane. (OS Map Exp 194 Ref 4024 and Ref 4123 or OS Map 167 Ref 4024 and Ref 4123.)

The story is that they were caught poaching trout from the River Rib. It is said that they died from food poisoning, due to consuming the stolen fish. The next due date is 2021.

However, a house at Cockhampstead, may be formerly Cockhampstead Priory, is sometimes open to the public under the National Gardens Scheme. There is a moat around a small island in the grounds. Perhaps this is where the monks fished. It is a stone's throw from Braughing Friars. According to Harry Ludlam, in his book, *The Mummy of Birchen Bower and other Ghost Stories*, back in the 1920s there were still elderly villagers living who swore that they saw the ghosts every five years. The ghostly monks, if seen, portend a good harvest.

Friars Road leads to Braughing Friars. Here you may encounter a ghostly monk.

Around Christmas time, the spirit of a tall lady dressed in a chic two-piece suit (possibly of Edwardian fashion) with her hair swept back in a bun, materialises in Braughing village. She appears perfectly solid, then suddenly vanishes. She has also been observed at other times of the year.

Legend

A man thought to be dead was being carried in his coffin to his funeral. The cortège was travelling down Fleece Lane to the church, when a pallbearer slipped. The coffin was dropped. Noises were heard from inside and on opening the lid, the supposedly deceased man sat up! He lived a number of years and raised a family. However, his Will now contained two requests. One was that a shilling be given to a poor man to sweep Fleece Lane to the church gate, and a shilling to be paid for the tolling of the funeral bell. I am reliably told by my friend, a resident of Braughing, that every 2nd October, village children still sweep Fleece Lane and a bell is tolled.

About a Mile South of Braughing Is Standon

A cottage opposite The Bell pub has a mischievous spirit that moves things around.

I visited The Star a few years ago and felt a presence in the dining area. (I also experienced other phenomena about which I cannot write.) I asked if the inn was haunted and the publican steered me towards a framed newspaper article on the wall, which I had not noticed. The cutting explained about the ghosts that haunt the pub. Apparently, a lady with a red hat haunts the dining area. The phantoms frequent the bar after closing. The men wear tricorn hats. There is a beautiful woman of Mediterranean appearance, laughing with the phantom men who sup from tankards. Sometimes there is a voluptuous woman present, and the small sounds of music. A past publican was witness to this scene one night, but as soon as he entered the bar the spectacle vanished.

Notes of Interest

On the corner of the High Street and Papermill Lane is a large pudding stone, which is a lump of glacial conglomerate consisting of flint pebbles held together with silica matrix. Pudding stones are valued in folklore as it is believed they ward off the evil eye and witchcraft.

The Camden Town murder was the talk of the country in 1907, and just over a hundred years later it is still considered to be one of the most famous unsolved murder cases.

Emily Dimmock alias Phyllis Dimmock, was born at The Bell Inn, Standon in 1884. Emily was a prostitute, and found with her throat cut in lodgings in St Paul's Road,

Camden, North London. The artist Walter Sickert painted a number of pictures entitled the Camden Town Murders, based on Jack the Ripper victims. Sickert had been put forward as a suspect. It is unlikely that Emily was a Ripper victim, as the Ripper murders took place in 1888, nineteen years before.

John Barber wrote an informative booklet in 2003 on Emily Dimmock. He told me that Emily's father, William, said that his daughter Rose, was visited by Emily's ghost at 3.00 a.m. on 12th September 1907. The police surgeon gave the time of death as between 5.00 a.m. and 6.00 a.m. but weirdly a court barrister kept referring to the time of death as 3.00 a.m. Also, newspapers reported of a medium who had been visited by Emily's spirit at 3.00 a.m.

Tour Eleven
From Cottered to Rushden, Ardley, Walkern, Benington and Aston

OS Maps 166 and 167
Cyclical and Notable Dates Walkern – 31st January

From Buntingford take the A507 to Cottered

Near a new housing estate you may espy a ghostly old tramp shuffling along the road, who suddenly evaporates. The sight of him brings good luck to the witnesses.

The Bull Inn is said to be haunted by a lady who crosses the bar area. A previous landlady fell down the very steep cellar steps, and later died of her injuries, but the ghost is not thought to be her.

Now take the minor roads north to Rushden.

The Moon & Stars Pub has a ghost who interferes with the beer pump in the basement.

Another ghost in this area is a departed gravedigger, who sits on the bench near the 'phone box' at the Green. He likes to turn up if there is funeral cortege passing by.

Villagers have seen the spectre of 'old Percy' in his garden. He has sideburns and wears an artist's smock.

A woman carrying a flower basket frequents the village hall, only to disappear.

Approximately half a mile north at Offley Green telephone exchange, people feel uneasy at night. It is said that this was built on a former plague pit. The spirit of a murdered little boy walks this road.

Take the Minor Roads South to Ardley

Moor Green Farm to the east once had poltergeist phenomena.

To the West Is Walkern

Fairview Cottage, opposite the Robin Hood pub, is haunted by a doctor and an ostler. The ostler was a very punctilious man in life. He always stabled his horses at the rear of the property (which was three-terraced cottages originally) at 9.00 p.m. Previous occupants of Fairview Cottage could set their watch by the ghost's arrival at 9.00 p.m. of an evening.

The area around the church is reputedly haunted by Jane Wenham, who was the last 'witch' to stand trial in England. Her cottage still stands (obviously refurbished) on the approach to the church near the ford. I have been reliably informed by someone who lived in Walkern as a boy that children were always nervous playing around the vicinity. Children can be more susceptible to ghostly atmosphere.

History Notes

Jane Wenham was a wise woman, well known in Walkern and surrounding villages. At the age of approximately seventy, she was the last woman to be condemned as a witch (1711) but was not executed. The judge doubted her guilt but the jury brought in a verdict of guilty. He was therefore forced to condemn her to death, but he managed to delay the execution. Meanwhile, there were two factions, those who believed her to be a witch and those who did not and questioned the idea of witchcraft generally. Pamphlets were published arguing for both sides.

Eventually, she was pardoned by Queen Anne and vindicated but could no longer live in Walkern, due to the villagers' fervent belief that she was a witch. There had been some very strange incidents.

Jane married twice, and when her second husband, Edward Wenham, left her, he asked for the Town Crier to impart that he was 'no longer responsible for her proceedings'. Not long after, he died, some said due to witchcraft.

Jane was accused of causing the death of livestock, and putting the evil eye on a young man when he refused to give her some straw. He subsequently was accused of stealing straw at Munder's Hill, after wading through streams and disregarding bridges, having been bewitched.

She was supposed to have cast a spell on a teenage girl, Anne Thorn, by various incantations and working a magic on her clothes. This girl had a knee injury, but apparently felt compelled to run eight miles, over fences and gates. The blighted clothes were burnt, and Jane then appeared at the girl's door. This apparently proved she was a witch, as burning revokes the spell and the witch then appears. Anne recovered.

Anne later met Jane on the road, and Jane then rebuked her for accusing her of witchcraft. After that, Anne suffered from fits and fell into a ditch, hurting her knee again. When better, she had the compulsion to run around like a mad thing, and eventually tried to drown herself. Finally, she was cured by prayer.

Jane was apprehended and searched for witch's marks. None were found, but on being stuck with a pin, she did not bleed. However, she could not recite the Lord's Prayer.

Other witnesses came forward to say Jane had murdered the wife of her second husband's friend, after Jane's and Edward's separation. Also that she had put the evil eye on a farmer who refused to give her some turnips. His sheep died, and another did headstands!

A Reverend Strutt managed to get Jane to admit that she had been a witch for sixteen years, that her familiar was a cat, and that she had three other female accomplices in Walkern.

People said that strange cats appeared whose faces resembled Mistress Wenham. When shooed away, they ran towards Jane's abode.

Jane was accused by one neighbour of killing a baby, nine years earlier.

It would seem that any misfortune in the village, in years gone by, was caused by Jane's spells. Any illness, family tragedy, farming problems or money difficulties were the result of her wicked spells.

She lived in Gilston for some years due to a benefactor, and when he died she moved to Hertingfordbury. Here she died on 11th January 1730 having lived nineteen years after the trial. She is buried in the churchyard.

Jane's story is a fascinating and troubled one. For a full account see *The Witches of Hertfordshire* by Simon Walker.

To this day some people still have vehement feelings about her. A letter in a local Hertfordshire magazine in 1968 indicated that although she was reprieved, the evidence was weighted against her. There was lack of sympathy for her at the trial due to events that had happened in the past of an alarming kind. The writer in 1968 must have thought that she was a witch, and the jury in 1711 was out for vengeance for past deeds, whether or not she was guilty on that occasion.

This case led to the 1735 Witchcraft Act abolishing the death penalty for witches.

'Rough Music' was a custom where the populace took justice into their own hands. The wrongdoer could be a nagging wife, a wife beater, a woman of easy virtue or some other offender. The local people would punish the culprit without referring to the law. The procedure was called Rough Music due to the din or uproar by clanging pots and pans and other noisy implements.

In Walkern on January 31, 1848 a posse seized a pregnant local woman who was known to be promiscuous. She apparently had said that she would name the father of her child. In 1848, before DNA testing, this was a serious matter. There was no foolproof method in those days of determining paternity. The man named would be responsible for rearing the offspring. A gang of local men decided that rough music and a ducking would keep her quiet.

The authorities were 'tipped off'. The police tried to stop the brawl, and the outcome was that three policemen were badly injured. Some said that the police had dealt with this clumsily. All but one of the accused was sentenced to six months imprisonment.

Local feeling, including some justices, was that the woman was known to be indiscriminate, and the sentences on the men, harsh. Opinions were that the police should not have interfered with this custom.

The ducking could have taken place in the River Beane on the south side of the village. The ford near the church would have been too shallow, presuming the waterways were the same in those days as now.

To the Southeast Is Benington

I have visited the church in Benington numerous times, and on at least two occasions I have experienced a very uncomfortable sensation of being watched. I am compelled to leave the church and feel as if an invisible something or someone is following me up the church path. My feet gather pace until I reach the gate, where the impression evaporates. It is almost as if I am being 'warned off'.

The Bell pub has a mischievous ghost who takes a dislike to building or decorating work being carried out on the property, especially if it involves the detachment of the front door. The spirit's anger is shown by emanating obnoxious smells around the region of the door, and shifting mirrors and pictures in upstairs rooms. When the old door is replaced and redecoration is finished, the haunting ceases.

History Note

Today, Benington has not altered much from 1871. The principal employment would have been farming. The main criminal offences would have been drunkenness or theft. Poaching, however, was considered to be a serious offence back then.

PC Benjamin Snow came to Benington in 1868 with his family.

James Chapman's family lived at Luffenhall, just north of Walkern. He would leave them for weeks on end and lived in Wood Green, North London where he travelled selling game.

Police were told to look out for James Chapman who was believed to be in the area. There were a number of offences outstanding. He was known to be a brute.

Chapman was indeed in the area and he met a young farm labourer, James Gilby, on the Whempstead Road. Chapman asked him who the local gamekeeper was. Gilby told him and they walked together towards Benington. Gilby saw that Chapman was carrying a gun. Chapman asked Gilby to wait a moment and then disappeared. Gilby heard a shot and Chapman came back with blood on his fingers. They carried on and Gilby gave directions to Green End.

At that point, PC Snow came into view. The farmhand hurried up the lane passed the policeman. As he looked back, he saw Snow grab Chapman's jacket. Gilby ran home scared that Chapman had been poaching and the police would think Gilby an accomplice.

A little later PC Snow, holding a handkerchief to his face, spoke to a man in his garden and said that he had been shot. Snow walked on.

Snow met another villager, and by this time was unintelligible. There was a trace of blood near his ear, and the villager enquired as to whether he had earache. Snow was only able to say 'shot'.

Snow arrived home and his wife sent for the doctor, who found a large bruise on the left side of Snow's head. The wound was small, and there was a lot of blood accumulating under the skin. Now the officer was incoherent. The doctor stayed for an hour and on returning later found PC Snow to be dead.

Inspector Reynolds, the constable's superior, visited Benington the next day. He found signs of a struggle in the snow, and followed the tracks of footprints. The prints were distinctive in that the shoes had a peculiar pattern of nails where they had been mended, and the wearer walked in a straddle like manner, like Chapman.

Chapman was arrested at Wood Green, and a gun and boots with soles similar to the pattern found in the snow in Benington.

The inquest was held at The Bell on the same day Chapman was arrested for murder.

Chapman was found guilty of manslaughter on a legal technicality.

The grave of PC Benjamin Snow can be seen in Benington churchyard, to the southeast of the church. The stone stands near a yew bush, but the lettering is illegible.

For a full account see *Crime in Hertfordshire Vol 2* by Simon Walker.

Note of Interest

Benington is probably most people's idea of a perfect English village, with its pretty timber framed cottages, inn, pond, church and manor house. There was a castle in the twelfth century where the Georgian manor house Benington Lordship now stands. Some ruins and pieces of the castle are still to be seen, and the lovely gardens are open to the public on certain days.

To the Southwest Is Aston

A house on the Benington Road is haunted by a lady who appears at the top of the stairs.

Approximately half a mile south of Aston is Astonbury Wood. Here, a knight in armour has been seen riding and then vanish.

Tour Twelve
From Waterford to Watton-at-Stone and Hooks Cross

OS Map 166

North of Hertford on the A119 is Waterford.

Here you may see the ghost of a beautiful young woman wearing a white fluttering gown who floats from the churchyard across the road into the recreation ground only to disappear. The apparition usually occurs after midnight.

Spectres have been seen toiling in the fields and traversing the road.

The spirit of a man in khaki clothing and a casual style hat with a brim also frequents the area.

Note of Interest

The stained glass in the church of St Michael and All Angels was designed by the William Morris Company. The designs were by different eminent artists, Morris, Barne-Jones, Phillip Webb and Ford Madox Brown.

Continue to Watton at Stone

The church is in an impressive setting laying back off the road. The area around the church is haunted by a grey lady at least twice a year. According to tradition, she threw herself from the tower when she was rejected by her lover.

Frogmore Hall near Watton at Stone is haunted by the sounds of children's happy voices and laughter, which gradually diminish in a room off the main hall.

A phantom lady believed to be a former resident walks down the staircase, leaving a pungent fragrance of lavender. She is believed to have committed suicide by hanging herself in the tower.

An old man wearing dark clothes and a cloak slowly walks the gallery above the main hall. It is assumed to be the spectre of a former reverend, as a chapel was once above the main hall.

A coach and horse moves past the main entrance towards the stables.

The original Hall was closer to the river, but was demolished due to damp conditions; the present Hall has been built on higher ground. In the older building, the ghost of a woman would stand at a window looking and waiting for her husband to come home from war. He never came, and so broken-hearted, she killed herself.

Continue on the A602 to Hooks Cross

Here you may see three ghostly women standing on the roadside kerb, silhouetted against the setting sun. (OS Map 166 Ref 2720.)

Tour Thirteen

From Datchworth to Burnham Green, Bull's Green, Woolmer Green and Tewin

OS Map 166 and OS Exp 182
Cyclical and Notable Dates – Datchworth – May
Bulls Green – 28th, December
Tewin – 31st December

Datchworth is considered to be the most haunted village in Hertfordshire.

Ghostly farmers and labourers, wearing ancient style clothing, toil in the adjacent fields.

The whipping post at Datchworth Green was last used, allegedly, on 27th July 1665. It is still here surrounded by railings but the stocks and cage are long gone.

A ghostly woman dressed in old-fashioned clothes, has been seen standing by the swings. Her feet float above ground level.

The sound of galloping horses and the screeching of a metal coach can be heard, and the sense of this phenomena rushing past is felt, but nothing is seen.

An old woman collecting sticks has been observed at twilight.

The Plough Inn has a departed spirit who appears in a mirror. He is believed to be Jacque who lived circa 1700s.

There is a ghostly cart carrying the dead bodies (supposedly of the Eaves family) which has been seen on the Green, and travels up Rectory Lane towards the churchyard. No horses are visible. But all one sees are the white, dead limbs of arms and legs trailing out of the back. Some people say the cart is seen and heard lurching up the hill, others that it slides silently with the jolting cadavers hanging out. Another theory is that the poor dead wretches are plague victims. (OS Map 166 Ref 2619 or OS Exp 182 Ref 2619.)

History Note

This true story is not only shocking but also shows the cruelty and callousness of human nature in that era, and moves one to anger even now.

The harvest of 1768 was blighted and famine and unemployment was rife. On 23rd January 1769, four persons were found dead. In a 'poor house' situated on the edge of Datchworth Green, believed to be the opposite end from the whipping post. It was little more than a hut, of just one room, without floor or ceiling, holes in the roof, and no glass at the windows.

The emaciated bodies lying on the filthy straw were James Eaves, his wife and two children. The woman and children were naked and the man in rags. A small boy was found crawling around in the straw was unable to say how long the others had been dead.

Neighbours said the family had been ill for about three weeks, and no smoke had been seen from the chimney for two. Local hearsay was that the family had gaol fever (typhus), and therefore no one wanted to make enquiries or look through the windows.

The parish overseers of the poor showed no interest in this starving family. Mrs Eaves asked a neighbour to buy twigs for fuel, sugar and a candle, which she did, and left it for them. The family was not checked upon again.

Another neighbour said that the boy who survived (wearing a sack) was asked why he did not go into service. He replied that the parish would not clothe him and no one would employ him because he was naked.

Mrs Eaves had been seen going to a pond to fill a kettle, about ten days before. She had fallen, and crawled back to the hut, leaving the kettle behind. Not a soul came to help.

Furthermore, just before Christmas, another son had visited the Eaves family and found them to be ill and starving. They asked him to go to the overseer's house and ask for help. The overseer and his wife refused aid, the wife saying, "Let them die and be damned!" The son wanted to check on his parents a few days later, but his employer would not allow him the time off.

The overseers claimed that the Eaves died of typhus not neglect and malnutrition, stating that a previous resident of the hovel had died of the disease. If so, why were the family put into an infected dwelling?

There was another building in Datchworth used as a poor house, and the family there were also in a situation of extreme neglect similar to the Eaves'.

A man named Thicknesse who knew the Eaves' plight saw the bodies being taken for swift burial by the parish constable. Thicknesse had already written to the overseer of the poor and the churchwarden insisting that the coroner look at them. He suspected a conspiracy. The coroner indicated that there were only two verdicts applicable – either that the Eaves family died of natural causes, or they had been murdered.

The bodies were then examined by a doctor, who said that he was surprised no physician had been called before their deaths. He had never seen bodies so wasted and agreed there were signs of neglect.

In May 1769 the court of the King's Bench moved against overseers, regarding their treatment of the poor.

The villagers for many years tried to claim the events took place in nearby Burnham Green, probably because they were ashamed of their own behaviour, and that of their rector, and overseers towards the Eaves family. So, the attitudes of the neighbours, the rector who was ultimately responsible for his parishioners, the overseers and the son's unhelpful employer, all added to the misery and abandonment of this family. The consequence being that a man, a woman and three children were left almost naked, in a filthy 'shack' with holes in the roof and walls, in the middle of winter, and to starve to death.

Thicknesse published a pamphlet about the case, the proceeds of which went to the sole survivor, William Eaves.

Ghostly Incidents Continued...

Unlit Rectory Lane to this day can be an unnerving place. Footsteps have been reported but no one is seen. The sound of a vehicle or something travelling at speed 'whooshes' up the lane and then fades away.

At the top of the lane sits All Saints Church. I visited this churchyard one warm sunny afternoon, and felt very uneasy. Nothing happened, but I was wary, and my husband felt 'edgy'. However, the churchyard is haunted by chattering sounds, and shadowy figures weave in and out of the gravestones. (OS Map 166 Ref 2619.)

A property near Pond House in Hollybush Lane is haunted by a woman with striking red hair. She wears vividly coloured clothing and is accompanied by the sound of tinkling bells.

Nearby, Bury Lane has a spirit of a man in black who stares through cottage windows.

I may have seen the ghost of Hawkins Hall Lane. The reputed ghost is a little old lady who shambles along. She wears black and appears to have a hunched back, but if you view her from the front, she is headless. They say she walks in a purposeful way and is seen at evening or at night.

One night my husband and I were with friends, Lisa and Steve Hockley, on a ghost hunt investigation in Datchworth. We had kept vigil outside the church for some time and witnessed nothing. (OS Map166 Ref 2619.) We decided to move on down Hawkins Hall Lane, where we saw a small old woman walking a dog. She had a torch to guide her way. This was approximately 2.00 a.m. My friends insisted that this was the ghost. I laughed and expressed the view that I had never heard of the ghost walking a dog and possessing a torch. My friends insisted, and we drove past and saw her again. We could not see her face and she appeared to have a hunched back, or be stooped agedly. She wore grey or dark clothing. We drove past yet again and she trudged on with a small white dog in a determined fashion. When we looked again she was gone. She was nowhere to be seen, and not a light on in the few houses in the street. The logical explanation is that maybe she was frightened of us, constantly driving past her, and did not put a light on, on entering her home.

The more I think about it, the more I wonder if I indeed did see the ghost of Hawkins Hall Lane. But why would a ghost need a torch? On the other hand, the little old ladies of Datchworth have some strange habits, if they walk their dogs at 2.00 a.m. in a dark, deserted lane (OS Map 166 Ref 2619).

Mardleybury Manor, at Woolmer Green is haunted by a poltergeist that throws clothes and objects around. Various unexplained noises have been heard, such as crunching, cracking, bangs and heavy breathing. Items are moved around.

Opposite the building is Mardleybury Pond. Here a phantom woman is seen. She is young, with long blonde hair, and a flowing cloak. According to a handed down tale, she lived at the Manor, and coming home from a party one night, her coach driver approached the sharp corner of the road at speed and overturned the coach. She was overthrown into the pond and drowned. (OS Map 166 Ref 2618 or OS Exp 182 Ref 2618.)

Motorists have encountered her on many occasions, the driver having to brake suddenly as she darts across the road. She seems to favour lone drivers. An unaccountable white mist has been seen hovering over the pond.

Nearby, Whitehorse Lane is haunted by the spectre of a headless white horse. The pub sign on the White Horse Inn at the top of the lane shows a white horse minus a head. Ghostly galloping hooves can be heard from the direction of Burnham Green. Apparently during the Civil War, Cromwell's men beheaded a cavalier on his farm here, and they tried to steal his beautiful, white horse. The horse resisted and so they beheaded the steed also. It is rumoured that animals become agitated in this area. (OS166 Ref 2617 or OS Exp 182 Ref 2617.)

Note of Interest

The names of the lanes in this 'neck of the woods' are indicative of times past – Turpin's Ride, Hangman's Lane, Robbery Bottom and Hanging Hill Wood.

Clibbon's Post can be found at the side of the Bull's Green to Bramfield Road, on the edge of Brickground Woods on the right-hand side if travelling from north to south. (OS Map 166 Ref 2716 or OS Exp 182 Ref 2716.) It is here that Walter Clibbon is buried. This is the true story of Walter and his three sons who were violent villainous footpads of the late eighteenth century.

They used to frequent country fairs and Hertford Market, selling pies and cakes. The Clibbon family lived at Babbs Green, near Wareside, and Walter had a baker's shop in Hertford. Walter, his wife and sons used the sale of cakes and pies as a cover as they went through the crowded market places looking for traders who appeared to be making a profit. At the end of the day they would drink in the taverns with other trades people, then lay in wait with blackened faces, ready to pounce on their victims, as they wended their way home.

On Saturday 28th December 1782 Walter, his son Joseph, and an accomplice secreted themselves in Oaken Valley Bottom, near Bull's Green. William Whittenbury came by in his horse and cart, and was robbed by the men. Whittenbury went to his uncle's home in Queen Hoo Hall. His uncle, cousin, a servant and dog, set out to find the robbers, as they knew that other members of the Whittenbury family were due home.

Indeed they came across the Clibbon gang robbing the Whittenbury brothers! Thinking that the new arrivals were further victims, Clibbon and his cronies attacked them also.

After a vicious and bloody struggle, Walter was shot by the servant. Walter Clibbon's body was dragged in plough chains to the Horns Inn, where he was clubbed to death, and placed in the barn overnight. The pub and barn are still in existence (although the existing barn cannot be the original). (OS Map 166 Ref 2717 or OS Exp 182 Ref 2717.)

Many people next day came to see the body of the robber they had feared. This was the man who appeared to be a jovial fellow tradesman, and who, in fact, was a vicious and heartless robber. Tradition says that a crowd then tied Clibbon by his heels to a horse and was dragged up and down the lane much to the onlooker's delight.

It was decided not to bury him on consecrated ground, and so he was buried where he was captured and shot – a wooden stake through his heart.

To this day, people say they can sometimes make out the indistinct form of a horse pulling a contorted body along the lane towards The Horns. At other times just the groans of the scoundrel, and the sounds of horses are heard.

My husband, Jack, and I with Lisa and Steve Hockley spent an evening in The Horns, and asked the bar staff if the pub was haunted. They replied in the negative, but then one barmaid came back to us, and out of earshot of the others, said that the barn had a creepy atmosphere. Staff did not like to go there, and at one time were forbidden to do so.

Note of Interest

On the way to Bramfield there is a footpath named Chain Walk on the left leading to Bramfield Woods. A little way along is Sally Rainbow's Dell. (OS Exp 182 Ref 2916.) Sally was a local witch who made her home out of a cave in a chalk pit in the Dell. Nearby farmers were so fearful of her that they appeased her every whim, and paid her regular amounts of money so that she would not put wicked spells on them or their livestock.

Dick Turpin used the Dell to hide his booty knowing of the local's fear of the place.

The stretch of road near Clibbon's Post has another ghost. It has been reported that a woman wearing white Victorian clothes steps out into the road. A driver hit her and then saw a man come out of the wood, pick up the injured woman and carry her into the woods, whereupon they vanish.

To the East Is Tewin

Villagers talk of a beautiful ghostly blonde young woman, who looks distressed, seen on the roads surrounding Tewin Wood. Her clothes are muddy, and creased as if she has travelled a long journey, and she clasps a grey cloak around her. The apparition just melts away.

The Plume of Feathers is likely to be the most haunted pub in Hertfordshire. There are a plethora of phantoms here.

The ghost of a grey lady may be the woman who was bricked up behind the fireplace. The tale is that sometime in the seventeenth century, her husband came home from the war after two years' absence, and found her to be pregnant. He then murdered her and disposed of the body in this way. A ghostly lady with long hair has also been witnessed. A spectral little girl is seen at the top of the cellar steps. Is she the ghostly prankster who locks staff in the cellar, or lights and extinguishes candles, especially around table eight?

Staff and customers say there is an eerie feeling in the ladies' toilet. Two spooky men appear to prop up a bar that no longer exists.

Lights turn on and off, electrical implements malfunction, and the ovens in the kitchen turn on and off of their own accord. Even corkscrews have been known to swing at speed on hooks around the bar, and something unseen messes up the cutlery on laid tables.

Lady Ann Grimston of Gorhambury died in 1733 and is buried at St Peter's Church. She is alleged to have said that if there were life after death, seven trees would grow out of her grave. A tree does in fact grow out of her tomb, and seven sturdy branches have broken the masonry. Her burial place is encircled by broken, rotting railings, overgrown with weeds and brambles, and the tomb is subsiding slightly. Her ghost is often seen flitting around the churchyard. A good time to see her is New Year's Eve.

At nearby Tewin Water, the ghost of beautiful Lady Cathcart ambles through the trees. This lady is also buried at Tewin Church, but her restless spirit haunts Tewin Water House.

The rustling sound of a crinoline has been heard in the aisle of the church. Some say this is the presence of Lady Sabine.

Tour Fourteen

From Baldock to Bygrave, Caldecote, Ashwell, Hinxworth and Clophill

OS Maps 166 and 153 OS Exp 193
Cyclical and Notable Dates Hinxworth – Autumn

At Baldock, an apparition of a man thought to be Rector John Smith wanders around the churchyard and sometimes is seen sitting at the back of the pews. This is the John Smith that deciphered Samuel Pepys' shorthand.

In Church Street, the vision of an old man in old-fashioned garb walks.

St Mary's House in Church Street domiciles the spirit of a boy said to have been killed by falling scaffolding. He favours the kitchen.

The Cock Inn at the end of the High Street is haunted by three troublesome ghosts who move items around on the shelves in the bar. A picture was seen to fling itself off the wall and smash.

The Orange Tree has a nuisance poltergeist.

The George & Dragon on the crossroads is haunted by something in the upstairs rooms.

The ghost of Elizabeth haunts room 10 at the Rose & Crown. She plays with children staying at the inn, and it is the children to whom she has told her name. Footsteps and noises like moving furniture are heard, but there is nothing to account for these sounds. The cellar and the kitchen are reputedly haunted by Shock Oliver, a highwayman of the eighteenth century. His presence has also been felt in the bar.

Also, the tormented soul of a housemaid who committed suicide dwells in one of the bedrooms. An old lady with white hair perambulates a corridor.

A ghostly cavalier prowls around Il Forno Italian Restaurant.

A sweet and gift shop has a mischievous spirit who likes to rearrange the goods. The door of the shop opens and an invisible someone enters.

Next door, a ghost cooks meals prepared previously, even though the gas hob is off. Microwave ovens and hairdryers switch on and off through no human agency.

A Victorian boy and girl dwell at Cost Cutters, and a violent ghost who throws people against the wall lives here. Ouch!

The Pembroke Road area has many haunted houses. One where a Roman soldier appears at the top of the stairs. There are footsteps, and doors open and close by themselves. Another Roman soldier frequents a bedroom, but he is only visible from the knees up, and he walks through a wall.

A Victorian cottage in Pembroke Road has a spook that moves clothes around. A teddy bear placed on a chair fell sideways just as a depression appeared in a cushion. This same invisible occupant sits on the bed at night.

Raban Court on the crossroads, is an old, timbered building. There is a kindly ghost here whose presence soothes unwell residents to sleep. There is also the smell of tobacco, and a jester appears.

A house in Bell Row, near the zebra crossing suffered from ghastly ghostly unpleasant smells. Doors swing open and animals are scared.

A housing estate is haunted by Roman soldiers, and a Roman military man has frightened drivers on the Clothall Road. Archaeologists have confirmed that this area was once a Roman burial ground. Corpses were unearthed. Some were buried face down. These may be the troubled spirits that haunt.

Off the A507 to the East Is Bygrave

A pedlar haunts Bygrave Farm House, who was murdered here, and a mother and child. When major refurbishment was being carried out to the house, an old well shaft was found in the garden. Here a headless skeleton was unearthed. The skeletal remains of a woman and child were discovered under the drawing room floor. A lone skull was found at a farm in Wallington. 'Coincidentally' a farmer Fossey had moved from Bygrave Farm House to the one at Wallington.

A headless pedlar was seen stepping along the Bygrave Road. He has not been seen for many a year – but just maybe… There is no history as to the fate of the woman and child.

Retrace your journey onto the A507. Go north and to the east via Newnham is Caldecote.

A spiteful and dangerous entity haunts the Manor House.

A housekeeper working alone was pushed down the stairs by unseen hands.

A lady in black has been seen and strange noises emanate from the cellar.

Go back to Newnham and Then Go Northeast to Ashwell

A headless black figure floats silently around the churchyard of St Mary's. This may be a remnant of a plague victim, thrown into a plague pit in the cemetery in medieval times.

History Note

Ashwell was known as the county's plague village, due to the number of deaths. Ashwell was a very large town at one time. Graffiti can be seen on the north wall of the church tower, about five feet up. It indicates the beginning of the Black Death in June 1300. Three feet below, another inscription records the plague of 1349, and the great storm of St Maur's Day – 15th January 1361.

A spectral coach and two horses startle late night motorists on the Ashwell to Bygrave Road.

Bear House is haunted by a seated old man enjoying his ale.

At Tower Cottage in Swan Street, there was a tunnel which linked the cottage to the tower of St Mary's Church. The cottage is haunted by the sounds of a baby crying, obnoxious phantom odours, taps turned on, cupboards and doors flung open, drawers unclosed and a tall lady. Other terrifying phenomenon has occurred here.

From Ashwell, Take the Minor Roads to Hinxworth

The Manor House here, Hinxworth Place, is haunted by a procession of monks who walk through the walls. A lone monk has been spied in the courtyard. Footsteps are heard on a stairway which no longer exists.

Mysterious screams, thuds, a crying baby and water pouring from the pump are heard, mainly on autumn evenings. Allegedly in the 1800s, the owners of the house went out one evening leaving their baby with a nursemaid. A servant boy frightened the nursemaid by dressing up as a ghost and making groaning noises. She attacked the 'ghost' with a poker. He consequently fell down a flight of stairs. The cook tried to revive him by flushing cold water over his head from the pump, but to no avail. He was already dead.

Clophill is in Bedfordshire, but you could include this site on this tour as it is only a few miles from Hinxworth, via Shefford, and it is such a fascinating place. Take the lanes westerly to the A1. Travel south to Stotfold, and then pick up the A507 to Henlow and Shefford. After Shefford, look out for the right turn to Clophill.

The site is St Mary's Church ruins' (OS Map 153 Ref 0938) near Deadman's Hill which is on the A6.

These gaunt eerie ruins near Clophill village are reached by footpath (although cars can access the track here). I visited this site one hot, sunny, summer afternoon, and I have never been so scared. The atmosphere was sultry, silent, the air was oppressive, and no birds sang in this remote place.

In the past, there were two churches in Clophill. The villagers only having use for one, St Mary's was decommissioned in the 1950s. Eventually, the decaying ruins were used for Black Masses or Necromancy on the solstices and at times of a full moon. Graves were desecrated, bones and skulls placed around the ruins and strange symbols daubed on the crumbling walls.

In order to prevent further ghoulish sacrilege, the gravestones were moved to form a circle around the perimeter of the churchyard. The burial ground was covered in turf and allowed to run to grass and weed. Thus, one cannot see where the bodies remain in the uneven terrain. This gives the church a rather stark, 'stubbornly implanted' appearance.

There was a medieval leper colony on this site before the church was built here. Some local villagers think that the ruins are haunted by Sophie Mendham who died in 1893, but why is unclear as her grave is not the only one to have been desecrated. Also, a hooded monk on horseback carrying a lantern has been seen. He may be making his way to Chicksands Priory which is only two miles to the east (also haunted – now a military base).

People have described this place as having an overwhelming evil aura. Maybe the occultists, the leper colony, and other forces have contributed to make this a primary spot for paranormal phenomena.

When I visited with my husband, we sensed this but not strongly at first. It was as if the malevolence was building up, and we had the distinct impression that we were being watched or 'staked out', as if we were prey. The build-up of malign atmosphere was almost palpable, and it was this that was so terrifying. We did not hang around for long, but whilst we were there a man hurriedly walked along the footpath adjacent to the churchyard. He looked neither right nor left, did not appear to want to acknowledge our presence, kept his eyes to the ground, and scurried away. He appeared to be frightened and seemed to want to get past the place as quickly as possible. We did go back with Lisa and Steve Hockley, our 'ghost hunting' friends, about six months later. Again, there was a pernicious feeling but not as strongly. Perhaps we felt there was safety in numbers – but that was the philosophy of the Sabine women, and look what happened to them!

Tour Fifteen
From Letchworth to St Ippollitts, Little Wymondley and Weston

OS Map 166. OS Exp 193
Cyclical and Notable Dates-Weston 12th August

Letchworth is to the west of Baldock.

A four-hundred-year-old house named Scudamore at Letchworth Corner reputedly has ghostly footsteps. Animals are aware of a presence.

A ghost thought to be Reverend William Alington haunts Letchworth Hall – now a hotel. He was the previous owner of the Hall, and the dark figure glides across the ballroom and the upstairs landing. Apparently, he was dismissed from office for drinking and improper behaviour with his parishioners.

An apparition of a lady wearing a grey coat and with black hair startles drivers on the Willian Road towards Letchworth Gate. She looks quite solid, and walks steadfastly into oncoming traffic. As drivers veer out of her way, she vanishes.

Willian is a district of Letchworth, and the Post Office here is haunted by a little boy dressed dapperly with a bowtie. Ghostly chuckling and conversations are perceived and poltergeist activity ensues.

The Fox & Duck pub next door also has supernatural activity in this sixteenth century inn. The spectre of a woman appears in the kitchen, hallway and on the stairs. She is about five feet tall, and likes to tidy up beer mats and ashtrays. If you are in her path, she will not stop. She will walk right through you. She was also witnessed by the manager imitating his mannerisms in a mirror while he was combing his hair! She is normally considered a friendly fetch, but there are feelings of something bad in the cellar.

In the early hours of the morning, children can be heard and seen playing in a former school playground, now a private residence, in the area.

A ghostly jogger may be seen in Willian, usually at dusk. He has fair, wavy hair, and red and white running gear. He wears a nasty, threatening expression and exudes a sense of menace. It has been reported that he suddenly runs across the front of moving vehicles and disappears into the hedge at the side of the road, or into nearby fields.

Note of Interest

Laurence Olivier, the famous late actor, lived at Letchworth as a boy.

(You may wish to visit Weston now, and not at the end of the tour.)

To the south is St Ippollitts.

History Note

In the medieval era, knights and pilgrims would bring their horses into the church of St Ippolyts to be blessed, before riding off to the Crusades. St Ippolyts was a healer of horses.

Take the minor roads east to Little Wymondley.

Little Wymondley Priory was founded by an Augustinian order connected to the Knights Templar. The Templars were a religious and military organisation that fought in the Crusades.

The Priory is haunted by a prior and chanting monks. There is said to be a stone with a stain that cannot be removed, and is thought to be blood.

There was an underground tunnel from here to Delamere, a house in Great Wymondley, once owned by Cardinal Wolsey. The tunnel has now been blocked off but in the past was an area of consternation and horror to the local children.

There are remains of a moat, and a refurbished ancient barn. In the 1990s some photographs were taken of the barn roof and a white, misty image like a warrior monk horseback appeared on the developed print. Nothing was seen when the photograph was taken which is genuine. There were no technical faults with the camera, and no shaft of light penetrating the barn could have caused this effect.

The Ghost Club Society conducted an investigation here in 2002. They heard unexplained scraping noises, and a blue, smoky image appeared in the roof, in the spot caught on the camera. Also, orbs and mist were seen in the bar area. (The barn is now used for salubrious weddings and functions.)

To the Northeast Is Weston (Weston Is Southeast of Baldock)

A spectral coach and horses races down Lannock Hill. (OS 166 Ref 2430 and OS Exp 193 Ref 2430.) Due to the lights of the carriage lamps, passengers can just be made out inside. As it reaches the foot of the hill it turns over into a chalk pit and fades away. It is said that a newly married couple were killed when their coach and horses bolted, and the carriage crashed here. The re-enactment is said to appear at midnight every 12th August.

N.B. Jack's Hill is to the south of here – 'just around the corner' – See gravely, tour seventeen.

Tour Sixteen
Hitchin

OS Map 166 and OS Exp 193
Cyclical and notable dates – Priory 15th June
Mill on outskirts September evenings

The Priory has a phantom lady in a long, grey dress who loiters in the grounds.

The most famous Priory ghost is that of a Cavalier named Goring. He fell in love with a girl from a Roundhead family living at High Down House in nearby Pirton. He was visiting the lady when Parliamentarian troops started to seek out Royalists. He escaped via an underground tunnel and hid in a hollow wych elm. (Both tunnel and elm are believed to be in existence.) He was found, then slashed to pieces and decapitated. His fiancé watched helplessly from a room over the porch. Tradition says that she died from shock, and this same room is haunted by a beautiful woman. Every 15th June a headless Cavalier rides from High Down House to the Priory on a white horse, and then scampers down the avenue clasping his severed head to his breast.

Other Priory ghosts are a group of people in old-fashioned garb playing cards, and a woman in a red cloak and black hat who suddenly disappears. Also, spectral monks have been seen, cold spots felt, and a woman wearing a white, short-sleeved blouse with a pearl pendant around her neck who drifts up the stairs. The phantom is only seen above her waist.

You may espy a battalion of Roman soldiers who march through the grounds at night, together with the sound of their marching feet and a babble of voices.

When refurbishment was being carried out at The Cock Hotel in High Street, a skeleton of a cat was found under the bar floor. In the distant past, dead cats were buried in the foundations or bricked up in walls of buildings as a good luck charm. However, this property is haunted by a spooky cat!

The Poundland store, 9/10 High Street, is reputedly haunted by a lady accompanied by a strong fragrance of lavender. In the past, lavender was distilled at this very spot.

The Tea and Coffee shop in Market Place has a ghost who likes to impersonate the owner's voice and call staff downstairs. When they arrive, the place is empty and the owner elsewhere, who had not called them.

Bar Amigo, 23 Market Place, has a ghostly, old man and little girl with arms intertwined, who walk through a wall.

Shops in St Mary's Square are haunted by poltergeist activity. Nearby, Queen Street was once known as Dead Street because not one person residing here survived the plague of 1665. Furthermore, in the nineteenth century the churchyard was fenced off and the gates locked at night, as it was the haunt of body-snatchers.

The attic of Howells newsagents that used to be in Churchyard, is haunted by a young man in Edwardian costume. You will only see him for a minute before he disappears. He apparently does not like children, as when they are in the shop he stamps on the stairs. Also, a small child was 'pushed' down the stairs and animals avoid the top floor.

Aram's Alley, where the ghost of Eugene Aram, scholar, friend of the gentry and murderer – is said to walk.

The Sun Hotel has a ballroom which is said to be haunted by the ghost of Lord Havisham, dressed in eighteenth-century evening attire. He was a hunting and fishing enthusiast and he is sometimes seen in other parts of the hotel with a fish under his arm. He allegedly committed suicide due to gambling debts. He also haunts one of the bedrooms, and hotel staff are not allowed to say which one, as the apparition is so terrifying.

The hooded figure of a monk frequents the bar, and the alarming wraith of a woman appears elsewhere.

Room 10 is haunted by a woman who tries to suffocate guests by lying across their faces.

The dumbwaiter apparatus goes up and down of its own volition. Voices have been heard in the night under the archway outside – 'Mind yer 'ead', 'Mind yer 'ead!' This is where the coach and horses used to drive through.

The car park area was once a bowling green, and people walking across here have reported being struck on the shins or ankles by a heavy, unseen object. Also, the clanking thud of bowling balls can be heard on occasions. Some say this is a re-enactment of a game played by two clergymen who regularly played here.

The upper floor of 10 and 11 Sun Street were at one time used as an apartment. Here, the menacing ghost is a dark hooded entity that whispers the occupant's name, or will pin them to the bed by their throat. It has been seen kneeling by a resident's bed and when challenged, the apparition slid through the floorboards to the storey beneath. The poltergeist activity that occurred here was so vicious and threatening that the bedroom in question was never used again by the plagued family.

A house on the corner of Sun Street and Bridge Street is haunted by a soldier billeted here in the Civil War.

Number 37 Bridge Street experiences eerie bumps, thuds and crashes. A figure of a woman upstairs in one of the bedrooms walks out of one wall across the room and through another wall. She wears period costume. It transpired that during renovations, a door had been found behind plaster where the woman emerged and again a door behind a plastered wall where the apparition disappears.

In Bucklersbury, number 8a is a flat above Hawkins shop. Here, phantom footsteps and scratching noises are heard. There are cold spots, a woman's spirit in a blue gown and a tall, thin man of malevolent appearance is seen. Other menacing happenings are explained here in brief, but for a full account please read *Ghostly Hertfordshire* by Damien O'Dell. They are almost first-hand accounts as they happened to a friend of his and I find them quite chilling.

Very much in précis – a Civil War soldier appears – a very big man in a red tunic with a beard and a scar on his face. This apparition is not reflected in a mirror.

An eerie presence will join a gathering of friends, and then leave the room, the others wondering who it was, as all persons are accounted for.

There is a plethora of other phenomena, like an invisible creature snarling loudly, further scrabbling noises and paranormal attacks, with physical marks as proof.

The George pub in Bucklersbury also has ghostly footsteps, and a very uneasy feeling in the cellar, where apparently, the pub's dogs, cats and staff refuse to enter at night – well, at least after 11.00 p.m.

The Red Hart has the ghost of an old man who sits in an armchair in a bedroom. Poltergeist activity occurs here. This was the site of the last public hanging in the town.

A legless lady walks Halls Yard, an alley off Tilehouse Street. She is legless – not because of drinking spirits – sorry! – but because in the past the ground was much lower than today.

The Cooper's Arms was previously a farm and before that an ecclesiastical property (note some of the window arches). Here resides another phantom feline. Also a one legged monk has been seen 'sprinting' out of the pub to the other side of the road. Beer tankards move on their own, and the cellar door has an atmosphere of menace. Strangely, surveyors have reported that on measuring the building inside and out, there is a seven-foot unexplainable difference.

George Chapman the Tudor poet and playwright supposedly haunts a house in Tilehouse Street, and a nineteenth century midshipman in blue uniform walks through walls at number eighty-four.

There is a flat above a shop in Bancroft which is haunted by a cat (yet another one – Hitchin is crawling with spooky cats!). Estate Agents confess that it is difficult to let. Apparently, tenants have stated that they have been scratched on the legs by invisible claws.

Number 30, Bancroft, now a private residence, accommodates a departed soul of a little old lady. The house was formerly a workhouse, but the ghost seems to belong to a previous era, as she wears a Tudor ruff and gown.

Legend has it that a sad, mournful widow drowned herself in a pond between the Pirton and Offley Roads. Her saturated spirit may be seen emerging from the Priory grounds into Charlton Road.

A wooded area adjacent to Holwell village just to the north of Hitchin is haunted by Roman soldiers seated around a campfire, their armour and army accoutrements on the ground at their side. Although they are dressed in short tunics, they are transparent.

A mill just outside Hitchin is haunted by a screaming girl in the process of being attacked (some reports say, raped). On September evenings a girl and a man are seen struggling at a window, even though that room now has no floor. I believe this was first reported in print by the late Peter Underwood, a former president of the Ghost Club. (He later founded the Ghost Club Society.) He does not care to say where the mill stands. Maybe this is to protect the owner's privacy or anonymity. Or the mill may not be in existence now. However, there are a number of mills on the fringe of Hitchin. (OS EXP 193.) If you wish to investigate this incident and visit various mills to try and ascertain which one, please be respectful of people's property and privacy.

Please see the Hatfield tour two, for the ghostly man in black who prevented a train crash near Hitchin.

Tour Seventeen
From Graveley to Stevenage, Old Knebworth and Knebworth

OS Map 166 OS Exp 193

Note of Interest

'Rook's Nest' the home of the author E.M. Forster as a child, can be found up a 'backwater' to the north of Stevenage. He used Rook's Nest and a housekeeper, Mrs Poston, as 'models' for his novel 'Howard's End'. This is a private residence and not open to the public.

Jack's Hill at Graveley just north of Stevenage is haunted by a soldier, complete with helmet, visor, and holding a pikestaff. (OS Exp 193 Ref 2329.)

(Lanark's Hill is 'just around the corner' to the north of here – See Weston on tour fifteen.)

A ghostly knight rides out of St Nicholas Churchyard, Stevenage, and down the hill only to vanish.

The grounds of The Grange School, which was built on the site of a coach house, are haunted by a stableman dressed in riding livery, who gazes at the building. He is believed to have been killed when a coach house was razed to the ground. Animals avoid the house. Now, the building has been converted into housing.

Body snatching (or grave robbing) was big business in the eighteenth century. One man who feared his corpse would be taken after his demise, and used for scientific dissection to educate student doctors, was grocer Henry Trigg. His Will dictated that his lead coffin should be placed in the rafters of his house. The house became the Castle Inn and then the NatWest Bank. The bank then closed in 2015 in the Stevenage Old Town. His coffin has rested in the rafters of the barn at the back since 1724, and it is muted that it is still there. His ghost, donning a striped apron, is seen to drift through a wall.

The Old Town to the northeast of Stevenage is the haunt of a very large spectral black dog. Possibly the same dog frequents Six Hills Barrow and Whomerley Wood (OS Map 166 Ref 2423 or Exp 193 Ref 2423).

Some people have sighted a pack of phantom hounds.

Supernatural dogs – or demon dogs – usually black – have been seen all over Britain.

You will 'meet' more of them on other tours, especially the Essex tours. They have been given various titles depending on the area and the folklore. Please see the glossary of terms for further details on their fascinating names.

Six Hills Barrows are alongside of the old North Road and west of London Road at a junction with Six Hills Way. The burrows are Roman burial grounds.

Adjacent to Whomerley Wood is Monkswood. (OS Exp 193 Ref 2423.) Unsurprisingly, phantom monks have been observed here. It is believed that a monastery once stood at this vicinity, which was burnt down and the religious community murdered.

Indeed, some say the monks are buried under the avenue of trees. Also, a hellhound has been seen here.

Stevenage Leisure Park hosts the ghost of a man kicked to death. Also, strange noises are heard, and a black shadowy figure flickers and shoots about.

Note of Interest

The Fox twins were born in 1857 – Albert Ebenezer and Ebenezer Albert! They lived in Symonds Green on the fringe of Stevenage to the west. Even their mother could not tell the identical boys apart.

They started poaching at the age of eleven. For a long time they would trespass and steal separately. If Ebenezer were caught he would give Albert's name and vice versa – not unlike the Kray twins of the East End of London – Ronnie and Reggie. This was successful until 1904 when they could be identified by their fingerprints.

For a period they undertook honest toil, and were employed with others, building Stevenage Police Station. However, it was not long before they were gracing the very cells they had assisted building.

On one occasion, Ebenezer hit a gamekeeper in order to avoid arrest. For this he was given ten years imprisonment for grievous bodily harm. He was never the same again, and resided for a while in the workhouse, before he died in 1926 aged sixty-nine. Albert lived for another eleven years and they are both buried in St Nicholas' churchyard.

They were remembered with 'affection' by all divisions of the law due to their good manners and ingenious lies to avoid prosecution. They were also seen as characters by many people due to their outlandish capers. For example, Albert paid off a fine from the sale of ill-gotten gains taken from the estate belonging to the magistrate. Also, the lady of the manor paid him money and gave him a brace of pheasants weekly to keep him away from her estate.

In total, Ebenezer had eighty-two, and Albert one-hundred and eighteen poaching convictions.

Photographs show them with identical bowler hats, moustaches, scarves, jackets, and buttoned the same way. Wearing cheeky grins, their faces were not to be trusted.

Knebworth House stands on the site of a Tudor mansion. Knebworth's owner rebuilt the ancestral home into a gothic style mansion here in the nineteenth century. It is the perfect stage setting for many a film, TV series or commercial. The building is a stereotype for a 'House of Horror'.

Spinning Jenny used to haunt a part of the house, now demolished. She was locked up in one of the towers, some say to keep her away from her sweetheart. She whiled away the time by spinning, but the imprisonment affected her mind and she died. It was reported that one could still hear her spinning in a room of the unused turret.

However, her ghost is now seen in the park and the gardens. There is some basis of the story of Jenny Spinner in fact, as allegedly there is mention of her in old documents.

Edward Bulwer Lytton was a writer, occultist and politician. His passion was the restoration of Knebworth House, and he added weird embellishments of turrets, towers, gargoyles and stone winged dragons. He is not seen but his presence is strongly felt, especially in his old rooms and the stairs. It is said that cleaners prefer to work in pairs here. Other ghosts are a girl with long blonde hair, a lady that haunts the gallery and another mystery female. There are tales of mysterious happenings around the lakes at night.

The sight of the 'yellow boy' (or radiant boy) is an ill omen to all who encounter him, especially residents of the house. He is said to appear in a golden light, with long yellow hair, and will indicate the manner of the onlooker's death by mime.

For a good account and history of Knebworth House read *Britain's Haunted Heritage* by J A Brooks.

Just to the south of Knebworth is Nup End. Here, a farmhouse and nearby offices are haunted by a farmer. Poltergeist activity occurs. A phantom man walks briskly at the side of the house over new flowerbeds. He wears a white shirt with deep cuffs and large buttons. Smoky shapes have been observed inside the building.

The road from Knebworth House lodge gate to Codicote is haunted by a Second World War tank. The helmeted soldier gesticulates from the open hatch to other motorists to beware of a phantom air raid.

Tour Eighteen

From Harpenden to Wheathampstead, Nomansland, Ayot St Lawrence, (Old) Welwyn, Codicote, Whitwell, Bendish, Rabley Heath, St Paul's Walden and Minsden

OS Map 166 OS Exp 193 OS Exp 182
Cyclical and Notable Dates – Old Welwyn – 24th December
Whitwell – 24th December
Minsden – 31st December

Harpenden was once known by the enchanting name of 'Valley of the Nightingales'.

Once, when on a business course, I stayed at the Harpenden House Hotel, overlooking Harpenden Common. I was lucky to be allocated one of the better bedrooms at the front of the building. A Georgian style room with a huge bay window. I was often away on courses or conferences so was quite used to being on my own in a strange place. However, when settling down to sleep, the room seemed to take on a sinister, creepy ambience. There was not a presence as such in the room, but the atmosphere seemed to change. The furniture and curtains looked the same, so this was not a time slip. I slept with the light on.

Next morning I mentioned this to a colleague on the course. She was a no-nonsense businesswoman and I expected her to laugh and tell me to pull myself together. To my astonishment, she said that she believed in the supernatural, and could she look at the room. We ventured back but all was normal with the sunlight flooding through the beautiful ornate windows. I stayed for the rest of the week in that room, but always slept with the light on which seemed to ease but not eradicate the strange feeling. I was so busy on the business course that it did not occur to me to ask the hotel staff if the room or the hotel was haunted, but upon talking to the course coordinators, they did say that The Silver Cup Inn was reputedly haunted. At the time of writing, there is a plan to convert the hotel into housing.

It has been noted by a number of authors that The Silver Cup public house (seventeenth century), also situated near the common is haunted by a lady wearing grey. In addition, a cottage behind this pub is haunted by a young, First World War soldier.

An old factory near the Silver Cup has a misty spook that opens and closes doors. Further along is a cottage where a man drifts through a wall into the next-door property. When building works were being carried out, a door was discovered on exactly the spot where the ghost walks through.

Harpenden Hall is troubled by strange noises on the stairs, unearthly footsteps, and shadowy shapes dart across the landing. There is also a vision of a lady who wears a long dress but does not possess any feet.

The Cross Keys public house, houses ghostly medieval monks. Their heads are shaven and they wear dark robes of thick material. The pub has suffered from poltergeist activity.

In Rose Cottage at Church Green, the apparition of a young girl shifts furniture around, looking for her illegitimate baby. She is supposed to have murdered her child and then committed suicide. Strange noises also occur here.

An apparition of a woman with long hair in a grey shroud frequents Bowers House situated behind the High Street.

An old hag loiters in Agdell Path. This footpath is adjacent to fields and leads to Agdell Cottage in Hatching Green. She is also seen in the area around Rothamstead, and on the common. She allegedly lived in a dell in Hagdell Field. (OS Map 166 Ref 1312 or OS Exp 182 Ref 1312.)

Take the B653 to Wheathampstead

The Elephant and Castle public house in Amwell Lane is haunted by the presence of a former licensee who murdered his wife and then committed suicide. His presence is felt in the area over the taproom. Furthermore, a spectral woman in a black dress with golden hair and pearls stands on the landing. She holds out her hands as if pleading or begging.

As mentioned before the B651 to St Albans is haunted by Roman soldiers. See the St Albans tour four.

Marshalls Heath Lane (OS Exp 182 Ref 1614) is a winding, unlit, lonely road, flanked by woodland and fields, leading to isolated farms.

In December 1957, Ann Noblett, aged seventeen, was last seen alighting from a bus in Lower Luton Road. Her body was found a month later in Rose Grove Wood at Whitwell. The macabre story is as follows: Forensic scientists established that she had been strangled, stripped and then redressed in the same clothes. She was then secreted in an industrial freezer. She was discovered frozen solid with her hands placed across her chest and still wearing her spectacles. Her purse lay nearby with no money missing. Her case remains unsolved, as the police have found no motive for her killing and no murderers have been detected.

Her ghost started to manifest seventeen years later in Marshalls Heath Lane at a business premises near her past home. Locked doors would open, she was seen near some sheds and then vanished into thin air, people were touched by unseen hands, and a cat hissed and arched its back at something invisible.

Nomansland is a large expanse of wasteland to the south of Wheathampstead.

The most famous ghost connected with Nomansland is Katherine Ferrers – the Wicked Lady.

She was born at Markyate Cell, Katherine Fanshawe, in the 1600s. When she was aged around thirteen, she was made to marry Ralph Ferrers, aged sixteen (the age of twelve being the legal age to marry).

Apparently her family were uncaring, and she found herself to be very solitary. In order to relieve her boredom she became a highwaywoman. She dressed in man's clothing complete with thigh high boots and tricorn hat. However, one night her luck ended its run and she was shot.

Her spirit is said to haunt Nomansland Common, particularly near The Wicked Lady public house, where she is supposed to have met her demise.

She, on her spectral black horse has been witnessed galloping over this heathland. Ghostly galloping hooves were heard by a man walking his dog at night along Ferrers Lane. (OS Exp 182 Ref 1612.) Also, another person heard similar sounds which came so close to him he could have touched the speeding steed, only nothing could be seen. Many people have experienced the phenomena, and dogs react to these spectral sounds by barking or shivering at the unseen horse.

Tradition says that Katherine would ride to the Tin Pot pub at Gustard Wood, north of Wheathampstead, to change into her highwayman's attire. The room that she used is said to accommodate her presence. (OS Exp 182 Ref 1716.)

For further information on Katherine Ferrers see Markyate, tour nineteen.

To the Northeast of Gustard Wood Is Ayot St Lawrence

The house of George Bernard Shaw, the renowned twentieth-century playwright, Shaw's Corner, is haunted by the said gentleman. The building and grounds are now owned by the National Trust, and everything has been left just as it was in his day. It is like walking into a time slip, and perhaps it is this as to why one feels his presence. His footsteps have been heard and he has called out to a housekeeper.

Shaw's friend T E Lawrence (Lawrence of Arabia) visited him here, and it is said that he too haunts the place. His motorbike has been heard in the narrow winding lanes, just as it has near his home in Clouds Hill, Dorset, also a National Trust property.

The Brocket Arms, circa 1378, was originally built as a monk's hostel for the local church which is now an ivy clad ruin further down the lane. It was also a stopover point for pilgrims on their way to St Alban's.

There is a tunnel which runs from the cellar of the Brocket Arms to the church. At the time of the Reformation, a monk was trying to reach the tunnel when Henry 8th's men who were in the area (to collect Katherine Parr, his sixth wife, who lived at Ayot St Lawrence, to take her to London) seized him, and hanged him from a beam. The beam in the pub has a hook on it to indicate where the unfortunate monk was suspended. There is also a poem on the wall describing the monk's demise.

The monk haunts mainly the bar area. He is known to be friendly, and a good time to meet him is usually around the three weeks either side of Christmas.

One hotel guest thought he was talking to a man in a dressing gown, whereas he had been conversing to a monk in a brown habit. Would a sixteenth-century monk know modern English? Apparently this is not an apocryphal tale.

The monk has a gaunt, old face, sometimes indistinct. Footsteps, thuds and bangs are heard as well as a conversation between a group of ghostly men.

There may have been a hellish fire here at some time, as one hotel guest awoke to find scorch marks on her feet, and another visitor awoke to find a burning monk standing by his bed! Sometimes, but rarely, people experience the feelings of panic and claustrophobia in certain parts of the old building.

Bedroom number four is haunted by the presence of a lady who took several days to die after having been run over by a horse and cart in the village.

Note of Interest

Names of places surrounding Ayot St Lawrence are indicative of the past – Prior's Wood, Abbotshay and Brimstone Wood.

To the southeast (OS Exp 182 Ref 2213), you may bump into an old-fashioned car which suddenly appears parked under some trees at Ayot Green. It disappears just as abruptly. The car registration number is MU 1468 and belonged to Albert Rouse. He led a chequered life being a 'Casanova' with the women, and when things got too complicated, he wanted to fake his own death. He kidnapped and murdered a tramp, drove to Northamptonshire and set fire to his car. He made the fatal mistake of leaving his identity disk in his briefcase forgetting to attach it to the vagrant.

Just north of Ayot St Lawrence is Brimstone Wood.

Find the Manor house and just past Brimstone Wood is a thicket of trees, reached by footpath, where a witch was reputedly burnt, and she now haunts here. (OS Exp 182 Ref 1917.)

Take the Lanes to the East Where You Will Find (Old) Welwyn

To the east is Lockleys, now Sherrardswood School (OS Exp 182 Ref 2315). The ghosts here are of Dowager Lady Shee who ascends the tulip wood staircase, a previous owner George Dering sitting on a tree stump overlooking the bowling alley, and an artist complete with spectral easel.

A blonde lady in white haunts the road adjacent to the school.

Mill Lane in Welwyn village is the haunt of an old man who lived in a caravan on wasteland here. He made his living reading and writing letters for illiterate fairground travellers. There was not much income in this occupation and he died a pauper on Christmas Eve. Three days later a letter arrived, saying he had inherited a lot of money. Each Christmas Eve his ghost is seen knocking on village doors.

Guessens House is situated opposite the church. Here you may glimpse a young woman emerge from the wall at Guessens House and cross the road to the church. She is believed to be Lady Betty Lee who lived in the house in 1731. She has blonde, curly hair, and is dressed in white, with a grey shawl and sunbonnet. Could this be the same shade witnessed near Sherrardswood school?

Legend

Digswell is to the east and it is here at the Red Lion on Digswell Hill that you may be shown the seat where Dick Turpin sat near the fire.

The Next Stop Is Codicote to the Northeast

Travel up the B656 and just before Codicote on the east side of the road is Sissevernes Farm.

A previous family member loved the old farmhouse so much that he asked to be buried here. He obviously loves it still as he now wanders around the place. You may get a view of the farm from Rabley Heath Road, on the right-hand side. It is a private property.

Continue up Rabley Heath Road and fork right and you will enter the village of Rabley Heath. Ninningswood Cottage at one time was a pest house. The pest house domiciled the victims of the plague and smallpox. There is said to be a plague pit nearby. (It is said that even to this day no construction can take place, or the ground be disturbed, on a past plague pit. For example, a tube line on the London Underground descends to a further level so as not to travel through a past plague pit. Also, graves surround an area of grass which was a plague pit in the churchyard of St Margaret's, Horsmonden, Kent. I mentioned this to a gravedigger when I visited Horsmonden a few years ago, and he said that he was not aware that that had been a plague pit, but he had always wondered why he was not allowed to dig there.)

Smells of breakfast being cooked – eggs and bacon – emanate from the deserted kitchen of this house, even when the property has been vacant for some time.

Retrace your steps and continue to Codicote church. Here you will find the grave of John Gootheridge. He was the victim of grave robbers. The body snatchers were disturbed, and the old man had to be buried a second time, hence the wording above his resting place.

A shrouded wraith wanders around the gravestones and may follow you. An old, red-faced woman with her hair in tiny ringlets prowls between the tombs. A young girl known as 'Little Norah' looks for something in the area of Gootheridge's grave.

Rose Cottage is haunted by spectral hounds.

At the top of the village take a minor road to the left to Whitwell.

At the summit of Bury Hill, on a Tuesday, you may smell fish frying. This is probably old Betty Deacon cooking her sprats or mackerel.

The medieval Bull Inn can be found at the foot of the hill in the village. The skeleton of an officer from the time of the Napoleonic Wars was discovered in a walled up cupboard. He used to haunt the old inn but after being given a Christian burial, his soul seems to be troubled no more, as he has not been seen again. All this happened in the 1930s.

At wintertime and usually Christmas Eve, if you travel out of Whitwell up Bendish Lane, on the left towards Breachwood Green, you may hear the sound of a spirit woodman's axe and timber falling. (OS 166 Ref 1522.) Yet however quietly and quickly you enter the copse, no tree feller or felled trees will be found.

The village of Bendish is haunted by its old squire on horseback. (OS Map 166 Ref 1621.)

Go back to Whitwell and turn onto the B651 to St Paul's Walden.

The apparition of a woman who killed herself by drowning in a pond frequents the church, where you may hear the tones of the old village choir.

Tan House has screaming departed souls.

If you walk down Mill Hill at night, you are likely to be followed by phantom footsteps all the way to the River Mimram.

On the way to Minsden along the B651 is where a spectral speeding coach and horses driven by a headless coachman is seen.

At the end of the B651 at a T-junction, turn left onto the B656 and just a little way along on the left is the Rusty Gun public house, formally The Royal Oak. This area is known as Chapelfoot. At the rear of the pub is a footpath to the isolated and eerie ruins of Minsden chapel. (There is also access from a bridle way off the B651 opposite Hill End Farm.)

The chapel lies in the heart of a small wood, and is therefore not visible from the road or path. It was built as a chapel of ease for pilgrims on the way to St Alban's Abbey in the fourteenth century. It fell into disrepair but the quaint ruins became a popular venue for weddings in the eighteenth century. However, when some masonry fell during a wedding ceremony, the use for this purpose ceased and it has remained a ruin to this day.

Historian Reginald Hine was so intrigued with, and loved the place, he leased it from the Church Authorities for his lifetime. His splintered tombstone is hidden under nettles and brambles. Some say his ashes were scattered around the crumbling ruins, others that his body lies here.

The main haunting is of a monk. The phenomenon begins with the tolling of a bell. (There are no bells on site now.) As the sound subsides, the monk appears under an ivy-covered arch. He walks with a stoop as if in prayer or deep thought, and silently ascends non-existent steps. Some then hear heavenly music, like an enchanting lament, but just as soon as it is audible, it is gone.

The ghost was captured on film in 1907. Some believe it is a fake but the Society for Psychical Research think not. Others in recent times have taken photographs at this location and strange shapes and glowing mists not visible to the eye have been produced.

Dogs and horses are aware of something strange, and one has the marked impression of being watched.

Reginald Hine's ghost now protectively haunts, together with a murdered nun. Where she fits in to the story is a mystery.

Also Dame Margery, a fourteenth century benefactress of the chapel appears, and a flute-playing boy. Is it he who provides the ghostly melody?

Peter Underwood kept vigil here one All Soul's Eve (Halloween), 31st October, which is the purported date for the monk to materialise. At 01.45 a.m. he saw a white cross appear, fade, and then reappear. It was a crux decussata (X-shaped). He admitted that it could have been a trick of the light or moonlit shadows, but it was certainly very odd.

At least two authors, on visiting the site, during the day, have reported signs of occult practices. Flowers arranged around candle stubs, together with other remaining evidence of pagan rites. These were in May and August, which are the festival times of Beltane and Lammas of the 'old religion'. So it would seem that the ruins are sometimes used for nefarious purposes.

Tour Nineteen
Lilley to Markyate

OS map 166 OS Exp 182 OS Exp 183

To the northeast of Luton lies the village of Lilley.

The Lilley Arms has a variety of ghosts. Poltergeist phenomenon happens here, and orbs of light have been witnessed.

Something does not like Christmas decorations in the bar, and staff have seen them twist and fall as if being pulled down by an unseen hand. When this happens, the room becomes so cold that one's breath can be seen.

On one occasion a paranormal investigation was being carried out at the Crooked Barn at the rear of the pub. A medium asked if anyone had committed suicide here. At that instance the video cameraman felt as if his face was being stretched back and the whole of his body was enveloped in something as if trying to make him taller. He was so frightened he stopped filming, and then a long, lank figure appeared lying on the floor.

The pub was previously named the Sugar Loaf, and about two-hundred years ago there was a fire which may have killed people.

Tom Connisbee a previous landlord has been spied sitting in a chair in the corner of the restaurant. Candles have been found alight when no one had lit them around his seat. He is also thought to be the playful phantom who pokes people in the back.

A shepherd haunts the yard outside, including a former handyman, a deaf and dumb girl, an eighteenth century postman and a small girl who plays in the orchard.

Children are very susceptible at seeing ghosts, often without fear. A small boy, fairly recently saw the ghost of the shepherd, and a 'see-through dog'.

To the Southwest of Luton Are Markyate and Markyate Cell

On the A5 near Markyate sits the Packhorse Inn. Here a vision in white, believed to be a cricketer, has often been seen. Two taxi drivers had witnessed the spectre, and one of them collided with the man dressed in white who stepped out in front of his car. On inspecting the area and his vehicle, there was no body, nor bumps and scratches on the taxi. The same apparition has been seen in the village of Markyate.

The B 4540, off the A5, runs along the side of Markyate Cell. A white, hooded spectre walks by the fence and then disappears.

At a spot on the A5 adjacent to Markyate Cell, a person on horseback and another person who staggers, cross the busy road in front of oncoming traffic. Next, the image scatters into thousands of tiny pieces and then dissolves.

The most notorious ghost of Markyate Cell is the 'Wicked Lady' Katherine Ferrers – see Nomansland on the previous tour.

Markyate Cell is a beautiful neo-Jacobean mansion, four miles north of Markyate village on the A5. The house was a priory (hence the name cell) before the Reformation. Katherine Ferrers lived at Markyate in the eighteenth century. She is believed to have led a double life of sedate lady by day, and ruthless highwaywoman by night, although there is no factual evidence to prove this. She would don male attire, a tricorn hat and mask, sneak down a secret staircase, and on her black horse rob travellers around Markyate and Nomansland near Wheathampstead. Katherine would also shin up a tree with branches overhanging the road and leap onto her prey.

The first person to be robbed was her sister-in-law shortly after she had dined at the Cell. When her husband heard the next day that his sister had been robbed at gunpoint, and her jewellery taken, he put up a reward to capture the highwayman, not knowing that the ruffian was his wife.

As explained before, in Tour eighteen, Katherine came from a wealthy family and married into the aristocratic Fanshawe household of Ware Park. She was around the age of thirteen and Thomas Fanshawe, sixteen.

She found country life tedious, and the marriage was not a happy one. When a young woman she went back to her childhood home at Markyate. Although, as Damien O'Dell points out in his book *Ghostly Hertfordshire*, at the time she is purported to have committed these crimes, Markyate was owned by Thomas Coppin. However, archive material for that era is rather piecemeal, and therefore may not be reliable.

Her ghost astride her spectral horse has been seen and heard galloping on the 'old' roads which were north-south staging posts for coaches to and from London. The taverns (coaching inns) providing the change of horses. In fact, Markyate was one of the staging posts from London to the North West, the old Roman road, Watling Street runs through it. Witnesses have been reporting these sightings for over three-hundred years.

Generations of Markyate Cell owners have met her shade in the house, particularly in a corner of the kitchen near the chimney where the entrance to the concealed stairway was situated. She is frequently seen on the main staircase late at night, and so often that one owner would wish her 'Good Night'.

Neighbours report their horses, unexplainably sweating and foaming at the mouth in the morning, as if they have been galloping through the night.

On one occasion she is said to have caused pandemonium at a tea party held at Markyate. Tables were overturned, cakes, sandwiches, glasses, plates and china scattered all over the lawns. Such was the shock of the guests having bolted in fear, when they saw Katherine swinging on the branches of an oak, wearing a saucy grin.

Katherine continued her secret life for a few years.

She is said to have been beautiful, with flaming red hair and piercing green eyes. Legend has it that she met handsome farmer Ralph Chaplin, as they tried to rob the same stagecoach, and decided to become partners in crime. They were probably lovers, as Katherine could hardly contain her grief when Ralph was caught and hanged.

According to O'Dell, there is no record of a farmer Ralph Chaplin in the historical archives, but according to Simon Walker (Crime is Hertfordshire Vol II) she was involved with a Jerry Jackson re Ralph Chapman, who may have been one and the same person.

She is supposed to have shot a 'policeman' during one of her escapades. Her adventures ceased when she was shot on Nomansland Common. Somehow she inched her way home, but she died as she reached the hidden stairs. Still in her male attire, the secret double life she led was now revealed.

The door to the stairs and secret den was sealed up, whilst her appalled husband buried her at Ware Parish Church, but not in the Fanshawe family vault.

There was a fire in 1840, which destroyed much of the building, and Katherine's vexed spirit was blamed. Fire fighters swore they had seen Katherine swinging on the branches of a nearby sycamore tree. However, when rebuilding work was being carried out, a heavy door was found. It was broken down only to discover a concealed spring that would have opened it. This led to the secret stairs and now empty room where she changed her clothing. Weird moans and sighs were audible.

She has been seen in Markyate village. Observers describe the apparition as having long hair, slim, wearing thigh high boots and a dark cloak.

Archives note that Katherine was buried on 13th June 1660. She was supposed to have been aged twenty-six, but I understand there is no record of her date of birth. O'Dell (*Ghostly Hertfordshire*) states that the cause of her death is unknown, but that she probably died in childbirth or due to a miscarriage. This may well be true. Author John Barber told me that when he was researching the history of Lady Ferrers (sometimes known as Kathleen Ferrers), he received a letter from a member of the family (now living abroad) indicating that the family would like the highwaywoman stories to be true, but they believed that she may have died in childbirth or as a result of miscarriage, as coincidentally O'Dell suggests.

The fortune she garnered has yet to be found. However, there is a childish little rhyme, which has been handed down over time, to give us a clue as to the whereabouts of her hoard.

Near the cell there is a well,

Near the well there is a tree,

And 'neath the tree the treasure be.

Nevertheless, there is no proof either way as to whether the tales about the 'Wicked Lady Ferrers' are true or false. Something or somebody haunts Markyate Cell, the village, Nomansland and its environs, and too many people have reported sightings since her death up to now. The descriptions of the manifestations give credence to them being Katherine. As for supernatural sightings in general, they cannot all be put down to people's overactive imagination.

There may be another spirit that haunts Markyate Cell. When builders were repairing a wall, they all saw a nun walking towards a gate in the wall. The rusty gate hinges had not been used for years, and overgrown brambles and nettles indicated this. She was also seen many times in the area around St John's Church. Is this a re-enactment of when the Cell was a religious establishment in 1145?

Tour Twenty
From Royston to Barley, Barkway, Nuthampstead and Therfield

OS Map 154

Note of Interest

There is a mysterious cave hidden beneath Melbourne Street, in the town.

The cave was discovered by accident in 1742, when a butter market occupied the site. A new bench was being lodged when workman found a buried millstone. On digging out the stone, a vertical shaft was exposed with the holes for human access. The shaft is the entrance to the cave. The millstone had been used as a seal and the date 1347 had been engraved on the wall.

The bell-shaped cave is thirty feet underground but the dome is only twelve inches below the road.

Some historians and archaeologists believe the cave was used by the Knights Templar. These were the warrior monks known for their association with the Crusades. There is a school of thought, however, that the cave is much older and carries pagan markings.

The cave is decorated with weird symbols linked to the Templars. It is known that the Templars established the town of Baldock in the twelfth century. They called it Bandac, the ancient name for Baghdad in memory of their campaigns in the Holy Land. The Knights Templar are also connected with Temple Dinsley on the site of the Princess Helena College, and Weston.

The strange carvings are unrefined and almost childlike. Some of the figures are out of proportion, and akin to the Cerne Abbas Giant in Dorset (but without the phallus). In amongst the haphazard scratches, numbers, letters, graffiti and indentations are said to be figures of Saint Christopher, Saint Catherine with her wheel and Saint Lawrence, amongst others.

The cave is situated where ley lines are said to cross. Ley lines are invisible earth energy lines, which too are a mystery. Could this site have been chosen for the cave? Interestingly, there is one of exact shape and proportions in Jerusalem.

The Celts as well as the Templars were aware of magnetic earth currents. Royston stands on a junction of two Roman roads, The Icknield Way and Ermine Street.

The Icknield Way spreads from the West Country to East Anglia. The ley line known as Saint Michael's and Saint Mary's line mainly follows this route. It starts from the East Anglian coast and ends at Saint Michael's Mount in Cornwall. During the pagan rites of Beltane, at the time of May Day, fires would have been lit along this line in order to synchronise with the sun's rays at dawn.

Ley lines link up with many churches, tumuli and ancient monuments like Avebury stone circle, Stonehenge, the Rollright Stones and the Abbey ruins at Bury St Edmunds.

Is this a science we have forgotten? It is said that many of our churches are built upon original pagan sites, which followed the ley lines.

The cave is not open all year to ensure preservation, but you can visit weekends and Bank Holidays from Easter Saturday to the end of September 2.30–5 p.m. There is an entrance fee. However, it is best to check the internet for opening times. The cave underwent extensive conservation work in 2014, where chalk-eating worms were eradicated!

The sound of chopping wood emanates from a building that was the old Post Office next to Royston cave. At one time, night workers refused to do their shift, as there was also the sound of doors banging, but all were wide open. Sceptics believed the sounds were echoes from the cave.

Opposite at the Manor House there are unexplained reports of breaking glass and door banging.

The old Oxfam shop premises in the High Street (at the time of writing) is a shoe repairs and suffered from poltergeist phenomena. Footsteps were heard from within unoccupied rooms.

Problems may have stemmed from a former owner, when the shop was a grocers. He hanged himself in the cellar from a hook, which is said to be still there. The ghostly grocer's troubled spirit had been seen in a flat upstairs, and the temperature drops when he is around – a typical ghostly eventuality.

A grey lady inhabits the offices of a firm of solicitors at 17 High Street. One of the upstairs rooms known as the Tudor room has an oppressive feeling to it, and it is here that bones were discovered under the floorboards.

The North Star Inn at one time had a poltergeist, and the publican's dog would howl at a blank wall. Obviously, the pooch could see or sense something humans could not. At other times the pet would rush from the room with hairs standing on end. On other occasions something malodorous would surround the bed with wafts of chillingly cold air. A terrible fire took place at the pub in 2012, and the building was derelict for some time. There was talk that it would be converted into apartments.

Ghostly footsteps are heard at night in Angel Pavement Shopping Mall where the old haunted Angel pub once stood.

A premises in King Street is haunted by an old woman.

Banyers Hotel on Melbourne Street is haunted by a Cavalier who, if you meet him, will remove his cape and bow with a flourish. He particularly favours room numbers one and four.

Some years ago I met friends for dinner at the Banyers, and we were given a dining room to ourselves as there was another function going on. The service and food was good and we had a pleasant evening, but although Britain was experiencing a heat wave, this dining room was decidedly chilly, and had an uninviting, gloomy atmosphere. As soon as I entered my car to drive home, the 'heaviness' lifted.

There are also reports of a phantom baby's cries, spectral voices and poltergeist activity.

Take the B1039 to Barley

The pub sign for the Fox and Hounds is very unusual in that it stretches across the road, showing images of a fox being chased by hounds. The pub has been haunted by disembodied footsteps for decades.

Note of Interest

Nearby, there is a timber framed 'cage' or lockup which is believed to be seventeenth century. Here, drunks and miscreants were confined.

To the South Is Barkway

The ghost at the Chaise and Pair public house was very welcome by the staff as he changed the barrels in the cellar. He had been seen at night. The pub is now a private residence.

The Wheatsheaf domiciled the ghost of a man almost beaten to death in a boxing match. He was brought here to die, and his moans and sighs of pain awaiting death were still heard. He also frequents the graveyard. The Wheatsheaf too is now a private residence known as the 'Old Coach House'.

At nearby Nuthampstead, the invisible ghost at the Woodman pub moves a chair up to a table in the bar, or stands next to customers who are aware of his presence. The sixteenth century inn also has the ghost of a little old lady with striking silver hair.

There is a picture which always falls from the wall. It is of an American B17 bomber which made an amazing return to the Nuthampstead air base, in the Second World War, after a large hole had been blown in the plane.

Retrace your steps to the A10 and take the lane westwards to Therfield.

The Fox and Duck is reputed to have been haunted by a former deceased landlord. Staff and customers witnessed a host of poltergeist activity but villagers were unwilling to talk about the happenings to strangers. On one occasion the police were called, and they too heard footsteps which appeared to be coming from unoccupied rooms. However, a search of the premises proved fruitless. I spoke to a member of bar staff a little while ago, but she had not experienced anything supernatural.

Note of Interest

Therfield Heath to the west of Royston has a number of ancient long barrows. On Money Hill Barrow the charred remains of a child aged about two years were found in an ornate cinerary urn. The barrow is fifteen feet high and one-hundred feet in diameter, and was a family tomb of the Bronze Age. Nobles were buried with their horses in both Bronze and Iron Ages, together with other animals to provide sustenance in the afterlife, much like the ancient Egyptians.

Tour Twenty-One
Bishop's Stortford

OS Map 167
Cyclical and Notable dates – 23rd December Boar's Head

The two most talked about mysteries of Bishop's Stortford are the tunnels and the grey lady.

The grey lady has haunted Bishop's Stortford for hundreds of years, and she 'pops up' in shops, pubs, offices and even the police station. The main area of the haunting is an east/west 'line' from Windhill, to High Street, down to Bridge Street, although her presence (presumably it is she) has been felt at properties in North Street and Potter Street. Interestingly, these haunts follow the line of an underground tunnel which is purported to run from Windhill down to the River Stort.

The identity of the grey lady is unknown, but her spirit frequents, The Old Monastery on Windhill, now occupied by businesses, the Boar's Head, The George Hotel, the Oxfam shop, the Black Lion, The Star, Nockolds offices, solicitors in Market Square and the old Tissimans Menswear building. Her ghost has been described as both terrifying and vicious.

Underneath Bishop's Stortford's roads and pavements lies a labyrinth of ancient, dark tunnels – allegedly. There are tunnels, but probably not as many as some would have us believe. There definitely is an underground passageway at the Charis Centre in Water Lane, another bricked-up entrance to a tunnel at the Boar's Head, a shaft which probably leads to a tunnel at Cooper's Store, and damp dripping underground corridors at the NatWest Bank.

Tradition says that a tunnel runs from St Michael's Church, across the road to the Boar's Head (seventeenth century) and connects up with the George Hotel (fifteenth century) on the corner of North Street and High Street. It then runs down Bridge Street to the Star (sixteenth century) and carries on to the Waytemore Castle mound across the river. This may be true, but some believe the tunnels stop at the foot of Bridge Street, as it would be very difficult to dig under the river.

A former vicar at St Michael's church indicated that he had heard of the tunnels but there is no evidence. The church does not even have a crypt. (This was probably originally a pagan site and there has always been a church here. The church that stands here now dates back to 1400 in parts.)

At the NatWest Bank there are a series of weird underground corridors. Each has up to twelve open-fronted alcoves, or cells, like small square rooms, on two levels. At the end of the upper level there are rusty metal cages. Each has hooks and holes through the brickwork.

The tunnels were longer but now the entrances have been bricked up. There are many businesses that have locked iron gates and bricked-up archways in their cellars.

A mysterious, very large figure swathed in black lurches amongst the gravestones in St Michael's churchyard at night.

At the rear of the old Monastery and St Joseph's Catholic Church, once known as Windhill House, in Windhill there are large grounds. Here Captain Winter and his yeomanry camped, at the time just before the Napoleonic Wars. He was accidentally shot by one of his own men, and his ghost haunts the area. There is a tombstone in the churchyard of a Ralph Winter, died 1802 aged sixty-three. The grey lady wanders here.

Across the road is the Boar's Head (circa 1630). A huge wooden beam that spans the fireplace is said to come from the church. The pub has been exorcised three times in the past, because of malevolent entities. The grey lady is said to have answered questions during an Ouija board session. She said her name was Sarah, and that she had been raped and murdered by the Squire's son on a Saturday, 23rd December, in the past. She begged the group to pray to help her pass over in peace. The date of the séance was Saturday 23rd December, in the 1970s!

Poltergeist activity has been experienced here, and a while back, a bar full of people witnessed the grey lady float by.

Room 27 at The George Hotel is reputedly haunted and has a small cupboard set into the wall with an old oak door, which has not been opened for decades. The handle is two-hundred years old, and because the building is Grade Two listed, a former publican was wary of forcing it. So no one knows what lies behind it. The grey lady haunts this room, and manifests as a swirling, grey mist. The temperature of the room becomes icy and the atmosphere, hostile. Guests feel as if they are being watched, as eerily the door opens of its own volition. She has materialised fully in Room 27. She appears bending over the bed with her arms raised as if in despair. She apparently vanished when a guest screamed.

Once an army officer occupied the room and was found next morning sleeping in his vehicle in the car park, such was the oppressive aura of the room.

Apparently, Americans like booking into Room 27. It is not unusual for visitors to vacate the room in the middle of the night.

It is rumoured that a workman abandoned his job and scarpered; he was so scared of the ambience outside Room 27.

A white mass lurks in the cellar. Beer taps, water taps and lights turn themselves on and off. This is all put down to the grey lady, and often happens on busy nights.

In 1998 during refurbishment of thirty rooms, plumbers found two more rooms that staff did not know existed. These are now bathrooms.

The George has been a hostelry since the 1400s. The original pub sign was the George and Dragon but now shows the Hanovarian George 111.

There are more rooms behind the Oxfam Shop over the cobbled courtyard. There is a ramp to the first floor. These were stables where horses were kept on upper floors.

The George was a coaching inn where travellers in the fifteenth century en route from London to Cambridge could change horses or stay.

It is now Bishop's Stortford's oldest inn, and the third oldest in Hertfordshire. Charles 1st is believed to have dined here, on his way to Newmarket.

The restaurant chain Prezzo has bought the ground floor of The George, which is where the bar would have been, and what was the cellar is now the restaurant's toilets. I have been told by a couple of people that the toilets have a very creepy atmosphere.

A cage where felons were incarcerated awaiting trial, stood outside The George in 1630, and was moved to a site opposite The White Horse, now Pizza Express, where it remained until the early nineteenth century. The only sanitation was a bucket.

I do not know if this next story is true, but I was once told that a policeman had been locked in one of the cells at the police station (situated on the corner of High Street and

Basbow Lane), by the grey lady. The police station is most definitely haunted, by bangs, footsteps and poltergeist activity, according to a policeman who was stationed there for over thirty years.

The Oxfam shop next to The George is another stamping ground for the grey lady. Objects are thrown downstairs and footsteps heard in empty rooms.

Tissiman & Co., Menswear, now Alexandra Wood (fourteenth century in parts), a beamed Tudor building situated in between The Boar's Head and The George is where the grey lady has been seen on many occasions. Some time ago this old building was a café, and was haunted by the sound of children playing and laughing accompanied by the apparition of the grey lady at the foot of the stairs. There was also the unexplainable smell of burning wood. As explained above, this lovely old shop has now closed after trading for four-hundred years, and the premises has been converted into flats, offices and retail units.

Part of the building of Coopers Hardware Store was once a grand house owned by the nephew of the famous hanging judge Bishop Bonner. The store is the only trace of the Bishop of London's Palace, circa sixteenth century. Ornate plaster decorations known as pargetting can still be seen on the ceiling at the front of the store. Pargetting is common around East Anglia, but is normally found on external roughcast plastered walls of buildings.

Bonner was the notorious persecutor of Protestants and stayed at the house from time to time. Here he would hold court and pass judgement on those accused of heresy. If found guilty they would be taken to the gaol at Waytemore Castle.

Here she is again! The grey lady has been seen in the store by a previous owner when he was working late one night.

Disembodied footsteps are heard.

A while ago human bones were discovered and were given a decent burial. This would normally put an unquiet spirit to rest, but haunting continues.

Strange noises seem to come from various corners of the building, including one almighty crash and the sound of someone running, but no explanation could be found.

The grey lady has been described as having a vicious streak, and I can attest to this theory (see Alliance & Leicester further on in this tour). Workmen were often on the premises at night when the store was closed to customers. On a certain occasion they were aware of a menacing presence, and heard a loud scraping sound behind them. When they looked they found gashes in the plaster they had just finished. So deep were the lacerations, they must have been made by something strong or in a hateful temper.

Heavy items have been known to jump off shelves, and plants thrown around, sometimes aimed at people. Poltergeist activity takes place in general, including nuts and bolts skimming through the air. Workers' tools have been kicked and thrown by something unseen.

The ghost of a past employee dressed in the brown uniform of yesteryear was seen in January 2013, and the grey lady was seen gliding between the display stands in October of that year.

Across the road at the Black Lion (seventeenth century) a little girl in Victorian clothing skips around. She likes to hide mobile phones and keys. Sometimes only her footsteps are evidence of her presence. A person staying at the inn one night saw a door handle of his room turn, the door opened, and something invisible joined him in bed! The mattress moved with the weight of whoever or whatever it was.

In Tudor times, coffins were stored at The Black Lion.

A cook at The Black Lion refused to work there for the rest of the day, when a pencil threw across the room, which appeared to be aimed at her. Consequently, no food was served that day.

The Black Lion and the Boar's Head caught fire the same night; locals put this down to the grey lady.

It is said that a bridge used to span the road from Coopers to The Black Lion, but some historians say there is no evidence of this. Apparently in medieval times, the centre of Bridge Street was an open sewer, so maybe there was a bridge here, so people could get from one side to the other. A man in old-fashioned garb has been seen crossing the road, only he is three feet above ground level. Could this be where the bridge once was? There was a Mill Bridge which stood opposite the entrance to Jackson Square where the pedestrian crossing is now. The bridge was a thoroughfare across the River Stort before it was diverted in the 1960s.

The Star in Bridge Street is where a cleaner met the grey lady, as she was in the way of the ghost's path. Also, spectral knocking noises are made from a small bar adjacent to the main bar.

Between The Star and Coopers is Water Lane. The Lemon Tree Restaurant building is around four-hundred years old, and was once three-terraced cottages with part of the premises being a dairy. The river, before it was diverted, came right up to the door at the back. This is where the dairy produce was put on barges and taken up the river to other towns and to London. The doorway has now been blocked up and made into an alcove. The table in the alcove is number thirteen. This is a sheer coincidence that the table should be numbered thus. One evening, the proprietor was taking an order from a diner at table thirteen when she felt a coldness swish past her. The diner stopped in mid-sentence and said, "Did you feel that?" The proprietor said that she did, but the diner's companion felt nothing. The feeling was like when you say someone has just walked over your grave. The restaurant has many nooks and crannies and apparently a few people have felt a shivery presence in the middle section. It may be that many people have experienced phenomena but not said anything to the staff.

The vacuum cleaner sets itself off in an upstairs room when no one has been near the appliance. Part of the upstairs is now an apartment, and one of the chefs was running a bath. He went to the bedroom to answer his mobile phone and turned off the running water beforehand. When he went back into the bathroom, the bath was full to the brim of very hot, almost boiling water.

A young lady connected to the establishment hates going down to the creepy cellar when asked to fetch something. Also, chairs were placed in a circle down there. When the cellar was next visited, the chairs had been moved out of alignment. No person working in The Lemon Tree was responsible for this. When the owner was working in the cellar, she had only turned her back for a few seconds, when all the doors to the fridges, freezers and cupboards were found open. The equipment down there is of all different shapes and sizes, yet the doors were simultaneously opened. She told me that she found this most unsettling, especially as she asked staff if they had played a trick on her, although that would have been difficult, as there would not have been time to act this out, but they were dumbfounded and a little frightened at what had just happened. When she is in the cellar and alone in the building, she can hear footsteps on the floor above, which is the restaurant area.

She has also heard footsteps in other parts of the premises, and has gone around calling out, "Who is there?" It is not obvious whether the tread is that of a male or female. Other staff members have heard them also. They sense the spook is that of a woman. However, a ghostly woman is believed to walk from the bar through the restaurant to the far end of the building. It is here that the owner feels as if someone is walking towards her.

There are rumours that there are tunnels under the cellar that link up with Coopers and the castle, but there is no evidence of this. The restaurant has been in existence for over twenty years, and the proprietors feel that the ghost or ghosts are part of the fabric of the place. They feel that the haunting is benign apart from the boiling water episode.

The Cock Inn, circa 1540, stands at the Hockerill crossroads. This is a haunt of Dick Turpin who would have had escape routes in four directions. Two-hundred years ago the pub was a court and jail. This may not be on the grey lady's patrol, but an old woman or a grey lady has been haunting here. Other ghosts are a mischievous young girl who haunts the cellar, a young woman who waits for her soldier husband, a man in Civil War clothing and a serving lass. Strange lights, dark images and poltergeist phenomena occur.

There is a dark maze of underground tunnels under this building too. The entrances have been sealed up, but a newspaper article dated 2001 mentions that the last time one of these was opened, the workmen saw a woman's shoe just lying there in the dark. The entrance was secured again very swiftly.

Some of the dwellings in Hockerill Street have the sound of marching in the bedrooms and downstairs. When a young man went to investigate, he could only get four rungs up the stairs as something unseen was holding him back.

I was delighted when the Alliance & Leicester transferred me to manage their Bishop's Stortford and Ware branches. Both old market towns are steeped in history, and have their individual appeal.

The Alliance and Leicester premises at 32 Potter Street, now a coffee shop, had some strange incidents.

When I first arrived there, the Building Society only operated from the ground floor, although it owned all of the three-storied building. The first and second floors were accessed at the rear of the building via an outside metal staircase. It was part of the security procedure to check on these unused floors periodically, and staff would do so in pairs, never alone.

The rooms up there always felt very creepy and were left empty except for a few boxes of obsolete files. One day on inspection, items seemed to have been moved. So we strategically placed certain files and objects and drew a line exactly where their edges touched the surface of the floor or windowsill as a marker. On the next inspection we found they had most definitely moved, as they were outside the markings. No one else could gain entry to that part of the building, and there was a rigmarole of security procedures to go through to obtain the keys. The only windows were at the front of the building and they were intact. We informed our premises department at Head Office, and they were at a loss what to advise. In order to be helpful, they suggested putting a padlock and extra security measures on the entrance door up there.

The workman we employed to carry out these improvements informed us that every time he reached for a tool which he had placed on the floor beside him, it was not there. He found it in one of the rooms. He was only working on the front door and hallway. He then found the door shut, which he had left wide open. He eventually finished the job but told us that he had never worked anywhere so spooky, and that he would not work there again. He looked quite ashen faced.

Also unexplainable cooking smells, like that of boiled beef and carrots would permeate the ground floor, always around nine-thirty in the morning. Premises nearby were not responsible for the cause.

A couple of years later the Alliance & Leicester gained planning permission to use one of the two floors above for business use.

Before the substantial refurbishment took place, the normal security checks on the upper floors were carried out. One day when I was at the Ware branch, I received a telephone call from a staff member at the Bishop's Stortford office asking me if I or a surveyor had torn wallpaper from the walls, as part of the ongoing enquiries and plans. I had not, nor had any surveyor from Head Office.

When I inspected the area concerned, I was quite shocked. The wallpaper had been ripped in jagged strips, and there were deep scratch marks as if claws or talons had gouged out the plaster. As no human agency was responsible, and a structural fault was not found, we put this down to the same ghost that had been tampering with the files.

I wanted to find out more but some of the staff were becoming frightened, and as Building Society Managers are supposed to be level-headed people not given to flights of fancy, I decided to leave it alone. It was years later that I read of the claw marks at Coopers, then Maslens, in Betty Puttick's book *Ghosts of Hertfordshire*.

However, I could not leave the matter alone for long. Whilst the refurbishment was going on, the branch functioned from a temporary site in the town. Spasmodically, I would visit to enquire how the work was progressing. The builders informed me that there were some strange events. An office-style chair on wheels, suddenly skated across a level floor, mugs of tea would vanish along with tools and toolboxes, and something liked blowing fuses. One evening I visited and the workmen left leaving one chap talking to me. He was then most insistent that I stay whilst he locked up as he was frightened of being there alone.

When we were established in the renovated site (the back outside iron staircase was now incorporated inside of the building) we did not have any further problems until one day when we had to perform some routine security checks.

The Society had not gained permission for business use of the third floor, and so metal grills had been inserted at the windows and a heavy, metal door placed between the second and third floors. This meant that it would be almost impossible for an intruder to gain access to the top floor, and we did not have to inspect it every day.

On this particular day, a member of staff and I opened the metal door and were only a few rungs up the stairs when we heard footsteps above. We both made a sign to the other indicating that we had heard something and crept down, locked the door and called the police.

We accompanied the police to the top floor, but it was empty and there was nothing to account for the sounds we heard. One of the policemen asked if we had a ghost. I, feeling rather foolish, replied in the affirmative. He just shrugged his shoulders as if to say, well there you are then, and wrote something in his notebook. Whether he wrote this woman is a nutter, I do not know!

One evening I was having drinks in a local bar with business associates when a local lady solicitor at Nockolds suddenly remembered that she had left her briefcase in her office. She was scared to enter the building after dark in case she encountered the grey lady. The famous town spook haunts these offices that extend over the shops in Market Square.

A policeman in the 1930s reported the apparition of a man standing at the junction of Northgate End and Hadham Road. As the officer approached, the man vanished before the constable's eyes.

A house in Mary Park Gardens on the fringe of the town had an oppressive atmosphere and suffered from poltergeist activity.

Waytemore Castle, 913 AD, is now just a mound (a very large one) and remnants of the moat now circle the bungalow in the Castle Gardens. Skeletons were unearthed in

1999. The site was used as a prison until 1649, and housed eighty miscreants. The first prisoner recorded in 1234.

A man now deceased, saw what he thinks was the grey lady in Castle Gardens, near the mound. She was gliding along, but only had one leg. She was swinging a false leg with her hand. He never ventured there again.

Also a man told me that when he was a teenager, he and his friend witnessed the grey lady in Castle Gardens. She emerged from the castle mound, crossed in front of the war memorial, and then disappeared into a hedge.

A couple driving on the A120 near the St Michael's Mead roundabout saw a group of people sauntering across the road at 10.00 p.m. at night. They were in silhouette with no discerning facial features. They, just casually, walked across the road completely unaware of oncoming traffic, and wandered into the heavily wooded trees at the side of the road, where there is no path, and no street lighting. They did not have a torch to guide their way. A weird place to be walking at that time of night, and dangerous. The people who told me this are very level headed, but they felt that there was something unworldly about what they had witnessed.

Notes of Interest

The Half Moon public house, circa 1642, still has old stables, which can be seen in the garden.

In the 1800s the workhouse was at Hockerill with a separate barn for vagrants. This was then sold and the union workhouse was built at Haymeads in 1837. The inmates were the village and town paupers. It was later the town's hospital and is now apartments.

Maze Green Road was once named Pest House Lane. This probably originated from the sixteenth century plague, known as Pestis or Pestilence. The pest house was situated at the top of the road away from the town. However, in medieval times every town had its mazel or leper house, so the green at the top of the road may have been the site of the mazel – hence Maze Green Road.

A peephole was found at 6 Bridge Street, now a charity shop. When the seal was pulled, one could see a long way up and down the road.

Bishop's Stortford has unfortunately lost three of its most disreputable inns. The Reindeer stood on the corner of Market Square and High Street, and was kept as a brothel and 'a place of good entertainment'. Samuel Pepys made several entries in his diary in reference to it. The establishment was run by a certain Betty Ainsworth, who had so bad a reputation in Cambridge, she was forced to move to Bishop's Stortford. Pepys wrote that he 'had taken knowledge of her' implying that their relationship was a sexual one. The site is now occupied by the Tourist Information Centre.

The Grapes was demolished in 1966, and a modern building now occupies the site, housing a bakers and dentist, on the southwest corner of Potter Street and Apton Road. The original building was sixteenth century but in 1895, the inn's landlord was George Chapman. His real name was Severin Klosowski, and he ran the pub with his 'wife' Bessie Taylor, whom he had originally employed as a barmaid. The marriage ceremony was bogus and she later died under mysterious circumstances, as had two of his previous wives. He was found guilty of poisoning all three women, and hanged in 1902. The flag at The Grapes was flown at halfmast. It was rumoured that he was wanted for murders in Russia. In 1888 he was a Jack the Ripper suspect.

The Dog's Head in the Pot, pub sign usually indicated that the landlady was a slut, and an inn of this name stood in Market Square, at the back leading to the rear entrance of what is now a doctor's surgery. There are some very old buildings, probably old houses and stables, now private residences and tearooms, in this little backwater.

There was a weekly cattle market which took place at Northgate End and was described in 1767 as the finest in England. This was discontinued in the 1960s.

Cecil Rhodes, the founder of Rhodesia, now Zimbabwe, was born and educated in Bishop's Stortford. His former house is now the town's museum, theatre and arts centre.

Thorley is a small hamlet just two miles west of Bishop's Stortford. (Thorley Park, a housing estate lies adjacent to the old Thorley hamlet.) This sleepy little backwater can be approached via St James' Way, into Obrey Way, and then through the sign-posted lanes. There is an ancient church, a converted barn which is now a community centre, some cottages, a pond and Thorley Hall Farm. The peaceful churchyard has some very old, interesting headstones and tombs. The church in parts is thirteenth century.

More tunnels! In 1903 a worker digging a hole for a tree, discovered by accident, a subterranean passage, believed to have been built to connect Thorley Hall with Sawbridgeworth's Shingle Hall. The tunnel runs almost due north for twenty feet (6 m) before turning at an acute angle, and then runs southeast for another thirty feet (9 m) where the roof has given way. Apparently, the man digging said the air exuded from said tunnel was so foul he felt compelled to desist.

Thorley Hall Manor house was owned by the famous hanging judge, Lord Chief Justice Ellenborough. In 1810 a bill was proposed in the House of Lords, to abolish the death penalty for shoplifting and burglary. Ellenborough opposed on the grounds that people would be marooned on their property, for fear that all of their possessions would be stolen if they should leave.

Dick Whittington, Lord Mayor of London lived at Thorley.

Harry Roberts killed three unarmed policemen in Shepherds Bush, West London in August 1966. He put a bullet in a policeman's eye, then shot another in the back. He watched an accomplice shoot a third officer in the head. Roberts hid in Mathams Wood, situated between Thorley and Sawbridgeworth. Some boys had seen a camouflaged tent and a man they thought was tramp, but had not connected this with the fugitive. He was on the run for ninety-six days. After a tip off, over three-hundred police searched the area and Roberts was finally arrested at Blounts Farm.

At the time of writing, he is still in prison. He has been let out on parole, but caused trouble. Yet another appeal for his release has been quashed, such is the feeling against him in legal quarters.

Map of Bishop's Stortford

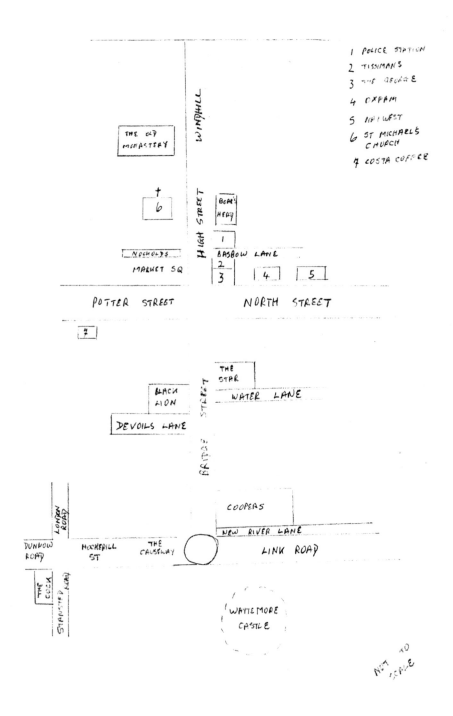

Tour Twenty-Two
From Birchanger to Stansted Mountfitchet, Manuden, Ugley, Henham and Quendon

OS Map 167 OS Exp 193 OS Exp 194 OS Exp 195
Cyclical and Notable Dates – Quendon 19th May
Stansted Mountfitchet around Christmas time.

Legend

From Bishop's Stortford take the B1383 to Birchanger village to the northeast of the town. Legend has it that there is an underground tunnel that led from St Mary's church to Birchanger Place. Part of Birchanger Place is now an estate called Harrisons. Some people believe the tunnel went to the Cottage (seventeenth century). (OS Map 167 Ref 5022.) The churchyard can have a gloomy quality to it.

Retrace your steps to the B1383 and travel a little way further north to Stansted Mountfitchet. The sites on this tour are on the Hertfordshire/Essex border. Although essentially Essex, they follow on conveniently from Bishop's Stortford (and have a Bishop's Stortford postcode).

Yet another grey lady!

This one is seen on the black bridge which crosses the railway near Mountfitchet station, according to local hearsay.

A ghost was captured on film at The Kings Arms in Station Road by the chef. He was trying out his new mobile phone and took a picture of the bar, and an ectoplasmic figure could be seen amongst the drinkers. Thinking there must be a fault or a trick of the light, he took another but this time there was nothing there amongst the customers.

Apparently glasses nowhere near the edge of the bar fall off, but do not usually smash, a guest left his hotel room in the middle of the night due to spooky feelings, the cellar is reported to have an eerie atmosphere, and a Victorian lady has been seen. Is this the same lady that haunts the nearby bridge, mentioned above? The pub dates back in parts to the sixteenth century.

Stansted Mountfitchet Castle is a reconstructed wooden motte and bailey, which has been built on the site of the old castle.

The plot has the ghost of a one-armed knight, affectionately named Sidney. He haunts the grand hall which is located in the 'medieval village', just outside the main castle gate.

There has been a castle on this site since Viking times, and supernatural phenomena have been reported here for years.

A balding man dressed in a white robe watches staff. Some say his intention is to protect rather than frighten people. A number of employees claim to have seen him.

In March 2002, flickering lights in the visitor centre was a cause for concern and a qualified electricians could find no electrical fault. A priest who specialised in unquiet spirits was called in. Workers said that when the lights went on and off, they felt spooky and did not like to work alone.

Stansted Mountfitchet village is in two parts. The upper part is either side of the main road to Cambridge. The lower part can be found at the foot of Chapel Hill. A cottage in Lower Road near the Dog and Duck public house is haunted. Apparently the property was one larger house, but is now two dwellings. The occupier hears footsteps ascend the stairs and proceed along the landing. These sounds are definitely in his cottage and are nothing to do with next door, as their landing is in the opposite direction.

A scented candle propelled across the room and came to rest at his feet, whilst he was watching television. A relative who claims to be a psychic told him, as soon as she entered the house that the place was haunted. She sensed a ghostly little boy.

The manifestations usually happen around Christmas time.

The Arthur Findlay College at Stansted Hall is just up the road towards Burton End. This imposing building now houses a college for the studies of psychic science and related subjects. It is known locally as 'Spooks Hall'. The college provides lectures, psychic demonstrations and private sittings. Courses run throughout the year, and include such subjects as hypnosis, stress relief, psychic phenomena, and dreams. The public can go to the services or attend the open week. There is a shop, restaurant and bar. (OS Map 167 Ref 5225.) It is rumoured that a phantom coach and horses travels down the driveway and then disappears into the lake.

Take the Minor Roads Northeast to Manuden

Manuden now only has one pub. The Yew Tree is said to have two ghosts, but who they are or how they haunt is unclear. They are said to haunt the hotel annexes. Current patrons and hotel staff are not aware of these spooks. (OS Map 167 Ref 4926.) In 2015 the upper floor was being renovated but the new manager did not like to go up there as she could hear voices and strange noises.

A seventeenth century timbered house, now used as offices was at one time known as The Jolly Waggoners. It is alleged that when it was a private residence, a ghost used to awaken the occupants by pulling at their arms with ice-cold hands, and turning lights on and off.

Note of Interest

William Wade (Waad) was examiner at the Tower of London. He was responsible for the incarceration and interrogation of Guy Fawkes and Sir Walter Raleigh. He retired to Battles Hall, which he inherited from his first wife, who died in childbirth, aged nineteen. He was known to be a spiteful person. He unceasingly victimised a Catholic, Thomas Crawley, who lived at Manuden Hall. According to Richard Symonds, a historian, wrote in 1639, that Wade had fifteen children by his second lady... all were imperfect. Those that were straight and handsome were dumb and deaf... those of them who could speak were lame and crooked. A plaque marks the place of his burial in the village church.

Cut easterly across the county, approximately a couple of miles, to Ugley.

Customers at The Chequers pub (OS Exp 195 Ref 5130) have heard a re-enactment of an argument between Camille Holland, and her bigamist husband Samuel Dougal. See Quendon on this tour.

A petite woman in Victorian dress has been seen walking around the pub. Is this the troubled spirit of murdered Camille? She emerges from the fireplace and floats across the room towards the toilets, her feet about twelve inches above the floor. The floor level was lowered in recent times for fire prevention reasons.

Pub staff are nervous of the apparition, and maintenance staff who work when the pub is closed at night are very wary. A few workmen refuse to enter the place after dark.

The featureless ghost, in a long black dress, frequents the old kitchen area and has been seen on many occasions.

When the publican first moved here, there was a window outside that could not be located within. It was later revealed that a room had been boarded up, but a face still appeared at the window.

It is rumoured that a Viking burial ground is located at the rear of the building, and that may account for some of the phenomena.

There is no reported haunting at the isolated St Peter's Church at Ugley. Nevertheless, I visited here one bleak winter's day and it certainly looked forbidding; there was a brooding air about the place, and it was so quiet you could hear a pin drop. (OS Map 167 Ref 5128.)

Legend

The Pharisees or Fairies Hole is situated in an underground passage halfway between Ugley Hall and Rickling Hall. The passage is supposed to connect the two, both of which are built on ancient sites. A groom at Ugley said he could hear a coach passing half a mile away as it crossed over the old Cambridge Road at the Pharisees Hole. It was also muted that the echo of falling bricks is heard through the tunnel at Rickling Hall.

Go East Again to Henham

The Rectory at this quintessentially English village is rumoured to be haunted by an Elizabethan lady whose portrait hangs there.

Pledgdon Hall is haunted by a little girl who died in a fire many years ago.

Retrace your journey and onto the B1383, turn right in the direction of Newport, you will find Quendon.

Here too the church is in a lonely spot, and lies almost due north from Ugley Church. I visited here with my husband to take photographs of the church for a painting. We both had the distinct impression that we were being watched, although we were the only humans around at the time.

Perhaps there is some connection between the two churches, in that they are geographically 'aligned', maybe on a ley line, only a mile or so apart, and the whole locality appears to be charged with something supernatural or esoteric. See what you think. (OS Map 167 Ref 5130.)

Go south approximately half a mile and turn right into Brick Kiln Lane, away from Rickling Green and towards Rickling. A little way past the church turn right, sign posted for Wicken Bonhunt and on the left lay both Moat Farm and Coldham's Farm.

Camille Holland was a wealthy spinster aged fifty-six when she met her future husband Herbert Samuel Dougal, aged fifty-five.

Dougal posed as an ex-army officer, and Camille, although having had a sheltered life, was prudent. He suggested after their marriage that they buy Coldham's Farm. Camille had that strange quality of the naïve coupled with the canny. (The Fool card in the Tarot deck of divination cards, can be defined as the wisest dunce.) She insisted that the purchase was registered in her name, and so she must have had some sense of self-preservation – all to no avail, alas. The couple moved in and called their new home The Moat Farm.

Three weeks later on the 19th May Camille mysteriously disappeared. They had gone out in a pony and trap but Dougal arrived home alone. He told the maid, Florence, that his wife had gone to London and would be back soon.

During that evening he went out several times telling Florence that he was to meet Camille at the station, and then that he had received a letter from her saying that she had decided to stay, to take a little holiday.

Florence left that morning as she did not want to stay in the house alone with him, as he had made passes at her, and at one time tried to get into bed with her.

After her disappearance, there were a number of attractive 'maids' employed at the house, and one was espied by villagers riding a bicycle naked in the grounds.

Then, Dougal's third wife moved in, claiming to be his widowed daughter. Cheques purported to have been signed by Camille were cashed in the Bank in Bishop's Stortford nearly four years later.

Villagers became suspicious and thought that perhaps Camille was a prisoner in her own home. Police made discreet enquiries.

It transpired that Dougal had shot Camille and weighted her body in a drainage ditch. Her body was discovered by a labourer digging six feet below when his spade cut through a lady's boot, containing the bones of a human foot. Police took over and Camille's body was revealed wearing a black dress.

Dougal was found guilty and executed in 1903. Strangely, Dougal used to frequent The Grapes in Bishop's Stortford – described as a rowdy house – and was put to death the same year as George Chapman, the licensee. (See the Bishop's Stortford tour, twenty-one.)

A local blacksmith passing the empty house heard a piano being played. Was Camille the ghostly pianist? Future residents have heard bangs and crashes in the house and barn, plus the sound of doors opening and closing, although bolted. There is a heavy studied door on the landing. This would open and close of its own accord. If it was locked it would find a way to open. Are the doors opening and closing the ghostly re-enactment of Dougal leaving and entering the property that fateful night? He admitted that after killing Camille, he had to have a few brandies at the house as Dutch courage, because he could not deal with weighting her body in the ditch.

Just as he was about to be hanged, he was asked again whether he was guilty or not guilty. As the trap door jerked open, he was heard to declare 'guilty'. Is the lady dressed in black that haunts The Chequers at Ugley Camille? Local newspapers at the time dubbed the case as The Clavering Mystery, but the farm is in the vicinity of nearby Quendon.

Tour Twenty-Three
From Little Hadham to Albury, Furneux Pelham, Stocking Pelham, Brent Pelham, Clavering and Newport

OS Map 167 OS Exp 194
Cyclical and notable Dates – Newport 24th December and October
Clavering Spring

Take the A120 from Bishop's Stortford (the old Roman Road – Stane Street) towards Little Hadham.

Just before the brow of the hill on the right sits Hadham Hall. The Hall originally dates back to the eleventh century, but a grander building was constructed in the fifteenth century. The Hall was owned by the Capel family in the sixteenth century. More recently it was a school, then a health club, and now it is a complex of prestigious, renovated private properties.

It is here that the spectre of Elizabeth, Lady Capel gazes out of a window. A phantom gardener and dog, together with a ghostly horse and cart amble silently around the grounds.

The next turning on the right is Church End, and it is this area where the original medieval village once stood, which also stretched across the A120 to Stone House Farm.

St Cecilia's Church is very old and dates back to early medieval times. There are good views across the countryside at the end of the cemetery. (OS Map 167 Ref.4422.)

A friend said that when visiting the church and churchyard they had a very uncomfortable feeling, like they were intruding on something, and also felt as if they were being watched. Somewhat like my experience at Benington, Ugley and Quendon churches.

Now carry on down the hill and at the traffic lights turn left to Little Hadham. The Nag's Head Inn is haunted by a lady in white. A previous landlady told me that one morning she was descending the stairs to make her first cup of coffee for the day, when at the foot of the stairs she saw a cavalier. He was dressed in green and brown, and on seeing her, doffed his plumed hat, and with a flourish, bowed to greet her, as if to say 'Good Morning'. Then he disappeared. She also at another time saw a young woman, who could have been a maid, wearing a long white apron.

Retrace your steps and at the Little Hadham traffic lights turn left, and up the hill there is a turning on the right to Albury (sign posted). Here an old house, formerly moated, is where a Mrs Marsh was murdered in mysterious circumstances. There was no clue as to her murderer, other than a broken bottle and empty crate found on her body. From time to time, the phantom scene of the murder is played out including the sound of breaking glass.

103

You will now come to a T-junction. Turn left, carry on, and eventually fork left, then take a right turn into Barleycroft End, at Furneux Pelham. (Furneux is pronounced by the locals as 'Fernox' and not as one would pronounce it in French.)

If you care to go straight across the crossroads at The Brewery Tap pub, you will drive into a track/bridleway that leads to Violets Lane Ford. Villagers say that at this spot at night one can hear whispering. (OS Exp 194 Ref 4327.)

If you care not to venture there, turn left at the Brewery Tap and on the right is the church of St Mary the Virgin, with a diamond shaped warning sign on its tower. There is a gilt figure of time, bearing a scythe with an hourglass. Underneath are the words 'Time Flies Mind Your Business'. The word 'own' was removed in 1906. The church is haunted by a man who sits in the front pew, believed to be a Mr Arnott. The heavy tread of his footsteps have been heard pacing down the aisle, and then the church door slams shut.

Note of Interest

On January 7, 2004 Riley Workman was shot dead on his doorstep by a twelve-bore shotgun when he answered the side door of his home in The Causeway, Furneux Pelham.

It was about eight o'clock that evening when neighbours heard a shot but thought nothing of it as in the countryside to hear a gun going off is not unusual. Someone is either shooting game or rabbits.

Lt. Col. Robert Workman known as Riley was found by his carer the next morning. Foul play was not suspected by paramedics, police and a GP, but when the undertakers arrived to move the corpse, it was evident that he had been blasted by a shotgun.

Previously, an emergency 999 call was made from a public telephone box in the nearby village Braughing (pronounced Braffing) at 04.57 a.m. about nine hours after the crime. The caller asked for an ambulance to attend Hollyhock Cottage in Furneux Pelham. Interestingly, the man spelt out the village name as F.U.R.N.E.A.U.X. It is known locally as F.U.R.N.E.U.X. but the village sign does have an 'A'. Voice analysts concluded that the caller was a man aged over fifty years, with a rural accent, which may have come from Hertfordshire. A transcript of the 999 call was on the television news and 'Crimewatch'. My personal view is that the accent is from The Cotswolds or West Country. I have never heard a native of Hertfordshire with that dialect. Also, I feel the voice sounded like a man of over seventy years of age. Interestingly, Riley spent some time, years ago, in the Oxford/Cotswolds area.

An ambulance crew was dispatched to Furneux Pelham but was unable to find Hollyhock Cottage, the reason being that the property was named Cock House. Col. Workman's deceased wife had named the cottage 'Hollyhock' at one time for a short while, but the property reverted to its original name of Cock House as there is a cockerel weather vane on the chimney.

So, if the Colonel was murdered, why was an ambulance requested later? Was it a pang of conscience? Was the caller a relative or friend of the murderer?

Villagers described Riley as a polite old man, who kept himself to himself. He had been devoted to his wife, Joanna, and nursed her unceasingly after spinal surgery. The widower was a war veteran attached to the Royal Green Jackets. The couple had no children, and Riley's stepdaughter had died a year before his wife's demise.

Police arrested a local rat-catcher who was released without charge, and pursued many lines of enquiry which ended in blind alleys. Apparently, Riley had had a series of gay affairs in the 1960s when homosexuality was illegal.

Then in 2011 the local rat-catcher, in prison for the murder of traveller Fred Moss, whose body has never been found, bragged to a cellmate that he was a hitman, and had been hired to execute Riley. If that was the case, what was the motive of the hirer? Was it a spurned lover from years ago? Also, how would someone from Riley's past know of a hitman who lived a mile away from Riley in Stocking Pelham?

It seems unlikely that it was a bungled burglary, as there was £10,000 worth of silverware in the property and nothing was stolen. Was Riley involved in something clandestine when in the army, or his subsequent antiques business? A shotgun is an unlikely weapon for a hitman or professional killer. There were no disputes with villagers and none were traced in the past.

It was muted that villagers were concerned that the killer is in their midst. No car was heard pulling away after the shot. However, a bridle path leads from the back of the cottage to Braughing. Only a local person would know that, and maps are not that clear for a stranger to the area to follow. So it could have been someone from the village or surroundings, but why would they send an ambulance to Hollyhock Cottage when they would know the house was named Cock House?

The rat-catcher/pest controller was Christopher Nudds, who had changed his surname to Docherty –Puncheon, was found guilty of this murder and given another thirty-two years in jail. (He has since changed his surname to Xavier.)

There is a school of thought that Xavier killed Fred Moss, because he knew too much about the murder of Riley Workman, and had to be silenced. It is muted that there had been a homosexual friendship between Col. Workman and Xavier.

Chris Xavier has since made a request for an appeal, but Lord Brian Leveson has said, "We don't accept that this sentence is either wrong in principle or manifestly excessive... the case is unarguable."

Why was the telephone call made from Braughing, and who made it? I cannot find on the internet or from newspaper articles, that this question has been answered. Was it answered in Court? Maybe in time all will be revealed, or perhaps we shall never know.

Note of Interest

At nearby Stocking Pelham in 1969, Muriel McKay was imprisoned by the Hosein brothers for a month on Rooks Farm, she then disappeared without trace.

They had planned to capture the wife of a newspaper mogul and demand £1m ransom. They abducted the wrong woman.

Arthur Hosein had delusions of grandeur, tried to join the local hunt and was known as 'King Hosein', locally. Arthur had noticed a chauffeur driven Rolls Royce in London. He took note of the registration number, and Nizamodeen Hosein, his brother, traced its owner via County Hall records. The car was owned by the News of the World, and the keeper of the car was the Chairman Rupert Murdoch.

The Murdochs were away in Australia and had lent the car to the Deputy Chairman Alick McKay.

They followed the car one evening from the Fleet Street offices to a prestigious Georgian-style property in Wimbledon, which they thought was Murdoch's house.

A few days later they overpowered Muriel and took her away. Alick arrived home, found a roll of twine, sticking plaster tape and a billhook. The latter being a farming implement used for hedging and ditching, shaped somewhat like a sabre only chunkier and shorter, like an axe.

The first two weeks after the abduction on the 29th December 1969, nothing was heard from the kidnappers, probably because they were shocked by the publicity.

Telephone calls demanding ransom money then ensued over the next three weeks. Three letters arrived from Mrs McKay as proof of life, and then stopped.

Fingerprints on a letter sent to the News of the World were identified as that of Arthur Hosein.

The brothers called themselves 'Mafia 3' or 'M3' for short. The following modus operandi was extremely amateurish. They liaised with the McKay's son Ian, and told him to leave the ransom money at a telephone box on the A10, Cambridge Road. He was then directed to another telephone box with further instructions to go to the area of High Cross at a junction with a road to Dane End, where false flowers would be left as markers. A detective posing as Ian left a suitcase with the money. Other detectives kept watch but no one came to collect the money.

A few days later there was another telephone call from the Hoseins. This time they would only deal with Alick, as they did not trust Ian. A similar procedure with telephone boxes was played out which finished at a point near Bishop's Stortford.

A security officer driving past, who had nothing to do with the investigation, was suspicious of the two suitcases standing alone next to false flowers. He called the local police from a telephone box, and then returned to keep watch over the suitcases.

The Hosein brothers drove around and saw a number of police cars in the area. So they drove off without once again collecting the money.

The police noted the Hosein's car registration number, which was registered to Arthur Hosein at Rooks Farm, Stocking Pelham.

Previously on the 1st January 1970, a close friend of the McKay family flew to Utrecht to meet Dutch clairvoyant Gerard Croisset. He took with him a photograph of Muriel, together with a map of London and the Home Counties. His psychic powers had been used successfully on many occasions around the globe. The psychic's description of Muriel's hiding place, proved to be uncannily correct. He described a white barn, surrounded by trees and another green barn. Amongst other details he indicated the kidnappers had taken a direction of north, northeast out of London, and that if she was not found within fourteen days she would be dead.

Police followed the 'clues' given, which led them to a deserted farm on the Hertfordshire/Essex border. The farmhouse was just south of Bishop's Stortford, and approximately five miles from Rooks Farm as the crow flies.

At the trial, a neighbouring farmer said that his billhook had gone missing in the October after visiting Rooks Farm. He was shown the exhibit of the billhook which he positively identified as his.

No trace of Muriel McKay was found at the farm. However, paper flowers, other evidence and notepaper incriminated the Hoseins.

Whether Muriel died on the farm or how she met her death remains a mystery. There were macabre rumours that they had cut her up and fed her to the pigs, but there was no evidence to support this. No bones were found, and the pigs were tested for remnants of Cortisone which she had been prescribed.

Muriel may not have been kept on the farm, and may have died from natural causes, brought on by the bitterly cold winter and her lack of prescribed medicine.

Arthur Hosein received twenty-five years and Nizam fifteen years for murder, and for blackmail and threatening letters, they each received fourteen and ten years respectively, to run concurrently.

Rooks Farm was eventually sold and the name changed. It lay near to the Cock Inn. This lovely, old pub was destroyed by fire in 2008, and new houses have been built on the site.

Note of Interest

To the northwest is the attractive village of Brent Pelham where the original stocks and whipping post are to be found outside the church.

Take the B1038 in an easterly direction over the border into Essex, to Clavering.

Maybe on a Friday night when the lilacs are in bloom, at twilight, you may see a courting couple on a small bridge at a place called Kings Water, at Stickling Green.

The bridge was originally a three-plank wide bridge, but now the lane crosses the stream. (OS Map 167 Ref 4732.)

The young man sits, as if on the top of the rail of the bridge (now a brick wall), with his arm around a girl's shoulders. The girl wears a pretty cream-coloured dress with a pattern of tiny roses in groups of three. Around her shoulders is a diaphanous white shawl. Her dress has a large flounce or panel at the bottom.

They have been seen by many over the years. There is a wonderful peaceful feeling when they are around.

Clavering is a straggling, charming village which is mainly one long road, which leads from the church up to The Cricketers. Surrounding areas such as Starlings Green, Roast Green, and Stickling Green are all part of Clavering. The area near the church, Middle Street, is a quaint little corner, and a footpath from across the footbridge leads across the meadows up to Kings Water.

A phantom coach and horses has been seen travelling from Wicken Bonhunt to Clavering.

According to hearsay, one of the bungalows near the school is haunted. When people argue, bad things tend to happen, and sometimes they feel as if they are being strangled.

Legend

A lady who died in the seventeenth century said that if there was heaven or hell, an ash and maple would grow above her grave, and accordingly she would be in heaven or hell. An ash tree grew and split the tombstone.

Carry on Eastward to Newport on the B1038

There is a phantom coach that travels from Saffron Walden through Newport on the B 1383, at night. This is probably the same one seen in Clavering and Wicken Bonhunt.

The Crown House at Bridge End is a very unusual dwelling. The huge shell porch dates back to 1692, but the house may be much older.

It is rumoured that Nell Gwynne and Charles 2nd stayed here on their way to Newmarket races.

One Christmas Eve the lower half of a man's body, attired in knee breeches, long hose, buckled shoes and a leather apron was witnessed. A door opens and closes at this time of its own accord. Apparently, the premises was once an inn. The apparition seen fits in with an eighteenth century innkeeper. Maybe the floor level has been altered, and that is why only half an image is witnessed.

There is an alley that leads from Wicken Road to Church Street in Elephant Green, in Newport. One dark October night in 1978, three ladies decided to take a short cut into Church Street using the alley. There was lighting at both ends of the passage but not in the middle where there is a slight bend, and therefore quite dark. As they walked up the alley, they saw a man dressed as a Cavalier wearing a plumed hat, cape and sword drift, along. The women flattened themselves against the wall as he passed. When they reached the top, they were overcome with curiosity. Was it someone in fancy dress? They ran back down to see if they could see him, but he was nowhere to be seen on Wicken Road. It has been said that this passage may have been a former corpse way.

Note of Interest

According to legend, one year a travelling circus passed through Newport and an elephant died as it crossed the green near the church. What became of the elephant's corpse? Was it buried here? Anyway, that is how this delightful little 'backwater' is named Elephant Green. No – it is not haunted by an elephant!

Tour Twenty-Four
From Much Hadham to Widford and Hunsdon

OS Map 167
Cyclical and Notable Dates-Much Hadham13[th] February

From Bishop's Stortford take the B1004 to Much Hadham

Historic Much Hadham village is mainly one long road that leads from Little Hadham to Widford. Set in the Hertfordshire countryside, the style of village cottages and houses are the first hint of East Anglia. On driving from Ware to Bishop's Stortford, it is at this olde-worlde village that the countryside starts to subtly change.

A pink five-hundred-year-old cottage has been troubled by a poltergeist. The building was the King's Head Inn for more than two-hundred and fifty years.

A story is that a ghostly black box materialises. The middle room always feels freezing cold. Local hearsay is that some owners would not stay there for the first six months of ownership for fear of the ghost, until the vicar had exorcised it. Apparently, the ghost has frightened every owner for years and years.

The Forge Museum has some wonderful ancient wall paintings, and in this particular room a phantom small boy has been felt brushing against people's legs.

There is a ghost named Henry who has a huge moustache.

One year I had an art exhibition at The Forge and I was invited to a Christmas Party on the premises. My husband was getting drinks from the kitchen and I was standing by myself in a room full of people whom I did not know. I was wondering how I could politely interrupt a group's conversation and introduce myself when I felt two sharp prods on my back shoulder. I turned around expecting to meet the 'prodder', but there was no one there. I looked around and everyone was huddled in groups of animated conversation. I then thought someone was playing a joke, but there was no sign of this, no one looking at me out of the corner of their eye to see my reaction. My husband came back with the drinks accompanied by the curator of the museum. I told her what had happened, and she indicated that it was quite normal and was probably one of the playful ghosts.

Patrons of The Bull not far from The Forge on the same side of the road have also been poked and prodded by something unseen. Perhaps it is the same ghost. The landlord says the ghost is a young girl. It would seem that there are two ghosts, as a member of staff saw the hazy apparition of a man wearing a large hat and cloak drift across the bar.

The Old Red Lion building is circa 1450. Dick Turpin is said to have escaped from here via a secret passage that led to a priest's hole, where now there is a carved head of a monk.

In 1923 during redecoration, Tudor panelling was found around a chimney and crumbling staircase. This opened up a passage along the upstairs rooms, but no doorway into them. A further search revealed a collection of bones belonging to a girl of seventeen years or younger.

The Red Lion is now converted into apartments, and has kept its name.

There is a ghost of a man in a brocade coat, knee breeches and buckled shoes.

Moat Farm at Kettle Green is on the fringe of Much Hadham. Here every 13th February, the shade of the Moat Lady rises from said moat to lure people to their deaths.

This menacing spook is believed to have been murdered and her baby flung into the moat. When the moat was drained, her bones were discovered and she was given a Christian burial. However, the troubled spirit still creeps about searching for a human victim every St Valentine's Eve. I met the owner of Moat Farm in 2004.He had lived there for twenty-six years and was non-committal as to whether he had seen the ghost, but he was not sceptical.

Note of Interest

The summer palace belonging to the Bishops of London lies at the foot of Winding Hill near the church. The building has been converted into private dwellings. Five-hundred years ago, Katherine, widow of Henry 5th, gave birth to Edmund her son by Owen Tudor. Edmund's son was Henry 7th, father to Henry 8th.

Carry on through Much Hadham southerly to Widford. There is a sharp bend and Blakesware Manor is on the right-hand side of the road.

Blakesware Manor on the B1004 is haunted by two children who float up the stairs at midnight. These are known as the 'babes in the wood' who inexplicably vanished under dubious circumstances.

Note of Interest

Elderly husband and wife Camp lived in a remote cottage between Stanstead and Hunsdon. They were burgled by two thugs who beat Mr Camp with a heavy stick, and cut his neck and legs, and Mrs Camp's stays (whalebone corsets) were cut through to her skin. They were threatened that if they did not hand over their valuables the thieves would cut their throats. No money or valuables were handed over and the robbers left with a few items. The ruffians then announced they were leaving them to bleed to death.

How they were caught is not clear, but Mrs Camp identified them. One came from Hoddesdon, the other from Ware. They were both hanged on Friday 13th January 1800. The portable gallows was carried from Hertford and set up in a field near the Camp's house. Ten-thousand people are supposed to have witnessed the execution. As soon as the capital punishment was over, the executioner and his assistant went to dinner at Widford.

Note of Interest

Due south of Widford lies Hunsdon.

At Hunsdon House, three children of Henry 8th were lodged here and attended the church. The King liked Hunsdon as there was plenty of hunting, the country air was good for his progeny and he could escape from plague-ridden London.

The future Elizabeth 1st was at Hunsdon when her mother Anne Boleyn was arrested. Edward and Elizabeth spent much of the last decade here before he succeeded Henry 8th as king.

This was Mary Tudor's (Bloody Mary) main residence as a girl, whilst Elizabeth was at Ashridge.

Tour Twenty-Five
From Perry Green to Allens Green, High Wych and Sawbridgeworth

OS Map 167
Cyclical and Notable Dates-Sawbridgeworth1st November

From Bishop's Stortford take the B1004 towards Much Hadham. About just over a mile along the lane, take the left, turn opposite Hadham Golf Club (sign posted Sawbridgeworth, Green Tye, Allens Green), and a little way along on the left is Warren Farm. Here on the lane you may spy an American airman. This may be the shade of a pilot who crashed his plane in a field at nearby Green Tye. There were a number of airfields in this district during World War Two.

Carry on Through Green Tye to Perry Green

Here a corner house is haunted by a man and a child. The child was drowned in a pond in the garden.

A little further on, on the left you will come across The Hoops Inn (seventeenth century). Before the inn was refurbished, I was told by the landlady that, a ghostly something likes to play with the sound system, and the beer pumps do strange things, but there is nothing wrong with them when checked.

The pub has since been modernised but the spooks are still active. When staff were upstairs in a meeting one day, they heard the distinct sound of furniture being moved in the empty and closed restaurant below. On inspection, nothing was out of place, and there was no one there. On another occasion, three members were at their duties in the bar area. All three heard someone say 'Excuse me'. They turned to see who had spoken, but there was not a soul in sight.

Retrace your journey to the crossroads, turn right and follow signs for Allens Green. On the way you will see a number of Second World War bunkers. (If you continue on this road to Spellbrook, there are more.) Along these lanes at night, a ghostly soldier (maybe the same chap seen near Warren Farm – witnesses may confuse the uniforms if the image is indistinct) is seen hitching a lift. If you stop, he disappears into thin air.

In addition, along these lanes a mounted Cavalry Officer has been seen. His great coat is spread over his horse at the back.

Just past Blounts Farm (see Thorley on the Bishop's Stortford tour twenty-one) turn right into a long, straight lane that leads to Allens Green. The countryside is very flat, and ideal for airstrips during the 1939/45 war. There are haunted houses and underground passages. Maybe these link up with Thorley Hall and Shingle Hall (approximately one mile northeast of here).

Carry on and you will come to High Wych. (Wych is pronounced as to rhyme with 'white' and not enunciated as 'witch' or 'wick'.)

111

Opposite the green is an old house named Wych Croft which was believed to be haunted. The nature of the haunting has been lost in the annals of time.

To the west lies Sawbridgeworth

Down Bell Street, there is a shop that used to be three, seventeenth-century cottages. In the flat above, the spirits of two women dressed in gypsy garments appear in the afternoons. One wears a bright green cloak. There is a wild animal and a little boy with a cut over his eye.

The most celebrated and outlandish ghost story in connection with Sawbridgeworth is that of Sir John Joscelyne of Hyde Hall.

Hyde Hall is to be found just over the level crossing to the left away from the town. The building is now a home for the elderly, but it has been a school, and was once owned by the singer Suzie Quatro.

Sir John was an eccentric who wanted to be buried with his favourite horse in the churchyard. This, the horrified vicar refused to do. So, Sir John (some reports say Sir Strange Joscelyne) left instructions that on his demise he was to be buried without a coffin nor shroud, his horse slaughtered and buried with him in the grounds of Hyde Hall. Sir John was buried near the Grand Avenue, within a circle of Yew trees. His instructions were also that an ox be butchered at the wake to feed to the poor of the parish. There is no record as to whether his horse accompanied him in the grave. However, tradition says that every 1st November, the anniversary of his death, Sir John rides along the Avenue up to the Hall, at breakneck speed, on his white steed.

The house is also haunted by a man and a small girl.

Tour Twenty-Six
From Tring to Long Marston, Wigginton, Pendley Beeches, Aldbury, Berkhamstead and Little Gaddesdon

OS Map 165
Cyclical and Notable Dates-Pendley Beeches – 1st May
Wigginton – 31st December
Gubblecote – 23rd August

A lady is seen gliding above ground level down the drive of Elm House, in Tring, and a grey lady is witnessed on recreation ground at Grove

A coach and horses crosses the railway line between Tring railway station and the signal box.

A large, spectral, black dog with eyes aflame, and a man on a white horse are seen on the roads around Tring railway station.

The Old Roman road, Akeman Street, runs from Tring to Aylesbury, and Roman soldiers in full battle dress march here. At Buckland, just off this road, a phantom farmer leans on a gate, from Buckland Wharf to the Rothschild Arms. He wears a smock and leggings.

Pendley Beeches is an area between Tring town centre and the station. Boadicea's chariot, sometimes seen on the 1st May, has been witnessed, the sight of which is considered bad luck. A tall man wearing a top hat and cloak, minus his legs from the knees down, frequents this area.

Half a mile or so north of Tring you will find Little Tring. A ghostly bicycle lamp appears on the bridge, believed to have belonged to a postman who disappeared on his round of Wilstone and Puttenham.

Wigginton lies to the southeast of Tring

The Common is haunted by a ghostly Roman army, and Oliver Cromwell's men who were camped on this site, manifest and manoeuvre. Also, on New Year's Eve a coach with a headless driver and four headless horses are seen some years.

Two harmless old people were taken by a mob and swum in a pond at Long Marston, just north of Buckland, as a test for witchcraft (OS Map 165 Ref 8915). They were stripped, and their thumbs were tied to their toes. They were thrown three times and dragged along in the muddy water. (The pond no longer exists.) It was a belief that a witch could not sink. If the accused drowned, they were deemed innocent. If they floated, they were guilty and then hanged or burnt at the stake.

The couple in their seventies both died after this ordeal. The main offender and leader of the savage witch hunters, Thomas Colley, was arrested and tried. He was taken on 23rd August 1751 to Gubblecote Cross (OS 165 Ref 9014) and hanged. His body was then hung in chains and left to rot.

Some say you may meet the ghost of the murdered woman in Astrope Lane, Long Marston, and that you may also meet Colley's ghost at Gubblecote. The sound of clanking chains and the groaning wood of the gibbet may be heard. A black dog with fiery eyes somehow connected with Colley haunts the area.

The road from Tring (via the railway station) into Aldbury is haunted by a man on horseback, who is both seen and heard. However, a coach and horses is also heard but not seen on this road, believed to belong to Simon Harcourt, Lord Aldbury.

Yet another black phantom hound pads around here.

The old stocks and whipping post are to be found adjacent to Aldbury pond. Go through the village, past The Greyhound public house, in a northerly direction, and on the left is a golf course which was Stocks Estate. Opposite, in the woods, three poachers battered to death by two gamekeepers. Now the wood is haunted but it is unclear if by the poachers, or gamekeepers, or all.

To the southeast of Aldbury you will find Berkhamstead. Oliver Cromwell's troops during the Civil War launched an artillery attack on Berkhamstead Castle, which was destroyed by their cannon. At dusk occasionally, in a lane named Soldiers Bottom, a squad of Roundheads are observed going about their tasks.

There have been sightings in the town centre of people in period dress. A wealthy looking woman wearing a grey dress, pinched at the waist and wide on the hip has been witnessed. She disappears in a trice. Other sightings include a boy in a flat cap running, and an old man either ill or drunk who carries a stone bottle with a handle. He is seen in an area which was the poor end of town known as 'Ragged Row'.

The five-hundred-year-old Crown Hotel is haunted by a ghostly lady in a rocking chair in the cellar. She may be responsible for poltergeist activity here.

Another poltergeist caused mayhem in a cottage at Piccotts End, and a monk manifested in a Georgian house next door. Wall paintings were discovered believed to be the work of Bonhommes monks from the Ashridge Estate.

Take the B4506 North out of Berkhamstead to Little Gaddesdon

The Manor House, at one time known as The Priory, is haunted by William Jarman. He was a churchwarden who fell in love with a woman from Ashridge. Rebuffed, he committed suicide. He drowned himself and now haunts the pond. Lights of candles would dip and extinguish; now the same thing happens to electric lights in the eighteenth century Manor House overlooking the green.

He rides out at night to Blue Pit Pond opposite the Manor House. After a fresh fall of snow, the wheel tracks of his carriage are imprinted from the old stables to the mansion.

At Gallows Hill (OS 165 Ref 9717), there are sounds of a creaking and clanking past gibbet, and a phantom grey man walks silently here.

Tour Twenty-Seven

From Chelmsford to Great Baddow, Roxwell, Mashbury, Great Waltham, Pleshey, White Roding, Hatfield Heath, Hatfield Broad Oak and Little Hallingbury

OS Map 167 and OS Exp 183
Cyclical and Notable Dates – Chelmsford – December
Great Baddow – 20th December

A small number of sites on the Essex border have already been explored in the Hertfordshire Tours. Now Essex can be visited fully, and we start with the County Town of Chelmsford. You may wish to investigate Chelmsford and Great Baddow, and leave the other sites on this tour for another time.

Chelmsford is the County Town and Administrative Headquarters for Essex. Essex has the sad reputation of having condemned more witches than any other English county. Major witch trials took place at Chelmsford (the assizes) from 1566 onwards.

Springfield is now a district of Chelmsford. Springfield Place is to be found to the east of Springfield Hall, and was once named Springfield Lawn on account of the huge lawn in the front of the house.

The house boasts an underground chamber, probably a priest's hole, and a large bedroom known as the blue room or ghost room, which is always locked. High up on the walls are a series of cupboards which are never opened, coupled with trap doors, dark corridors and bricked-up windows.

A mother and child once occupied the blue room. The mother awoke to hear the child laugh and exclaim, "Funny man!" The funny man was a grotesque dwarf standing with folded arms and his back to the fire. Does he reside in one of the high cupboards? It is said that he also haunts the churchyard. A local paper recorded a sighting in 1946, but has he emerged again? More recent witnesses may not have reported the phenomena.

Money problems, death and marriage difficulties are some of the main reasons why houses are sold. It would be hard to buy a property where sadness has not occurred at some juncture. If a property is newly built, it can take on impressions of tragedies left behind by what was on the site before, even if there were green fields! In a very old house, one would expect a number of disagreeable incidents over time.

In Chelmsford there is a medieval house that comes up for sale regularly. Occupants do not stay much more than five years. There have been a number of divorces and deaths. A particular tragedy is that of a baby drowned in the moat. Maybe some houses are unlucky or cursed.

A moated house that has remained anonymous in Essex has a history of poltergeist phenomena, and a menacing, chilling presence. A nun is said to have been stabbed to death with a carving knife, and her wan face peers out from a window. The succession of owners does not stay long. The house is nearly always up for sale and builders who know nothing of the history will not work after dark. I wonder if these two moated houses are one and the same. Having said that, their whereabouts have not been divulged, and there are numerous ancient moated properties in Essex.

An angry nun haunts All Saints church.

A helpful ghost shows visitors around the Civic Theatre. He is believed to be a technician who met with a fateful accident in Duke Street, and his footsteps are heard on the empty stage. There is a melancholic feeling on the balcony and the stairs to the wardrobe.

On Christmas week, a phantom butterfly appears in one performance.

A tall ashen-faced man wearing a top hat and cloak glides down Patching Hall Lane, and then disappears.

A shopping centre on the site of the old Spotted Dog pub is haunted by a troublesome spirit that throws cardboard boxes around.

Note of Interest

In August 1938 a twenty-two year old young woman burst into flames after a dance at the Shire Hall, Chelmsford. It was generally believed that someone had dropped a lit cigarette end, and the girl's long dress of white tulle, and satin petticoat had caught fire – although there was no evidence to support this. She had been standing in a queue to collect her coat at the time.

The girl died in hospital from complications after the burns. The coroner could find no cause for the sudden fire. There were various tests on the garment, some with cigarettes and lighters, but the dress did not ignite, only smouldered.

Was this a case of spontaneous human combustion? Many people do not believe the phenomena exists .However, in all parts of the world, and for many years there have been cases of spontaneous human combustion. People usually die from the phenomena, either immediately or later in hospital. Those that have survived are unable to explain what happened to them, nor can witnesses. In most cases, not all the body has been consumed by fire. In fact, in some cases, there is a mound of ashes, and just half a leg, foot and shoe of the victim remain.

Scientists are confounded. In the eighteenth century, a woman burst into flames in front of her daughter – in 1904 a woman in Scotland was burned 'to ashes' sitting in her chair, the rest of the room unaffected – in 1930 a New York woman burnt to death although her clothing was untouched, in her own home – in 1938 a girl dancing in a Soho nightclub suddenly caught fire, the flames emanating from her shoulders, back and chest. Dickens wrote of spontaneous human combustion in his novel *Bleak House*.

So what did happen to the woman in Chelmsford?

Great Baddow is a suburb of Chelmsford and lies to the southeast.

Molram's Lane is haunted by the ghost of Maria aka Mollie Ram. She was a 'white' witch but some feared her and one night she was set upon by a rabble from Sandon. She was beaten to death, and her spirit still walks along Molram's Lane, Southend Road and Sandon Road, up to Grace's Cross (OS Exp 183 Ref 7405).

At St Mary's Church, a monk floats down the aisle and leaves through a door on the west side. He is supposed to follow the route of tunnels underneath the building. Also, soldiers from the Civil War era loiter outside the church.

Every 20th December at the White Horse Inn, phantom footsteps descend the attic stairs.

Take the A1060 out of Chelmsford to Roxwell

At Thieves Corner, the ghost of a sheep stealer who was hanged here possibly haunts the spot. (OS Exp 183 Ref 6707 or OS Map 167 Ref 6707.)

Further along the A1060, turn right onto a minor road to Good Easter, and then carry on to Mashbury. At the seventeenth century Fox Inn, in Fox Lane, the sounds of a spectral coach and horses pulled up outside. The clinking of a harness and the heavy tread of wheels crunched on the gravel up to the entrance. An invisible person's presence was felt at the bar, and poltergeist activity had occurred. This is one of Essex's 'lost pubs', as it is now a private residence. One wonders if the occupants experience any supernatural activity.

To the Northeast via the Lanes You Will Come to Great Waltham

A grey cat haunts the Beehive public house in Barrack Lane. The spectral moggie sprints down a corridor, through a wall into a bathroom. The pub's resident poltergeist brakes glasses. (OS Map 167 Ref 6913.)

To the Northwest Is Pleshey

At Pleshey Mount Farm, a nun is said to frequent the outside, but the reason for the haunt is unknown.

Retrace your journey westwards, drive through Good Easter, and take the minor roads back onto the A1060, and turn right towards the Rodings.

At White Roding you will find the sixteenth century Black Horse Inn. The ghost of an old woman totters into the bar then suddenly vanishes. Sporadically, strange noises are heard and glasses slide along the bar. Lights that have been switched off are found on again. At the gable end of the building there are two windows, but only one is visible from the outside. A false ceiling had been put in as the high roof made the area cold. This upper window area has been blocked off. The only way to gain access is through a trapdoor in the bar. Yet, on occasions this upper window is lit from inside. There is no electricity or any form of lighting.

One of the ghosts is a pianist. Beautiful but strange music can be heard in the middle of the night, even though there is no piano now. When there was a piano in the bar, the landlord would creep down to catch the ghostly pianist, but as soon as he entered the room, the melodious strains would stop, and the piano lid was closed.

Carry on Along This Road to Hatfield Heath

In 2006 an orb was photographed hovering over a grave in the churchyard of Holy Trinity Church. Orbs are considered to be a human soul or a ball of light or energy from the departed. The local minister said that he had not known of ghostly activity here before.

Opposite the church is a junior school. A past caretaker reported that his cleaners had had spooky experiences. Whilst vacuuming, the appliance had been turned off from the plug in the wall. At other times, parts of the vacuum equipment were found not where they had been left.

Take the B183 northeast to Hatfield Broad Oak.

If you enter this lovely, old village (very East Anglian in character) at twilight, it is easy to imagine the place in medieval times. I have been told that there are ghosts here, but no villager seems keen to tell me who, what, where or when! However, the only piece of hearsay I managed to glean is that there is a grey lady who wanders around outside the country butchers (famous for Broad Oak Sausages) at Cage End.

Go back to the A1060 and carry on in a southeasterly direction and you will come to the magnificent Down Hall Hotel. (OS Exp 183 Ref 5213.) The ghost of a woman known locally as the Lavender Lady haunts the bedrooms of the hotel. The apparition is preceded by a strong smell of lavender. She is not always seen, but one knows she is around by her olfactory presence.

Also years ago when a new wing was being built at the hotel, a builder was killed in a tragic accident. He is sometimes seen sitting on a bed doing up his shoelaces.

Now retrace your journey back on the A1060, go right through the village of Hatfield Heath, and take a right fork towards Bishop's Stortford. About half a mile along on the left on a bend is a thatched house which lays back off the road. This was formerly the Sutton Arms. The building is well over five-hundred years old. The Sutton Arms was named after Thomas Sutton, who came from an Elizabethan wealthy family. One of the Sutton boys fell in love with a serving maid who spurned his advances. Piqued, he killed her in a fit of rage. His ghost is desperate for forgiveness and young women visiting the pub – now a private residence – have been given a ring by a handsome young man. He greets them in the vestibule between the two bars. As soon as the young ladies show the ring to another person, it vanishes. The good-looking stranger cannot be found.

Other reports are that he walks upstairs on creaking floors with a large bag of gold.

Steve Hockley, my friend, used to be a fireman in the district, and he told me that the passageways upstairs are so narrow, one cannot walk normally. One has to edge along sideways on.

Another ghost haunts the road just outside this house. A taxi carrying fares hit what he thought was a young woman wearing 1970s style clothing one night. However, there was no bump or impact; to the astonishment to all in the taxi, she went straight through the car and out the other side.

Tour Twenty-Eight
Colchester

OS Map 168
Cyclical and Notable Dates. Colchester Castle – May

Outside Colchester on Stane Street, on the old Roman Road now the B1408, and the area nearby, a troop of ghostly Roman soldiers are seen marching across the roads and through hedgerows. They are believed to be the ninth legion on their way to Lincoln.

Colchester Castle is now a museum, and one can visit the room where Matthew Hopkins interrogated some of his prisoners. (See Mistly and Manningtree tour forty-seven.)

The Castle is said to be haunted by James Parnell held in captivity in May 1656, who was made to climb a rope every time his food was left for him. He fell to his death and now haunts the dungeon. A rash individual once stayed the night in the dungeons for a bet, only to surface the next morning out of his wits.

Nearby at Hollytrees Museum, which houses toys and dolls, the Gun Room is haunted by Anne Lisle, whose portrait hangs nearby. Her clacking footsteps are heard running in and out of the Gun Room. Children are particularly susceptible in seeing her. Staff are used to hearing her footfall when the museum is closed to the public.

At night, faces appear at windows at the back of the premises.

Not far away at East Lodge, the wraith of a white lady has been seen on the stairs and darts from room to room, then dissolves into nothing. There is always a strong smell of scent when she is around.

The apparition of a cavalier walks down East Street, and vanishes when he arrives at Siege House. Staff will only work in pairs in one of the rooms. He also haunts a house near Crouch Street, and at Headgate Court. The shade of a puritan haunts the siege area.

The Hostel of The Good Shepherd 87 on East Hill, later called Cambridge Lodge, suffers from ghostly footsteps, shuffling sounds, and doors opening and closing in empty rooms. Although the place has been exorcised, phenomena still continue.

Around the ruins of St Botolph's Priory, a dark phantom lurks, smiles and then vanishes.

Essex County Hospital has a spectral nun, who once gave a child patient a toffee, then faded from view.

Three soldiers on separate occasions were afflicted with a comatose condition by an unseen power, at Colchester Barracks.

The charred body of a soldier was found in a hayloft in Mill Street. His legs and boots were untouched as was the surrounding area – a case of spontaneous human combustion? (See Chelmsford tour twenty-seven.)

O'Neill's pub has the spectre of an old man who wears a peak cap. He walks through walls and fiddles around with taps in the cellar.

Alice Catherine Mellor (or Miller) was murdered in 1633. She shares her haunt with a monk who died in a fire at The Red Lion Hotel. The hotel is circa fifteenth century and was frequented by Oliver Cromwell when alive. Alice, a chambermaid, was offered her freedom by a magistrate who seduced her. However, when she was pregnant by him, he beat and killed her, and threw her body from an upstairs window. She appears all over the hotel, but especially in a rocking chair in one of the bedrooms. Alice is blamed for any poltergeist activity. She has been known to play with children staying at the Red Lion.

The monk appears in one of the function rooms, together with a woman and child. Black shapes dart about. There are cold spots and beds shake in certain rooms. Room seven is the most haunted.

In Victoria Road, fairies were seen dancing around a tree stump. Apparently, the spectator took a photograph as proof.

To the north of the town was Severalls Hospital, later a mental asylum. Here the grounds were haunted by featureless, spectral gardeners. They seem to favour rainy days. The site has now been redeveloped.

At the south of Colchester lies Charlotte's Well at Berechurch Hall. The apparition of a beautiful woman has been seen in the vicinity of the well.

A number of homes in Defoe Crescent have been haunted by phenomena such as dark, faceless shadows, and the sound of children playing.

Another featureless ghost of a man wanders in Greenstead Woods to the east.

Maldon Road lies to the southwest. Here a family were compelled to leave their home after four years of poltergeist activity, and supernatural disturbances, such as ghostly running footsteps, strange reflections in windows and mirrors and a door clamped shut by a shadowy image. One night, all electrical appliances were unplugged. Iron Age and Roman settlements flank either side of the road, plus church ruins near the zoo.

Mersea Road runs from Colchester to Mersea Island. The Mermaid public house is now a private residence. It stands next to the Odd One Out. A man was shot in the back garden of the pub, and he now haunts the top of the stairs in the house.

A driver glancing in her rear view mirror saw a teenage boy in the back seat of her car. Astonished, she turned to see who it was, but the seat was empty. On looking in the mirror again, the spook was still there.

Edith Wright was murdered by her stepson, Kevin Wright. She was savagely beaten, stabbed, then drowned in the bath, at Lilac Court on the Greenstead Estate. He then pushed her body under the bed. She was found two days later.

Her other son Geoffrey was in Saint Bartholomew's Hospital at the time of the murder. One night he was found under a bed in the ward, and his face was inexplicably badly bruised and tender. Geoffrey was informed the next day of his mother's demise.

After leaving hospital he read the post mortem report on his mother, and was stunned to read that not only was his mother's body found under a bed, but also that she had extensive bruising down the right side of her face.

The Stanway area is haunted by a man wearing a raincoat, who walks at a swift pace, with his hands in his pockets, as if he wants to get out of the rain. He is seen in Turkey Cock Lane emerging from a hedge and gradually dissolves as he nears the old London Road.

Map of Colchester

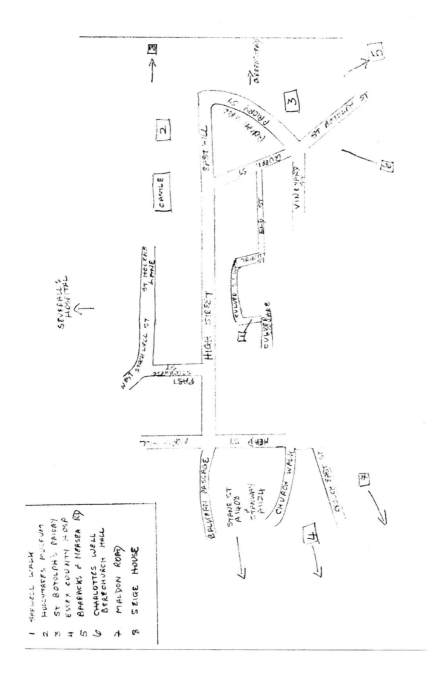

Tour Twenty-Nine
From Harlow to Gilston and Nazeing

OS Map 167 and Exp 174

The remains of Latton Priory, now part of Latton Priory Farm, in Harlow, are haunted by a monk who jumped from the top of the church, according to hearsay. (OS Map 167 Ref 4606 and Exp 174 Ref 4606.)

The doors of the barn were once part of the Priory Church. These are said to open every night at midnight. Also, each night a man on a white horse rides around the moat, according to tradition.

Many sources say The Green Man public house at Mulberry Green, Old Harlow, is reputedly haunted by a bereaved mother searching for her child who died mysteriously in a fire.

Just outside Harlow to the northwest lies Gilston.

The Plume of Feathers sits at Pye Corner where three roads meet. Here, there used to be a gallows. Many executions took place on this spot, but if the weather was inclement, the hanging would be carried out in an upstairs room at the pub. An electrician was working in the attic room when he suddenly downed tools and fled, the atmosphere was so spooky.

Glasses have been lined up on the floor behind the bar, and the fruit machine found in the middle of the bar. It is too heavy to lift.

A seat at the fireplace has a strange feeling to some who sit in it. Legend has it that a stagecoach pulled in to the inn one raw winter's night, with a frozen passenger in the back. They sat him by the fire to warm up but he was already dead.

If you drive up Gilston Lane to the left of the Plume of Feathers, you enter a peaceful world, a far cry from the 'new town' of Harlow, a stone's throw away. The road flanked by farmland, narrows as you reach St Mary's church. There are a few red-bricked Victorian cottages adjacent. I knew someone who lived in one of these, and she told me that one day she saw some phantom farmers wandering around the silos near her home. The strange thing was, their faces were black when they should have been flesh coloured/white, and their clothing was white when it should have been dark – a bit like a photograph negative.

Jane Wenham lived at Gilston after her trial for witchcraft. (See Walkern tour eleven.)

To the southwest of Harlow you will find Nazeing.

At Nazeingbury House, believed to be the home of Katherine Parr, sixth wife of Henry 8th, in a room at the top of the house, there is a cupboard which exudes a strong smell of musk, and a ghostly lady occupies the place. Katherine Parr?

Although there is no evidence to substantiate that Queen Katherine lived at Nazeingbury, her mother Maud Parr had a connection with Nazeing Common. Nazeingbury Mansion is near the crossroads in Lower Nazeing.

Tour Thirty
From Epping Forest to Theydon Mount, Theydon Garnon, North Weald Bassett

OS Map 167 OS Exp 174
Cyclical and Notable Dates Theydon Mount – 31st May

At one time Epping Forest stretched from Bow, East London to nearly Cambridge and to the fringes of Colchester. Although it is now only a fraction of the size, the beautiful woodland is an oasis of flora and fauna, surrounded by the built up areas of Loughton, Waltham Abbey, Chigwell and Epping.

As in days gone by, it may not be a place to linger after dark. The Forest was home to gypsies who made their living by telling fortunes, also to witches like Old Mother Jenkins, the Goose Charmer. Farmers paid her, as soon as their goslings hatched, fearing their geese would not fatten without her goodwill.

The Forest was home to gangs of highwayman and bandits, such as the Waltham Blacks and the Gregory Gang. Dick Turpin at one time was a member of the Gregory Gang, until he teamed up with the notorious 'Captain' Tom King. Turpin and King would hide in a well-hidden cave and rob anyone passing by. There was nothing glamorous about Dick Turpin. He was squalid and cruel, with a scowling pockmarked face, a flat nose and thick lips.

In more modern times due to its close proximity to the Metropolis, the Forest was a safe place for London gangs to dispose of a body! Many a soul has been dumped or buried here.

The aforementioned cave is to be found near High Beach (OS Exp 174 Ref 4097) and Turpin's ghost has been seen riding the tracks and lanes around here on his horse Black Bess. Also, a white shadowy shape hovers near the entrance to the cave. The same, or similar misty form is seen on the tracks near High Beach. High Beach in later years was known as 'the Cockney's Paradise', as East Londoners would spend a day in the countryside here.

Gilwell Park on the edge of the Forest to the west is haunted by a grey lady. (OS Exp 174 Ref 3896.) You can take in this site on tour thirty-one if you prefer, and please see that tour for further details.

Another ghost said to haunt the Forest is that of Queen Boudicea. She haunts Amesbury Banks where she was tied up and flogged whilst her daughters were raped in front of her. (OS Exp 174 Ref 4400.) There are no reports of her spirit being witnessed at Cobbins Brook (OS Exp 174 Refs 3800 and 3901), where she poisoned herself.

Strawberry Hill ponds is probably where a servant girl drowned herself with her baby, after being dishonoured by her employer. Arms are said to emerge from the water at various ponds around here. (OS Exp 174 Ref 4196.) One particular pond was noted for a number of suicides and murders. Elliott O'Donnell, author, and authority of ghosts, allegedly spent a night by one of the pools, and witnessed a re-enactment of a murder. The victim's ghostly body was dumped in the pond.

In Monk Wood situated between Epping New Road and Goldings Hill, hooded monks are seen wandering amongst the trees.

An area of the Forest unofficially called Hangman's Hill is situated near High Beach. It is my opinion that the tiny road is near the church opposite Mott Street. An apparition of a man hanging from the boughs of a tree appears from time to time. However, others say that Hangman's Hill is situated on a junction with Avey Lane and Pynestgreen Lane. This is where, if you take your handbrake off your stationary car, it will appear to travel uphill defying the laws of gravity. This is of course an optical illusion.

From Epping Forest go through Epping Village and take a right turn towards Coopersale. Carry on to Fiddlers Hamlet. At the T-junction turn left to Theydon Mount. Just as you descend a hill there is a bend, and on the right is Hill Hall.

Sixteenth century Hill Hall stands behind wrought iron gates at the end of a long driveway. A variety of ghosts inhabit here.

A grey lady flits here and there, and when Hill Hall was a temporary hospital, she haunted the nurses quarters. The matron witnessed her on several occasions, and if she said there was a ghost, there definitely was a ghost! Who the grey-haired phantom was is an enigma.

Another spectre is that of a beautiful young woman dressed as a bride. There are two versions of this story. The first being that seven brothers courted the young lady. They fought a duel over her, and each one was killed. The second version is that the seven brothers disapproved of her fiancé and were killed in a duel one by one. Either way, there were some ineradicable bloodstains in a room known as the 'brother's room'. When the Hall was up for sale, this room was not open to view.

The sorrowful young lady, then dressed as a bride, committed suicide. People believe that if her ghost appears at midnight to a male owner of the Hall, he will meet with a violent death. According to Jessie Payne in *A Ghost Hunter's Guide to Essex*, this has happened at least twice.

There is a phantom black hound, but the canine's origins, or why the creature haunts is unknown.

The most startling apparition is a mustard-coloured coach and horses which makes its way down the drive every 31st May some time during the night. I have waited for this vision on three occasions, but, alas, did not see it.

At one time when the Hall was partly derelict, and the gates stuck open, one could wait in the grounds where a new drive intersects with the old. This anniversary is well known in the locality, and many people keep vigil between 9.00 p.m. and 2.00 a.m. in the hope of seeing something. I have done this. It was extraordinarily odd, peculiar and slightly crazy, to see, and be part of, a number of people, standing or sitting on the grass at either side of the drive, unknown to one another, silently waiting in the blackness, for a glimpse of a ghost – for hours.

Hill Hall has been used for a number of purposes over the years. In the war the premise was an agricultural camp, and a hospital. It then became an open prison for women in the 1960s. Christine Keeler, the woman who 'brought down the Tory Government' in 1963 was an inmate. It caught fire in 1969, and parts were in ruins for some time. Now it has been refurbished and divided into exclusive private dwellings. English Heritage has saved many of the beautiful sixteenth century wall paintings of mythical and biblical topics. It is open to the public for private tours arranged by English Heritage. (OS Map 167 Ref 4899.)

The stepmother of my work colleague saw the coach when travelling by car past the Hall, late one night. It floated through the gates, across the road into a field opposite, then vanished. It was only when it had disappeared that she realised it had floated, with wheels not visible, and that she must have seen an apparition.

Next – carry on along this lane, and you will come to a T-junction, turn right, then take the next right turn to Theydon Garnon.

Here, the church was the subject of a television programme in the past on hauntings and hearsay, I am told. This stark church in a remote setting does have a strange feeling about it. As to why a television programme was made I have not been able to ascertain.

Retrace your journey, and east of Epping is North Weald Bassett airfield, which has three ghosts.

The first is a woman who was killed when a bomb hit during the war. The WAAF member's footsteps are heard.

The second is a badly wounded airman who tries to make a telephone call.

The next is the spirit of a man who was blown into a tree during an explosion.

Tour Thirty-One
From Loughton to Waltham Abbey and Sewardstone

OS Maps 166 and 167 OS Exp 174

On Trap's Hill, Loughton (OS 167 Ref 4296), you may see Dick Turpin's ghost dragging a screaming woman behind his galloping horse. She leapt on him after he had stolen her jewels. This re-enactment happens three times a year.

The ubiquitous highwayman also haunts sixteenth century Alderton Hall at Loughton. This is where he tortured a woman by 'roasting' her in the fireplace (now bricked up) in order that she told him where her money could be found. The ghosts of Turpin and the woman haunt.

In addition, the phantom of a fair-haired man in a red cloak appears. He is quite clear and solid but then suddenly disappears. The house is also inhabited by the shade of a servant girl who was seduced by her employer. She killed herself in a nearby pond with her baby, and not long after, the squire's young son drowned also. (See Epping Forest tour thirty.) Disembodied running footsteps, and a piano being played are heard. One day a resident awoke to find a face peering intently at her, and take hold of her hand. It was a young girl who promptly evaporated. Occupants hear their name being called which cannot be accounted for. A private house in Oakwood Hill has a spiteful spirit who hurts living inhabitants by pushing them down the stairs. The phantom old man has been seen at the foot of the steps. Strange sounds and smells abound. (OS Map 167 Ref 4295.)

The top half of a ghostly soldier perambulates a small wooded path near Loughton Hall. At the Hall, the ghost of Mary, a servant, looks down at visitors from the first floor landing. She locks rooms from inside. Apparently, she froze to death. How or why is unclear.

She shares the Hall with two other ghosts, a man in black, and another attired in tweed.

Beech House at Loughton is frequented by Sir Francis, a cavalier, who fell in love with Lady Elizabeth. Her father disagreed with Sir Francis' political leanings and handed him over to Cromwell's men. Sir Francis looks wanly out of a first floor window whilst Elizabeth and her father roam around other rooms.

Approximately Five Miles East Is Waltham Abbey

The Abbey ruins are reputed to be haunted. People feel their coats being tugged by an invisible presence.

A ghostly monk loiters in the old stone archway.

Celestial music accompanied by a black shape is observed late at night with the unmistakable smell of incense. The entity dissolves as it walks past spectators.

According to legend, a local damsel committed suicide in the River Lea adjacent to the ruins, after being spurned by her lover. Her wraith haunts the abbey ruins. She beckons to people and then fades away. Whether this is the same ghost with a different story, I do not know, but a young woman is said to have drowned herself as she could not endure the attentions of a clergyman. Now she haunts the area which has a feeling of dread about it.

It is said that at the time of the Dissolution of the Monasteries, some monks were murdered here, and their bodies buried in a mass grave. The presence of these monks is felt by some, and plain chant is heard in the deserted ruins.

The ancient church of the Holy Cross, twelfth century, is to be found close to the ruins. A strange light has been seen from within the church at night when the services are over and the building locked. A long dead choir is audible. The luminous glow is more like a weird radiance. Those who witness this are overcome with a disturbing and utter sense of evil and terror.

If you walk to the right-hand side of the church you will come to the market square. I once had a strange experience here. It was market day and customers and vendors were busy in this bustling area. I suddenly felt that I had walked into another time. Everything seemed slightly hazy, people were dressed in old-fashioned clothing, nobody took any notice of me, and all was silent. It was like watching a video without the sound. I was by myself and so there was no one to substantiate this, and it only lasted a minute or so. I could not put an era on the clothing, but the women wore long dresses, of mainly duns and browns, as were the men's attire.

Just off the market square is the Green Dragon public house in Sun Street. This building is over four-hundred and fifty years old, and it is haunted by a cavalier. His apparition is preceded by shuffling footsteps and he seems to prefer lunch times to rendezvous.

To the South of Waltham Abbey Is Sewardstone

This is where Dick Turpin lived with his wife, Hester

The White House at Gilwell Park is known to be haunted. The nature of the manifestation is that a phantom man walks along a corridor and opens a bedroom door. The park is haunted by the shade of a grey lady. (OS Map 166 Ref 3896.) See Tour 30.

Note of Interest

Alfred Lord Tennyson wrote part of 'In Memoriam' at Sewardstone. The 'wild bells' are believed to be the bells of Waltham Abbey.

The poet John Clare was a patient at a lunatic asylum at Lippetts Hill. (OS Map 166 Ref 3997.)

Tour Thirty-Two

From Chipping Ongar to Greensted, Stanford Rivers, Fyfield, Bobbingworth, Moreton, High Laver, Magdalen Laver and Matching

OS Map 167 OS Exp 183
Cyclical and notable dates High Laver 24th December
Housham Hall 21st June

Chipping Ongar lies between Chelmsford and Harlow.

The King's Head is the oldest pub in Ongar, and is haunted by a presence that emits a green light.

Journey southerly and just on the edge of the village, turn right to Greensted (Juxta Ongar).

The enchanting ancient church of St Andrews is situated up a small track on the right. (OS Map 167. Ref 5303.) The church is Saxon in origin, and probably stands on a pagan site. People from all around the world come to visit this log church. A service is held every Sunday. Parishioners have been worshipping here for over thirteen-hundred years.

There is a crumbling wooden cross near the church gate. This is the grave of a cattle drover who bled to death after cutting his leg with a scythe. His ghost is said to stumble down the road to the Two Brewers Inn.

Other phantoms seen inside the church are a man dressed in black who stands by the organ, a milkmaid by the pulpit and two further ghostly shapes. A woman wearing dark clothing carrying a bible is said to haunt the path outside.

Fields adjacent to the church mark the site of ancient Roman fishponds. A Roman legion marches across the fields here. They are witnessed only from the knees up.

Drapers Corner (OS Exp 183 Ref 5302) which lies between Greensted Church and Drill House Inn at a T-junction is so named because a well-known sheep thief was hanged from an oak tree at this spot. His ghost hovers here. Two boys returning home from school saw a dead body swinging from the tree. The police attended the scene but the body had gone. One of the boys was so scared by this that he was struck dumb for twenty-four hours.

At Widows Farm, a lady in Victorian clothes prowls around the garden, usually in the afternoons. She looks quite life-like, and those observing her, thinking her to be a living person, are amused by her attire.

Take the lane south of Drapers Corner to Newhouse Farm where three ghosts are domiciled. One is an old lady who wakes up those sound asleep. Another is a farm labourer sporting a smock and hessian leggings and the third is an entity in the attic that produces strange hieroglyphics on the walls.

At Burrows Farm, a cupboard mysteriously opens. The arch-shaped cabinet is thought to have in the past, been a shrine connected with religious persecution. It is locked at night and the key put in another locker for safekeeping, but in the morning the door is open.

A poltergeist inhabits a back bedroom at Coleman's Farm. Footsteps are heard running through the bedrooms and half way down the stairs where they cease.

The lane from Coleman's Farm to Brook Cottages is still guarded by a spectral gamekeeper who was killed by his own gun, accidentally. His footsteps are still heard, in the cottage, on the lane, bridleway and footpath across the fields.

To the South Is Stanford Rivers Church

It is here that a headless monk paces around.

There was a past ritual to bury babies under the altar if they had been christened within the last month. Babies in swaddling clothes have been found at both Stanford Rivers and at Greensted.

Ongar Union Workhouse was at Stanford Rivers, and is now haunted by someone crying.

To the Northeast of Chipping Ongar Is Bobbingworth

Here the Poor House is haunted by three sobbing children. A soldier (in maybe Napoleonic uniform) stands under a tree.

A skeleton was found in a gravel pit nearby.

The White Hart Inn at nearby Moreton (just north) is haunted by a woman in a long dress. She is thought to have had a fatal accident in the building.

To the East Is Fyfield

Clatterford Hall is haunted by a little old lady carrying a basket.

To the Northwest Lies the Hamlet of High Laver

Here at Otes Pond, a house once stood owned by Abigail Masham, a lady in waiting to Queen Anne. On Christmas Eve a phantom carriage drives through the village, and stops where the house used to be. A sadly countenanced lady peers from the inside and then the apparition dissolves. Many people have kept vigil over the years but have seen nothing. That does not mean much! Remember, the length of time means nothing to a ghost. She may appear yet.

West of Here Is Magdalen Laver

A seven-hundred-year-old building, Wynters Armoury is haunted by a cavalier. It is believed he was murdered. He manifests by a cacophonous sound.

To the North Is Housham Hall

Another lady in a coach! According to hearsay, the ghost of a lady from the Hall travels in a coach to Matching Tye every midsummer day at dawn. (OS 167 Ref 5011.)

The Matching area falls into three parts. Matching Green, Matching Tye and Matching. 'Tye' means a crossroads, and 'green' is a clearing in the forest. Matching

Tye has some wonderful, old houses circling a small, grassed area. Augustus John, the artist, lived at Elm House next to the Chequers at Matching Green.

My favourite of the 'three Matching areas' is the church green at Matching. Reached by way of a class C lane, round a sharp bend which skirts the deep Matching lake, and on to a wide expanse of green, where sleepily sit a church, and ancient marriage feast room (circa 1480), and Matching Hall. This quiet secluded, charming backwater, off the beaten track, has not changed much since Saxon times. Every other year in September, a fete is held at this spot, with an art exhibition in the Feast Room.

However, I visited the church green, one sunny, midweek morning in order to take some photographs for some artwork. There was not a soul around. The silence was uncanny. I felt very wary, and had the definite sensation that I was being watched, by something or someone whom I could not see.

It is rumoured that the church at Matching is haunted. The ghost is affectionately known as 'Old George'. The door of the bell tower swings open through no human agency and the temperature drops to iciness. I know one of the bell ringers, and he told me that although the ghost is friendly, he always feels the hairs on the back of his neck 'stand up' when 'Old George' is around.

Tour Thirty-Three
Brentwood

OS Maps 167, OS Exp 175

On the A128, Ongar to Brentwood Road, you will find Langford Bridge. (OS 167 Ref 5501.) This was a tollbooth across the River Roding. Spasmodically, the sound of ghostly galloping horses can be heard.

The Fountain Head in Ingrave Road suffers with poltergeist activity.

At nearby Hutton, a district of Brentwood, in Hanging Hill Lane, a phantom woman wanders. In the eighteenth century mansion Hutton Hall, a ghostly grey lady dwells (Exp 175 Ref 6394).

A black Labrador dog haunts The Thatchers Arms at Great Warley, a mile or so to the southwest of Brentwood.

At the New World Inn, Great Warley, very few guests spend a second night in Room 14. There is a ticking noise for which no natural cause can be found, and a previous owner still inhabits the room. A phantom noisy party is sometimes heard, along with a spectre looking for something in a hurry.

Nearby is Warley Lea Farm. Here, a bailiff hanged himself and it is said his footsteps are heard on the stairs. There are other inexplicable noises.

A hooded monk floats above ground level at a Supermarket, Chapel High. If you touch him, he vanishes!

Brentwood town centre has a number of haunted pubs.

Number 133 High Street is the site of the old Seven Stars Inn. Here, some unpleasant poltergeist activity took place, which resulted in very aggressive behaviour from animals. There are hot and cold spots, and sometimes supernatural laughter manifests.

The Golden Fleece on the London Road is where poltergeist activity has taken place. A phantom monk has been seen reflected in a mirror, and disappears when the witness turns around. On looking in the mirror again, he is still there.

The White Hart at 93 High Street has a paranormal practical joker. The unseen entity taps people on the shoulder. Bar staff have reported walking into an indiscernible barrier or miasma.

The Swan Hotel in the High Street has 'classic paranormal symptoms. There may be one ghost or several. William Hunter is considered to be an unquiet spirit here. He spent his last few hours on earth at the Swan before being burnt at the stake for religious beliefs in 1555. Plates depicting theological scenes uncannily fall from the walls.

However, there is a plethora of other activity: furniture and chairs hauled around, knocking on doors by unseen fists, electrical equipment and lights turned on and off, the usual poltergeist activity like items going missing and turning up in strange places, and cold spots. Police found the building unlocked when it had definitely been secured at closing time. A beat constable had earlier checked the door and found it to be secure. No explanation could be found. On another occasion, the police arrived in the early hours of the morning to say that they had been informed by the telephone exchange that a call had been made but the receiver not replaced. On unlocking the bar, the telephone receiver was found to be lying on the floor, and no one had made a call.

Dogs are nervous, and howl.

Guy Lyon Playfair (*Haunted Pub Guide*) believes that poltergeists can follow people around from one home to another. He says he has evidence to suggest that the poltergeist syndrome can be contagious like diseases. This is an interesting theory. I think he may have a point. Many years ago I had a friend who was experiencing poltergeist activity in an old house. She moved to a modern dwelling but the phenomena continued.

Tour Thirty-Four

From Ingrave (Heronsgate) to Cranham, Horndon on the Hill, Orsett and East Tilbury

OS Map 177 OS Exp 175
Cyclical and Notable Dates Cranham – around Christmas time

Ingrave can be found on the A128 southeast of Brentwood, and Heronsgate is just beyond.

The Boar's Head near the green is possibly haunted by 'Spider Marshall' (see The Bear Inn at Stock tour thirty-five).

Carry on, on the A128 over the A12 interchange. Take the first turn on the right to Cranham via West Horndon.

St Mary's Lane is just outside Cranham (now Greater London). Here, a ghostly monk glides up the lane. He is only seen from the waist up. The cowled figure is usually seen around Christmas time.

Franks Wood near Moor Lane, now known as 'brickfields' is haunted by a very tall black shadowy shape that chases people in the wood.

Retrace your steps back to the A128 and travel south towards Orsett. On the left just before Orsett, take the turning to Horndon on the Hill.

A man rides a horse at breakneck speed down the Orsett Road and into Black Bush Lane causing accidents. (OS Exp 175 Ref 6583.)

At a road junction at Rookery Corner, a woman rises from a pond riding a donkey. They then cross the road and enter a wooded area. Many cyclists have had to swerve to avoid them, and have been injured.

Note of Interest

It is rumoured that Anne Boleyn was buried under a black marble slab either at Horndon on the Hill or beneath a similar slab at Salle. The slab at Salle (not far from her ancestral home of Blickling Hall) was lifted but no bones were found. However, she is supposed to haunt the church tower at Salle. She was executed at Tower Green, London, and many historians believe that her body was dumped in an old arrow box in the tower precincts.

Travel West over the A128 to Orsett

A phantom female in grey cloak frequents Blacksmiths Lane. It is said that a couple were murdered a long time ago by a highwayman, and now the girl haunts the area.

Travel South Towards Tilbury

Coal House Fort can be found on the banks of the River Thames at East Tilbury. Take the lanes to the east at Chadwell St Mary just north of Tilbury. (OS 177 Ref 6976.)

The building is notorious for spooks, and is popular with investigative teams.

The Fort is a Victorian coastal defence and is one of two forts. The other fort is maintained by the local authorities, as a tourist attraction, but Coal House has been neglected. It was originally built to defend London from a possible French invasion, but it was also used in both World Wars as a military establishment. The upkeep of this large building is maintained by a group of volunteers.

The volunteers have experienced some strange events, such as a re-enactment of a poker game in a room that now has no floor! Other phenomena are batteries draining immediately on entering certain areas, footsteps, heavy dragging sounds, mists, smells of garlic, a sweet citrus odour, and orbs seen in dark, dank, gloomy tunnels.

Ghosts witnessed are Beth who chuckles, and a man with burn scars on his face due to a weapon back firing. An entity nicknamed 'the clown' seems to take on different manifestations and 'moods' all in the intention of frightening people to keep away. Queen Elizabeth 1st is said to walk the corridors here.

At nearby Worlds End Fen, the mist hangs around the adjacent fields of a busy road. Here, three monks creep across the road, probably looking for the monastery that is believed to have stood in this vicinity.

The Worlds End Inn houses the ghost of an old highwayman, Swift Nick. He likes to restart fires which have been extinguished for hours.

Note of Interest

Queen Elizabeth 1st made her famous speech to the troops somewhere near Mill House Camp and Turnpike Cottages.

Tour Thirty-Five
From Ingatestone to Stock, Fryerning and Stondon Massey

OS Map 167, 177

The four-hundred-year-old Star Inn at Ingatestone has a menacing spirit that haunts an upstairs room. The atmosphere is forbidding, lights turn on and off and the door constantly opens and closes.

The building and outside are haunted by Toby, 'the devil dog of Ingatestone'. The black bulldog once lived at The Star and terrorised the cats and dogs of the district. The spirit of the dead dog haunts the pub and still tries to block people and animals walking up the lane. Due to taxidermy, Toby's lifelike head is kept on the wall in the bar.

Pierro's formerly Little Hammonds restaurant is reputedly haunted, mainly upstairs. The ladies' toilets have a creepy ambience.

At The Star Inn, two sisters left the pub after paying for a room, because the lights kept turning on and off, and their bedroom door constantly opened and closed of its own accord. There were no draughts. Also in the vicinity of The Star, a spectral small black dog bars your way.

Ingatestone railway station is the scene of disembodied footsteps. The footsteps ascend the stairs, cross the footbridge and descend the other side, then carry on along the platform.

The railway line between Shenfield and Ingatestone is haunted by a hand which bashes the seats on trains. The hand strikes the backs of the seats and appears brown in colour.

Beautiful Ingatestone Hall built by Sir William Petre in 1548 is haunted by Lady Katherine Grey, sister of Lady Jane Grey, the Nine Days' Queen. She is said to waft around the Lime Walk.

Sir William is believed to haunt the turret in the corner of the inner court, which gives access to the upper rooms.

There are two slightly different versions to this next anecdote involving the Lime Walk.

The first is that Bishop Benjamin Petre was saved from robbers in 1733 by his mongrel dog. The faithful canine now walks the path.

The second is that Bishop Petre's assailants were warned off by a large black dog which suddenly appeared. When the robbers had gone, the hound vanished.

From Ingatestone, take the lane to the east via Buttsbury. When you reach White Tyrrells you may espy a ghostly cavalier.

The Bear Inn at Stock is haunted by quite a character, Charlie 'Spider' Marshall. He was apparently very small, lacking in personal hygiene, wore grubby white riding breeches, a faded pink hunting coat, and a black, battered and stained velvet hunting cap. He was the Inn's ostler, and walked in a strange sideways, crablike manner. He was a show off and liked to shin up the inside of the chimney in one bar, cross the recess between the bars where bacon was placed for curing, and climb down the chimney in the other bar. Sometimes Spider would stay up in the bacon loft drinking his ale, and refuse to come down. He would be forced out of his hiding place by the pub's patrons lighting a straw fire and smoking him out.

One Christmas Eve he went up the chimney and never came down. His 'kippered' body is believed by some to still be there. Legend states that locals tried to hoodwink the clergy that they had retrieved Spider's body, but really the coffin was weighted with stones or some other matter. For some reason the parish minister disbelieved them, and so Spider Marshall was buried in haste in nearby waste ground, before any further questions could be asked.

His ghost ducks and darts about, and creeps around in the middle of the night. His footsteps can be heard on the creaking floorboards as he opens and closes doors, particularly when there is a new landlord.

The best atmospheric, and yet very funny, description of the pub and Spider Marshall is by James Wentworth Day in his book *Essex Ghosts*.

Broomwood Lane is haunted by an entity that breathes very heavily near one's face, but nothing is seen.

To the West of Ingatestone Is Fryerning Village

There are a few ponds which sit astride the main street in the village and one is haunted by a drowning man, and a witch who was swum here. Both died here at different times, and now haunt the area of the ponds.

Take the Lanes West to Stondon Massey

An image of a young woman in Edwardian dress, appears at the back gate of the Rectory, walks along Canons Walk, and into Courtfield Wood (OS Exp 183 Ref 5800 and Exp 183 Ref 5700). She may be the same ghost that haunts a bungalow near here.

Richard Jordan of Stondon Place is said to hover around the churchyard at night. After Jordan's burial, his corpse was found lying outside his coffin. After that his remains were chained down. However, this was normal practice in the nineteenth century to deter resurrection men, or body snatchers. The Jordan ghost is said to also haunt the Stondon Place area especially where the old gates stood, and has been seen floating by the Rectory.

My husband Jack, Steve and Lisa Hockley, and I, once kept watch outside the church one night in the hope of seeing at least one of the ghosts. All we saw was bats and moths!

Tour Thirty-Six
From Great Cornard to Bures, Alphamstone, Wormingford, Boxted, Earls Colne

OS Maps 155 and 168 OS Exp 195 and 196
Cyclical Date and Notable Dates: Boxted – 21st October

Great Cornard can be found to the southeast of Sudbury, on the Essex/Suffolk border. Here at Abbas Hall, a grey lady wanders. Many houses in Suffolk and this area of Essex are rendered in 'Suffolk Pink'. The Hall is built in the darker hue of this colour. Also, it is said that courting couples who parked in the vicinity of the Hall were troubled by the ghosts of monks, who had taken exception, to the canoodling. The unforgiving monks struck and shook the cars, much to the consternation of the lovers.

Bures can be found to the south of Great Cornard on the B1508.

The road that runs from Lamarsh to Bures has been haunted by a phosphorescent horseman who terrifies travellers between nightfall and daybreak.

A headless woman who carries her head crooked in her arm appears on the bridge at Craigs Brook at Mount Bures at midnight (OS Exp 196 Ref 9032).

Alphamstone to the northwest of Bures is where a spectral black dog haunts – especially at Sycamore Farm.

Travel South on to the B1508 to Wormingford

A phantom lady rides a white horse at Sandy Hill between Wormingford and Bures. (OS Exp 196 Ref 9232.)

Note of Interest

When building works were being carried out at the Crown Inn, Wormingford, two mummified cats, on either side of a chimney were found. They would have been put there for protection against the evil eye/witchcraft. The cats therefore date the inn to circa 1600, the period when Elizabeth Newman, the witch of Wormingford was tried for witchcraft.

Go via the lanes in an easterly direction to Boxted. There are two hamlets named Boxted in the same vicinity. The one you want is to the south of the two. Here you will find Betty Potter's Dip. Betty Potter was a witch who lived in a cottage at the side of the straight road, going south towards Colchester. She was supposed to cure people, and also she was accused of casting a spell on a wagonload of wheat travelling from Rivers Hall. (OS Exp196 Ref 0032 to 0030, and OS Exp 184 Ref 9929.) Matthew Hopkins wanted her to stand trial, but the squire's son and some ruffians seized her beforehand and hanged her from a nearby tree. Another version of the story is that she committed suicide.

She now haunts the tree and the little dip in the road, now known as Betty Potter's Dip. You may meet her at midnight on 21ˢᵗ October.

Retrace your steps back to Wormingford and to the southwest reached by the lanes, you will find Earls Colne.

A ghostly monk appears in the bar of the ancient Castle Inn. He probably hails from Earl's Colne Priory.

The remains of the Benedictine Priory are haunted by a non-existent bell that strikes at 2.00 a.m. although there have been no reported supernatural occurrences here for some time. (OS Exp 195 Ref 8528.)

Tour Thirty-Seven
From Billericay to Little Burstead

OS Map 177

Two ghosts haunt the former Cheyne Library, 118 High Street, which is now part of Waitrose Supermarket. The first is a little girl who ascends the stairs, and the second is a man who hanged himself after being robbed of his life savings.

Sixteenth-century St Aubyns House 3–5 Chapel Street is haunted by the sound of dragging footsteps, as if someone is lame or injured. At another time the sound was like someone walking and dragging something behind them, and doors opening and closing. A black, shadowy figure clings to the walls of the kitchen.

The Georgian building in the High Street, Burghstead Lodge, is now a Registry Office and Citizen's Advice Bureau, but at one time was a private residence. A nurse was employed to look after a young man who was critically ill. Three nights running a woman dressed in green silk whose face was covered by a black veil, appeared in the room. The young man became very agitated. On the third night the nurse lifted the veil of the ghostly visitor. She fainted, as under the veiled bonnet was a skull, and a demonic laugh echoed around the room. The young man died that night, and the nurse became mentally ill, and died three months later.

Apparently the room, which has a southwesterly aspect on the first floor, has a brooding air about it, but the green lady has not reappeared.

Once again, Dick Turpin turns up. Here he is said to haunt the stretch of road between the Mayflower Hospital and Hill House Drive. He appears as usual on horseback on this part of Stock Road.

To the southwest of Billericay, you will come to Little Burstead.

There have been reports of phantom footsteps, and a piano being played, when no pianist is present, at what was Hope House, Tower House School. Hope House has now been split into four properties.

Tour Thirty-Eight
From Great Dunmow to Great Easton, Tilty and Broxted

OS Map 167

One would expect the ancient town of Great Dunmow to have ghosts but I have been unable to find much phenomena.

According to a local newspaper, a seventeenth century house in Dunmow High Street was haunted by a playful spirit. When new owners moved in, they swept the floor before the carpet was laid, and the broom was propped against the wall. After the carpet fitters had finished, the lady could not find the broom. On exclaiming out loud, "Where's that broom?" she was flabbergasted to see it hurtling towards her.

Other strange incidents have occurred, lights have been found on when the owner absent, and disembodied footsteps heard.

It is rumoured that nearby Clock House is haunted, and has tunnels leading to the church.

Take the B184 towards Great Easton. Follow signs for the Gardens of Easton Lodge at Little Easton.

Great Easton Lodge was haunted by the Countess of Warwick. Her shade descended the stairs and frightened soldiers billeted there during the Second World War. One wonders if her ghost meanders around the gardens of Great Easton Lodge, which is open to the public.

Follow lanes northerly to Tilty.

A crumbling wall, believed to be part of the cloisters, in a tranquil field, is all that remains of the once imposing Tilty Abbey. The only building to have survived this ancient site is the church of St Mary the Virgin. It was in the twelfth century when Tilty was handed over to the Cistercian order of monks for an abbey.

A ghostly headless monk is sometimes seen wandering down Cherry (or Chawneth) Lane. In 1942 graves on the site were excavated. On lifting the lid of a thirteenth century stone coffin, a skeleton was found, intact, except the skull was missing. There was no indication that the grave had been interfered with in the past.

King John's men ransacked the abbey in 1215. The monks fought back, and maybe that is how the poor man came to be decapitated. Cherry Lane does have a strangeness about it.

In the past, several parts of the abbey remained and were used as farm buildings. The superstition was that if anyone demolished these buildings they would die within a month. A steward ordered the buildings to be destroyed, and sure enough he died within a month. His replacement ordered the demolition of the buildings, and he died within a month.

There are rumours that there are underground tunnels from the Abbey to Horham Hall. The Hall is open to the public. Check with the internet for details. OS Map 167 Ref 5829. See Tour thirty-nine.

Take the B1051 to the hamlet of Broxted.

Do you believe in fairies? No?

Here, it is said that mischievous elves, gnomes and fairies tamper with farm machinery. Apparently, the little people have been seen by sensible, hardworking, local farmers and residents. The fairy folk usually appear at dusk, dancing in a fairy ring, or sitting under toadstools. One couple came across a wry-faced goblin on entering a remote farmhouse. All sorts of strange things happen around Broxted which are put down to the little folk. Well, you never know...

Tour Thirty-Nine
From Thaxted to Wimbish, Hempstead and Hadstock

OS Maps 154 and 167 OS Exp 195 and 209
Cyclical and notable dates Hadstock – November

Our next tour starts at Thaxted and it is worth spending some time in this quaint historic town.

Nearby, Horham Hall is visited by Queen Elizabeth 1st. The click, click of her high-heeled shoes resound along the corridors here, although there have been no recent reports of this manifestation. (OS 167 Ref 5829.)

Cobblers Cottage and the almshouses next to the churchyard are reputedly haunted – or were in the past. Corpse lights have been seen in the churchyard and nearby fields leading up to the windmill.

Property that once belonged to the composer Gustav Holst is haunted by the sound of a phantom wearing carpet slippers, who trudges down the cellar stairs. These footsteps are said to belong to the miser who previously lived in the house, on his way to check his hidden stash of money down there. Look for the blue plaque to find the house.

The Gibbets crossroads is where a white horse carrying a headless rider has been seen.

Take the B 184 north out of Thaxted towards Saffron Walden.

At Carver Barracks, Wimbish (Exp 195 Ref 5634 or OS 154 Ref 5634) there is a building on the airfield which is haunted. Doors open and close by themselves.

Dick Turpin's spirit haunts Tiptofts Farm between Wimbish and Sewards End, where he is said to leap over the moat astride his horse, Black Bess.

To continue with the omnipresent Dick Turpin take the B1053 to Hempstead. The Bluebell Inn was where the highwayman was born, and his presence is sometimes felt here.

Continue to the northwest via the lanes through Ashdon up to Bartlow, turn left to Hadstock.

The Anglo Saxon parish church of St Botolph is said to stand on the point of where sixteen ley lines converge. Here, an old man haunts. Why he chooses to hang around, or who he was, is not known.

Note of Interest

The north door dates back to 1020, and it is the oldest church door in the country. Centuries ago a Dane tried to steal the church plate. He was whipped to death, and his skin nailed to the door as a warning. When the door was being repaired, a piece of skin was found under a hinge. Tests showed that it belonged to a blond man turning grey. This can now be seen at Saffron Walden Museum.

Part of the road between Hadstock and Saffron Walden, B1052, once formed part of the runway of an airfield. At this point in the road, one November evening a young female driver experienced a flash of light and the sound of a siren. Expecting the emergency services to appear at any moment, she glanced into her rear view mirror. She was shocked to see an American Air Force pilot in uniform sitting on the back seat. She stopped the car but on looking in the mirror again, the man had gone.

The young woman convinced herself that she had imagined the whole thing. However, a few days later, when cleaning her car, she came across a button on the back seat – a button belonging to an American Flying jacket!

Also on this stretch of road, an airman hitches a lift. If you slow down to look at him, you will see that he is headless.

In addition, if you see a fiery ball heading for the old control tower, you are watching a re-enactment of an airman shot down in flames here during the war.

At night, drivers on the B1052 have reported sightings of a huge spectral dog, known in the area as the Shug Monkey. The apparition is normally considered an ill omen. Apparently, it has the body of a black shaggy dog and the face of a monkey with luminous eyes. The creature walks on its hind legs, but it is also seen bounding at speed on all fours. If you risk searching for it, you are most likely to find it on this road just north of Linton, between Balsham and West Wratting, especially on a track named Scarlett's Lane. (OS 154 Ref 5951 or Exp 209 Ref 5951.)

One dark evening in winter, my friend Lisa and her mother were travelling between Little Walden and Saffron Walden, when suddenly a grey lady stepped out in front of their car. Lisa's mother slammed on the brakes but the woman had vanished. There is a slight bend in the road, and a small bridge, but there is no pavement for pedestrians, and it is a fairly uninhabited spot for people to walk. (OS 154 Ref 5440.)

Tour Forty
Saffron Walden

OS Map 154 OS Exp 195
Cyclical and Notable Dates Cross Keys Hotel 24th December
Castle Ruins – 24th December
Church – 24th April
Hill House – 6th January

The historic market town of Saffron Walden is one of the most attractive in Essex, and is best explored on foot.

There are numerous ghosts at the fifteenth century Cross Keys Hotel in the High Street which was Oliver Cromwell's headquarters for a while. It was then called 'The Whalebone'.

The ghost's footsteps are heard around Christmas time but especially between 11.00–12.00 p.m. on Christmas Eve. They are so heavy they make the ceiling shake. They are believed to belong to 'Ronnie the Roundhead', and emanate from the top of the stairs, travel along a passage and stop at a blank wall.

A monk has been seen in the building, and a poltergeist moves glasses and crockery.

A cavalier with curly hair and wearing breeches floats around.

In April 2005, two plumbers booked in to share a room. One went to sleep with the television on. He awoke and saw a man, whom he told to turn off the television, but his friend did not arrive until the next morning.

Further along near the Market Square, The Rose and Crown stood on the site of the arcade. This caught fire on Christmas Eve. Gluttons, the eatery, in the arcade had a lot of electrical failures which were put down to poltergeist activity. The walls still show the rings for tethering horses, as this is the site of the old stables. Decorators tried to remove the rings and this was when the poltergeist phenomena started.

Walk through the arcade and you will come out to the common. There is an area of raised ground in the far corner to the east, known as the turf maze. This is where there is a labyrinth – a mile of bricks underground. Hooded figures have been seen here, and strange lights. The lights are believed to be fairy lights or will-o'-the-wisp. (OS Exp 195 Ref 5438.) It is said that it was designed for penitent monks, who made their way to the centre on their knees.

Just up the hill near the common, you will find the twelfth century castle ruins. Geoffrey De Mandeville appears here on Christmas Eve along with two ghostly children.

Around the corner in the museum, phantom footsteps occur occasionally.

Now enter Church Street. On the left is The Grange which is reputedly haunted, by what or by whom is not known. The property has been empty for years and years.

Lankester Antiques on the corner of Church Street (now closed) was once the Sun Inn. This fascinating shop with interconnecting rooms, jam-packed with books and antiques, is associated with one of Cromwell's men. The soldier's presence is felt in some of the rooms where the temperature drops. My husband, Jack, felt some of the areas so supernaturally stifling he had to get out. Part of the building was once a café, called Cromwells. The owners next door complained to Lankasters of noises at night, like furniture being moved around. They could not sleep, and banged on the wall. Someone hammered back, and the noises continued. No one had been working late at night, and the whole episode remains unanswered.

Turn down the little street and the building on the corner of Market Square and this lane was The Kings Arms. The premise is haunted by female footsteps and a vision of a Victorian lady who looks out of a window with a malevolent expression.

Turn back, and carry on down Church Street to St Mary the Virgin church on the right. On St Mark's Eve, 24th April, you may see a procession of ghostly people who are going to die that year. Be careful – you might see your own doppelganger, and do not fall asleep – you may never wake up. Christmas Eve and the 24th of the month are key times to see ghosts and UFOs – allegedly.

Go through the passageway to Castle Street. One of the cottages here is haunted by the smell of roast beef.

In this road you will find the entrance to Bridge End Gardens. At night, the stone summerhouse has a bad atmosphere. Gardeners do not hang around as soon as dusk falls, and cameras and recording equipment fail here. There is a white/grey lady who prowls around the gardens, and people have experienced an uneasy feeling at twilight.

Walk in a westerly direction back to the High Street. The Saffron Hotel has a painting of a First World War soldier. The painting went missing and visitors were disturbed in their sleep by the apparition of a soldier. Unaccountably, the painting reappeared and the haunting ceased.

Walk down the High Street in a northerly direction, and you will come to Myddleton Place on the left. This short street is lined on both sides by old dwellings. On its northern end, the property was built for a rich merchant, but at one time was a mill (it is now a youth hostel). Footsteps are heard of the wicked miller, a drunk, who killed his wife by pulling up the floorboards and digging a hole – his wife fell in. Diagonally opposite on Castle Street is a quaint cottage with a window shaped like a spider's web. In Myddleton Place the ancient white dwelling on the left as you enter, was haunted by a headless man. At 4.00 a.m. a girl was awoken by her door opening. Her brothers saw the ghost, jumped on the bed and wrestled with it. One of the brothers ended up in hospital, he became so deranged.

The large Georgian house opposite (on the same side as the hostel) is haunted by an old man with a child, arm in arm. Are they grandfather and granddaughter?

Back on the main road just on the boundary of Bridge Street and the High Street, a policeman was murdered in 1827.His spirit is seen crossing the road.

The Eight Bells pub in Bridge Street has five ghosts. They emerge as shadowy figures in the restaurant, and a cold white mist in a bedroom.

Hill House on the High Street is haunted by a servant girl named Nelly Ketteridge. She was nineteen years old, and after finishing her day's work she set off to walk the six miles or so to her home in Elmdon. On the way she was caught in a snowstorm and her body was not found until six weeks later in a ditch between Wenden Lofts and Wendens Ambo. Now her ghost haunts Hill House. Since 6th January 1845, to this day, one can hear the swish of her petticoats as she walks along the corridor and in the bedrooms, followed by a waft of icy cold air.

The old Station House in Station Road (you may prefer to drive up here) is said to be haunted by a dark shadowy figure that thuds around the first floor of the old building. Footsteps are heard ascending and descending the stairs. There are strange cold spots.

Map of Saffron Walden

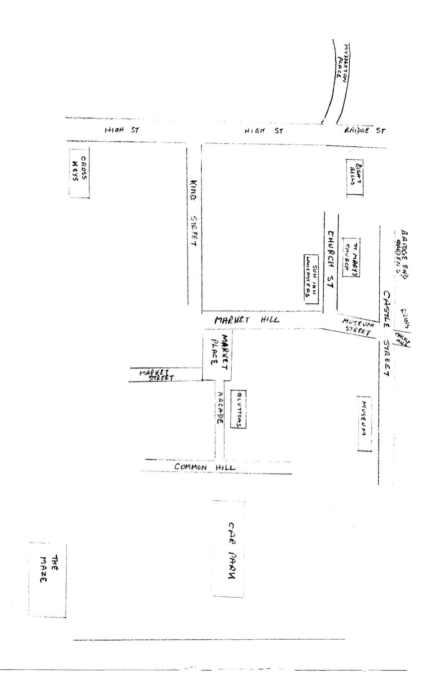

Tour Forty-One
From Audley End to Catmere End, Arkesden, Chrishall, Heydon and Hinxton

OS Maps 154 and 167 OS Exps 195 and 209

Audley End, near Saffron Walden, is a magnificent stately home owned by the late Lord Braybrooke. It is open to the public through English Heritage.

Occasionally, at night a spectral coach sets out from the Lion Gate. It traverses down Audley End Road and then turns right into Chestnut Avenue (OS Exp 195 Ref 5138 and Ref 5238). Is this the same ghostly carriage that travels down the B1383 at Newport? (See Newport on the Little Hadham tour twenty-three.)

The hamlet of Catmere End is to be found to the northwest of Audley End (OS 154 Ref 4939). There is a cottage built on the site of wooden cottages which were burned down. This cottage is almost one-hundred and fifty years old now, and is really two old cottages knocked into one. The building seems to have one 'bad end' and one 'good end'. The haunting appears to be of a strong smell of burning near the stairs, and the image of a weeping woman in a long dress and large hat. The same lady roams around the garden, and has been seen digging at a spot where foul odours emanate. Dogs avoid this part of the outside. Children's footsteps are heard, running at speed across the upstairs landing. Residents complain of being watched by something. These incidents all occur at the bad end of the house.

Visions of children staring at the house, a ghostly fire engine nearby, and infants with bulging eyes and their tongues hanging out of their mouths have been seen. Strange lights occur at night in the adjoining fields.

The Herts and Essex Observer printed a story in September 1907 concerning a family who were compelled to vacate their house due to poltergeist activity. The whereabouts of the property was merely described as 'in a village on the outskirts of Saffron Walden'. I wonder if this could be the same property in Catmere End.

To the Southwest Is Arkesden

Wood Hall viewed by footpath is haunted by an elderly lady believed to be Mrs Birch Wolfe.

To the Northwest Lies Chrishall

The old village was originally near the church which sits just outside the present village. The old village was completely destroyed by fire, which some say was started deliberately to eradicate the plague. The dead were buried in a pit marked by a yew tree, and at no time must that part of the churchyard be disturbed for interments. (See Rabley Heath tour eighteen, which mentions Horsmonden in Kent.) Misty wraiths are seen flitting around old graves. These are suspected to be ghosts of the victims who dance around the tree, as a warning to keep away from their burial place.

A Little Way to the Northwest Is Heydon

At an area known as Heydon ditch, many people have witnessed huge Saxon warrior men in battle. An archaeological dig revealed remains of Saxon soldiers who were extremely tall. (OS Exp 209 Ref 4241.)

To the north of Saffron Walden at Hinxton churchyard, a ghostly lady in a black dress with a very white face stands near a square stone vault.

Tour Forty-Two
From Finchingfield to Wethersfield and Great Bardfield

OS Maps154 and 167 OS Exp 195

The picturesque, 'chocolate box' village of Finchingfield can be found southeast of Saffron Walden on the B1053. Photographs of Finchingfield grace many an Essex calendar.

Spains Hall is haunted by the ghost of a boy aged about seven or eight, murdered by robbers in the late seventeenth century. The haunting has faded over time.

At Pump House the spectre of an old lady stares out of one of the windows.

Legend

There is a legend that at one cottage, a woman died and her body was laid out downstairs. Upstairs her relatives were sorting through her effects. They found a box containing strange little ornaments that resembled imps. Fearing witchcraft they threw these into the fire. On looking again at the corpse downstairs, they simply found a pile of ashes!

Notes of Interest

On the east side of the pond next to the bridge is the old workhouse, now a private residence.

A new resident repairing his cottage came across a curious stick implanted in the plaster of the wall. It was longer than a walking stick and had two carved snakes with anticlockwise and clockwise coils entwined. One theory is that the stick was used for beating witches. Another is that the witch stick was used in past times by white witches to ward off evil spells or the malign intentions of black witches. A fertility stick was also found embedded in the thatch. This stick is much shorter and has images of animals pertaining to spring.

Further along the B1053 is Wethersfield.

A cottage, named Old Lodge, on the Wethersfield Road from Braintree, set in a hollow on the left-hand side, overlooking fields on the B1053, is haunted by ghostly footsteps, bangs and crashes. Also, the apparitions of two policemen are witnessed. One smiles and is dressed in Victorian uniform with bushy whiskers, and the other is in modern uniform. They appear separately and both suddenly vanish.

The surrounding fields are haunted by a hooded monk, whose robes swish as he ambles along.

To the West Is Great Bardfield

Drivers and pedestrians are pursued by a grey shape in the lanes around Bardfield. Believed to be the misty shape of a man, the spirit emerges from behind trees.

Place House, Dunmow Road, a Tudor house, had a haunted bedroom. People felt the presence of an unhappy woman. There have not been reports of any phenomena since the room was exorcised. The ghost was thought to be Eleanor Bendlowes, wife of William Bendlowes, sergeant at law to Elizabeth 1st and builder of the house.

Note of Interest

In the past, many Essex villages had their own jail for miscreants. Great Bardfield has such a cage, on the B1057 just south of the long bridge (OS 167 Ref 6730).

Tour Forty-Three
From Borley to Belchamp Walter, Sible Hedingham, Ridgewell and Pentlow

OS Map 155
Cyclical and Notable Dates – Borley – all year, and 28th July
Road Junction with Liston, Foxearth and Rodbridge – 3rd December

Foxearth, Liston, Pentlow and Borley are to be found on the B1064, on the west bank of the River Stour in the county of Essex. These villages are generally thought to be of Suffolk, and the inhabitants have a tendency to consider themselves of Suffolk.

Where the road to Liston converges with the Foxearth to the Rodbridge Corner road, the B1064, one misty evening (3rd December), a spectral hooded figure suddenly ran in front of an oncoming vehicle, forcing the driver to slam on the brakes, leaving the passengers very shaken. There was no impact, and on checking for an injured person, there was no one to be seen.

So much has been written about Borley Rectory, 'the most haunted house in England', and subsequently the church and its environs. However, I will give a synopsis of the haunting of Borley for those new to the subject. It is difficult to know what to leave out, as the story is so fascinating and compelling.

Borley lies to the northwest of Sudbury, Suffolk. Take the B1064 north out of Sudbury to Rodbridge Corner. Turn left and cross the bridge over the River Stour, then turn left again, travel up the lane and Borley Church is on the right on the brow of the hill. (OS Map 155 Ref 8443.) You may need the map reference as at one time it would appear that all signposts to Borley had been removed.

Inhabitants discourage ghost hunters, by day or night, and say they are disturbed more by these visitors, than by anything supernatural. I was once given short shrift, and told to leave in no uncertain terms by a lady arranging flowers in the church, once she knew of my interest in ghosts. It was unfortunate that apparently, my enquiries followed an evening where lager louts had been running around the churchyard, and roaring around the lanes on motorbikes – supposedly phantom finding. I went to Foxearth Church later that day and the warden there agreed that peculiar things still happen at Borley.

The subject of the Borley ghosts is extraordinary and has caused much controversy. Even though the Rectory no longer stands (it was destroyed by fire in 1939), supernatural phenomena appears to have transferred to the church, which still attracts sightseers and ghost hunters. Indeed even as the house burnt, people said they could see ghosts at the windows walking amongst the flames.

A spectral nun has been reported walking in the gardens (four bungalows have been built on the site of the old Rectory grounds where the nun was seen regularly, known as 'the nun's walk') in the direction of the church. She may be seen at any time of year, but she seems to like 28th July in which to manifest.

The churchyard is said to be haunted by ghostly footsteps, and organ music can sometimes be heard coming from a locked and deserted church.

The haunting started with the incumbency of the Reverend Bull and his family. The children claimed to see the apparitions of a nun, and a ghostly coach. All sorts of strange events occurred. Also Harry Bull died in suspicious circumstances, but murder was never proven. However, the height of the phenomena was when the elderly Reverend Algernon Foyster, and his young attractive wife moved in. A malicious poltergeist scratched nasty messages on walls, and objects were thrown around. The nun still walked, and other phenomena continued.

Further haunting included a screaming girl, as she plummeted from the blue room window, a flying brick, and Harry Bull.

The phantom coach, seen by some villagers, uses the old road across fields.

Marianne Foyster had a 'colourful life', and a book on her interesting but – allegedly – dissolute life was published in 1992, *The Widow of Borley* by Robert Wood.

The aforementioned nun was supposed to have fallen in love with a monk. There is a theory that there was a convent at Bures and the Rectory is believed to have been built on the site of a monastery. The pair decided to elope but were caught. The novice was walled up alive.

Séances were held at the Rectory, and a different story came to light. The nun 'came through' and said that she was Marie Lairre, who came to Borley from Le Havre in the seventeenth century. She later married one of the Waldegraves, who lived in the house on the site of the Rectory. The Waldegrave tomb can be seen in the church. It transpired that the marriage was not happy, resulting in Waldegrave strangling her and burying her body beneath the cellar floor. Harry Price the renowned psychical researcher and author of *The Most Haunted House in England* and *The End of Borley Rectory*, led an excavation. The skeleton of a young woman was found. The remains were given a Christian burial at Liston.

Messages appeared scrawled on walls, requesting 'light', 'mass' and 'prayers'. Strange smells, bells rang, and uncanny noises continued.

Harry Price was accused of fraudulently causing missiles to fly around, and the Foysters were blamed for exaggerating the basic phenomena, the whole thing being a hoax. But supernatural phenomena still occurs at Borley. Just look at some of the more sensible blogs on the internet.

I have visited Borley on many occasions, and the area certainly has an oppressive, strange feeling, especially around the churchyard. Once when visiting the church, whilst inspecting the Waldegrave tomb, my husband, who is a levelheaded man, suddenly said that he could feel an evil presence, and he had to leave. I too felt wary.

The feeling did not fade until we had reached the bottom of the lane, almost as if the entity had joined us in the car. We both wondered if this was a case of autosuggestion, as we had recently seen a scary television documentary programme on Borley. We had visited the church and the area many times before, and had not felt panicky. So, perhaps our perceptions of something malevolent on this occasion were legitimate after all.

Borley has an enthralling history and anyone of the following characters are eligible to be one of the ghosts: the nun who was bricked up alive, a monk who was either hanged or beheaded, one or two coachmen either hanged or beheaded; Simon of Sudbury, beheaded; Sir Edward Waldegrave, died in the tower of London; John Deeks, unpleasant minister; Cavalier killed at Borley Green; Catholic priest, crucified in the churchyard and thrown down a well; his lover, a nun, murdered; Marie Lairre, strangled; Arabella Waldegrave, a spy murdered by her mother; Henrietta Waldegrave, a Stuart spy murdered by Nicholas Waldegrave; screaming girl, may be pushed out of a window. Two coachmen executed for murder; Harry Bull, poisoned by his wife; Lionel Foyster, poisoned. Furthermore, underground tunnels were discovered in the 1950s, and stone coffins in the crypt are often found to have been moved. The site sits at the intersection of four ley lines. There is a secret entrance to the crypt of the church disguised as a grave, and the fire may have been caused by supernatural means. Strange shapes and faces turn up on recent photographs.

Psychical research groups have visited Borley since the 1970s and television programmes produced. Tape recordings have been made of footsteps, sighs, grunts and other strange noises – at night when the building is empty and locked, the equipment having been placed in the building beforehand. I remember one spine-tingling TV programme (mentioned above) where two investigators were locked inside the church overnight, with a tape recorder and camera. Footsteps were heard on a wooden floor, the church floor is flagstoned. There were sighs, growls and snorts. Orbs started at the back of the church and advanced towards the spectators over the pews.

In 2004 two skeletons were found in a barn next to the church, by builders converting the barn into a dwelling. The bones were estimated to be both male aged around forty-five and seventeen, eleventh to thirteenth century. Part of a jaw bone was found when the Rectory was razed to the ground. Is there a link with these remains, as one of the skulls had a missing jaw bone?

The Borley story is intriguing with many levels, facets, truths, half-truths, untruths, history proven and unproven, legend, scientific evidence and fear.

There are many books on Borley, but in my opinion, the most informative are *The Enigma of Borley Rectory* by Ivan Banks, and *Borley Rectory – The Final Analysis* by Edward Babbs and Claudine Matthais.

So whether it be day or night, summer or winter, ghostly goings on are said to still occur, and people still flock to Borley hoping to experience something – much to the annoyance of the hamlet's residents.

And yes – the above is just a synopsis!

On leaving Borley take the lanes via Borley Green to Belchamp Walter (OS 155 Ref 8140).

Stephen Jenkins, a specialist in ley lines, was driving through Belchamp Walter (two miles from Borley), one 28th August with his wife. They were on the minor road north of Belchamp Walter Hall. Four men appeared suddenly in front of the car. They were monk-like, hooded, wearing long black robes, and carrying a coffin. Only one of their faces could be seen – it was a skull. Jenkins made a note of the time, 12.52 p.m. and went back the next day at exactly the same time and took a photograph at the same spot. When the film was developed, the image of a cloaked figure with a skull-like visage appeared on the print.

I have visited the lane, where I think the vision took place. It is fairly bleak open farmland with few trees, with nothing that could cast a shadow or account for such an outline.

There is a footpath that connects the back lane and Belchamp Walter. The footpath could follow the route of an old corpse way, and the vision has been of coffin bearers on their way to the church. I have taken photographs, and will continue to do so, having been disappointed so far.

Take the lanes southerly to the B1058, via Gestingthorpe and turn right to Castle Hedingham. Go through the village and at the T-junction turn left onto the A604 into Sible Hedingham.

The Bell Inn houses the spirit of an old man who knocks on doors. The ghost of a teenage girl with long dark hair haunts one of the bedrooms. It was her room in her lifetime and she wishes to stay here, according to a medium. The room is always cold, and she pulls bedclothes off sleepers.

The White Horse public house suffers from noisy, disembodied footsteps, and something unseen that scrapes past staff and customers. The doorbell is the old-fashioned type, where one pulls down a metal handle. Many times the bell has rung, and when the door is opened there is nobody there, but the bell is still moving. This happened on one occasion when it was snowing. The bell was still shaking but there were no footprints in the snow.

Note of Interest

An eccentric old man known as Dummy lived in Sible Hedingham in 1863. He was named thus because he could not speak. His tongue had been cut out, under what circumstances is not known.

He lived in a hut with three dogs. He was known to be a white witch. He wore three hats at a time, and sometimes three coats. He was thought to be French.

One night he was in The Swan in Sible Hedingham, when a woman from Ridgewell accused him of casting a spell on her as she had been ill. She had refused him a night's accommodation, and the spell, apparently, was his revenge.

He denied by signs that he had done no such thing. She struck the old man with a stick, shouting and screaming so that all in the crowded bar could hear. A riot then started. Old Dummy was manhandled and jostled. Finally, the rowdy crowd dragged him down to the stream at Watermill Lane. There, they threw him in the water. He tried to wade out on the other side, but the woman and others ran over some wooden planks which served as a bridge, and chucked him in again, in the deepest part.

Some of the crowd by now were of the opinion that they had had their fun, and one man pulled Dummy out. They left him on the riverbank to recover. The poor creature was terrified, exhausted, soaked to the skin and covered in mud, slime and weed. Eventually, he was helped home by two women. His persecutors disbanded not knowing that the whole episode had been witnessed by a ten-year-old girl.

Dummy, aged about eighty, died a month later in Halstead Workhouse, from trauma and disease of the lungs caused by injury and infection.

According to *The Times* the crowd had been sixty or seventy strong. The young girl gave evidence at Castle Hedingham petty sessions. The woman and another perpetrator were sent for trial at Chelmsford assizes, and both were sentenced to six months hard labour.

Swimming a witch was a barbaric custom anyway, but this was a crude attempt 'as a trial'. It would seem that no one observed as to whether the poor wretch sank or floated 'as judgement'. They took the law into their own hands with an urge for brutality and amusement, fuelled by ignorance and superstition. Poor 'old boy!'

Now Take the A604 to Ridgewell

Here on a disused airfield, a collection of old World War Two huts remain, accompanied by the supernatural sounds of crashing aeroplanes, shouting airmen and other weird noises.

Take the Lanes Eastward to Pentlow (OS 155 Ref 8144)

The Pentlow Tower is just visible from the road but lies on private property. Henry Dawson Bull, one of the Rectors of Borley, was born here. The tower was built in the grounds of what was the Pentlow Rectory. Allegedly if one climbs the one-hundred and fourteen steps to the top, on a clear day there is a view of over forty churches.

The folly is said to be haunted by weird, sinister laughter, and has cold spots, even in very warm weather.

Tour Forty-Four
From Braintree to Rayne, Great Leighs (Scrapfaggot Green), Faulkbourne, Cressing Temple, Cressing

OS Maps 167 and 168

The Angel Inn on Notley Road, Braintree, is haunted by a previous landlord who takes exception to alterations being made at the pub. Dogs howl when she is around. Lights are turned on, and glasses and bottles rearranged. Doors which had been locked are found open. A shadowy figure has been espied on the staircase.

A building on the Witham Road which was previously a convent is haunted by a screeching nun. Footsteps have been heard on the stairs.

A hairdresser driving from Braintree towards Dunmow on the old A120 at dusk, saw a woman standing at the side of the road. It was only when she had driven past that she realised the woman was two feet above the road – just hovering there.

From Braintree take the road westward to Rayne.

The Swan is said to be haunted by a lady weaver, who hanged herself from her loom, in an attic that had no windows at the rear of the house.

Ghostly footsteps are heard at twilight on the road at Rayne in the direction of Pods Brook.

From Rayne take the lanes southward to Great Leighs off the A131.

Ye Olde St Anne's Castle public house at Great Leighs is claimed to be the oldest inn in England. A spot known as Scrapfaggot Green where three roads meet on the A131, a triangular piece of green land is said to be the site of a witch's grave, near Drakes Lane.

Apparently, the word scrapfaggot means a witch. But does faggot refer to the heap of sticks for the burning of witches?

Legend tells that elderly Agnes Haven (allegedly the witch) had been burnt at the stake, and a great stone placed over her remains to stop her 'walking'. Later, the stone was removed to St Anne's Castle Inn where it was used for publicity.

Towards the end of World War Two the Americans cut down Dukes Wood and widened roads to make way for a new airfield. The Scrapfaggot stone was thrown into a ditch. This caused a major outbreak of ghostly phenomena, which still occur today, although to a much lesser degree.

A brewer's deliveryman refused to enter the cellar of the pub after meeting 'an evil something' down there. A teenage girl saw something nasty in the fireplace in the bar, and fainted.

There is a haunted room where sounds of knocks, thuds and scratching are coupled with draughts and clammy feelings. Black shapes are seen and cries of either a cat or a baby are heard. There is a legend that a child was murdered in front of its mother in this room.

Discarding the witch's stone seemed to also affect the whole community. Strange, illogical and mischievous things began to occur, which were more annoying rather than frightening, but defied logic:

- sheep strayed through unbroken hedges.
- hay ricks were overturned at night although there had been no windy weather
- church bells rang at odd times.
- geese vanished overnight with no sign of feathers or droppings, and no break in their pen. It was as if they had never existed.
- large scaffolding poles which were kept overnight in a yard were found to be strewn everywhere.
- very heavy paint pots which had been carefully placed outside a cottage, were found in the attic after a painstaking search.
- a dead chicken with a rung neck was found in a water butt. No one owned the bird.
- the huge boulder was found at the entrance to the Dog and Gun Inn. The publican did not know how it came to be there. It took four men to lift it out of the way.
- at Chadwicks Farm, wagons in the barn had been turned around in the night. There was very little space for manoeuvrability, and they were therefore removed from the barn with great difficulty in the morning.
- rabbits were removed from their hutches and placed with chickens in their coop.
- the stone went missing and was found at a turkey farm at Little Leighs. Remember it would take four men to lift it with great effort.
- haystacks were placed in another field
- the church clock went backwards.
- farm animals became sick
- gossip went around that thirty sheep and two horses were found dead.

It was rumoured that the witch's bones were discovered and the stone replaced. Her remains were interred in Little Waltham. However, records show that Agnes Haven was tried at Chelmsford assizes in July 1593 for casting spells on people, making them ill. She was found guilty and hanged not burnt at the stake. Also, there is no evidence that she was buried at Scrapfaggot Green, or that she is reburied at Little Waltham.

A church dignitary believes that Agnes Haven was never buried at Scrapfaggot Green but was interred outside the walls of Boreham Church. A known practice was to bury a witch on unhallowed ground. Bones were found just outside the confines of Boreham Church and were reburied in the churchyard in a secret grave.

The stone was replaced and the haunting diminished, but to this day the pub is haunted by something that whips off bedclothes, moves furniture around, and misty dark shapes encircle the bed in the haunted room.

In Great Leighs when three old cottages were being knocked into one abode, there were problems with one of the cottages. Building conversions went ahead well in two of the cottages, but the third had an atmosphere that was malevolent and rank. After a dog was cajoled to climb the stairs, the animal bolted out of the building, yelping.

A secret room which had been bricked up was found. The dark room smelled of potions brewed in the dim and distant past. The room was bare apart from a witch's hat and the mummified body of a cat. People surmised that this was the witch's house. But who blocked up the room, why, and when?

Travel via the lanes eastward to Faulkbourne. From there take the road towards Witham.

Around the area near Faulkbourne Hall the road is haunted by a man on a bicycle wearing a billycock hat. He is seen at twilight, and rides towards you. Also, a speeding cyclist knocks over living cyclists if they do not get out of his way. Is this the same ghost, or are there two spectral riders?

A room in the fifteenth century Faulkbourne Hall is reputedly haunted. The chamber is known as the Bishop's room because it has a priest's hole. Why it is haunted or by whom is unknown.

Take the Lanes North to Cressing

The church is haunted by a phantom organist during the wintertime, when the church is locked. The music is normally heard late at night or at dawn. This phenomena was reported some time ago.

Tour Forty-Five
From Maldon to Beeleigh Abbey, Danbury, Little Baddow, Boreham and Hatfield Peverel

OS Maps 167 and 168 OS Exp 183
Cyclical and Notable Dates Beeleigh Abbey – 13th April, 11th August, 22nd August

Maldon Marsh is haunted by an elemental at twilight.

Maldon Railway station has been closed since the 1960s. The building was converted into a pub, The Great Eastern, before being sold on. The track was dismantled. However, a white lady lingers around what would have been platform two. She groans as she floats along leaving an icy blast.

Bedroom and lavatory doors are held fast at The Kings Head, Maldon (circa eighteenth century), so that occupants cannot get out. After a great struggle the doors open, and phantom footsteps are heard running away down the corridor. When floorboards were removed at one time, a mass of human bones were found, belonging to more than one person. Some have suggested that this was the site of a former plague pit. There could be some truth in this, in that the churchyard is opposite, and plague victims would not be buried in the churchyard but nearby. Others have muted that a former landlord had killed his guests.

I have learnt of a story concerning a sixteenth century house in a lane in the Maldon vicinity, but I am not allowed to know the location. Apparently, the house is doomed to a miserable atmosphere, and residents do not stay long.

Two sisters lived at the property. The younger stole the elder's boyfriend and they later married. It is rumoured that the elder sister smothered the younger whilst she slept. The ghost is seen (which sister?) standing at an upstairs window. The unhappy spirit trudges around upstairs, children are sensitive to her presence, a servant fell or was pushed out of an upstairs window where the ghostly lady with long grey hair has been seen, and an entity pushes people down the drive, regardless of which way they wish to go.

Beeleigh Abbey lies to the west of Maldon. (OS 168 Ref 8307.)

A figure has been seen standing in the James Room. It is either a monk or the ghost of Sir John Gate. On 11th August 1553 he was held awaiting execution for supporting Lady Jane Grey on becoming Queen, and he was beheaded on 22nd August at the Tower of London. The ghost laments and moans throughout the building on every 11th and 22nd August. On the 22nd, the apparition is said to be headless.

In addition, an abbot is said to walk every 13th April.

People staying in the James Room have the sensation of being watched and the bed has been known to shake on several occasions.

Human skeletons in recent years were discovered in the mud of the abbey pond. It is not known who they were, or how they came to be there.

To the west you will find the pretty village of Danbury.

Here, The Griffin public house is haunted by a man wearing a tricorn hat. He sits at tables in the bar, then gets up and walks through a wall. The pub apparently has at least two other ghosts.

Danbury Common is haunted by a Roman soldier. (OS Exp 183 Ref 7804.)

Phantom monks have been witnessed in Well Lane. Something supernatural frequents Moor's Bridge, and Danbury Hill has a ghostly cyclist.

To the North of Danbury Lies Little Baddow

On moonlit nights, the ghost of Lady Alice Mildmay is seen at a pond, where she is said to have drowned.

Graces Walk is now a track, and she is said to haunt this area which leads up to the church (OS Exp 183 Ref 7507 and 7506). Horses have been known to shy at a certain point along Grace's Walk.

Another woman–some say this spectre is Lady Alice–is said to haunt Grace's Walk by the bridge crossing Sandon Brook. (OS Exp 183 Ref 7505.)

The canal/river area near Grace's Lane is haunted by ghostly footsteps, and other unexplainable noises. A couple moored in a narrow boat were so disturbed by the phenomena that they untied their vessel and left during the dead of night.

At Riffhams the ghost of a Catholic whose burial was delayed because of a lack of priests at the time of conflict between the Roman Catholics and the Church of England, haunts.

To the North Is Boreham

To the northwest across the A12, Anne Boleyn haunts New Hall. She has been seen in the corridors, and gaily flitting around the gardens, reminiscent of happier times with 'Good King Hal'. (OS Map 167 Ref 7310.)

Travel Along the A12 Eastward to Hatfield Peverel

The landlord of The Fox at Matching is also the licensee of The William Boosey at Hatfield Peverel. He said that there are two ghosts and many cold spots.

Legend has it that a driver on the B1137 met a spectral black dog at the driveway gates at Crix. The ghost dog was so unnerved at seeing a motor car, exploded, and set both him and the vehicle on fire. Another version is that a man driving a timber wagon hit out at the dog with his whip, whereupon the dog took its revenge by reducing the driver, wagon and horses to fiery dust.

Note of Interest

The first major trial for witchcraft was held at Chelmsford in 1566. Agnes Waterhouse, her daughter Joan and Elizabeth Francis all resided in Hatfield Peverel. They all at some point owned a cat named Satan. The ridiculous 'evidence' was that the cat spoke in a deep voice, and could turn into a toad or black dog. The cat killed a man who had spurned Elizabeth's propositions and later begot a husband and child for her. She then gave the cat to the Waterhouses, when the pet is supposed to have soured some butter and cheese, drowned cattle, and killed a man.

Elizabeth Francis was imprisoned for merely a year. Joan went free, but her mother, Agnes, was hanged as she confessed. What torture was put on this woman, one wonders, to draw out a confession. Elizabeth Francis, however, was hanged for witchcraft in 1579.

Tour Forty-Six

From Cold Norton to Woodham Ferrers, Latchingdon, Mayland, Steeple, Bradwell-on-Sea, Dengie Flats and North Fambridge

OS Maps 167168 OS Exp 175176

On this tour we enter an eerie area full of lonely creeks, where there is absolute silence other than the cries of curlews, skylarks and gulls, and where the wind moans over the flat land. Take a walk on the ragged coastline along the St Peter's Way on the Bradwell marshes. (OS Exp 176.) The Dengie Flatlands region can be particularly forbidding.

To Get There, First Go to Cold Norton, South of Maldon

Here, a small lady in Victorian clothing appears at 2.00 a.m. who, it is said, is the very essence of malevolence at De Laches.

To the southwest is Woodham Ferrers

Edwins Hall was once owned by Edwin Sandys, Archbishop of York in 1619. Here a girl has been seen flitting around the grounds. She is believed to have been drowned in the lake or moat. A cavalier also walks the grounds of the hall, and there is possibly something supernatural in the orchard.

To the east of Cold Norton you will find Latchingdon and Snoreham.

The lane between Latchingdon and Southminster has been haunted by a headless calf. It is also said to amble down the lane from Latchingdon past Snoreham Hall. There have been no reported sightings since World War Two. You never know though, the apparition may have been witnessed and not reported by people, for fear of ridicule.

Continue Eastward on a Class 'C' Road to Mayland

Legend has it that a woman rides a white horse in the sky – reminiscent of the Valkyries. For those who are not acquainted with Norse Mythology, the Valkyries were the handmaidens of the God Odin. On quick and nimble horses they rushed into the midst of battle and selected those to die. They then rode through the skies to Valhalla, a hall in heaven, where the slain were to spend eternity in bliss and in feasting, waited upon by the Valkyries. Mead and ale would be served in the skulls of the conquered.

Carry on to Steeple

The Star Inn (seventeenth century) is inundated with nooks and crannies. There are possibly secret rooms, and there is an old staircase to a cellar. It is rumoured that there are tunnels from the cellar to the church, and that bodies were buried in the underground passageways. Legend has it that a body is buried near an open fireplace. A ghostly soldier haunts the building.

Note of Interest

The Kray twins, the notorious London gangsters, used to take their holidays as youngsters in the St Lawrence Bay area. Their mother, Violet, used to frequent The Star.

Further east is Bradwell-on-Sea (Bradwell Juxta Mare), and St Peter's Chapel on the tip of the coast land.

Bradwell Lodge, once the village Rectory, is haunted by a butler and a child. Apparently the butler attempted suicide in a small room upstairs, but he actually died in the library. His footsteps are heard, and people do not like sleeping in the room.

The ghost of a child has been seen here, but it is not recorded whether boy or girl, and the reason for the haunting is unknown.

Take the right fork at Bradwell village church, past the mounting block outside the church gate and the village cage – see notes of interest. Drive along the lane as far as you can. This is the old Roman road. The road ends at Eastlands Farm. You need to park on the left, and then walk along the public footpath to the chapel of St Peter's ad Muram – St Peter's on the Wall.

The small chapel stands on the site of the Roman fort of Othona. The Romans built many forts along the eastern coast of Britain as fortresses and 'look outs' against the sudden attacks of the bloodthirsty Vikings.

The fortress also had a dock, evidence of which can be seen still. Here the triremes – war ships – were anchored in readiness for invasion.

After the fall of Rome, the 'sea wolves' of Scandinavia invaded. (This is relevant to the following ghost stories and other tours near here.)

In about 654 AD, St Cedd came down from Holy Island and built the chapel from the stones of the Roman fort. Over time the chapel decayed, became derelict and was used as a barn and a cow shed. During Victorian times, smugglers used the old chapel to store contraband. (More on smugglers on further tours.)

In the 1920s the chapel was reconsecrated and restored in keeping with the Saxon era. A skeleton was found, and evidence showed that the person had been a victim of human sacrifice.

Nearby, the coastguard's cottage is haunted by a seaman wearing a pea jacket with a double row of big buttons. He has a large nose and a sombre expression, and he peers through windows at the occupants. Sometimes he is seen inside, but he is invisible from the waist down. The temperature is ice cold when he is around, even during a heat wave. He has been known to punch an occupant in the jaw. The ghost is thought to be that of a previous inhabitant, a wild fowler known as 'King of the Fowlers'. He hated weekend trippers and bird watchers, who he felt disturbed his birds–his subjects– and were intruders on the landscape – his realm.

A Roman centurion rides a horse at breakneck speed from the area of Weymarks Farm towards the chapel. He and his horse are not seen but the pounding of galloping hooves is heard. Why the haunting is said to be of a Roman soldier is unclear. However, it would make sense as it is likely that a Roman horseman would travel at speed towards Othona to warn of an impending invasion, as there was a pharos – a high lookout tower based on Mersey Island. After receiving the signal, this would be the direct route for the horseman to take to Othona.

The old chapel is said to have a malign atmosphere, and sometimes a light is seen through the windows at night when the building should be in darkness. On inspection, no cause is found. Dark, indistinct shapes are said to be around. When I visited, it was a very hot day. I saw nothing unusual, but I did feel very cold, and found the ambience displeasing.

There is another galloping ghost (or is it the same one that rides from Weymarks) who has been seen travelling at high speed along the Roman road towards the church. The apparition is of a Roman soldier on horseback.

Notes of Interest

The cage/lockup at Bradwell village (1817) has restraining irons still in place, where local miscreants were kept in punishment.

A well-known family of witches by the name of Hart lived at Latchingdon. Tradition says that when one of the Hart witches died, hundreds of white mice ran screaming from the witch's house.

Retrace your steps as far as Mill End, and then turn left to Tillingham. Now take the class 'C' lanes southwards to the lonely Dengie Marshes. Please see tour fifty-two regarding a ghostly experience which may have been near Court Farm. There is some confusion as to whether the phenomena happened here or at Courts End.

On your return journey, at Cold Norton, drop south to North Fambridge.

The five-hundred-year-old Ferry Boat Inn has a mischievous ghost. He is an old man who has been seen by the publican and customers. He moves barmaids politely out of the way by the waist. He likes to let people know he is around when he is being spoken of, by moving bottles, glasses or furniture. He is inclined to turn lights on in the bars after closing, when the licensee has retired for the night.

Jack and I visited the pub with friends Lisa and Steve Hockley. Whilst eating in the Restaurant, Jack had a feeling like a cat or dog rubbing themselves around his knees and lower legs. On looking, there was nothing to be seen. Jack insisted that the feeling was real and definitely not his imagination. He kept looking for an animal. The landlady said this was likely to be the ghost playing a prank, and was probably in tune with Jack's sense of humour.

Tour Forty-Seven

From Mistley to Bradfield, Wix, Great Oakley, Manningtree, Lawford, Dedham, East Bergholt, Brantham

OS Maps 155 and 168
Cyclical and Notable Dates Lawford 1st November

Essex 'rejoices' in the title 'The Witch County'. There were more women hanged in Essex as witches than any other English county. Matthew Hopkins, the Witchfinder General, sentenced nineteen women in one day, and was responsible for hundreds of deaths. He tortured his victims into confession of witchcraft by depriving them of sleep, or applying thumbscrews (pilniewinks) or heated leg irons (caspie claws). Then, as stated before, they were bound by their left thumb tied to their right big toe, and vice versa, then ducked in a nearby pond or river. If they floated, they were a witch, and if they sank they were innocent. Lakes known as ducking ponds are not known for their ducks, but were where witches were swum or ducked in the water. Sometimes they were immersed in a 'ducking stool/chair'.

His assistant Mary Phillips would strip and search the victims for witch's or devil's marks. These being birthmarks, moles, warts or rashes. Hopkins and his assistant John Stearne would interrogate suspects, who in fear of torture would confess or accuse others, no matter how flimsy the 'evidence'.

Witch hysteria was stirred up by the populace's terror of torture inflicted upon the innocent. The fear of being accused as a witch, and the fear of being bewitched, quickly escalated throughout East Anglia.

The ubiquitous Matthew Hopkins haunts Mistley and Manningtree. According to parish records he was buried on Mistley Heath, and people claim to have seen his spirit around the site of a pond in which he may have drowned. Some say he was swum as just deserts for his cruelty and later died of an infection of the lungs.

The ghost of a short man dressed in old-fashioned garb, knee boots, and a stovepipe hat – the sort of apparel Hopkins would wear – has been seen near the lake at Mistley Place.

His shade has been witnessed at the Thorn Inn, where he and Stearne would carry out investigations. Hopkins has been seen elsewhere in Mistley, but at The Thorn Inn he sits in a chair in the attic, then stands and walks away.

Seafield Bay is just across the River Stour opposite Mistley. Here, the screams of tortured women accused of witchcraft are heard at night. The most agonising sound of screeching and wailing is said to be the lament of Elizabeth Clarke, a cripple, who was tortured, as were the others by the Witchfinder. Elizabeth's ghost appears on the shoreline.

A ghostly image loiters near the Swan fountain.

The Walls at Mistley are frequented by a headless coachman driving a hearse carrying a dead body.

There is a small hump-backed bridge along The Walls, known as Hopping Bridge. There have been many reports of a phantom pedestrian, who steps out into the road in front of oncoming traffic. When the driver slams on the brakes and stops, there is no one to be seen. Some who have seen this phantom believe it to be none other than our 'old friend' Matthew Hopkins as the apparition appears to be wearing the type of clothing he would have worn. Also, the figure runs across the road towards Mistley Place where Hopkins' ghost is said to manifest. A witness returned the next day to examine the area where the apparition disappeared, only to find an area of grass, thicker and darker, about the size of a grave. Some say that Hopkins was buried at Mistley Place and not Mistley Heath. Rumours abound about the nature of his death and his burial place. Legend has it that he died of consumption but it has also been muted that he emigrated to America.

Returning to the Thorn Hotel, there are stories of a serving wench who walks the passageways. A boy roams the rear of the premises. Apparently, he was pushed under a horse whilst fighting, and was trampled to death in the stables.

At the site of the Waggon and Horses, now a private residence, an unearthly face stares out of one of the windows – not believed to be Hopkins this time!

Now on to Bradfield which can be found southeast of Mistley.

Allegedly, Sir Harbottle Grimston, on dull, moonless nights, drives around the village in his coach and four. He lived at Bradfield Hall, Steam Mill Road, in Stuart times and was at one time speaker of the House of Commons. It is rumoured that there is a tunnel that runs from the Hall to Wix Abbey. Furthermore, a tunnel is believed to stretch from St Lawrence church to the river Stour previously used by smugglers.

Now on to Wix

At the crossroads in August 2007, Black Shuck, the demon dog was seen. The apparition occurred about 8.00 o'clock at night.

To the East Lies Great Oakley

The Maybush Inn is haunted by the sound of a child (presumably) playing marbles – the unmistakable sound of the little glass balls, rolling and clanking together. A fetching young woman wearing a kimono has also been observed.

Retrace your journey and now visit Manningtree, situated southwest of Mistley.

A Victorian gentleman haunts the Red Lion public house, as does Matthew Hopkins. The Witchfinder General appears in dark clothing with unkempt, unwashed hair, dark sparkling eyes, and a small beard and moustache.

The White Hart is said to be haunted by Hopkins, but he is only heard, not seen. Perhaps the haunting is by another entity as it is only heard.

This time it is a white canine that haunts the area. It is said that a white dog scampers down Mistley Hill near Manningtree. It portends a death to the Norman family.

To the West Lies Lawford

A haunting or a slip in time?

On All Souls Day a woman witnessed an assembly of monks in the church swaying incense burners and chanting. So, she had seen the monks, heard the singing and also smelled the incense. As all three senses were used this may suggest that the witness may have 'walked' into another time zone, rather than experienced a haunting.

The church is haunted by a shade of a bride. She has appeared in a number of group wedding photographs, standing behind the actual bride. She has been seen standing at the church gate wearing white and a thick material covering her face, her veil. Also, she has been observed running from the church, her veil like a white line flowing behind her. She bolts from the church door through the churchyard, often on the first of November, All Souls Day. This is a ghostly re-enactment of a bride waiting for her groom, only to receive the news that her husband had been thrown from his horse on his way to the wedding and killed. The bride then ran through the cemetery to her father's grave where she sobbed hysterically then died.

This improbable story is supposed to be true. A woman in Lawford walked down her garden path, and to her astonishment, saw a fairy! The creature was about twelve inches tall. It was an old lady, attired in a shawl, bonnet and buttoned boots. She was holding some tiny flowers. Apparently, bewildered, both women stared at each other. Then the elemental smiled, and floated away, waving goodbye.

Whilst researching stories for this guide, I have come across, surprisingly, quite a few tales concerning the little folk. I have only recounted another in a previous tour, but I just had to include this one as it is so extraordinary.

However, my late father, a no-nonsense army sergeant major, swore to me that when he was a boy, he saw a goblin.

Take the minor roads northwesterly to Dedham.

A departed boy, chimney sweep, still haunts Brook Street and environs.

Elsa was the last witch to be burnt at the stake in Essex. She was a serving wench at the Sun Hotel in the High Street. She is usually seen on the stairs at lunchtime. The manifestation is very fleeting, and although the witnesses say they only had a glimpse of her sitting on the stairs crying, it was definitely not their imagination. She tends to appear when the pub is busy, and staff do not have much time to take notice. It is said that if one waits to see a ghost, it will not appear, but when one's mind is preoccupied, or thinking about nothing in particular, that is when the paranormal is often experienced. (The drowsy state just before sleep is another example.)

She has also been seen outside the Inn wearing a dark-coloured cloak and carrying a parcel.

To the Northeast You Will Find East Bergholt (Sometimes This Is Classified as Suffolk)

Here the Friary and church are haunted, and according to Peter Underwood in his *A–Z of British Ghosts*, there is a 'distinct eerie atmosphere'. The building was originally a Benedictine convent. A door is said to open by itself routinely at 10.50 p.m. and the ambience would be extremely cold. Soldiers were stationed here in World War Two. A young soldier felt cold hands on his face, and his hair turned from black to white overnight. That particular room was then sealed up. There was another door at the Friary that the soldiers refused to use, and all would enter the building via another entrance the long way round.

Take the Lanes Westerly Towards Brantham

The lane linking Brantham to Bentley (north) is haunted by a headless monk. He is thought to have been an incumbent at Dodnash Priory. There is only a stone to mark where the priory stood. There is supposed to be treasure under it. (OS 155 Refs 1035, 1036, 1037.)

Tour Forty-Eight
From Chingford to Buckhurst Hill, Chigwell, Ilford

OS Map 177 and OS Exp 174
Cyclical and Notable dates – Chingford 31st December

Chingford lies to the south of Waltham Abbey off the A112.

A highwayman haunts the area around Richmond Avenue and The Avenue, Highams Park. He may be seen on New Year's Eve. (OS 177 Ref 3892.)

Chingford Hall is haunted by a hidden menace. Apparently a tramp once spent the night there and was found the next day to be out of his wits.

Nearby at Chingford Mount Cemetery (OS 177 Ref 3793), a phantom horseman dressed in black canters between the graves. On dismounting he disappears. Also people report feeling followed, and some have heard footsteps behind them, though no one is in sight.

At Friday Hill House on Simmons Lane, a ghostly man and a weeping woman in white haunt.

A grey lady gropes her way around the Highams Park. She is supposed to have drowned in the lake (OS 177 Ref 3992).

A spectral white deer haunts the vicinity.

A hotel near Queen Elizabeth's Hunting Lodge on Rangers Road (OS 177 Ref 3995), is haunted by Mary. She died in a fire in 1912, and her ghost haunts the rebuilt premises. Dogs are frightened of her and she has been spotted sitting on a bed on the upper floor.

Nearby to the east is Buckhurst Hill.

Black shuck scurries around the graveyard, the animal's intentions seem to be to frighten people. The dog then bounds over the churchyard wall into oncoming traffic.

A house in Bradwell Road was haunted by the spectre of a young girl that hid objects which turned up in prominent places weeks later. Unaccountable smells of perfume and cosmetics pervaded the main bedroom. When the family moved home, the ghost moved with them. The ghost was attached to the wardrobe that the mother had bought cheaply from an acquaintance. The phantom child was seen to emerge from the wardrobe. On investigating the history of the previous owners of the furniture, it transpired that their five-year-old daughter had died of cancer. The family had four children, and when each one reached the age of five, the haunting occurred.

Eventually, the wardrobe was given away. The mother, feeling guilty, confided in her doctor who assured her that another owner would only see the furniture as a wood and metal wardrobe. However, the 'new' owners started to experience supernatural activity and the wardrobe was destroyed. There have been no reports since, other than sometimes the house on Bradwell Road does have a suggestion of the smell of perfume, and on each occasion the family, within a day, has been informed of a death.

To the East Lies Chigwell

A house called The Marchings in Gravel Lane is haunted by a lady in white, a friend of King John – or so rumour has it.

Woolston Hall, now Epping Forest Country Club (OS Exp 174 Ref 4495 or OS 177 Ref 4495), when being renovated, builders would not work late at night to complete a contract. Agnes, a thirteen-year-old girl threw herself out of a third floor window. She only haunts men!

Take the A123 Southward to Ilford

The old fire station in Broadway is haunted by Geoffrey Netherwood, a former fire fighter. When the brigade moved to the new station in Romford Road, the ghost went with them. In life he was interested in ghosts and now haunts both sites.

Dick Turpin used to hide in Ilford at The Green Man Inn, now a private house. Occupants say that occasionally they would hear the sound of a galloping horse, but when they went outside there was nothing to account for it. An upstairs room had rings on the walls indicating this was once used as a first floor stable. This area is haunted as are the stables outside.

A poltergeist troubles residents at Perryman's Farm by removing pictures from walls.

Two spectral ladies dressed in 1920s style clothing on summer evenings walk through Valentines Park, near the Perth Road entrance.

Tour Forty-Nine
From Romford to Upminster, Hornchurch, Rainham, Aveley and West Thurrock

OS Map 177
Cyclical and Notable Dates – Romford 30th November
Rainham Hall Christmas Time

On St Andrew's Day at noon, 30th November, you may hear the spectral church bells of an ancient chapel that sank when the River Rom burst its banks, on Oldchurch Road.

The Romford Union workhouse was built in 1838, and now forms part of what was the Oldchurch Hospital. There is a plethora of supernatural phenomena here. Nurses in old-fashioned uniforms warned staff of upset children. Infants and babies were heard crying. Radios turned themselves on, and doors opened and closed on their own. People experienced panic attacks and the feeling of being watched. It has now been converted into housing. It would be interesting to see if the hauntings continue.

A woman in white climbs into a horse-drawn coach which then moves along and disappears. This occurs at The Manor, Harold Hill.

To the East Is Upminster

Somewhere between Upminster and Barking along the rail tracks, a number of passengers had a strange experience in the 1980s. As the train slowed, an old man with a lamp stared apprehensively at the train, from a brick building. He shone the green lantern as an 'all clear – proceed'.

A female passenger was surprised that a man of that age, possibly a septuagenarian, should be working (at night). On further investigation she discovered that the wall and the arch on which he was standing, no longer exists.

It would seem that the Victorian Railway worker was just as astonished to observe the train, as the passengers were to see him. Was this a 'slip in time' on both sides? Had the old man seen a glimpse of the future?

At Upminster theatre, people who sit in a certain seat in the auditorium feel as if they are being shoved. This may be connected with a suicide that occurred here. Also, footsteps and knocking noises have been heard.

A young girl in a white dress is believed to haunt the first floor corridor of Upminster Golf Club in Hall Lane. Legend has it that in Tudor times, she was kidnapped, raped and then bricked-up.

Hornchurch is situated between Romford and Upminster.

A house in Parkstone Avenue was haunted by a little girl in Edwardian clothing, who asks if she may have her ball back!

Rainham lies to the south.

This Rainham Hall should not be confused with Raynham Hall in Norfolk where the famous brown lady haunts and was allegedly photographed – that is another story.

The ghost of a tall man believed to be Colonel Mulliner, a previous occupier, appears in daylight dressed in Edwardian attire. He is a friendly chap. Apparently, he has not been seen for some time. This is a National Trust property and therefore is easily visited. Just because there have been no reported sightings does not mean that he is not around. People may not wish to register a sighting for fear of appearing foolish. You may see him yet.

A ghostly coach with headless horses and a decapitated driver sets out at midnight from the church. The passenger sits with his head in his lap. The journey ends near Bloors Place. Tradition says that a drink was put out at Christmas time for the headless travellers, and the glasses were found empty next day. (Look out for drunken foxes!) The haunting may stem from a legend that a Tudor gentleman seduced many wives, and the cuckolded husbands from the village banded together and decapitated him.

Bretons Manor, a Social Club now is situated at 411, Rainham Road, has a variety of spooks. Roman soldiers are said to march through walls in the basement. A lady in white loiters on the stairs. Martha Ayloff also haunts the stairway whilst Anne Ayloff, wearing a lavender coloured dress, appears in one of the rooms.

Now Travel Eastward to Aveley

A manor named Belhus was haunted by an elderly person in black silk and lace. Cold hands would be placed on people's shoulders. A maid haunted the upstairs passageways, and a shade in a black cloak wanders. According to Jessie Payne in her *Ghosts Hunter's Guide to Essex*, she says that the building was demolished in 1956. This site is now a golf course and country park, but there are buildings there. Maybe the ghosts still haunt and have transferred their manifestations to either the buildings or the grounds. (There is a footpath to Belhus Woods Country Park.) Ghosts have been known to transfer their activities – see Borley, tour forty-three.

Now drop south to west Thurrock where the Ship Inn is haunted by a previous publican. He was shot some time during the nineteenth century.

Tour Fifty

From Southend to Prittlewell, Hadleigh, Leigh-on-Sea and Westcliffe-on-Sea

OS Map 178 OS Exp 175

Southend has a variety of ghosts.

A grey luminous monk-like shape accompanied by a drop in temperature was exorcised from a property in Royal Terrace.

Porters mansion house, now owned by the Corporation and Mayor's offices, is haunted by an entity that taps people on the shoulder when no one else is present. Disembodied footsteps are also heard. Legend has it that there is a secret passage that leads to the sea.

A dwelling in Ambleside Avenue has a spirit who likes to sit on beds. The ghost is not seen but part of the bed depresses as if someone has just sat on it, and then it raises as if someone has got up.

Another dwelling, this time in Hartington Road, near Marine Parade, houses a frightening woman in Victorian dress.

A private house at Orchard Side, Eastwood, suffered from poltergeist activity, although not badly. A parent noticed their baby's eyes following an unseen presence around the room. As the child looked upward, two cards fell from a high shelf.

A spectral dog, the size of a calf, is said to haunt the roads around, Rochford, Ashingdon and Hullbridge, to Southend.

Eton House School, closed in 1993 and was originally known as Southchurch Lawn. Rumour has it that there was a tunnel under the building used for smuggling. Nelson and Lady Hamilton are said to have lodged here. Princess Charlotte when aged five ran out in front of a horse and missed death by a 'bat's squeak'. The smuggler who is supposed to have saved her, is said to haunt here. A ghost is believed to haunt the north side of the house carrying a lantern. In addition, the sound of someone plodding about sweeping, is heard. The school is now Alleyn Court Preparatory School, Wakering Road.

A Victorian building in Southchurch Road, now converted into apartments, was haunted by footsteps on the upper floor. Also, organ music would start up in the middle of the night. On investigation the next day in the empty apartment, on the floor above, three harmoniums were found. They could only be played by working the foot pedals.

Victoria Circus in the town is haunted by an old lady dressed in black who engages passers-by in conversation.

A tall man wearing a long coat walks to the end of Southend Pier and then vanishes. He is believed to have committed suicide.

A council house near Sutton Road was haunted by an old man who only a four-year-old boy could see. Poltergeist activity, someone calling the names of the inhabitants, footsteps and banging were just some of the phenomena.

Sutton Rectory on the fringe of Southend is haunted by ghostly footsteps.

An ancient house (circa four-hundred years old) somewhere in Southend is haunted by a beautiful lady with long, luxuriant auburn hair. She wears a long, white dress and may be a bride. Unfortunately, it would appear that the house owners wish the address to remain anonymous.

Another tantalising elusive 'address' near Southend is where a procession of ghostly monks are seen crossing a field. It was later discovered that a religious establishment used to be there.

A young girl killed in a motorcycle accident still hitches a lift. Those who have stopped say that she asks to go to Victoria Circus. She appears in a dishevelled state. Drivers en route have found that before they reach the destination she has disappeared. She appears near the arterial road and the Wickford Roundabout. Be careful, we do not want any more accidents whilst you are looking out for her!

Prittlewell is an area of Southend, and Prittlewell Priory and Museum may be found on OS Map 178 Ref 8787. Previously this was a Cluniac Priory, and one story tells of a monk who was involved with black magic. Another version is that he fell in love with a local girl and was murdered. In any case, when he appears, ducks squawk and birds become very noisy, agitated, and flutter about in a warning stance. An archaeological dig in the 1960s revealed a grave which showed markings suggesting that it was one of a dishonoured monk. A monk has been seen near the refectory, and another or the same one rises from the cloister garden. In addition, sounds of children emanate from a first floor room, which is empty.

There is a rather macabre story which tells of a Samuel Brown who died 15th November 1827, and is buried in Prittlewell churchyard. After his funeral, hordes of people would come to the graveyard and stand next to the tomb believing that they could hear sounds from under the earth. Had this poor man – aged thirty – been buried alive by mistake? Premature burial is a dreadful and horrifying thought.

A bungalow near the Priory is said to be haunted by an old lady in Victorian dress.

Note of Interest

This story could be considered humorous, but I doubt that it would have been to those involved.

The ceiling of the chancel at Prittlewell church is particularly beautiful. A sort of latter day wallpaper design in red and white with gilded cherubs. There is a well-documented story of an argument between five bell ringers and the vicar of St Mary's Prittlewell. In 1822 a new incumbent, the Reverend Doctor Frederick Nolan, settled.

Dr Nolan was an intellectual and a linguist having knowledge of twelve languages, at least five of which were archaic. The people of Prittlewell at the time were farming folk, not learned, and found their new vicar to be difficult to get to know.

The bell ringers of St Mary's were dedicated in that they started their exercise at five o'clock in the morning. No doubt a payment of ten shillings and a flagon of ale helped their diligence. Nolan and his wife gave permission for this to continue, but as time went on they found it difficult to bear as they lived next to the church. He asked if the bells could be rung at eight in the morning instead of five. The bell ringers refused. The six bells would peal from five a.m. until mid-morning. After eighteen years, Doctor Nolan had had enough. One day (14th June 1840) he could bear it no longer. He grabbed a kitchen knife, raced to the belfry and attempted to cut the bell ropes. A fight broke out. The case went to court. Dr Nolan then locked the church door and had a policeman as guard.

The bell ringers retaliated by throwing stones at the vicarage and shouting in a rowdy manner, consequently putting Nolan and his wife in fear of deadly assault, as this continued night after night. The pair then fired shots at the campanologists.

Dr Nolan complained to the ecclesiastical court, and in response the bell ringers burnt an effigy of Dr Nolan on Guy Fawkes Night. Five bell ringers who were summoned to court did not attend and consequently incurred fines. The fines were not paid and the ringleader (no pun intended) was imprisoned for thirteen weeks. Then peace was restored.

However, Dr Nolan was the incumbent at St Mary's for the next twenty-four years. A funny story? Not for Reverend Doctor Nolan.

Next Stop Hadleigh, Which Lies to the West of Southend

Hadleigh in Essex should not be confused with Hadleigh in Suffolk – something I have been guilty of many times.

One day, a brother and sister were walking from Leigh-on-Sea to Hadleigh, through a wood. A journey they had made many times, so they knew the wood well. On this occasion they came across a Georgian mansion which they had never seen before. They saw also a young girl with a large dog walk down the drive. When walking through the wood on further occasions they could not find the house. There was no other house in the vicinity that fitted the description, so their vision was unlikely to be a mirage. They were unable to find the house on old maps. It is also unlikely that their experience was another time dimension as the girl was wearing clothing relevant to the present day.

In the recent past, a cynic said that he believed he had found the house. He located it to be in a glade in the woods of Benfleet Downs. The house could be found via an inconspicuous path that leads from the main one from Leigh to Hadleigh. (Apparently, the wrong maps had been consulted in the first place.) However, the house discovered was not Georgian, which begged the questions, were the brother and sister sure of the style of the period, or was this indeed the house in question.

There have been other phenomena similar to this. Two women on holiday in Versaille, Paris, appeared to walk into a time warp. Two cottages were seen at Wallington, Surrey, which had been demolished years earlier. At Rougham in Suffolk, two people saw a Georgian mansion, when on a walk, only never to find the grand house again. A story uncannily similar to the Hadleigh 'missing' mansion.

The old schools at Hadleigh are haunted by dark moving shadows and running footsteps, bangs and crashes, and lights turning on and off. One person felt the presence to be resentful of them being there. Dark shadows flit around. I once experienced a similar feeling in an apartment in which I lived in Harrow on the Hill. I was at a dinner party in the penthouse, and returned to my apartment to fetch a book that I had been discussing. I had the distinct impression that something or someone did not want me to be there. The hostile feeling had gone on my return that night. I could go on ad infinitum about the spooky things that happened in that flat – another time maybe.

A shop that was a village stores in the High Street, is haunted by a previous owner – a little old lady. She has been seen walking at night from the churchyard across the High Street into her shop. She is buried in said church.

A woman in white haunts the ruins of Hadleigh Castle. If you meet her and she commands you to visit again you must attend. If not, she will seek you out and punch you in the face! She may ask to dance with you, but beware, because if she does not like your footwork, she will throw you into the dry moat below. A huge man in black, said to be the devil himself, appears.

At one time, strange lights were seen emanating from the castle, but it is now believed that these were made by smugglers hiding contraband. Smugglers used to say the area was haunted so that they could have the place to themselves.

'Cunning' Murrell a wise man, or white witch, or warlock, or cunning man, is buried in the churchyard. His ghost has been seen picking herbs. James Murrell 1780–1860 was the seventh son of a seventh son, or so he claimed. He was known for his knowledge of astrology, quack doctoring, exorcism and veterinary surgery. He could find lost property and foretell the future as well as look into the past with accuracy. He foretold correctly the exact time and date of his own death. His reputation was known more or less throughout the southeast of England. Murrell said that there would always be nine witches in Canewdon, and three in Hadleigh. He also said that there would be witches in Leigh-on-Sea for a hundred years. He is sometimes seen at dusk gathering herbs and flowers from the local hedgerows.

Note of Interest

Hadleigh Castle was built in 1232, but shrinking London clay caused subsidence. It now leans slightly. It was built as a 'look out' for a possible French invasion. However, it was often used to house royal wives. Queen Margaret, wife to Edward 1st, was granted the castle as part of her dowry. Edward 2nd's wife, Isabella 'The She Wolf of France' resided there. Henry 8th gave the castle to Catherine of Aragon, Anne of Cleves and Catherine Parr.

The artist Constable was enchanted by the castle and sketched it.

There are marvellous views from the castle across the Thames to the Kent shoreline.

Retrace your journey easterly to Leigh-on-Sea.

A school is haunted by a poltergeist that has fun turning lights on and off, and overturns chairs just as staff leave empty classrooms. A phantom sigh was heard, and photographs of children performing a school play showed orbs, which cannot be explained.

One day a cleaner said she saw the caretaker on the stairs and spoke to him, but he ignored her. On confronting him later, both parties were astonished, particularly the cleaner who went home in tears, as the caretaker had been at the far end of the building at the time, and certainly would not have ignored her. This is a classic case of a doppelganger sighting. The building has been exorcised twice, yet the haunting continues, but to a lesser degree.

At Prospect House, the spectre of a short small man wearing a long coat appears from time to time, accompanied by the smell of fish.

A man who committed suicide is said to haunt a building in Broadway West, before it became a bakery. Unexplained footsteps, wafts of air and objects moved are the usual phenomena. An employee ran from the bakery after witnessing something supernatural, never explaining what he saw.

Notes of Interest

Near to the Peter Boat Inn is Strand Wharf. This area was owned by Queen Anne Boleyn.

The Mayflower set sail with Essex pilgrims for Portsmouth and America from the wharf. There were no travellers from Leigh, as people felt the Mayflower was not seaworthy!

The original Peter Boat Inn was built in the fifteenth century, but was razed to the ground by fire in 1832.People of the town came out to help put out the inferno, but without success. It seems that beneath the beer cellar, a secret cellar was revealed jam-packed with smuggled goods. Apparently, the whole town was involved. Perhaps they were trying to save their booty as well as hiding their guilt.

Between St Clement's church and the Library gardens is Church Hill, a steep and attractive footpath leading to the picturesque old town. Here one can sense what Old Leigh must have been like in the past.

Leigh too had its witches, and it was here that there existed a very deep pond where women were tried. The area was known as Doom Pond. Cunning Murrell said there would be witches in Leigh for one-hundred years. That time is up, but some still believe there are witches here and in Canewdon.

Nearby is Westcliffe-on-Sea.

Here the Palace Theatre Arts Centre is haunted by George, a previous theatre manager. He had financial problems and hanged himself from the fly floor. He sometimes sits next to people in the audience during performances. A lady in white has also been observed.

Tour Fifty-One
From Wallasea Island to Paglesham, Canewdon, Ashingdon, Rochford and Great Stambridge

OS Map 178 and OS Exp 176

A German bomb in World War Two coupled with the tidal flood of 1953, annihilated Wallasea Island. The flood affected thousands of acres of the east coast, washed away the sea walls at Wallasea and Foulness, engulfed other islands, and drowned men and livestock. Farmhouses and barns were destroyed.

Today the area is flat, regimented agricultural parcels of land. Dilapidated barns are dotted here and there, akin to wrecked ships on a 'sea' of cornfields. It can be reached from the mainland by road and then footpaths around the sea wall. It can also be reached by ferry from Burnham on Crouch. At the time of writing, the RSPB has a project creating lagoons to introduce a habitat for marshland wildlife and combat the threats of flooding and climate change.

The Tyle Barn (or Tile Barn) was washed away in the flood – a dwelling that was said to be haunted by a demonic entity. It was known as the Devil's house. Cattle would stampede from the barn, and the house was always icily cold. The sound of something that had huge wings would thrash around, unseen, on the high ceilings. At these times there was a threatening sense of evil. One day a farmhand was passing the barn and heard someone calling him. On entering, there was no one. He then started to feel odd and trancelike. He picked up a piece of rope and heard a voice say, "Do it! Do it!" He was about to throw the rope which he had placed around his neck onto a beam and saw a creature of such malevolence and ugliness, the sight of which brought him to his senses, and he 'scarpered'. The demon was said to have been a familiar of Old Mother Redcap, the witch of Foulness.

The eerie landscape of the marshes and farmlands has now taken on the desolate, brooding atmosphere of the washed away Tyle Barn. This is a lonely tract of land with just gulls, skylarks, hares and the mournful wind for company. Interestingly, a section of the River Crouch is called Devil's Reach (OS Exp 176 Ref 9692).

Travel Westerly to Paglesham

Three hollow trees known as the 'three old widows' were haunted by a ghost. This may be a story put about by smugglers as £200s worth of silk was once found hidden there. Only two trees are left, but the site is on the bend of the road near East Hall. (OS Exp 176 Ref 9392.)

There is a story of a three-hundred-year-old cottage near the church that was said to be haunted. At one time, postcards were sold showing a skeleton at one of the windows, and tourists from miles around would flock to view the place. I am uncertain as to whether the cottage still stands. The building's beams were old ship's timbers. The map reference for the church is OS Exp 176 Ref 9293.

Now Drive North-Northwest to Canewdon

The ghost of a woman is said to advance from Canewdon's St Nicholas churchyard. She glides to the west gate. Here she stops for a moment and then travels rapidly down the lanes to the river. The story is that she was a witch and was executed.

Another version – or another ghost – rises from a tomb in the churchyard. She wears a crinoline and a poke bonnet. Some witnesses say she has no head – others say there is no face under the bonnet. A phantom lady in blue has been observed.

Regarding St Nicholas' church, there is an uncomfortable feeling around the west side of the church, and a strange ambience near the altar. When I visited, I felt very ill at ease and did not stay long.

The ghost of a young girl stands in the driveway of the vicarage.

A ghostly lady has been seen in Larkhill Road, her head swathed in a mist, and a man who encountered her said the impression she gave was that of a witch. Those that have seen her express their astonishment that she slides along at a phenomenal speed. Her perambulation usually comes to a halt at the river, but on one occasion she was seen at The Old Ferry House on the other side of the river, floating in front of the hearth – minus a head. Apparently, if you are in her path she will seize you, and propel you into the air out of her way.

Another spectre haunts Larkhill Road near Pudsey Hall Lane. A man with a red emblem on his clothing, believed to be a crusader (Red Cross usually on a white background) has often been seen.

The ghost of an executed witch is said to haunt the crossroads at Canewdon. An uncultivated field near the river is where witches met and is called 'Witches Field'.

A small evil elemental chased a motorcyclist on a lane in or around Canewdon. The presence kept up speed with the bike.

Steve Hockley, my friend, is a former fireman, medical first responder, and a no-nonsense down-to-earth man, felt as if he had walked into some sort of miasma (a bit like walking into a thick web) in the restaurant of the Anchor Inn, whilst we visited for lunch. The proprietor was aloof on the subject of ghosts and those that allegedly haunt the pub, but the waitress/cleaner said that she always felt as if she was being watched when cleaning upstairs.

Notes of Interest

King Canute landed with his Danish army nearby, hence the name Canewdon. His army defeated the Saxons at the battle of Ashingdon.

The church was allegedly built by Henry 5th to celebrate the victory at the battle of Agincourt 1415. The tower is said to be tall enough to be used as a beacon for ships.

The village lockup, a structure of wood and iron, and the village stocks stand near the church.

For centuries Canewdon was known as the village of witches – Essex the county of witches.

'Old Picky', George Pickinghill, witchmaster of Canewdon, lived in a cottage on the corner of the lane near The Anchor Inn. He was feared by the villagers and those who knew of him elsewhere. People of today would have difficulty in understanding the terror of sorcery and superstition. He was said to have the 'evil eye' and just one look from him and you were ill, until he touched you with his cane.

He never paid rent and neither beer nor clothing cost him a penny. Farmers bribed him with beer to stay away from their farms. People avoided him, unless they needed his help. He could find animals, property, and cure blighted crops.

He was said to blow on his wooden whistle, and his witches would appear – all of them, women. They would meet, amongst other places, in the churchyard. There would be chanting, ritual sex, magic and dancing. The old vicar was too frightened to confront them. A new clergyman was not so lenient when he heard the chanting and weird prayers. Armed with a riding crop he went to challenge them. When he arrived there was nothing to behold. All was dark and silent, except for thirteen white rabbits chomping on the grass. Any self-respecting witch should be able to 'shapeshift', or transform themselves into another being.

'Old Picky' died in 1909 in his nineties. He said that there would always be witches in Canewdon. Some believe there are witches here still. They may not shapeshift into rabbits, but perhaps practice some of the rituals and black arts. Crossed broomsticks against doors are a charm against witchcraft, and this custom was still being carried out in 2002!

Nearby Is Ashingdon

At Ashingdon Hill one may hear the moans and cries of wounded soldiers. The site is said to be of an old battleground.

The church of St Andrew's stands on Ashingdon Hill (OS 178 Ref 8693). This ancient building is believed to be haunted by various spooks. An extremely reliable source says spirits were seen in the chancel and nave, during services. The apparitions comprise of a beautiful lady enshrouded in a blue light, men in Danish armour, an oriental man in a purple robe, and a young monk dressed in brown habit and sandals.

An organist appeared at his own funeral, facing the congregation in the nave and later at his graveside during the committal.

A blood-curdling scream is sometimes heard near the church. It would seem that two men walking past the church had a violent argument. One murdered the other, and the killer committed suicide in an asylum. The scream is believed to be that of the murderer not his victim.

Note of Interest

A tailoress named Nellie Button known as a witch in Ashingdon put a curse on a young girl who wanted to take her custom elsewhere. The girl gradually became paralysed. When she promised to use the dressmaker again, she was gradually able to walk and speak again.

Drop South to Rochford

Rochford Hall (OS 178 Ref 8690) is one of the many places haunted by Anne Boleyn. She appears in white meandering around the grounds during the winter months. Many golfers can, apparently, attest to seeing her. Poachers avoid the twelve nights after Christmas as she is particularly active then, and the headless apparition is not a pleasant one. Ghostly footsteps have been heard within the Hall, and these have been attributed to Anne.

The lanes around Rochford are said to be haunted by the headless ghost of a witch dressed in a silk gown. Some say this is the spectre of Anne Boleyn as she was accused of witchcraft by King Henry 8th.

Houses in Rectory Road built on the site of an old mansion, have experienced poltergeist activity.

A room in an ancient house in East Street is said to be haunted. A virago of a wife tried her husband's patience by her constant unreasonable demands. He consequently locked her up is a very small room where she starved to death. If you witness her ghost, beware of her steely stare!

When undergoing refurbishment a thirteenth century building known as The Old House in South Street released some phenomena that had lain dormant. Builders reported ghostly activity. A little girl in a long white night-dress roams around, sometimes crying. A psychic, a historian, and a team of interested people kept vigil one night. They reported impressions of Puritan figures, a man in green velvet, and a little girl in Victorian dress holding a rag doll, amongst others.

The building is now council offices which I believe may be open to the public on Wednesdays between 14.00 to 16.30 hours. It is suggested you check on the internet to see if this still applies.

To the Northeast, Nearby, Is Great Stambridge

A ghostly, cowled figure creeps along the side of the road in the village. The apparition wears a large crucifix. Witnesses report that when the figure turned towards them, there was just a black void instead of a face.

Tour Fifty-Two
From Great Wakering to Little Wakering, Barling, Shoeburyness and Foulness

OS Map 178 and OS Exp 176

Great Wakering lies between Shoeburyness and Foulness. The area abounds with stories of witchcraft and ghosts.

Clement the baker hanged himself from a tree situated at a road junction known as Baker's Grave. (OS Exp 176 Ref 9387.) The tree no longer stands but his ghost still lingers.

Star Lane is haunted by black shuck and a ghostly young boy has been observed. There is a nasty bend on this road, the area is pitch black at night and there have been many accidents.

Note of Interest

In the distant past, the area being marshland and therefore very damp caused many diseases (chest conditions and rheumatics) and illnesses which were particularly harmful to the distaff side. This, in addition to the awful death rate of women through childbirth meant that there was a shortage of females. Women were persuaded from elsewhere in Essex to move here to make up the deficit. Although a damp area, the rainfall is the lowest in the country.

Nearby at Little Wakering Hall, Betty Bury's headless ghost shuffles around. She is also said to haunt the lane leading to the house. She has been seen or heard in Wick Meadow behind the church, and between the Hall and Wakering Wick. She has even been known to walk along the village street. She was a serving maid and is supposed to have hanged herself after being jilted.

Continue further up the road in a northerly direction, and you will come to Barling.

At Weir Pond which lies at the corner of Church Road, an elderly woman haunts. She wears a grey gown. Apparently, she has been seen frequently in present times. (OS Map 178 Ref 9289 and OS Exp 176 Ref 9289.)

Retrace your journey and drop south to Shoeburyness.

At North Shoebury (OS Exp 176 Ref 9486) on Poynters Lane near Crouchman's Farm, a man wearing a striped polo neck top and casual trousers steps in front of oncoming cars. Drivers are compelled to swerve to avoid hitting him. He then vanishes. The haunting is well known in the area.

A dwelling known as The Red House in Shoeburyness is haunted by a young girl. Tradition says that she cut her own throat to provoke her lover. Strange knockings and noises happen at night. When repairs to the roof were being carried out, builders claimed that there was a thick shroud of cobwebs housing a nest of the biggest spiders they had ever seen. A stone was dislodged in the garden revealing an old well where there was an entrance to an underground tunnel, which is rumoured to lead to Shoebury Manor. The well was filled in and the tunnel not investigated

The women's army barracks are built on the site of a property that was razed to the ground by fire. The new building is believed to be haunted by those who perished. They can be heard at night panting and gasping as they breathe in the smoke that killed them.

Somewhere in the surrounding countryside in a tree-lined road the sounds of workhorses' hooves on gravel are heard when no animal is in sight. It is said that one can feel their hot breath and smell the steeds. Apparently, where this phenomena occurs used to be a brickyard, and horses would drag the heavy bricks in carts.

A grey-haired old lady is rumoured to haunt a private dwelling in Caulfield Road.

Now Travel Eastward to Foulness Island

This is a lonely area and Courts End hamlet is in the middle of it – more or less. A wildfowler arranged to meet some colleagues before dawn on a winter's morning. The idea was to meet up in the hamlet and then set out on foot for the creeks. He waited for some time and noticed a party going on in the farmhouse, which appeared to still be going strong in the small hours. He decided to go and enquire as to whether they had seen his friends. He peered through the windows and to his astonishment saw people dressed in Victorian attire, dancing. There was a fiddler playing, but there was no sound from him or the people, absolute silence. When he knocked on the door, the scene vanished. So now there was not only silence but blackness. The house was empty. He went back to his car feeling very frightened. All he could hear in the dark was the quarrelling geese. A light went on in a neighbouring cottage and a man came out stacking milk churns. The wildfowler drove down to the farmer and asked who lived in the farmhouse. The house had been empty for years, he was told. The other wildfowlers never turned up.

The best description of this haunting is by the late James Wentworth Day in his *Essex Ghosts*. However, he describes Courts End as being in the Dengie Hundreds. If you look at the map OS Exp 176, there is a Courts Farm in the Dengie area but not a Courts End. (Tour forty-six.) Both Courts End and Courts Farm fit the description of the haunting. I wonder which is correct. See what you think.

At one time a ship was sunk just off the coast, and it can be seen, if the weather conditions are right, sailing through a field that was once covered by sea.

A pond in Foulness is visited by a pregnant serving maid, who drowned herself after being spurned by her lover, her employer.

Tour Fifty-Three

From Mersea Island to The Strood, Ray Island, Great Wigborough, Salcott cum Virley and Langenhoe

OS Map 168 and OS Exp 184

Mersea Island is one of the islets off the Essex coast, reached from the mainland by a causeway known as The Strood. It is best to contact the Colchester Tourist Office to find out when the tide washes over The Strood, as this is the only spit of connecting land. The island can be cut off at high tide for some hours, and you do not want to become stranded.

Mersea Island can be a disturbing but seductive place. Here there is a sense of isolation, influenced by the mainly flat landscape, creeks and broad skies. The marshes can be a silent brooding domain when the mist rolls in off the North Sea. Mersea is somehow a place apart.

The indented coastline of Essex, with its countless number of creeks, secret coves and secluded inlets, were ideal for smuggler's hidden contraband. The Peldon Rose Inn was said to have held more black market liquor than legal alcohol, in Victorian times. Mersea Island was no exception when it came to smuggling. You may hear many a tale of days gone by regarding pirates, pillagers and buccaneers in these parts. "Watch the wall my darling, as the gentlemen go by," warned poet, Rudyard Kipling (The Smuggler's Song). Yes, better to stare at the wall, so that you could not identify a smuggler's face, or witness that he was transporting 'Brandy for the parson', or 'baccy for the clerk, laces for a lady or letters for a spy'. Better to remain unknowing 'as the gentlemen go by'.

The Strood is haunted by a Roman centurion. (OS Exp 184 Ref 0115.) He marches from Barrow Hill, along the causeway onto the Colchester Road, and occasionally trudges on to Ray Island. Sometimes only the tramp of his feet is audible, but many have seen him, usually from the waist up, as he walks on the original level of the road. The modern road has been elevated. He is supposed to appear on moonlit nights. One night the landlady of the Peldon Rose was walking along the Strood, the tide washing the side of the road, and was followed by the jangling footsteps of a Roman soldier in armour. She met a friend on her travels who was shaking with fear, as he could hear the ghost but could not see him, although the spectre was close enough to touch.

There is another spectre – or the same one – who favours stormy nights. He is seen in full armour and would seem to be a Roman General. He marches towards The Strood at times of heavy rain, pauses and then fades away. He also starts his perambulations from Barrow Hill where Roman remains were found.

On Barrow Hill (OS Exp 184 Ref 0214) the ghostly sound of heavy wheels and horses have been heard for years and years. Also, at Barrow Hill Farm House, a poltergeist knocks on walls. At the top of the mound, two Danish brothers are said to re-enact a fight over a beautiful girl. They killed each other and the sounds of clashing swords can be heard at midnight.

The sound of Roman soldiers' tramping feet, legionaries fighting, and the vision of a Roman chariot and horses, have been observed by many across the island.

A cottage in The Lane is said to be haunted by the footsteps of the Rector who murdered his errant son, and then committed suicide in remorse.

Motorists have driven through a white mist in a human shape, but on inspection, there is no damage to the vehicle, and the road is deserted.

A woman dressed in a smock and wearing a tall hat, with a stick under her arm, has been seen by trustworthy witnesses. The witch-like female appears sitting on a wall at the corner of Colchester Road and High Street.

An old house which lays back off the East Mersea Road, with a pond in the front garden is, or was, haunted by two genteel ladies, believed to be a mother and daughter who once lived there.

The mudflats near Maydays Marsh and the Pyefleet Channel are said to be haunted by a huge man, who strides from the sea wall into the mist. (OS Exp 184 Ref 0315.)

A wrecked yacht was washed up on the beach near the church. A man tried to save the injured crew and after a long time he passed out due to exhaustion. When he regained consciousness, there was no evidence of a shipwreck or crew.

There have been sightings in Dawes Lane of a woman wearing a bonnet and long silk dress. There is no sound while she enters a nearby field, where crops and grass do not stir as she walks through. Then the vision vanishes.

At West Mersea, an elderly woman dressed in blue velvet haunts The White Hart Inn, as does a spectral dog whose habitat is the cellar.

West Mersea Hall is haunted by the sound of laughter from a female Roman friend of the Emperor Claudius. She is said to have drowned during a midnight swim. The Hall is built on the site of a Roman villa.

Between The Fox and the turning for Waldegraves Farm, a cloaked figure crosses the road and disappears into a hedge.

Ray Island lies to the west of The Strood in the tidal creek between the Ray and Strood Channels. (OS Exp 184 Ref 0014.) It is a remote salting where the inexperienced with creeks and mudflats can become marooned or drown. There is a trackway from The Strood to Ray Island but only the experienced can sometimes find it, and for the untrained it is better not to try.

Here a Roman soldier follows visitors.

Some time back, a young man camped out on Ray Island. He had a gun with him for shooting widgeon. He looked out of his tent and could see all over the island, so bright was the full moon. He decided to get some 'shuteye' as he intended to be up at the crack of dawn to bag some birds. He was just drifting off to sleep when he heard loud footsteps coming towards him. He could hear the boots squelching in the mud. Then the footsteps came up to the tent and stopped. The young man guessed it was another wildfowler, but then the footsteps trod right through the tent, inches away from his body, and faded away in the distance. The camper grabbed his gun and looked out, but there was nothing, just the saltings bathed in moonlight. As soon as it was daylight, the young man packed up and left.

Take the Left Fork When Coming off the Strood to Great Wigborough

At The Hyde (OS Exp 184 Ref 9615) the ghost of a witch still haunts. She is believed to have lived in Tudor times.

Carry on down Colchester Road to Salcott cum Virley

On the road between Guisnes Court (OS Exp 184 Ref 9411) and the Salcott crossroads (OS Exp 184 Ref 9413), a spectral black dog, larger than a Great Dane, with drooping ears and huge eyes that glow like bicycle lamps, pads around. (See tour fifty-six for further details.)

Interestingly, there is an uncannily similar description of an animal seen on 7th October 2008. This was reported to an organisation which logs sightings of alien big cats. These animals are said to be descendants of cats that were let loose after the Dangerous Wild Animals Act 1976, by keepers who could no longer adhere to the legislation, or, descendants of cats that escaped from travelling circuses which were a popular form of entertainment in Victorian times. There is no clear evidence as to how they come to be here, but they are out there. There are too many sightings by no-nonsense people, all over Britain, even allowing for mistaken identification or hoaxes.

A man was returning home from a late shift in Cambridge. His route was diverted by roadworks which took him into country lanes. The story is longer than detailed here, but he saw what he thought were car or motorbike reflectors. "They were really bright, blood red and shining just like car stop lights." The lights seemed to come straight at him, a couple of feet high, and then a huge black shape leapt into a field. The man jokingly asked if he had seen Black Shuck, but it would seem he seriously wanted to know what had such huge, red eyes.

There is a school of thought that these spectral dogs that have been seen throughout the centuries are in fact alien big cats. There have been other reports of the devil dogs with red, glowing eyes.

Note of Interest

At the church of St Edmund, East Mersea, there is a caged grave on the north side of the churchyard. Sarah Wrench was believed to be a witch, and a metal grill was put over her grave to stop her 'walking'. The north side of churchyards were kept for witches and suicides in times gone by.

Retrace your journey back through Great Wigborough and Peldon up to Langenhoe.

I have included this site in this gazetteer because it is such a fascinating story, even though there is little to see now. Like Borley, the building is no longer in existence, and the ghosts may have nestled elsewhere in the immediate area. All that is left to identify the spot is a neglected churchyard, which can be found near the Manor House.

In my opinion the best interpretation of events can be found in Peter Underwood's *Gazetteer of British Ghosts*, but here is my précis of incidents.

The rector of Langenhoe church at one time was Reverend Merryweather. He had not experienced anything supernatural, and was not interested in the subject, until he came to Langenhoe.

The first incident was some poltergeist activity, door slamming and locking by no human agency. Flowers that had been placed in a vase on a pew, were later found removed from the vase, and were lying on the seat. There were many incidents where the flowers appeared, disappeared, or were moved.

On one occasion Mr Merryweather visited the Manor House. He was shown over the house by the then owner. They entered an attractive bedroom; the lady of the house mentioned that she did not use the room as there was something odd about it, and left him alone. He stood admiring the view from the window, and as he turned, he 'moved into the unmistakable embrace of a naked young woman' – 'one wild frantic embrace and she was gone'. He was absolutely certain what had happened although he heard and saw nothing. There was no odour.

Thumps would be heard on a regular basis near the vestry door. Other poltergeist phenomena ensued, and disembodied voices were heard in the church.

There had been some trouble with a number of boys from the neighbouring village, and people had been mugged. So, Mr Merryweather decided to arm himself with an ornamental dagger (a present from Cyprus) whilst he visited his remotely situated church. He placed the implement firmly in his belt, hidden by his cassock. As he was standing in front of the altar he felt the dagger swiftly pulled from him. He heard a female voice say, "You are a cruel man," as the knife clattered to the floor.

Various noises including that of a human cough, and a tiny bell used in church services rang of its own accord. These were heard in the vicinity of a blocked-up door. The door was once a private portal to the church for members of the manor house.

On another occasion, during Holy Communion, Reverend Merryweather saw the ghost of a woman, aged about thirty. She was wearing a white or grey dress, and a veil. The apparition made its way from the north side of the church, across the chancel, to the southwest corner. She walked with a slight stoop, and wore an unhappy expression. She disappeared through a wall which seemed to swallow her up. She looked quite solid, but made no sound.

Around fifty years before these occurrences, Langenhoe church was badly damaged by an earthquake. Old photographs taken soon after, showing the damage, revealed a former doorway in the internal tower wall. This was where the Reverend saw the spectre dissolve into the wall, and not into the more recent doorway a few feet away. He did not know of these photographs at the time of the vision.

A variety of phenomena continued, including a female voice and a strong smell of violets throughout the whole building. This was autumn time, and of course violets are in bloom in springtime. Later on that particular autumn, the rector heard a woman singing plain chant, and then the heavy tread of a man's footsteps, walk along the nave. There was no logical explanation for these sounds.

Another day, workmen and Reverend Merryweather heard ghostly singing, and one Christmas Eve the Rector saw a man in a tweed suit vanish into the pulpit.

The girl with the veil appeared again during a service. She floated through the bricked-up door.

The Reverend heard a ghostly conversation which appeared to be involving three unseen people. The words were indistinct. There was a sigh and then silence.

Another phantom young lady was seen in the church wearing a cream-coloured dress. She had blue eyes and an oval shaped face that bore a melancholy look.

Apparently, stories of the haunting by a veiled young woman are decades old. A former rector is said to have killed his lover during one of their clandestine meetings.

Mr Merryweather was sincerely mystified and kept a diary of events. He had a quiet, uneventful life, in the supernatural sense away from the church.

The Langenhoe area once formed part of an estate owned by the Waldegrave family, which included the church, the Manor House, and a number of houses and cottages. It is alleged that each of these sites have experienced paranormal phenomena. Strangely, it is also interesting to note, that a Waldegrave family were prominent at Borley. The Waldegrave tomb can be seen in Borley church. (See Tour forty-three.)

When Reverend Merryweather retired, the living of Langenhoe joined with another parish nearby. Eventually, the church became derelict and was demolished.

Tour Fifty-Four
From Wivenhoe to Brightlingsea, St Osyth and Thorrington

OS Map 168
Cyclical and Notable Dates St Osyth 7th October
Thorrington June

Picturesque Wivenhoe can be found to the southeast of Colchester
A poltergeist haunts The Greyhound public house, which is situated in the High
Street opposite the park.

Travel Southerly to Brightlingsea

An atheist was buried just outside the church door in Brightlingsea churchyard in 1771.
He, on his deathbed, said that if there was a God, an ash tree would grow from my grave.
Years later his tombstone started to crack, and on investigation an ash tree was found
growing at the side of the tomb. In the 1940s it had flourished so much that the subsiding
tomb was becoming dangerous. The tree had to be removed and when raking away the
roots, the skeleton was disinterred. School boys took the skull to their science master.
The vicar soon retrieved it and the skull was reinterred on hallowed ground. There are
similar stories to this in Clavering in Essex, and Tewin in Hertfordshire.

Note of Interest

Brightlingsea is the only cinque port outside Kent and Sussex. These are the five ports
on the south coast with ancient privileges.

Nearby Lies St Osyth

Saint Osyth's Priory was founded in 1121. Osyth was the daughter of King Frithwald of
Mercia (the first Christian King of the Angles) and Queen Wilburga. She was betrothed
to King Sighere of Essex, but she decided to take the oath of chastity. Sighere gave her
the village of Chich, which was generous and gracious of him, considering. There, she
built a nunnery and became an abbess.

She was murdered in the year 653 by a Danish pagan sea captain because she refused
to renounce her faith and worship the Danish gods. Legend dictates that she was
decapitated. Her bones are laid to rest at the Priory, and she is said to walk each year on
7th October, carrying her head in her hands.

A ghostly monk in white carrying a candle is also seen at night.

At one time, the Priory was used as a convalescent home (1948 – 1980s). Poltergeist
activity occurred. A carpet nailed to the floor somehow threw a cleaner against a wall.
This was witnessed.

The Priory was used as a Nursing Home at one time. The ghost of a woman stands near the washing machine, and a monk has been seen in the laundry room. When he melts away, icy patches are left as evidence of his presence. The monk also walks through walls.

A group of patients were seated by a window, and all saw monks in a procession walk through the archway. A staff member could not see them. However, it was later learnt that where the vision took place was formerly a monks' graveyard.

The Priory is open to the public; check with the Tourist Office or on the Internet for times.

Hippisley Coxe in his book *Haunted Britain* says that there is a haunted well at St Osyth but he does not give the location or the character of the phenomena.

The road near the Priory gate is haunted by a ghostly hitchhiker who suddenly appears in the back seat of cars. A person slight of stature appears in the road and slowly dissolves.

An ancient cottage in St Osyth known as The Cage is haunted by a man in old-fashioned garb. The cottage was a jail until 1908, and is supposed to date back five-hundred years. The current owner fled the cottage in fear after poltergeist happenings and on seeing the ghost of a man standing over the cot of her baby son. Although the lone parent went to live with a friend, she still has a mortgage on the property and is paying this off by offering ghost tours and vigils. One person who kept observation one night was so terrified of the sound of scratching on walls, a foreboding atmosphere, the temperature plummeting, and a chain on a wall vibrating violently, that she left before daybreak. The paranormal activity was reported in the national newspapers in 2012.

One inmate of the gaol was believed to be Ursula Kemp (no relation to the author).

In 1921 two female skeletons were unearthed by a man digging in his garden. The elbows, knees and limbs were riveted through with irons, their heads buried towards the north. This was a practice to stop witches from 'walking' after death.

The skeletons may be of two witches hanged by Matthew Hopkins in 1645, or those of Ursula Kemp and Elizabeth Bennet, both executed for witchcraft in 1582. One female's remains are on display at the museum in Boscastle.

Shortly after the discovery, the man's house was burnt down and superstitious locals said that this was his punishment for having (accidentally) exhumed their bodies.

Go Northward on the B1027 to Thorrington

Here a phantom car waits beside the petrol pumps at a filling station and then slowly fades away. The apparition was caught on the garage's security video. Maybe a likely time to see it is on a June evening.

Tour Fifty-Five

From Walton on the Naze to Kirby-le-Soken, Thorpe-le-Soken, Weeley, Clacton, Holland-on-Sea, Great Holland, Little Holland, Frinton-on-Sea

OS Map 169 and OS Exp 184

A phantom fisherman strolls along the Walton on the Naze pier, and on one occasion a witness claims to have had a conversation with the ghost.

The promenade to the west of the pier is said to be haunted by a number of ghostly people meandering around.

The tower on the Naze was used as an observation post during World War Two. A soldier ran screaming from the building after seeing a ghost. It is believed that his superior officer covered up the event probably to avoid panic by the rest of the troop. (OS 169 Ref 2623.)

The ruins of Walton Hall are said to be haunted by the ghosts of smugglers who were caught and held as prisoners there.

Note of Interest

The old church at Walton on the Naze was engulfed by the sea due to coastal erosion in the late eighteenth century but the sounds of its bells can still be heard sometimes tolling under the briny, foretelling storms. In 1928, after a storm, the church suddenly reappeared owing to an uncharacteristic low tide. It was covered with shells and seaweed. People tried to cross over to it but were hindered by the 'sucking' sands and a fast incoming tide. The church was visible for only a few hours and then it was swallowed up by the sea again

Travel Inland on the B1034 to Kirby-le-Soken

Two spectral children haunt The Red Lion Inn. They have been seen playing in a front bedroom, and their phantom frolicking can be heard.

Carry on to Thorpe-le-Soken on the B1034 and then B1033.

On reaching the village take the B1414 on the left. This is Station Road. Take the first turning left after the station into Tan Lane.

Near the T-junction with Holland Road, many drivers have been forced to slam on their brakes to avoid hitting a pedestrian. Some say the man is in Victorian clothing and carries a stick, and at other times he is with a woman. No one has been able to identify the ghostly couple, who suddenly appear in front of cars. Sometimes there is a silvery mist around the hump-backed bridge. (Exp 184 possibly Ref 1718.)

Back in Thorpe-le-Soken, The Bell Inn is haunted by the spirit of the beautiful Kitty Canham. She married the Reverend Alexander Gough, but found life as a vicar's wife dull. She went to London and met the wealthy young aristocrat, Lord Dalmeny. Believing her to be a single young woman, the couple married. They travelled widely, but Kitty became very ill. She confessed her bigamy, and her dying wish was to return to Thorpe. Both her husbands attended her funeral.

The Bell is near the graveyard, and people believe the female ghost that has haunted the pub for the last two-hundred and fifty years is Kitty. She has been seen to walk through closed doors, plays mischievous jokes, and moves furniture around. A fire broke out in 2001, but a portrait of Kitty, which hangs over the fireplace, went unscathed.

A cottage near the war memorial is haunted by a man in chains.

The police station is frequented by a ghostly police officer in old-fashioned uniform, and unearthly whisperings are heard in empty cells.

Note of Interest

Sir William Gull, the eminent physician, is buried at Thorpe-le-Soken. This distinguished man's reputation has now been sullied by those who think he was Jack the Ripper.

He was born in 1816 on a barge moored at St Osyth Mill. Although a lowly start, he became one of the leading medical men of his era. He attended the Prince of Wales during a bad bout of typhus, and was physician to Queen Victoria. He was brought in to try and solve the poisoning of Charles Bravo – a famous unsolved fatal poisoning in the 'village' of Balham, now a district of South London, in 1876. He was a Fellow of the Royal Society, a Fellow of the Royal College of Physicians and Professor of Physiology at Guy's Hospital.

Some say that Sir William Gull was not buried at Thorpe, but was incarcerated in a lunatic asylum, that his coffin was in fact weighted down with stones, or even that another person's body was interred.

Gull and his wife are buried in a large grave, but some say it is too large for two bodies, and a third is buried there also. A rumour abounds that Gull was buried there many years later in secrecy, after his 'official' funeral on 3rd February 1890.

Why did these rumours start? There are some strange anomalies to consider.

His will was probated on his death in 1890, but it was probated again in 1897. There seems to be no legal reason for this to happen. This gives credence to the gossip that he had been locked away due to insanity and he really died in 1897.

When Gull died – in 1890 – his death certificate was signed by his son-in-law, Doctor Theodore Acland. There were other medical men in attendance when he allegedly died, yet the document was signed by a relative. This is not an illegal act, but irregular.

The Jack the Ripper murders took place at Whitechapel, London, in 1888. There has been much conjecture over the years as to the identity of Jack the Ripper. Information and evidence taken at the time has been lost, especially during the Blitz in World War Two.

The number of women he killed is debatable. Some say four women, others as many as nine. It depends whether some of the murders in the vicinity were attributed to Jack. However, five is usually the believed figure. The murders took place in smelly, dark alleyways and yards at night, except for Mary Kelly. The last of his victims. Mary was murdered in her lodgings. The butchery inflicted on this woman was sadistic and savage – a blood bath. Some experts have said that this may not have been a Ripper murder as the modus operandi was different. The crime was committed in a building, and the mutilations carried out were hellish, and would have taken hours to perform. Or had Jack finally satiated his bloodlust in this final slaying.

It is widely believed that the Ripper was a surgeon, or at least had medical knowledge. He had to work swiftly in the dark for fear of being caught. Organs were taken deftly from the victims without damaging other parts of anatomy.

In 1895 an American newspaper published a story about the medium Robert Lees. He mentioned that he had pointed out the house of an important physician to the police.

The physician, assuming the name of Thomas Mason, had been placed in a madhouse. (Gull was a member of the Masons.) His death had been made known, and a bogus funeral had taken place.

There is a theory that there was a conspiracy from on high, also connected to the Masons. Prince Albert Victor, Duke of Clarence, and Walter Sickert, the artist, used to frequent the 'more questionable' parts of London. On one of these jaunts, the bisexual Prince – his identity disguised – met Annie Crook and fell in love. They secretly married and had a baby girl. Soon Queen Victoria heard of the matter, and asked the prime minister, Lord Salisbury, to deal with the situation, as the Duke of Clarence (known as Eddie) could not marry a commoner or a Catholic.

The dwelling where Eddie and Annie were living in Cleveland Street was raided. Eddy was taken away in a carriage, and Annie in a separate conveyance. The baby girl, Alice Margaret, was taken away by her nursemaid Mary Kelly, who placed her in a convent.

Mary Kelly, down on her luck, took to gin and prostitution. She bragged to the other streetwalkers of her knowledge of the Prince, Annie and the baby.

So, the government had protected Eddie. Annie had been rendered to a zombie-like state after operations to her brain, supposedly performed by Gull in an effort to silence her. Now the government had to deal with Mary Kelly and her cronies who were spreading the word – hence the murders of the prostitutes. This is an unlikely scenario, and is ridiculed by many Ripperologists.

Gull at the time was seventy years of age, had had a stroke in 1887, and was forced, therefore, to retire. It is unlikely that this ailing, respectable, esteemed man would stoop to murder, especially in this perverted manner.

Nevertheless, there are mysteries surrounding Sir William Gull: his will, his burial and grave, and his alleged secret confinement in an asylum: but the world's most famous serial killer, Jack the Ripper, who murdered for Queen and country? I think not.

Now Take the B1033 Westerly out of Thorpe to Weeley

In the Manor House the ghost of a little, old lady dwells. She tidies up, cleans and dusts, but is inclined to leave her hairpins scattered about.

Hillside House allegedly has a ghost responsible for the deaths of two girls, each of whom fell down the stairs. Now the spirit of one of them re-enacts the tragedy. There is a local story that a rocking chair in the house was always in motion, so it was placed in the loft, where the movements could still be heard. It was then placed in a garden shed. In just a few days it was back in the loft, by no human hand, still rocking. When the house has been vacant, a face has been seen at the window.

A ghostly monk has been seen in the lane of Hillside House. He crosses the road and continues walking in the direction of Great Bentley

There is a pond near the church where one may hear the supernatural sounds of an accident involving a coach. (OS Map 169 Ref 1521 and Exp 184 Ref 1521.)

Take the A133 to Clacton

You will reach Great Clacton first. At the junction of St John's Road and London Road, a lone spectral horse crosses the roundabout and then disappears. Ghostly monks have been seen in St John's Road and environs. The Plough Inn is haunted by something that grasps hands, and people feel they are being watched.

The Ship Inn, situated in Valley Road, has a poltergeist.

A woman who once drowned herself appears in photographs taken at or near the Baptist Church in Pier Avenue, near the sea front.

A man exercising his dog along the beach, between Clacton and Jaywick, came across a severed arm. For some grisly reason he took it home before taking it to the police station. For some time afterwards his house was afflicted with bangs and knockings.

There are phantom footsteps, faint fraught voices, and the sound of a skirmish at the top of the stairs, at Carr's Farm House in Coppins Road.

Three German pilots with pale faces who crashed into a sand pit during the Second World War have been seen. The area is now a factory car park.

Old Lifeboat House has poltergeist activity.

A home care shop now stands on the site of the Old Kinema. The building has been haunted by an old man since the 1940s. He wears clothing akin to the old gangster era of the 1930s. Many employees and workmen have experienced the heavy phantom footsteps and doors opening and closing of their own accord.

A woman in Burrs Road was seated in a rocking chair cuddling a baby, when suddenly the chair rose up. She nearly hit her head on the ceiling. She managed to jump off and ran to the door, but it was stuck fast. Something unseen prevented her from leaving.

Take the Coast Road Eastward to Holland-on-Sea

The footpath between Oakwood Inn and Aylesbury Drive is haunted by a woman who wanders here leaving the scent of her perfume.

Travel Inland to Great Holland

There is an ancient burial ground near Little Holland Hall on the Frinton Road. Here, grey figures flit around the area. Locals believe they are either the spirits of smugglers or monks.

Six headless men supporting a coffin trudge over a field near Park Lane. Could this be part of an old corpse way track? (OS Exp 184 Ref 2020.) There is a similar story in Belchamp Walter – see tour forty-three.

Park Lane is where a blonde woman on horseback has been sighted. She drowned near here, and sometimes her lone white horse is witnessed (OS Exp 184 Ref 2020).

To the southeast is Treasure Holt Farm.

This ancient house boasts many ghosts. A woman dressed in a crinoline glides through the building. A woman with blonde hair sits before the fire. A cavalier loiters in the lounge. A ghostly monk walks above ground level in the gardens, and nearby, the apparition of a highwayman hangs from a tree.

To the East Lies Frinton-on-Sea

Studio B of the local radio station is haunted by a murdered man.

Tour Fifty-Six
From Tollesbury to Tolleshunt D'arcy, Tolleshunt Knights, Layer Marney, Copford

OS Map 168 and OS Exp 184
Cyclical and Notable Dates. Layer Marney – Easter to Mayand Christmas time

Tollesbury is situated on one of the Essex peninsulars north of the Blackwater estuary. The tinkling little streams and rivers in this area open up to magnificent skies. The quiet roads lead to snug little villages. Timbered houses, some with pargetting – combed patterns on the plasterwork – moated manors, and church towers uncompromisingly and resolutely implanted, all conspire to an idyllic atmosphere. The tides wash around Tollesbury's marina, flat marshes and oyster beds – a popular place for bird watchers and nature lovers.

The marshes around Tollesbury are said to be haunted by a phantom Druid.

Tollesbury churchyard is the habitat of a spectral white rabbit.

The re-enactment of what appears to be an accident takes place at Prentice Hall Lane (OS 168 Ref 9410). A young woman dressed in black is found lying, curled up on the road, but when drivers stop to help, she has gone.

Some of the older locals say that the area abounds with witches to this day, and are afraid of the 'evil eye', or being 'overlooked' – cast with a spell.

Take the B1023 towards Tolleshunt D'Arcy, about halfway along this road is Gorwell Hall. On this road near the Gorwell Hall entrance, a white lady is said to walk. This is where she was murdered – her throat was cut.

On the same stretch of road you may encounter Black Shuck. A demon dog or phantom hound may not seem much of a 'big deal' but there are many terrifying stories about this phenomena.

A young woman travelling from D'Arcy to Tollesbury to summon a midwife one winter night about 12.30 a.m. met the animal near the entrance to Gorwell Hall and Guisnes Court. The midwife told her to go on ahead. It was there again on her way back. This time instead of following her, the hound appeared to be dozing, and she managed to cycle past without disturbing the frightening beast.

The huge dog, about two and a half feet high, with red slobbering tongue, and eyes as large as saucers, is usually seen at night. Its sooty black coat is rough and unkempt. It is often first noticed lying in the middle of the road, and then accompanies the traveller, especially if he is on a pushbike, along the road. Sometimes the animal is so close, it almost impedes the cyclist, and at other times it hangs back but is always there – watching. His large paws make no sound, his head looking up at the rider is level with the handlebars. It then suddenly vanishes. People travelling in cars say that the dog is always at their side, or behind them no matter what speed they are doing. (OS 168 Ref 9411 and OS Exp. Ref 9411.)

The area of the entrance to Gorwell Hall is known locally as Jordan's Green. There is an old superstition that a man was buried at this spot with a stake through his heart.

Black Shuck has also been encountered on the B1026 – the road out of Tolleshunt D'Arcy to Great Wigborough.

You may come across the ghostly canine anywhere on this stretch of road but particularly at the Salcott cum Virley crossroads. (Mentioned briefly in tour fifty-three.) The devil dog is met along here at dusk, where it plagues pedestrians and cyclists by growling with bared teeth with a grin-like expression. Several brave or panicky witnesses have tried to scare off the animal. It just disappears before their eyes. If you speak to some of the older folk around here about Black Shuck, they are very unlikely to laugh at you. If you meet this great shaggy dog, you will no doubt enquire if anyone owns a dog like that in these parts. Do not be surprised if the answer is in the negative, and to be warned not to travel at dusk. (OS 168 Ref 9413 and OS Exp 184 Ref 9413.) Apparently, whatever you do, do not run!

Notes of Interest

Marjorie Allingham, the crime writer, lived at Tolleshunt D'Arcy.

White House Farm (private residence) situated in Pages Lane just off the Tollesbury Road B1023 was once the scene of multiple murders.

The White House Farm massacre took place in a region where villagers' families had lived for centuries. The area is of quiet villages and old market towns. There was little of the nightlife and the jet set lifestyle of which handsome Jeremy Bamber craved. He killed to inherit, and nearly got away with murder.

On 7th August 1985 at 3.26 a.m. Jeremy Bamber told the police duty officer at Chelmsford (not a 999 emergency call) that he had just received a fraught telephone call from his father. He heard a shot and the line had gone dead, and when he redialled, he got the engaged tone. His father was supposed to have said that Jeremy's sister had gone hysterical with a gun.

Armed police surrounded the building, which was quiet. Police made loudspeaker appeals which were met with silence. Jeremy Bamber arrived moments later from the village of Goldhanger where he lived.

He explained that the gun was a rifle that was kept for shooting rabbits. He and his half-sister Sheila Caffell, known as Bambi, were adopted.

Neville and June Bamber adopted both Jeremy and Sheila at three months of age. The attractive former model was staying at White House Farm with her twin sons Daniel and Nicholas.

Bamber told police that his sister had had nervous breakdowns in the past, was separated from her husband Colin, and had now gone mad. He explained the four-hundred-acre farm was owned by his parents, and jotted down a plan of the house.

Police were concerned for their own safety and the risk to any family member being held hostage. Consequently, the surveillance went on through the night, and the police finally forced entry at 7.30 a.m.

Their eyes were met with carnage. Sixty-one-year-old Neville was lying near the telephone. He had been beaten and shot six times in the head, neck and arm. The room was in chaos. There had obviously been a violent quarrel.

The twin toddler boys lay in bed. Both had been shot numerous times.

June's body was spread on the floor. She had been killed by a shower of bullets.

Sheila was found in June's bedroom with one bullet wound to her throat, and another bullet had passed through her jaw to her brain, but she had no marks on her to indicate a fight.

Bamber's adoptive parents were churchgoers, and he often described them as religious fanatics. Jeremy however, enjoyed fast women, fast cars and a louche lifestyle.

Bamber's comments about Sheila's mental state were not exaggerated. It was common knowledge that she believed herself to be a white witch, or the Virgin Mary, and that the twins were evil and plotting against her. Otherwise she was a sweet, quiet, pretty, introverted girl. However, villagers expressed that they were unaware that Sheila knew how to shoot.

So, the police's opinion was that Sheila had killed everyone and then turned the gun on herself. Suave Jeremy played the grieving son, and had to be supported by his girlfriend, Julie Mugford, at the funerals.

Then on the day of the special service for the family held at St Nicholas Church, Tolleshunt D'Arcy, Bamber spent the time drinking pink champagne with his pals and flirting with the waitresses.

Meanwhile, a relative and a villager together made their own search of White House Farm, and found a hidden silencer. Also, at this time, a pathologist reported that Sheila could not have killed herself using a silencer, as her short arms would not be able to reach the trigger, let alone shoot herself twice. The gun length would be forty-nine inches and Sheila's arms would have to be thirty-six inches long. Specks of blood were found on the silencer, and of course Sheila could not have shot herself and then hidden the silencer in a cupboard.

Bamber soon after went on holiday with a friend from New Zealand and not his girlfriend.

Julie, now freed from her controlling, commanding, mesmerising lover, now had time to reflect. She told Essex police that: Jeremy had been planning to kill his parents for months; he thought that he could commit the perfect murder; he was originally going to drug them, shoot them and then set the house on fire, but the property was underinsured and valuable antiques would be destroyed. He detested his mother; he had rung her (Julie) the day before the murders saying that he was going to carry out the massacre. Julie told him not to be foolish but did not forewarn the family. She explained that she did not really want to believe it; she was frightened, and thought Jeremy might hurt her.

Bamber was arrested when he and his friend arrived back at Dover from St Tropez. He was then charged with the five murders.

At the trial, the jury found him guilty with a majority of 10 – 2. He was sentenced to five concurrent murder sentences.

Julie Mugford emigrated to Australia.

Immediately after the trial, the Home Secretary ordered an investigation into the way Essex police had handled the case. There were a number of basic and fundamental police procedures which appear to not have been carried out properly. Essex police admitted that they had originally been duped by Bamber, but denied that their handling of the case had been slapdash.

Curiously, White House Farm does seem to have been cursed. The Bamber family slaughter was not the first visitation of bane. An earlier owner was found drowned in a horse trough and another hanged himself there.

Jeremy Bamber has made a number of appeals over the years, and to this day claims he is innocent.

Now a legend, facts, and a haunting:

Legend

Take the minor road from Salcott cum Virley towards Tolleshunt Knights and on the right lies Barn Hall.

There are several versions to the old legend that Barn Hall was to be built a mile away from where it now stands. The devil came each night and pulled it down, and eventually threw a huge timber across the fields, and the house was built where the beam landed. The devil swore that he would have the owner's soul whether he was buried inside or outside the church.

Fact

There is a knight buried half in and half out of a wall at All Saints Church, Tolleshunt Knights, known as the Bushes Church (OS Exp 184 Ref 9213).

Fact

There is an ancient beam kept in the cellar of Barn Hall – probably fifteenth century and from an old ship.

Haunting

The field where the devil is supposed to have thrown the beam is known as Moat Field. A farmer ploughing late at night with tractor lights on, experienced forbidding black shapes that chased him on his tractor from the field. Something threw itself at the door of the vehicle. On arriving back home the tractor was found to have deep 'claw' marks and dents on the door. Locals say the field is haunted. The site may be near (OS Exp 184 Ref 9414).

A farmhouse in this vicinity was 'heavily' haunted. The area abounds with stories of ghosts, witches and mysteries amongst the tucked away hamlets and salty mud flats. There is an area known as Devil's Wood near the crossroads at Salcott and Virley. It is said that smugglers made up the stories about Devil's Wood, to keep the locals away, as they used to hide booty there.

North of Tolleshunt Knights is the Layer Marney Tower (OS 168 Ref 9217). Open to the public certain times.

Reached at the end of a quiet lane, the enormous Tudor gatehouse is of twin towers and eight storeys high.

This fascinating building is haunted by Lord Marney who died in 1593 before he had finished building it. He scares people who are in his way as he descends the staircase.

During the period between Easter and May, Lord Marney's voice may be heard reverberating around Layer Marney Church, and at Christmas time a ghostly headless chicken runs around the gravestones.

As for the tower, once you have seen it you will never forget it.

When I visited I asked one of the staff if the place was haunted. She replied, "What would you like? If you want it to be haunted, I'll say yes; if not, I'll say no." When I said I just wanted the truth, she said that she had not experienced anything.

Take the Minor Roads Northward Towards Copford

The spectre of the stern and cruel Bishop Bonner, the last Roman Catholic Bishop of London, manifests in Copford Church. He is believed to be buried under the High Altar steps. Adjacent Copford Hall was the residence of the Bishops of London. It is rumoured that Bonner hid some of the church plate from the reformers. It is supposed to be stashed in a secret tunnel between the Hall and the Church. Church cleaners have heard footsteps walking up the aisle to the pulpit. He slams a book and then the church door. Other ghostly activity has been recorded. (OS 168 Ref 9322.)

Tour Fifty-Seven
From Coggeshall to Feering, Kelvedon and Messing

OS Map 168 and OS Exp 195

Coggeshall is a picturesque village which dates back to medieval times, famous for its wool and cloth industry. Pargetting and woodcarvings can be found on the ancient merchant's houses. The finest example is Paycocke's House which is a National Trust property and open to the public.

Number forty-seven Church Street was once an inn and then a bakery. This 'rabbit warren' of an old house was being renovated into a private dwelling when a secret room was discovered, which was then incorporated into the living area. From then on, a strange presence pervaded the building. Doors would open and slam shut of their own accord. Strange odours would pervade rooms, and footsteps were heard in empty corridors. There would be sudden drops of temperature and a weird mist would hover up and down the stairs.

An American woman and her husband settled in Coggeshall. She had a recurring dream about a grave. She could see herself tending to the burial place and earth slipping through her fingers. She thought about the dream constantly as she felt someone was trying to tell her something. She became so obsessed that she was prescribed tranquillisers. Then one day she decided to take a shortcut through St Peter's churchyard, a different route from the norm, and suddenly saw the grave in her dream. The plot belonged to 'the wife of Henry Coggeshall of New York'. The grave was overgrown and the tombstone, dirty.

She cleaned the stone, tidied the grave, bought plants and generally tended it. The American lady dispensed with her tranquillisers. How did the wife of Henry Coggeshall come to be buried in the village of Coggeshall, and how did she contact the other American living in Coggeshall through dreams?

At Guild House, Market End, a small attic chamber is haunted by a little old man, and mysterious lights roam around the room.

The White Hart at Market End is home to a spectre dressed in blue velvet. A poltergeist makes scratching noises, puts chairs on tables and plays with hot water taps in the kitchens.

Cradle House, roughly a mile north of this little town, near Markhall Old Rectory, was once used by monks for covert meetings. The house, now divided into two cottages, is a warren of secret passageways. Monks in white habits have been seen to enter the gardens through a gate near the stream. They are said to dance in the grounds.

There are vague reports of people seeing or sensing something at nearby Gate House.

Also, Robins Brook runs through this vicinity. Robin was a sixteenth century woodcutter. His ghost is said to wander here and sometimes his axe can be heard. He is also said to haunt the environs of the Abbey further south. The Abbey ruins may be found off the road that leads to Feering (OS 168 Ref 8424 and OS Exp 195 Ref 8424). Apart from Robin, a ghostly monk walks. Ashen-faced and wrinkled, he carries a lit taper and meanders along the banks of the river. Ghostly Templars have been reported here since 1176.

Take the Southerly Road to Feering

Here the gory ghost of John Hardman may be seen at Feering Church. He was killed in the Zulu wars. He is witnessed by the wall near the pulpit clutching a bloody wound near his stomach.

Approximately a mile to the south lies Kelvedon.

The Railway Station at one time was haunted by disembodied footsteps, always at 04.55 a.m. Now the old Victorian station has been modernised; the footsteps are no longer heard

Marks Hall, now demolished was once haunted by Cromwell's men. During the siege of Colchester, Cromwell is believed to have made the Hall his headquarters. In 1941 a hundred men were billeted there. The colonel reported men informed him that the Jacobean wing was haunted. A sixty-foot dining room was added in 1702, and ghostly singing had been heard there. Although the Jacobean country house has been demolished, one can walk around the gardens and arboretum known as Marks Hall Estate. (OS Map 168 Ref 8425.)

To the east you will find Messing.
The sounds of music and chanting are heard when the church is unoccupied.

Tour Fifty-Eight
From Basildon to Langdon Hills and Vange

OS Map 178 OS Exp 175
Cyclical and Notable Dates Basildon – January

Basildon (New Town) lies to the west of Southend.

The vicinity around the church of the Holy Cross is haunted by a red-robed and hooded figure. Believed by some to be one of the two rectors expelled at the time of the Reformation, the apparition drifts through solid obstacles in its path.

The melancholy spectre was sighted by different workers from a nearby factory on separate occasions. Indeed a female cyclist claims to have ridden right through the shade when it stopped abruptly in front of her one misty morning. The crimson clad monk emerges from some foliage, floats silently across the road and melts away amongst the gravestones of the church. Other times the figure has been seen crossing the highway heading towards Laindon church. Sceptics maintain that the vision was a hoax. An image produced from a projector onto the mist created the illusion. This 'logical explanation' seems unlikely as the hoaxers would have to be hidden with their equipment on numerous mornings. Surely, they would have been discovered – but who knows.

Unaccountable footsteps have been heard near the church porch.

The entrance of Church Lane at Crays Hill was haunted by a spirit that threw people over the hedge. Also, another ghost said to frequent this area is that of a little girl who was killed by being thrown from a pony and trap. (OS Exp 175 Ref 7192 or OS 178 Ref 7192.)

Alley seventeen of the Ambassador Bowling Club is haunted by a man wearing blue overalls. The machinery is noted for being unreliable, and the ambient temperature often drops unexpectedly.

A weeping woman dressed in a school crossing uniform carrying a 'stop' sign haunts the Laindon area. Once seen she slowly fades away.

An old house, Goldsmith's Manor lies to the south of Langdon Hills, and to the southwest of Basildon.

The fetch of a lady wearing a beige, pleated dress appears from time to time in the hallway. Dogs sense her presence.

Vange, an area of Basildon to the south of the town, has a variety of ghostly phenomena.

Mysterious spooky voices are heard at Hill Farm.

The vicinity around the level crossing on the Fobbing road south of the A13 is haunted by a white gliding image. It stands on the pavement by the barrier, or wafts towards the Five Bells Inn from the direction of Vange church (OS Exp 175 Ref 7288 and OS 178 Ref 7288).

Strange lights have been observed on Vange Marshes. These 'Jack o' Lantern' sparks may be due to the combustion of gases from rotting vegetable substances on marshy ground imbedded with natural chemicals.

The road from Vange to Fobbing is the haunt of the Devil Dog Black Shuck. It silently pads around near the entrance to White Hall Farm.

Tour Fifty-Nine
From Stanford-le-Hope to Mucking, Corringham, Coryton and Fobbing

OS Map 178 OS Exp 175

Stanford-le-Hope can be found on the north bank of the River Thames in Essex.

A family in Abbotts Drive were driven frantic by a male ghost. The entity tapped on windows, moved objects around, hid cooking ingredients, appeared on the doorstep, thumped around, stamped about, breathed on family member's necks, and there was a feeling of being watched all the time. It was thought that either the ghost had been brought to the house by a member of the family, or the haunting was connected with Abbotts Hall as the house was built on the site.

Rookery Corner was once haunted by a young woman wearing a three-cornered hat, who rode a white horse through the pond at midnight. She has not been seen for many years – but you never know – time means nothing to a ghost.

In Saint Clere's Hall dwells the spirit of a servant girl, amongst other souls of the dead. (OS 178 Ref 6881.)

There is not much to see now at Mucking, Corringham, and Coryton, but you can sample the atmosphere if you decide to visit.

At nearby Mucking, the creeks can be very eerie, and a face of a suicide used to appear at windows at Mucking Hall.

To the east of Stanford-le-Hope you will find Corringham.

Corringham marshes may still be home to the supernatural where an ancient house once stood which was known in the area to be haunted. The house was in ruins in the 1980s. The nature of the haunting is unknown.

Carry on down the A1014 to Coryton

At an oil depot an employee fell to his death. The ghost wears a safety helmet and overalls.

Retrace your journey along the A1014 dual carriageway, and take the turn northwards for Fobbing. (You may have to go as far as the roundabout and double back.) The area around the old wharf ruins is said to be haunted. There is an oppressive atmosphere at times and the entity assaults walkers.

People have reported strange noises, and the sounds of rattling chains in the vineyards near Fobbing church.

Also an Elizabethan house manifests and then vanishes, on a hill leading from Corringham to Fobbing.

As mentioned in the previous tour, the road from Vange to Fobbing is the patrol of Black Shuck. Take the minor road northward and then onto the double roundabout intersection, then take the right turn onto the B1464 to Vange, if you want to catch sight of the canine.

Tour Sixty
From Wickford to Runwell, Rettendon and East Hanningfield

OS Maps 167 and 178 OS Exp 175
Cyclical and notable dates Runwell January to April
Runwell Hall area – 31st December

An apparition of a girl killed in a motorbike accident appears at Wickford roundabout. Her ghost has been seen thumbing a lift. She asks motorists to go to Southend, but vanishes before reaching their destination

A ghostly coach carrying a woman in old-fashioned clothing has also been seen here, believed by some to be Anne Boleyn.

Runwell north of Wickford takes its name from the Running Well (OS Map 167 Ref 7596 and Exp 175 Ref 7596).

Runwell Hall, now demolished but presumably in the proximity of Runwell Hall Farm to the west of the A30 had a visitation every New Year's Eve by a spectral coach and horses which pulled up at the door. A ghostly lady would be seen to leave the carriage, she would then walk towards the Hall, whereupon a spectral butler opens the door. This apparition may return to the area.

The parish church of 'Our Lady of the Running Well' boasts a phantom monk with a scarred face wearing a black habit prowls. He is usually seen between January and April.

The monk or chaplain is believed to be Rainaldus, who was an evil character and practised Black Magic. He had an altercation with the Devil. Legend dictates that he left his hand mark burnt into the wood on the door. The door does have a mark resembling a claw like a left hand. The Devil is supposed only to use his left hand when dealing with the living. Rainaldus was reduced to a foul-smelling, squelching, swirling black liquid, in the midst of which was a stone in the shape of a skull.

Folk lore apart, the haunting continues.

Before the skull-like stone was deposited in Southend Museum, it was interred in the doorstep of the north porch. This area was always cold even in hot weather.

The entity has been seen by many over the years, up to the recent past. Sometimes a black shadow is seen to stand beside the telephone box, not far from the church, and drifts along the fence.

Rainaldus' ghost has been observed in broad daylight, on numerous occasions following different living members of the clergy. He shuffles along, stooping, wearing a grey or brown robe with a wide leather belt. He has angular features, and wispy sideburns and beard.

He has been seen in the churchyard with other ghostly clerical figures. Another witness described the spook as having a scar on his face, piercing eyes, and was accompanied by a priest wearing a cassock.

The church is also haunted by other supernatural phenomena. Footsteps are heard in the turret. Sounds of furniture being chopped up, believed to be a re-enactment of Roundhead soldiers destroying the original rood screen by axes.

Lady Anne Sulyard is said to move from pew to pew, unsure where to sit or kneel, as she behaved in life. Her presence is made aware by creaking sounds amongst the seats.

Nearby, the road that runs from Rettendon to East Hanningfield is haunted by a farmer with his pony and trap (OS 167 Ref 7698 to Ref 7700).

Tour Sixty-One
Rayleigh, Hockley, Hawkwell, Hullbridge and Brandy Hole

OS Map 178 168 and OS Exp 175
Cyclical and Notable Dates
Brandy Hole – October

Rayleigh is to be found northwest of Southend.

Rayleigh Lodge, The Chase, Rayleigh, was once a hunting lodge in the reign of Henry 8th, but now has more of a Georgian appearance. It was a private house until 1964, and is now a hostelry. The ghost is a young woman who had an affair with the Lord of the Manor which resulted in pregnancy. She is thought to have drowned herself in a nearby pond. She is seen wearing a dark, trailing dress and hat, and appears in the restaurant and the bar which was previously a gunroom.

A former toyshop is haunted by a woman who died in a fire.

A girl hitchhiker signals vehicles to stop on the A127. She asks to be taken to Blinking Owl Café, and vanishes just before reaching her destination. She and her boyfriend were killed on a motorbike after leaving the café.

Just to the north of Rayleigh is Hockley.

A coach with four white horses carrying a beautiful lady dressed in white haunts. A ghostly re-enactment of an accident occurs outside the church where the tragedy happened. After losing control of the horses, the coach driver and his passenger were killed. The woman waves a white gloved hand at any passer-by, as the coach tries to slow down, and then it swerves and crashes.

Shapes have been observed around the tower, and the atmosphere around the church is generally forbidding.

The Bull Inn, a popular busy pub is haunted by something that turns up after closing, usually between 2 and 3 a.m.

Witchcraft and Black Magic rites, it is rumoured, were once carried out in Hockley Woods. Also, there are sounds of a dreadful air crash and screams for help, but nothing is found on inspection.

The B1013 is the haunt of Black Shuck. The large black dog silently follows pedestrians and then quite suddenly vanishes. Sighting of the animal is considered to portend of doom or death. It usually roams on foggy nights in the proximity of the church (OS 178 Ref 8492).

The village of Hawkwell lies to the south east of Hockley.

At Clements Hall the phantom must have been known to the family pet dog, as the canine would run up to ghostly sounds wagging its tail. Normally, dogs bristle and wail in the presence of spirits.

In addition Anne Boleyn is said to walk the passageways, minus her head of course! (OS 178 Ref 8592 and Exp 8592.)

A glowing presence in the shape of a female drifts through the woods adjacent to Belchamps camping area (Exp175 Ref 8391 and OS 178 Ref 8391).

Take the lanes through and out of Hockley north westerly to Hullbridge.

Here taxi drivers have reported the spectre of a young girl in a black cloak along Ferry Road.

Nearby to the east is Brandy Hole (OS 168 Ref 8295 and Exp175 Ref 8295) so named due to where smugglers stashed their contraband after sailing up the Crouch estuary.

A seaman wearing a blue sweater frequents the district. He is visible only from the waist up, and seen on misty evenings at dusk around October.

Tour Sixty-Two

From Bowers Gifford to North Benfleet, South Benfleet, Benfleet Creek, Canvey Island and Thundersley

OS Map 178 OS Exp 175

St Margaret's Church at Bowers Gifford is off the beaten track. It sits alone on the marshes and flat lands amongst the pylons. It can be reached by footpath, but if driving you have to turn off the multi roundabout on the A13 at Thundersley, and then take the B1464 to Bowers Gifford. Take the first turning on the left, follow the road over the motorway and the church can be found at the end where the lane terminates. (OS 178 Ref 7587 and OS Exp 175 Ref 7587.)

Organ music has been heard at night when the church is deserted. A visitor to the church one afternoon heard the organ start up, but there was no organist. A little old man sporting a white beard is said to appear on occasions.

When I visited I found the gloomy atmosphere uncomfortable but saw and heard nothing. A tramp had made his 'camp' nearby, and had been living there for a few months, but he had not observed any phenomena.

The ghost of an old woman is said to wander along Pound Lane, which leads from the village of Bowers Gifford to North Benfleet.

There is a small woodland which is known as 'Screeching Boy's Wood'. A young ploughboy was murdered here, some say decapitated. His ghost sits on a gate at the entrance to the wood, and screams. (OS 178 Ref 7691 and OS Exp 175 Ref 7691.)

A family travelling by car all witnessed a teenage girl hit by their vehicle on a roundabout in North Benfleet. The occupants inspected the car and searched the road, but there was no injured girl or damage to the car.

In South Benfleet the Anchor public house has phantom pirates in the attic.

The Conservative Club in the High Street is haunted by a woman said to be Lady Hamilton, ever waiting for Horatio Nelson. She perambulates the corridors.

A large man thought to be a Viking warrior walks across the mud at Benfleet Creek on moonlit nights. He wears a steel helmet with winged appendages that glint in the moonlight, from under which long blond hair flows, and a moustache that hangs down to his chin. A leather jerkin covers his tunic, and he has cross gartering below his knees. He makes long strides, almost like sliding over the mud. An experienced seaman knows not to thrust his feet into the mud or he will get sucked down and stuck. (OS 178 Ref 7885.)

Long ago there was a battle between the Danes and the Saxons. The fleet of long ships were anchored in Benfleet Creek. The Saxons set fire to them leaving the Danes stranded. Many were slaughtered. This is probably the ghost of one of the warriors searching for a ship to take him home, according to Wentworth Day in his book of *Essex Ghosts*.

It must be eerie to see this huge man silently wading across the mud flats, with just the sound of the seabirds plaintively mewing overhead. He is mainly observed at Canvey Point to the east of the island.

Canvey Island Lies to the South of Benfleet Creek

At Knightswick Farm a nun is said to walk on the farmland and then gradually sink into the ground. Legend has it that there was once a chapel here.

An old Dutchman is said to stroll from Benfleet along Church Parade, through some gardens to Oysterfleet, then from Winter Gardens to Waterside Farm. He wears a pointed hat, buckled shoes, knee breeches with rosettes at the sides, and carries a bag over his shoulder. He is often seen at dusk (OS 178 Refs 7885 and 7884, and OS Exp 175 Refs 7885 and 7884).

The ghost of a young woman whose sailor fiancé was lost at sea is said to manifest along Hole Haven Road. She is believed to have been a serving wench at the Lobster Smack Inn, which is the oldest building on Canvey, and mentioned in Charles Dickens' *Great Expectations*.

Note of Interest

In the seventeenth century, a Dutch engineer, Cornelius Vermuyden built the first sea walls. He employed many workers from the Netherlands, some staying on after the work had finished. The King allowed them to build a church so that they could worship in their own language. Two Dutch cottages still exist, one is privately owned, the other, a museum.

The catastrophic East Coast Floods of 1953 destroyed much of Canvey. The Red Cow pub was used as an Army HQ. The army rescued the inhabitants from rooftops, and repaired sea walls. Many people perished. The pub was renamed the King Canute, famed for ordering the waves to recede.

To the North of Benfleet Is Thundersley

Jarvis Hall near Bread and Cheese Hill has a slope named The Devil's Steps. There is, or was, a barn where sleep is impossible. The ghosts of priests hiding from soldiers because their religion was banned, haunt.

The area around Thundersley Parish Church is haunted by the cry of a murdered man although his cries have not been heard for some time.

A property in Selbourne Road was domiciled by a screaming spirit in hobnail boots.

A farmer's daughter who drowned herself in a pond at Upper Wybarns's Farm because her father would not allow her to marry the man she loved, appears dripping wet at the second stile leading to Dawes Heath from the London Road (OS Exp 175 Ref 8188). She will stare at you with unseeing eyes.

A cottage near the church is troubled by the sound of bugles, usually at the time of the new moon. Subsequent residents of the cottage have heard the bugles not knowing of its haunted history. The bugles have, so it is rumoured, something to do with the Crimean War.

Glossary of Terms

Apparition

The manifestation of a ghost. They can be transparent, luminous or misty shapes. They can also appear quite solid and have been mistaken for the living.

Black Spectral Dog / Demon Dog

Phantom dogs thought to be custodians of parochial areas. They can portend death or are an ill omen. Folklore has given them many names:

East Anglia – Old Shoch, Shucky Dog, Black Shuck, Shug Monkey, Scarfe, Galleytrot.

Lincolnshire – Hairy Jack
Leicestershire – Shag Dog
Lancashire – Trash, Shriker
Yorkshire – Barguest, Barghest
Westmoreland – Cappel
Staffordshire – Padfoot
Midlands – Hooter
Sussex – Gytrack, Grattack
Somerset – Gurt Dog, Great Dog
Wales – Gwylligi
Scotland – Muckle Black Tyke
Isle of Man – Moddey Doo
Jersey – Le tchan de Bouole

Cold Spot

A sharply defined area of intense coldness (but not a draught) of which one can step in and out. Usually about the width of a human body.

Corpse Lights / Corpse Candles

Usually small flickering lights that forebode death, and show the way the corpse would take.

Corpse Way

The old routes across country where coffins would have been carried for burial at church. It was supposed that wherever a dead body passed became a public thoroughfare.

Crisis Apparition

Spirit of a person seen near the time of their death, or a live person in crisis.

Disembodied Footsteps

The re-enactment of an incident or habit. There are so many reports of ghostly footsteps that they cannot always be put down to a misconception. The sounds have been so convincing that the witness immediately seeks out the cause.

Doppelganger

An image seen of a person in one place when they are in fact in another. Also two identical images of the same person doing the same thing. Can be regarded as a portent of death.

Fetch

A person's double or ghost.

Grey Lady

The apparition of a woman, which appears as a misty, grey, shadowy figure. They may be solid or transparent. Grey ladies are usually associated with a tragedy, and are frequently seen.

Ley Lines

Invisible lines or tracks of energy, supposedly linking the mystical and religious sites. Places may have been built on these 'paths', due to past knowledge that has now been forgotten over time.

Orbs

Floating supernatural circles of light.

Paranormal

Outside the range of normal explanation.

Poltergeist

An entity that manifests by rappings, knockings, throwing items, stones and furniture around, hiding objects that appear again in the same place or another. Poltergeists some believe draw their energy from pubescent or adolescent youth. Poltergeist is a word of German origin meaning 'noisy spirit'– poltern = noisy and geist = ghost.

Where poltergeist activity has been noted on the tours in this book, I have not specified every individual detail as the manifestations presented are more or less always the same, as explained above.

Presence

The sense of something ghostly but unseen.

Time Slip

Going through another time dimension, past or future.

Will-o'-the-Wisp/Jack-o'-Lantern

A small light or phosphorescence, often seen over marshland after dark.

Wraith

A person's double, or a thin vapour.

Bibliography and Recommended Reading

A Gazetteer of British Ghosts. Peter Underwood. Souvenir Press, 1971.

A Ghost Hunter's Guide to Essex. Jesse K Payne. Ian Henry Publications, 1995.

Big Cats in Britain Yearbook 2009. Mark Fraser. BCIB Publishing, 2009.

Borley Rectory: The Final Analysis. Edward Babbs and Claudine Matthais. Six Martletts Publishing, 2003.

Brewer's Dictionary of Phrase and Fable-Revised Edition. Cassell London, 1971.

Britain's Haunted Heritage. J A Brooks. Jarrold, 1990.

Crime in Hertfordshire: Vol 1. Simon Walker. The Book Castle. 2002

Crime in Hertfordshire: Murder and Misdemeanour Vol. 2. Simon Walker. The Book Castle, 2003.

Dark Journey. David Farrant. British Psychic and Occult Soc., 2004.

Discovering Ghosts. Leon Metcalfe. Shire Publications, 1972.

East Anglian Curiosities. Rick O'Brien. The Dovecote Press Ltd., 1992 reprint 1998.

Elizabeth. Dr David Starkey. Chatto and Windus, 2000.

Essex Ghosts. James Wentworth-Day. Spurbooks Ltd, 1973.

Essex Tales of Mystery and Murder. W H Johnson. Countryside Books, 2001.

Folklore of Hertfordshire. Doris Jones-Baker. Rowman and Littlefield, 1977.

Ghostly Hertfordshire. Damien O'Dell. Pen Press Publishers, 2005.

Ghosts and Haunted Places. Peter Underwood. Judy Piatkus Publishers Ltd, 1996.

Ghosts and How to See Them. Peter Underwood. Caxton, 1996; Anaya Publishers, 1993.

Ghost Hunter's Guide to Britain. John and Anne Spencer. Harpur Collins, 2000.

Ghosts of East Anglia. H Mills West. Countryside Books, 1984.

Ghosts of Essex. Betty Puttick. Countryside Books, 1997.

Ghosts of Hertfordshire. Betty Puttick. Countryside Books, 1997.

Ghosts of Old England. Terence Whitaker. Robert Hale London, 1987.

Ghosts over Britain. Peter Moss. Book Club Associated, 1977.

Gothick Hertfordshire. Jennifer Westwood. Shire Publications, 1989.

Haunted Christmas: Yuletide Ghosts and other Spooky Holiday Happenings. Mary Beth Crain. Rowman & Littlefield, 2009.

Haunted Britain. A D Hippisley-Coxe. Hutchinson & Co, 1973.

Haunted East Anglia. Joan Forman. Jarrold Publishing, 1974.

Haunted England. Christina Hole. Fitzhouse Books, 1990.

Haunted Hertfordshire: A Ghostly Gazetteer. Ruth Stratton and Nicholas Cornell. The Book Castle, 2003.

Haunted Inns and Taverns. Andrew Green. Shire Publications Album 319.

Haunted Land. Paul Devereux. Piatkus, 2001.

Haunts and Hauntings. Edited Russell Beach. Publications Division of the Automobile Association, 1974.

Hertfordshire Tales of Mystery and Murder. Betty Puttick. Countryside Books, 2001.

Katherine Swynford. Alison Weir. Vintage, 2008.

Our Haunted Kingdom. Andrew Green. Fontana, 1974.

Folklore Myths and Legends of Britain. Reader's Digest Assoc. Ltd., 1973.

Readers Digest Touring Guide to Great Britain. 1992

Supernatural Britain. Peter Hough. Piatkus Books, 1995.

Supernatural England. Betty Puttick. Countryside Books, 2002.

Tales from Four Shires. John Houghton. The Book Castle, 1994.

The A–Z of British Ghosts. Peter Underwood. Chancellor Press, 1992.

The Borley Rectory Companion. Paul Adams, Eddie Brazil, Peter Underwood. The History Press, 2009.

The Encyclopedia of Ghosts and Spirits. John and Anne Spencer. Headline Book Publishers, 1992.

The Enigma of Borley Rectory. Ivan Banks. Foulsham Publishing House, 1996.

The Essex Village Book. Women's Institute. Countryside Books, 1988.

The Ghost-Hunting Casebook. Natalie Osborne-Thomason. Octopus Publishing Group, 1999.

The Haunted Pub Guide. Guy Lyon Playfair. Harrap Ltd, 1985.

The Hertfordshire Village Book. Women's Institute. Countryside Books, 1986.

The Realm of Ghosts. Eric Maple. Pan Books 1967/1971 Robert Hale, 1964.

The Mummy of Birchen Bower and Other Stories. Harry Ludlam. W Foulsham & Co., 1966.

The Suffolk Village Book. Women's Institute. Countryside Books, 1991.

The Witches of Hertfordshire. Simon Walker. Tempus Publishing. 2004

This Haunted Isle. Peter Underwood. Harrap Ltd., 1993

Witchcraft in England. Christina Hole. Fitzhouse Books, 1990.

50 Great Ghost Stories. John Canning. Souvenir Press Ltd., 1971.

Periodicals and Newspapers

Fortean Times

Issue 283, 'Ghostwatch' Jan 2012. Alan Murdie. Phantom Houses P16-17.

Issue 293, 'Ghostwatch' Oct 2012. Alan Murdie. St Osyth's Priory P18-19.

Issue 294, 'Ghostwatch' Nov 2012. Alan Murdie. Betty Potter's Dip P21

Issue 303, 'Witch Scrapfaggot Green' July 2013. Robert Halliday P30-33

Issue 340, 'Letters' May 2016. Local Ghosts P67

Issue 327, 'Unlocking the Cage' May 2015. John Fraser P34-37

Issue 332. 'Ghostwatch'. Oct 2015. Alan Murdie. Great Cornard P20

Paranormal Magazine, November 2010

Hertfordshire Life Magazine,	November 2002
	December 2003
	February 2004
	March 2004
	April 2004
	June 2004
	March 2005
	December 2005
	January 2009
	January 2016
Essex Life Magazine,	January 2002
	October 2002

October 2003
January 2004
March 2005
June 2004
October 2016

Murder Casebook No.7: Marshall Cavendish Ltd., Weekly Publication 1990.
Murder Casebook No.17: Marshall Cavendish Ltd., Weekly Publication 1990.
Crimes and Punishment Magazine No.4: Phoebus Publishing, 1975.
Crimes and Punishment Magazine No. 34: Pheobus Publishing, 1975.
The Camden Town Murder, John Barber: self-published pamphlet first issued 2003.
Daily Mail, 16 July 1994.
Daily Star, 17 May 2012.
Daily Telegraph, 3 March 2001.
Daily Telegraph, 9 February 2002.
Paranormal News, 2005.
Journal Frederick Barwell 'For whom the bell tolls' November 2002 P18-21
Journal William Tyler. 'As gentlemen go by.' May 2004. P16-17
Southend Evening Echo, 29 October 2004
Jacqueline Benton. 'The Curse of the Essex Coast.' (Magazine article)
Herts and Essex Observer,   November 1996
                              25 June 1998
                              27 April 2000
                              20 June 2000
                              31 May 2001
                              12 July 2001
                              14 December 2001
                              March 2002
                              February 2003
                              3 April 2003
                              1 May 2003
                              8 May 2003
                              15 May 2003
                              31 July 2003
                              9 Oct 2003
                              16 October 2003
                              17 June 2004
                              6 January 2005
                              12 January 2006
                              20 September 2007
                              13 March 2008
                              29 November 2012

Ghost Club Magazine, Summer 2004, Chairman's letter.
Web Sites
www.eerieplace.com/haunted-places-clacton
www.eerieplace.com/haunted-places-hertford
www.errieplace.com/haunted-gallows-hill-hertford
www.errieplace.com/haunted-ghosts-of-epping-forest

www.spookyisles.com/2014/05/5-haunted-places-tovisitinhertford
http://en.wikipedia.org/wiki/hertford
www.hertford.net/history/gaol.asp
www.paranormaldatabase.com/hertfordshire/hertdata.php

www.paranormaldatabase.com/essex/esspages/essedata.php
www.mysterymag.com/yourexperience (no longer active)
www.compassion-in-business.co.uk/cityscape/brickendon.
www.stalbansreview.co.uk/nostalgia/crimelibrary/annenoblett
https://archive.birchanger.com
www.hiddenea.com/essexb.htm
www.guardian.co.uk(who killed the colonel of Cockhouse)
www.hauntedexperiences.com/haunted-hotels-of-essex

www.nazeing-glass-factoryshop.co.uk/PBCPPlayer.asp?ID=1286791
www.ourstevenage.org.uk/?s=henry+trigg
www.stortfordhistory.co.uk/guide
Other
Ghost Walk and Talk at Saffron Walden. Alan Murdie. Aug 2005.
The Ghost Hunters Documentary 1975
Lecture Keith Mawby – Bishop's Stortford/Ghost Club/circa 2004
Lecture Edward Babbs Ghost Club Marble Arch April 2004
Ghost Club Investigation (Thundridge) July 2004
Great British Ghosts TV Series 1 Episode 4 2011 Michaela Strachan
Ghost Club Investigations. 'Coal House Fort.' 4 October 2003
17 April 2004
Ghost Club Investigation. 'Old church Hospital Site, Romford.' circa 2005
'The Murder of Lieu. Col. Robert Workman'
Herts/Essex Observer 15th January 2004
                              22nd January 2004
                              29th January 2004
                              5th February 2004
                              15th April 2004
                              16th December 2004
                              22nd December 2004
                              5th January 2006
                              2nd March 2006
                              11th October 2012
                              18th October 2012
                              25th October 2012
                              31st October 2013
                              5th December 2013
Sunday Telegraph 11th January 2004

Daily Mail 13th January 2004
The above newspaper articles are where I have obtained the information on this case. There are circa forty other newspaper articles on this case, too numerous to be mentioned here. The source of the information can be provided to anyone wishing to know.

The author will be happy to provide details to anyone wishing to know the source of a haunting.

Illustrations

Salisbury Hotel

Red cloaked knight Enfield

A lady haunts Braughing village

The Fox and Hounds Barley

Devil dog Alphamstone

Belchamp Walter Monks

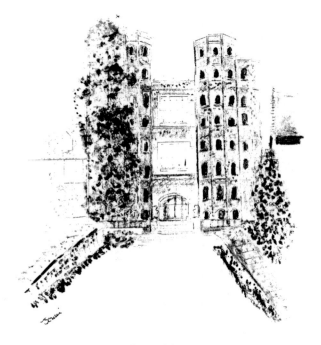

Layer Marney

Viking at Benfleet Creek